P9-CJZ-326

DUKE

Also by Rozlan Mohd Noor

21 Immortals

DUKE

INSPECTOR MISLAN AND THE EXPRESSWAY MURDERS

ROZLAN MOHD NOOR

An Arcade CrimeWise Book

First North American Edition

Visit our website at www.arcadepub.com.

10 9 8 7 6 5 4 3 2 1

Library of Congress Cataloging-in-Publication Data is available on file.
Library of Congress Control Number: 2020948613

Cover design by Erin Seaward-Hiatt
Cover photography: © Nojustice/Getty Images (figure and police lights); © Ignitius Kong/EyeEm/Getty Images (Kuala Lumpur skyline)

ISBN: 978-1-950691-41-8
Ebook ISBN: 978-1-951627-60-7

Printed in the United States of America

DUKE

1

A black Mercedes E200 cruises in the slow lane toward the city on the wet and slippery surface of the DUKE—the Duta–Ulu Klang Expressway. Its occupants are in cheerful conversation accompanied by a soft medley of Hari Raya songs from the radio. It is an exceptionally quiet night, hot and humid after a late evening shower. The traffic on the expressway is lighter than usual, with speeding cars taking advantage of the fact that most city dwellers are still at dinner or are at the mosque for the supplementary Tarawih prayers during the holy month of Ramadan. The Mercedes E200, however, is traveling at a leisurely pace, in no hurry to get to its destination.

A female passenger in the car trailing it is astounded by a bright flash of reddish glow that is immediately followed by a muffled bang from inside the Mercedes. She sees the Mercedes losing speed, swerve hard to the right, jerk, and roll forward. Then a second bright reddish glow flashes, followed by another muffled bang, and the car comes to a rest, hitting the safety guardrail at the road divider. It is at the eleventh milestone marker. The driver of the trailing car hits his brakes and veers left, narrowly escaping a collision, and swears "Idiot!" As he maneuvers past the black Mercedes, the woman in the passenger seat sees a third bright reddish glow and hears the final muffled bang.

"Did you see that?" the passenger asks her husband.

"See what?" he answers, still cursing under his breath at the idiot driving the Mercedes.

"Those bright flashes in the Mercedes."

"No."

"What about the explosions, did you hear them?"

"No!"

"There was a bright flash and a bang just before the car swerved, then another and another as we passed it," the wife says excitedly, turning in her seat to look back at the Mercedes.

"You probably saw reflections of fireworks from the flats down there, you know, the rocket type that shoots up and explodes. Sound travels far at night," the husband says, trashing his wife's claim.

"No, I'm sure it was from inside the Mercedes. Aren't you stopping to help?" she asks, turning to gaze at her husband.

The husband glances at his rearview mirror.

"It is only a minor accident, I'm sure he's all right. Probably drunk," the husband says, taking another glance in the rearview mirror.

The wife sighs, disappointed at her husband's attitude. She turns around and looks back again, concerned.

"The driver could be injured."

"Serves him right for driving like an idiot. Look, we have a long journey, and I don't want to waste half the night at the hospital or the police station. Unless you want to change your mind and spend Raya here with my parents?" the husband growls. "I didn't think so. Anyway, I'm sure someone will stop to help." He takes another peek at the rearview mirror, "There, you see, people are already stopping."

The wife continues to stare at the fast-vanishing black Mercedes as her husband steps on the accelerator to continue the long journey back to their hometown.

Several passing cars stop to investigate. More follow suit, and before long both sides of the once-quiet expressway turn into a free-for-all parking lot. Traffic is moving at a snail's pace. Drivers slow down as they and their passengers gawk. The ones who play the lottery jot down the license plate numbers of the unfortunate vehicle, which could be a winning number to bet on—someone's misfortune could well be your fortune.

The emergency lanes are soon packed with parked cars, accident-chasing tow trucks, motorcycles, and curious motorists on their way home. With the right lane blocked, vehicles have to squeeze left through the bumper-to-bumper crawl, causing tempers to flare, feverish honking, and swearing with middle-finger gestures.

A Good Samaritan who had stopped to lend a hand peeks inside the black Mercedes and retreats in shock. He calls 999 to report two bodies covered in blood inside a car on the DUKE. A Mobile Patrol Vehicle (MPV) is dispatched immediately by Operations Center.

One of the patrolmen shines his flashlight into the car and shouts to his partner, "Ali, better get the station to send an IO."

"Yes, I've already called the Traffic Police," Lance Corporal Ali replies.

"No, call the investigating officer on duty. I think we have a double homicide here."

Lance Corporal Ali calls the district police headquarters, gives their location, and requests for the investigation officer on duty to report a possible double homicide. Ali also requests another MPV to help with traffic control and the growing number of onlookers.

"I think we should instruct the other MPV to redirect traffic down the slip road and block access through here," Ali suggests.

"Yes, why don't you do that? I'll get the caller to sit inside the patrol car. I'm sure the IO would like to talk to him. Where the hell is he, anyway?" Lance Corporal Yatim snarls. "Ali, can you check with the station again?"

"Just did, they said he's on his way."

"On the way, on the way . . . For all you know, he's not even at the station," Yatim grumbles.

The Kuala Lumpur Police Contingent Forensics (D10) team headed by Inspector Lily Chin arrives at the scene and asks for the investigating officer. Yatim tells her that he's on his way.

"Who's the IO?"

"Ali, who's the IO?" he asks his partner.

"Inspector Murad."

Lily is just about done when district investigation officer, Inspector Murad, arrives.

"Amoi, what happened here?" *Amoi* is the generic term used by non-Chinese to address a young Chinese woman.

"Not good news. Two deceased—gunshots. Murad, I need to call in Forensic HQ. Here, put on these gloves."

After Murad puts them on, she hands him the wallet and handbag.

"Why?" Murad asks, looking at the items.

"This is more than we can handle. That guy was an executive chairman of a company, and she was his managing director. Two corporate figures shot in a car, nothing stolen. Money, cell phones, valuables all untouched. That's always a bad sign."

"You think this was a hit?"

"I don't know, but it's better to be safe."

"Okay, I'll call Major Crimes to see if they're willing to look at this."

"You mean Special Investigations?"

"Yeah, Special investigations Unit, I can never get used to the new name. I still think Major Crimes is a more fitting name for D9. More oomph," he says with a tiny smile.

2

Inspector Mislan Latif and Detective Sergeant Johan Kamarudin of the Special Investigations Unit (D9) arrive just as Chew Beng Song and his team from Crime Forensics HQ are unpacking their equipment.

"Hey, Chew, what brings you here? I thought D10 is handling this."

"Lily called for help, said they're not equipped to handle this. What brings you here?"

"District thinks it might be a case of public interest. Usual thing, trying to pass the buck," Mislan sniggers. "Let's see what this is all about."

Inspectors Murad and Lily Chin greet them as they walk under the crime-scene tape held up by a patrolman.

"What do we have here?" Mislan asks.

"A male victim, Mahadi Mokshin, sixty, executive chairman of MM Harapan Holdings, address in Bukit Damansara, Kuala Lumpur. A female victim, Zaleha Jalani, thirty-four, managing director of Rakan MM Harapan Sdn Bhd, address in Beverly Heights, Ampang," Murad says, briefing him. "MPV checked the vehicle. It's registered to the male victim. Talked to the caller, but he says he didn't witness the accident. When he got here, the car had already crashed into the railing. He stopped to help, but when he saw the two bodies, he called 999. We got the call around 20:48 hours."

"Why are you referring to the deceased as victims?" Mislan asks, curious. "You figure there's foul play?"

"No, but what do you want me to refer to them as?"

"The deceased, until you know for certain there was foul play."

"OK, the deceased."

"Any other witnesses?"

"If there were, they're long gone. Hari Raya's what, three days away. It's back-to-hometown time. I suspect those who saw the incident would've simply continued with their journey."

The holy month of Ramadan and the Hari Raya celebration, as Eid is known here, is one of the biggest events in Malaysia, as the majority of its population is Malay-Muslim. A week or so before Hari Raya most of the city dwellers, especially in Kuala Lumpur, start preparing and leaving for their hometowns. This is especially so for those from the East Coast states like Kelantan, Terengganu, and Pahang and those from the northern states like Kedah. States that are Malay-dominated.

"Jo, can you interview the caller? See if he saw or noticed anything worth following up on. Is the car the way it was? I mean, did anyone move or do anything to it?"

"Apart from the responding MPV, we're the first to arrive," Lily answers. "The car was locked from the inside and we had to break in. The key was in the ignition, headlights, radio, air-con, and alarm were on, but the engine was dead."

"By dead, do you mean it had stalled or was the ignition turned off?" Mislan asks.

"Stalled. The key was in the On position. I believe the engine stalled on impact," Lily says.

"What about the deceased?" Chew asks.

"The male has a single GSW to the head and the female one GSW to the head and another to the chest. That's gunshot wound," Lily says for Murad's benefit.

"Yes, thanks for the education."

"We found a Walther PPK .32 and three casings. I'm pretty sure it was the weapon used. Nothing stolen—wallet, handbag, and valuables all intact. I guess Crime Forensic is better equipped for this than us," Lily says to Chew.

"Let's see what we can do. Can you tell your guys to hand over whatever they've bagged to my boys?"

"With pleasure," Lily replies, signaling to her assistants.

Chew, Mislan, and Johan approach the black Mercedes E200, and the Forensics supervisor switches on his flashlight. The body of the male deceased is on the right, in the driver's seat. The safety belt unstrapped, with the head and torso facing front but slumped a little to the left, toward the passenger seat. A small hole, no larger than the girth of a pencil, is on his lower right temple close to the ear. There is a patch of dried blood around the hole with the stain running down the cheek. The side and front of the deceased's shirt are damp with blood. His left hand hangs between the seats, and his right rests on his lap. The female deceased's body is also not buckled in. Her head is tilted to the right, resting below the jaw of the male deceased. Her upright torso faces the front, slightly angled toward the steering wheel. Two gunshot wounds are visible—one on the right temple and another in the center of the chest. The right side of her face is covered with dried blood, and her dress is damp. Blood spatters dot the cream leather seats, windows, dashboard, windshield, and the inner roof. The smell of blood and death fill the interior, overpowering the lemon fragrance from the car's air freshener.

"What do you think happened here?" Johan asks.

"Hard to say," Chew replies, as he bends over carefully into the car's interior on the driver's side.

"Didn't Lily say the car was locked?"

"Yes, we had to slim-jim the door open," Lily says.

"The alarm?" Johan asks.

"The key was on the On mode, so the alarm was not on," she explains.

"If the car was locked, and the ignition key was on, they must have been the only two people in the car," Johan suggests.

"I suppose so."

"Lily, did you get all the photographs?" Chew shouts above the traffic noise.

"Yup."

"OK for me to move the deceased and exhibits, then?"

"Yes, unless you want your boys to have another go at it?"

"OK, let's do that, just to be sure. Not that I don't trust your work," Chew adds, making sure Lily's people hear him.

He signals to his photographer to have another go at the interior.

"Chew, is that the gun?" Mislan asks.

"Yes."

"Hmmm. Anything on the back seat?"

"A box of tissues."

"Lily, were the victims moved?" Mislan asks.

"No, why?"

"Is this the way they were, when you got here?"

"Unless they moved themselves, because none of my guys did."

"Who recovered the victims' handbag and wallet?"

"I did," Lily admits.

"You think this is murder-suicide?" Murad inquires.

"I don't know, what makes you think that?"

"Only two of them in a locked car, it's the victim's own gun . . . sorry, the male deceased's own gun, what else could it be?"

"How do you know that's the male deceased's handgun?" Mislan asks.

"I'm just assuming. They're only two of them in the car, who else could it belong to?"

"Murad, since you think this is suicide cum murder, I suggest you take this on for now. I'll brief my boss and see what she says. Chew, to be on the safe side, I'd rather you handled the forensics instead of D10 in case this turns into something unexpected. I have a bad feeling about this, but it's not my call. Where are you sending the victims?"

"KL General Hospital, it's nearer," Murad says.

"You think it's not suicide cum murder?" Chew asks.

Mislan gives a noncommittal shrug.

"Okay, let me know if something comes up. In the meantime, Johan and I will check out what we can find out about the two deceased. We'll do whatever we can at this hour, so we'll know a little more when we brief the boss."

3

WHEN JOHAN STARTS THE car, Mislan turns the air-conditioning on at full blast, leans back, and waits for the interior to cool before resetting the thermostat to 73 degrees Fahrenheit.

"It's humid tonight. I'm all sweaty and sticky," he remarks.

"It's that time of year. Where do you want to start, male or female?" Johan says.

"The female deceased's address is Beverly Heights, right?"

"Number 3, Jalan 2A, Beverly Heights."

"That's close by, let's start there."

They exit the expressway to the DUKE and make a U-turn back toward the city and cut left to Beverly Heights. At the guardhouse, Johan flashes his police authority card and asks the security guard for directions. It is a middle high-end suburban-gated community housing estate. The roads are lined with bungalows and semidetached houses with the minimum of two cars under the carport and in the driveways.

"It's close to ten, you think they're still awake?" Johan asks.

"It's the fasting month, I'm sure they're up."

Walking up to the front gate, Johan rings the bell and waits. After about thirty seconds, he rings the bell again. The porch lights up and the front door opens. A woman appears at the grille of the front door and looks at them.

"Who's that?" Her diction sounds Indonesian.

"Police," Johan replies, holding his card above the gate.

"Hold on, ya," the woman responds and the door closes.

A minute passes before the front door opens again, followed by the grille, and two women step out to the porch. The automatic gate swings open, and the two D9 officers walk up the driveway. Johan displays his authority card for identification again.

"As-salamu-alaikum," Johan greets the women, *peace be upon you*. "I'm Detective Sergeant Johan and this is Inspector Mislan."

Together the elderly women reply, mu-alaikum-salam—*peace be upon you, too.*

"What's going on?" one of the women asks anxiously.

"Is this Mrs. Zaleha Jalani's house?"

"Miss," she corrects him. "Yes, it is. Is there a problem? Is she in some kind of trouble?"

"And, ma'am, you are?"

"I'm her mother, Khatijah."

"May we come in?"

"Sorry. Yes, yes, please come in," Khatijah says, stepping aside. "Something has happened to my child, hasn't it?" she says, her anxiety mounting.

"I think it's better for you to sit down," Johan suggests.

"Is your husband home?" Mislan asks.

"My husband has passed away. Has something happened to Leha?" she asks again.

"Your daughter has been in an accident—"

Before Johan can finish his sentence, the women wail, "Ya Allah, Leha's gone," and hug one another, crying and weeping.

The two D9 officers wait for the initial shock to pass. This is the part of police work Mislan dislikes the most. No matter how many times he has done it, he can never get used to it. This is one task where experience does not make it any easier. There is no easy way to tell parents that their child is dead.

"When, where, what happened?" Khatijah meekly asks, as if uncertain she really wants to know.

"The best we can say for now is that it happened around 8:30 tonight. She and Mr. Mahadi were found dead in a car on the expressway. Do you—"

The word "dead" triggers a fresh bout of wailing, again stopping Johan mid-sentence. When the wailing subsides, Johan continues, "It's too early for us to determine what happened, and we're still at the stage of preliminary investigations." He pauses, letting her digest his reply. "Do you know who Mr. Mahadi was?"

"Leha's partner."

"Business partner?"

"Yes."

"Do you know where they went or were going tonight?"

"She said she was breaking fast with him, but I don't know where. How did it happen?"

"We're still trying to put the facts together. Were Miss Zaleha and Mr. Mahadi . . . mmm . . . together?"

The women look at Johan.

"I mean, were they a couple?"

"She didn't tell me anything, but she talked about him a lot."

"Was Miss Zaleha ever married?" Mislan asks.

"No, why?"

"Was she seeing anyone?"

"She didn't tell me, but I know they were seeing one another. A mother can sense these things."

"How long had they been together?"

"Leha brought him to the house about two years ago, when we first moved in. So, I guess they must have been together longer than that."

"Was Mr. Mahadi married?"

Khatijah nods.

"I told her it was not proper to go out with a married man, but she kept saying it was business. I could tell it was more than business."

"Did you disapprove of their relationship?" Johan asks.

"Sergeant, it's not a question of approval. I'm a woman and a mother. I know how a wife feels when there is a third person in a marriage. If it's Leha's fate to be the second wife to a married man, so be it. But if she had a choice, she shouldn't. That's my opinion, but I'm from the old school."

Johan agrees with her.

"Is it possible for us to see Miss Zaleha's room?" Mislan asks.

She nods, stands, and leads them upstairs.

Careful Lan, this is where it all begins, Mislan warns himself. *Your first step into the deceased's life—the beginning of nightmares, of intimacy that can only be exorcised through closure.* He fights back the urge to sit this one out, to let Johan handle it alone. Standing at the deceased's bedroom door, he watches as his assistant walks into Zaleha's room, into her past, her hopes and dreams, a world he knows they will almost certainly obsess over. *If this was indeed a murder-suicide, she must have been the victim. But what could she have done to be murdered by her business partner? If it was a lovers' suicide pact, what drove her to it?* Without realizing it, Mislan takes a few steps into the room, drawn by the desire to understand.

Zaleha, being the man of the house, occupied the master bedroom. The room is modestly furnished with a queen-sized bed, a built-in wardrobe, and a dressing table. In one corner, there is a stand with an LCD TV, an ASTRO cable-network decoder, and a Blu-ray player. A digital clock-radio and two framed photos sit on the nightstand. One of the photos is of her with her parents, and the other is of her with a few others including the male deceased. They were seated around a dining table, probably in a posh restaurant, with the Sydney Opera House in the background. The deceased were not seated next to each other, but from their eyes you can see they were smiling to each other.

"Mrs. Khatijah, may we look around to see if your daughter left anything that might help us to understand the incident better?" Johan asks.

"I really don't feel it is right for me to let you go through her stuff. There might be things here better left private to her," the mother says, unsure if she should allow it or if she has the right to stop the police.

"We understand, but it could help our investigation. We'll do it in your presence," Mislan assures her.

Khatijah is silent for a moment then nods her consent. They start with the wardrobe. The victim's dresses are meticulously arranged according to style and length. The drawers in the wardrobe are just as systematically compartmentalized, with the clothes folded tidily. Everything has a place and everything is in its place. The dressing table drawers reveal many pieces of custom-made jewelry and accessories. *An organized person.* He points to a carrying case leaning against the dressing table.

"May we take a look inside?" Again, he notes the doubt on the mother's face and adds, "It's all right. We won't take anything without your consent."

She picks up the briefcase, lays it on the bed, and nods again. Johan unzips it, extracts the contents, and carefully spreads them on the bed. Mislan picks up a planner he sees and leafs through it while his assistant examines the rest.

"Do you know what business Miss Zaleha's company was in?"

"Construction, I think."

"Did she mention any of her concerns to you?"

"No, she was not the type to discuss such matters with me or her siblings."

"Do you know if she had any enemies?"

Khatijah shakes her head.

"How about her moods? Was she disturbed or depressed?"

"Leha was always cheerful, full of life, and always optimistic about everything. I dread to think what would've happened to me and the family when my husband passed away if it hadn't been for Leha."

"What about friends? Did she have a close friend, someone she confided in?'

"I guess that would have to be Ayn, they were close."

"Do you have Ayn's full name and contact number?" Johan asks.

"It's in my cell phone."

"May I hold on to this planner for a while? I'll return it as soon as I'm done," Mislan says.

"Why?"

"There might be something in here that could help us understand her movements, the people she met, or the schedule she kept. We may need to talk to some of them."

She is reluctant but agrees.

"Does she have a laptop, a computer?"

"Yes."

"I don't see one here."

"Maybe she left it in the office or her car. Why?"

"We'd like to look at it, too. It may contain information that could be helpful."

"Let me check the car," she says, leading them downstairs.

Johan retrieves a laptop from the passenger seat.

"Thank you. I'll return the diary and laptop as soon as I'm done with them. Thank you for your time. Again, please accept our condolences. Miss Zaleha's body will be sent to the Kuala Lumpur Hospital. Inspector Murad from Sentul police is the investigating officer for this case, but you can call me on this number should you need any assistance. Please call Inspector Murad on this number to arrange for the release of the body."

4

Driving out of Beverly Heights, the D9 officers are quiet. Mislan lights a cigarette, lowers the window, and stares out into the dark. As they hit the Middle Ring Road 2, Johan asks if he wants to visit Mahadi's family in Bukit Damansara. Mislan turns away from the window and looks at the clock on the dashboard.

"It's already close to midnight, and by the time we locate the house it'll be late. I'm sure Murad would have contacted the family already. Let's stop for a drink and I'll check with him."

"Anyplace, in particular?"

"Kampung Baru, I'm hungry."

Stopping at one of the many roadside stalls along Jalan Raja Alang in Kampung Baru, Mislan calls Inspector Murad. He is informed that the bodies are already in the Kuala Lumpur Hospital morgue. The deceased's vehicle is with Chew in the Forensics garage, and Mahadi's family has been notified.

"Where are you guys?" Murad asks.

"In Kampung Baru having dinner," Mislan tells him. "How're you classifying the case?"

"My SIO said to go with 302 for now."

So his senior investigating officer is going with murder. "What did you brief him to come to such a classification?"

"Nothing, just what was at the scene," Murad says defensively.

"I know what you guys are trying to do," Mislan says with a chuckle.

"What?"

"Offload the case. Let me know if something breaks."

"Sure. Is Special investigations not taking this case?"

"What did your SIO say?"

"The first words from his mouth: Can we pass this on?" Murad says, followed by laughter.

Mislan chuckles. "I'll let you know tomorrow after I brief my boss."

Just as he terminates the call, his cell phone rings.

"Mislan," he answers, taking a sip of his iced black coffee.

"Sir, we got an armed robbery at Petronas gas station on Jalan Peel. Four men, most likely Malay."

"Casualties?"

"One casualty reported, minor injury, pistol-whipped."

"Okay, thanks."

"What was that?" Johan asks.

"Armed robbery; Petronas station, Jalan Peel. . . . Let's skip dinner."

Johan drives out of Kampung Baru, makes a right onto Jalan Tun Razak, and drives past the Royal Selangor Golf Club straight to the Kampung Pandan roundabout. At the roundabout, he takes the slip-off at 10 o'clock to the Petronas gas station about five hundred yards up the road.

"You think it's the Wira gang?" Johan asks as he pulls into the station.

"Every time a festival is around the corner, every Amat, Ah Chong, Muthu, and enforcement officer will try to make a quick buck. It could be anybody."

"Festive season robberies," Johan says, "I think the gangs have some sort of understanding. Before Raya, the Malay gangs do their thing, robbing petrol kiosks, breaking into houses, and snatching purses. Before Chinese New Year, Chinese gangs target goldsmiths, gambling dens, and girlie bars."

"How about Deepavali and Christmas?"

Johan laughs. "I've not figured that out yet."

The gas station is crowded with holiday-makers filling their tanks, curious onlookers, and uniformed police personnel. Johan honks to move the crowd away and parks the car. Stepping out, the officers give the surroundings the once-over. The roads around the area are quiet, but all the mamak—Indian-Muslim—stalls and restaurants are full of customers, young and old.

"Jo, did the caller who called in about the DUKE incident know any of the other onlookers? I mean, did he speak to them or recognize them?"

"I didn't ask."

"You have his contact details, in case we need to talk to him again?"

"Yeah, he works at the Setapak army camp."

In the convenience store, Mislan sees two station employees at the counter with several armed policemen. A Special Investigations detective approaches them.

"Good evening, sir."

"Evening. Who's the IO?"

"Inspector Kula," the detective replies, jerking his head toward the convenience store.

"Losses?"

"RM1,200, two cell phones, some cigarettes and beers. Four men drove up to the pump, two went into the store pretending to pay for the petrol and to buy drinks. Then one of them pulled a gun and emptied the cash register while the other grabbed the rest of the stuff. The cashier tried to resist and was whipped across the head with the butt of the gun. Nothing serious, just minor injuries. Both workers are Bangladeshi."

"They must be legal," Johan remarks.

The detective looks at him, puzzled.

"Otherwise, they would've bolted before the police arrived."

"CCTV?"

"Dummies. The workers got the car registration number. We ran it. False."

"Description?"

"Husin showed them some photos, and the cashier picked out one of them, a former member of the Green Screwdriver gang nicknamed Din Mayat—Din the Corpse."

"I thought the Green Screwdriver gang specialized in housebreaking," Johan says.

"They do, but Din Mayat is an ex. Maybe he joined another gang, or started a new one," the detective explains.

"Has Ops been notified?" Mislan asks.

"Yes."

"Okay, let's see what the investigating officer thinks."

As they are walking toward the convenience store, the inspector's cell phone rings.

"Mislan."

"Mislan, Murad here. The male victim's family has just arrived with a few big guns. You may want to be here."

"Who are they?"

"I recognize one as someone in politics. I don't know his name, but I've seen him on TV."

"Has he said anything?"

"I think they're looking for me. I was in the toilet when they arrived. When I saw them as I was walking back to the morgue, I decided to keep my distance and observe. Are you coming?" Murad asks, sounding desperate.

"I've got an armed robbery. Why don't you find out what they want? I'll be down once I'm done here."

"OK."

The district investigating officer sounds relieved.

"Murad, don't agree to any of their requests, especially for the release of bodies until the postmortem is done. Who's the pathologist?"

"OK. The pathologist is Dr. Matthews. I've not worked with him before."

"OK. Play it by the book." Terminating the call, Mislan says, "Jo, can you handle things here? I have to run down to the hospital. Murad says some big shots are there for the deceased."

"No problem. You want me to come down after finishing here?"

"Yes, do that and keep the car. I'll get one of the MPVs to drive me. And Jo, get ASP Ghani's special project team in on this, too, I'm sure he'd love to make this his project."

It is 1:15 a.m. and the hospital complex is quiet and deserted except for the Emergency & Trauma Center. The Medical Forensics facility building is at the back. When the MPV approaches the building, Mislan sees several media vehicles lining the road. He tells the MPV to drive past the main gate and stop a distance away. Getting out, he casually strolls back toward the gate, checking out the surroundings and trying not to attract attention. He observes quite a number of black Toyota Vellfires, the luxury multipurpose vehicle, and black Toyota Harrier SUVs, the Southeast Asia version of Lexus, parked along the road close to the gate. In the tiny Medical Forensic compound, he counts three Mercedes and two BMWs parked irresponsibly, blocking the access. Two milling crowds, one at the ambulance parking shed and another at the entrance to the morgue. He makes out the crowd at the ambulance parking to be media crew with their cameras, microphones, and digital recorders, while the crowd at the morgue is made up of the deceaseds' families and friends.

Standing by the gate, Mislan searches the crowd at the morgue for Inspector Murad, when he feels a tap on his shoulder. Turning around, it is Rodziah, the crime reporter who likes to be called Audi, like the car.

"Not now," Mislan tells her sternly.

"Just for a minute, I'm sure you'll want to hear this," she says, pulling him away by his arm into the shadow.

"What?"

"The deceased, do you know who they are?"

"Why?"

"Do you know who came here twenty minutes ago?" Audi asks, jerking her head toward the cars in the compound.

"Surprise me."

"Tan Sri Kudin Kudus, a big-shot powerbroker politician, and some of his cronies. He's more popularly known as Tan Sri KK or Kabel Kuat—Strong Cable, referring to political connections." Tan Sri is a title conferred by the king to deserving recipients who have contributed greatly to the nation.

"So?"

"You don't know who he is, do you?"

"Nope. Should I?"

"I guess in your case, ignorance makes you courageous." Audi chuckles.

"No. In my case, ignorance allows me to do my job."

"OK, I know you don't give a shit about politics, but just for your info, he's somebody big. So, my dear Inspector, your victims must have been people who'd have made the news. You may want to tread with caution . . . you know, kowtow a little. I'm telling you this because we're friends. You treated me right the last time, and I respect that."

"Thanks for the warning. Did you know the victims?"

"I overheard some media guys saying he was high up in the food chain in Selangor state."

"Meaning?"

"Front man, proxy holder, you know, someone that manages the war chests of those in public office. But that's only media talk. Half of it is street gossip. Anyway, store that information somewhere in your head."

"Shit, that's all Murad needs, political interference. Thanks for the info, Audi."

"No sweat, you treat me right, I treat you right," Audi says and waggles away, giving him a wink.

"Why aren't you with them?" Mislan calls after her, pointing to the media crowd.

"I don't work with packs, I hunt alone," Audi says, grinning. "And I got an insider."

"Who's your insider?"

"You, Inspector," Audi says, with a laugh.

Mislan watches Audi weave her way between the black Toyota Vellfire MPVs and black Toyota Harriers, disappearing into the night. He remembers Johan once told him that the political termites can be identified by their vehicles—those driving Vellfires are one rung up the food chain from those driving Harriers. It is an unwritten code for the ruling political party but known to all its members: from Harrier to Vellfire to BMW to Mercedes, and it had to be black.

5

Mislan is in no mood to deal with politicians and political termites. He has very little regard for this breed of people and what they stand for. He steps between two Toyota Vellfires, leans against one, and lights a cigarette. Taking out his cell phone, he calls Inspector Murad.

"Where are you?"

"In the morgue with Tan Sri—"

"Can you step out a minute?" Mislan asks, cutting off Murad mid-sentence.

"I'm with—"

"I don't care who you're with," Mislan snaps.

"OK, where are you?"

"Outside the gate, behind the first Vellfire."

A couple of minutes pass, and Mislan sees Inspector Murad walking out of the gate, looking left and right. He steps away from behind the MPVs and waves him over.

"Why are you out here?" Murad asks.

"What's going on in there?" Mislan ignores the inspector's question.

"What do you think is happening?" Murad answers fretfully.

"Now you know why I'm out here," Mislan replies with a smile. "Is your SIO in there?"

Inspector Murad shakes his head.

"Hmmm."

Mislan has empathy for what it feels like to be an investigating officer abandoned by his superior.

He takes another peek at the crowd, which seems to have grown. A couple of luxury cars have joined those already there in the tiny compound. *Who the hell is the deceased?*

"Have you found out who the deceased is?"

"I heard them talking, and I think he was the proxy director or shareholder for some politicians."

"Who?"

"Don't know, they don't mention names."

"Who are inside there?"

"Tan Sri KK and I think an assemblyman, because I heard one of them calling him YB."

"You didn't ask?"

"They're all talking among themselves like I don't exist. Half of them are on cell phones talking as if they're at a political rally, and the others are barking orders."

"It is past 1 a.m., I'm sure the case hit the midnight news. That's why there's such a big crowd. I'll take a risk and call my boss to see if she wants to take this on."

Stepping away from the investigating officer, Mislan makes a call to the head of Special Investigations Unit. On the second ring, she answers the call.

"Ma'am, sorry to call you at this hour."

"It's OK, I'm not asleep yet. What's up?" Superintendent of Police Samsiah Hassan asks.

"There was a double homicide on the DUKE around 8 something, two deceased, a male and a female—"

"I caught it on the midnight news. What about it?"

"It has the makings of a media sensation. I'm at the morgue, and there's a Tan Sri Kudin Kudus, an assemblyman, and dozens of political lackeys here. One media person has told me the male deceased was a political crony in Selangor."

"You mean Tan Sri KK?"

"You know him?"

"By reputation. And you're thinking?"

"I'm thinking maybe we'd like to step in."

"And we want to step in because?"

"District has classified it as 302, initially they're leaning toward murder-suicide. I have a bad feeling about this case, and the presence of these guys is one of the reasons."

"I don't care about them. What are the other indicators?"

"Well for one, the deceased is a sixty-year-old Muslim male; two, this is Ramadan. I know many Muslims would like to die during Ramadan but not by suicide. I mean, not even an ignorant Muslim like me."

"I'll take note of your religious point of views. Now, convince me with evidence," she says.

"As I said, the deceased was in his sixties. A man of that age would have passed the age of suicide. He'd be inclined to take any good or bad that comes his way with understanding."

Mislan can hear the head of Special Investigations chuckling.

"I also take note of your psychoanalytical abilities, although I'm not sure of your credentials for that. Lan, tell me your gut feeling as my investigator."

He snickers. "Everything about the scene, it doesn't add up, but it'll take too long to brief you over the phone."

"Who's the IO?"

"Inspector Murad from Sentul police."

"And the SIO's instruction?"

"The standard . . . Can we push it?"

"OK, tell Murad we are taking the case until we can clear your doubts. And Lan, since we're looking into it, you can start referring to them as victims and not deceased."

"OK," Mislan answers with a chuckle. "Ma'am, sorry to have disturbed you. Good night."

"Night, Ustaz Dr. Mislan."

Walking back to Inspector Murad, he says, "OK, let's go and do some work. This case for the time being is under D9. Once we know more, my boss will decide."

Murad beams. "Thanks."

"Don't thank me yet, it may well fall back onto your lap."

The two officers push their way through the crowd at the morgue entrance. The media sees them and instantly rush toward the morgue with cameras flashing and calls of *Are you the IO of the case? Can you give us a comment on what happened?* The officers ignore them and shove open the heavy morgue door.

Morgues are kept cold, sting with the smell of disinfectant, and are normally still, especially at this hour of the morning. Yet this is like a circus, crowded and noisy—people are either talking to one another or on their cell phones. The room is not cold due to the overcrowding and body heat, and the smell of disinfectant is overwhelmed by body odor.

Inspector Murad points out Tan Sri KK and the assemblyman who are talking to the forensic pathologist, dramatically pointing at the empty autopsy table and at the crowd outside. Mislan nudges Murad forward.

"You take the lead, there's something I need to do."

The big shots stop talking as the police officers approach them, much to the relief of the forensic pathologist.

"Which of you is in charge?" KK asks, before the officers reach the group.

Mislan pushes Murad forward and steps back.

"I've asked the doctor here to expedite the postmortem, so the bodies can be released soon. Their families are grieving and waiting," KK continues.

"I understand and will do my best," Murad answers timidly.

While the Tan Sri and YB confront Murad, Mislan sneaks around them, stands next to the forensic pathologist, looks at his name tag, and extends his hand.

"Doctor Matthews, I'm Inspector Mislan from D9."

"Inspector, are you the investigator?"

He leads Dr. Matthews away from the group.

"Yes. Doc, I'm not trying to tell you how to do your job, but I'm sure you can see the situation here. Everything we do will be watched closely, so take your time and exercise care."

"Who are the deceased?"

"I don't know yet, but, whoever they are, they deserve all that we can do for them."

"I understand."

Mislan sees Murad meekly pointing toward him while explaining something to the two men. He walks over to them.

"He says you're in charge," KK says, frowning.

"Yes, I am, and who might you be?"

"Tan Sri Kudin Kudus, and this is Assemblyman Ibrahim Taib. I've spoken to your boss, and he tells me the bodies can be released tonight," KK replies in an intimidating tone.

"I'm sorry, Tan Sri and YB. I'm sensitive to the grieving families, but I'll not be able to release the bodies until the autopsies are completed."

YB stands for *Yang Berhormat* (the Honorable), used in addressing an assemblyman or member of parliament.

"Did you not hear me? I spoke to your boss and he said they'll be released tonight."

"I heard you, but unless my boss instructs me directly, I'm powerless. In the meantime, I would appreciate it very much if Tan Sri, YB, and the rest would cooperate by clearing the morgue so Dr. Matthews can start working. The earlier the doctor starts, the sooner we can release the bodies. By the way, who did you call?"

"Datuk Jalil, the Selangor police chief."

"This is Kuala Lumpur's case, and Selangor has nothing to do with it," he says. "If you'll excuse us," and he ushers them to the door.

Seeing the big shots coming out of the morgue, the media rushes forward to bombard them with questions. Tan Sri KK and Assemblyman Ibrahim gladly offer themselves for questions, while Mislan slinks back into the morgue, closing the door behind him.

Just then, Johan enters. Jerking his head toward the door, he whispers to his boss, "That's Tan Sri KK and YB Ibrahim."

"Know them?"

"Only by reputation. What are they here for? Family of the deceased?"

"The usual, Jo. By the way, we can refer to them as victims."

Johan looks at his boss with raised eyebrows. "It's our case?"

"For now. I need you and Murad to interview some of those people outside and find out whatever you can about the vics. Their business, relationships, political connections, anything worth following up on. I spoke to ma'am, and she has agreed to take this on until we can get a clearer picture."

As Inspector Murad and Johan head for the door, Mislan calls after them, "Watch your step, be careful of snakes."

Johan laughs.

"I want to stick around for the autopsy. How did it go at the Petronas station?"

"ASP Ghani's team came, and I took off."

Turning to Dr. Matthew, Mislan says, "OK, let's start."

6

Mislan watches as the doctor and his assistant remove the personal belongings and clothing of the male victim, bagging and tagging them. The black plastic body bag is replaced with the white hospital sheets, giving the cadaver a little more respectability. He watches as a CT scanner is rolled next to the cadaver, the assistant operating the machine while Dr. Matthews views the monitor. As he expected, the bullet is lodged within the cranium.

The scanner is wheeled away from the autopsy table and the external examination begins. As he examines, the forensic pathologist speaks into a hanging microphone and writes notes on a clipboard. His assistant snaps a photo every time the forensic pathologist dictates an observation or when told to do so. Swabs of the entry wound and the hair around it, the back of both hands, and between the thumb and index finger are taken for gunshot residue analysis. The examination is methodical, with the tiniest foreign item found on the body collected for analysis. The care and respect the pathologist displays in handling the cadaver fascinate Mislan. The silent respect, the courtesy of telling the cadaver what he is about to do and why, blows him away. *If only the living were treated with the same respect.*

After the initial external examination, the cadaver undergoes a thorough washing. Another external examination starts with more speaking into the overhead microphone and photographs.

"Doc, is it possible to establish the bullet's entry trajectory?" Mislan asks.

"I can."

The doctor walks to the cabinets lining the wall and returns with what looks like a chopstick. He slowly inserts it into the wound. The chopstick-like instrument protrudes from the wound at a fifty-five-degree upward angle. The assistant takes a snapshot of this.

"What are you looking for? Perhaps, I can focus on that?"

"I don't know, Doc, I'm still fishing. Would you say the angle is right for a self-inflicted shot?"

"There is no forensic literature on the 'right' angle for a self-inflicted wound. But in my experience, which is not much, fifty-five degrees upward is within an acceptable range. Usually, the ones that I've seen are between a forty- and ninety-degree upward angle. More than ninety degrees would be a downward angle and questionable."

"Why is that?"

"It's hard to imagine a person shooting himself downward," Dr. Matthews says with a smile.

"Yeah, downward shot is more like execution style."

Dr. Matthew looks at the officer, puzzled.

"Can I step out for a smoke?"

"I could use one, too, but I've got my hands full right now."

"Is there a back door? I don't want to attract any attention," Mislan says, referring to the crowd outside.

"Through there," Dr. Matthews says, pointing.

Mislan cracks the side door open and peeks out at the dark narrow path between the buildings. It is almost 2:20 a.m., and he can still hear the crowd from the other side of the building. It sounds like the crowd has grown larger and more restless. It must be the fasting month, he figures. Malays normally stay awake until Sahur between 5 to 6 in the morning, which will be the last meal before fasting for the day. He makes a call to his assistant and asks him and Murad to meet him at the back of the morgue. Waiting for them, he lights a cigarette.

"So, Inspector, was I right?"

"Shit Audi, you gave me a fright. Where did you come from?"

"Over there," she says, pointing to a passage leading to the main building. "I know this place well, every passage and every staircase. So, was I right?"

"I don't know, could be."

"You can't smoke here, this is a hospital," she admonishes him.

He gives her a does-it-look-like-I-give-a-shit look.

She smiles. "Can I have a cig?"

"I didn't know you smoked," he says, handing her the pack.

"Trying to quit. Has the autopsy started?"

He nods.

"Who's the forensic pathologist?"

"Dr. Matthews."

"What are the dead saying?"

"Nothing yet, it has just started."

"Don't bullshit me. You wouldn't be out here if it had just started. You would be watching it like a starving lion. Come on, you can trust me."

"I'm not bullshitting you. It's the truth, it's just started. Look Audi, I have nothing yet. At this stage, you probably know more than me. I need to speak to my guys. Can you give us some space?"

"Don't worry about me, pretend I'm not here," she says, grinning.

He gives her a get-lost stare. She smiles, stubs out her cigarette, and walks toward the waiting crowd, saying, "I'll call you later."

Once Audi is out of range, he asks, "Anything interesting?"

"As you said, the male victim is a top crony in Selangor, heads several companies involved in mainly government projects. Some say the victims were married, others say they're lovers, but one thing's sure, they all say she was managing one of the companies," Murad says.

"Mahadi was married with four children, three male and one female. The eldest, Hashim, is a managing director in one of the vic's subsidiaries; the second, Latiff, is an accountant with a multinational; the third, Mokthar, is a businessman, but we're not too sure what kind of business. The youngest, Laila, has no known occupation. The wife, Rahimah, is a housewife," Johan briefs him. "I don't think we can get anything of substance here."

The inspector looks at Johan.

"Most here are party members simply exchanging gossip. The family's keeping mum. KK and the YB are hovering over them like mother crocodiles."

"The whole family's here?"

"Only the boys. The wife and daughter are not."

"Jo, call in a couple of detectives to mingle with the crowd, to pick up on the gossip. They might find something to follow up later."

"OK, will do."

"Murad, you want to split?"

"I should. I left two complainants at the station. I hope they're still there."

"I'm going to check on the autopsy. Let me know when the detectives arrive, then we can leave." Mislan walks toward the door. "Jo, did you see the female vic's family around?"

"No, just the male vic's."

"Just as I thought."

Mislan reenters to the autopsy room just as Dr. Matthews is opening the deceased's chest. The sudden change in the temperature from the hot and humid air outside to the cold morgue interior makes him shiver. The forensic pathologist notices the inspector shiver, thinking it was because of the open-chest cadaver, and he smiles.

"Not a pretty sight, eh?"

"Never is, Doc. Are you doing both tonight?"

"I don't think so. I'll finish with him and get the next shift to do her."

"Who's on next?"

"Dr. Bakar Sulaiman."

"Doc, how long can you hang on to the deceased, before releasing them?"

"As long as we need to complete whatever we have to do. Why?"

"I need you to hang on to the bodies for a while until I talk with our Forensics people. Shouldn't be too long. Think you can do that?"

"I don't see why not."

"Great. Doc. Is it OK if I bring Dr. Safia from HUKM to have a look at the bodies?"

"Any particular reason?"

"I hope you don't take this the wrong way. I've got a bad feeling that this case . . . how shall I put it?"

"Front-page news."

"I was about to say something else, but front-page news sounds more respectful."

"It's unusual for an outside forensic pathologist to review our case unless challenged in court or requested by the family. I guess, if it helps in your investigation . . . I have no problem with it. I don't know about Dr. Bakar. I suggest you talk to him or you can put in a formal request through the hospital administration."

"I just think a fresh pair of eyes might help me understand. I don't comprehend medical jargon. It's more for me to understand, nothing official."

"Like I said, I'm OK with it, but you have to check with Dr. Bakar for the other deceased. Call me when you bring Dr. Safia, so I can be around."

"Sure, thank you. I've got to run now, and thank you again, Doc."

7

The Special Investigations office is starting to look more like an Indian barbershop, with colorful greeting cards pinned on the notice board and hung across corners. Reflective green-and-gold-colored Hari Raya greetings are strung across the door. The festive mood is certainly felt. Almost all the civilian clerical staff are on leave, and those remaining are not in the mood for work. Since the office staff is mostly Malay-Muslim, Hari Raya is a big deal. Even investigation teams are down to two teams.

Mislan has never been a festive person, has never been able to get into the flow, but since his wife left, he has been trying to adjust for the sake of his son. He wants Daniel to understand the Hari Raya spirit and enjoy it like other kids. When Lynn was around, she handled that by taking Daniel back to her hometown to spend Hari Raya with her parents. Last year, he had spent Hari Raya with Daniel at McDonald's and watching *Monster Fish*. Earlier this week he called his ex-wife and suggested that Daniel spend Hari Raya with her. She promised to think about it and let him know. Mislan knows he's going to miss his son, especially on the eve and morning of Hari Raya, but he's happy that Daniel will get to celebrate the festival like other fortunate kids around the world.

The front desk clerk shouts from the doorway announcing that morning prayer is about to begin. Mislan gathers his notepad and walks to the meeting room. There are only two of them for the meeting, and the atmosphere feels strangely quiet without the usual joking, boasting, and bitching. The head of Special Investigations walks in, takes her seat at the head of the table, and looks around.

"It's that time of the year, again," she remarks. "Right, what do we have?"

"One armed robbery at Petronas, Jalan Peel, by four Malay men. One of the vics was injured, pistol-whipped. Losses: RM1,236, eighteen packs of cigarettes and ten cans of beer worth RM208.20. One of the victims picked out a former Green Screwdriver gang member, Mohammad Din Mohamed Tahir aka Din Mayat from the mugshots shown. Special Project was informed, and maybe ASP Ghani would like to take over this case as his project. The district IO is Inspector Kulaselvam."

"Green Screwdriver, isn't that the Indonesian-Malaysian gang that specialized in housebreaking?"

"Yes."

"I thought that gang was wiped out two years ago."

"They were, but Din Mayat is an ex-member, probably just out of prison," Mislan says. "One double murder on the DUKE, vics are Mahadi Mokshin, sixty, executive chairman of MM Harapan Holding, and Zaleha Jalani, thirty-four, managing director of Rakan MM Harapan Sdn. Bhd. The male vic has one gunshot wound to the head, the female vic has one to the head and one to the chest. Nothing was stolen. We can rule out a botched robbery. A Walther PPK .32 and three empty casings were found in the car. I've checked with the Firearm System. The pistol is registered to the male vic. The bodies have been sent to HKL and the car taken to Forensics HQ."

"Anything else?"

"Only these two," Mislan says.

"Are you leading the DUKE case?" Inspector Tee asks.

"Looks like it, for now at least."

"Right, is there anything else?" Superintendent Samsiah inquires.

The two investigators shake their heads, and the morning prayer is adjourned. As they leave the meeting room, Superintendent Samsiah signals to Mislan to see her in her office. He tells Johan to join them.

"Morning, ma'am," Johan greets her.

"Morning, Jo. You said something was bothering you about the DUKE scene, what was it?" she asks Mislan, getting to the point.

"A few things. First, the car's position."

"Explain."

"The car coming to rest against the road divider in the middle of the road, the driver's side. OK, try and follow this logic. If the driver is holding the steering wheel with his right hand, when startled, he will jerk the steering wheel clockwise veering the car to the right on the driver's side . . . Agreed?" Mislan says, as he demonstrates by holding an imaginary steering wheel and jerking the steering wheel downward — clockwise. "That's unless he's an idiot and holds the steering wheel way on the left, crossing his hand across his body, like this. Nobody drives that way."

Superintendent Samsiah remains noncommittal, but Johan nods.

"And if his left hand is on the wheel, it would when jerked be counterclockwise. It's a common reflex," he continues, with a similar demonstration.

"And?"

"My guess is the vic was driving with his right hand on the wheel."

"OK, what else?"

"Next is the position of the gun. It was found at the base of the gearshift, in the middle of the car."

"And it should be?"

"I noticed the male vic wearing a watch on his left hand. Most right-handed men wear their watch on their left hand, and I'm sure the same goes for women. If he was right-handed, the gun would most likely be on the right side of the car between the driver's seat and the door."

"He could be right-handed, but in this case shoots with his left."

"It's possible, except for one thing."

"That is?"

"He was shot in the right temple."

"Jo, do you have an answer to that?" Superintendent Samsiah asks.

Johan shakes his head and smiles.

"So, you're saying it's not murder-suicide."

"I'm saying, let's be sure before we decide. What's puzzling is that the car was locked from the inside, and Inspector Lily Chin from D10 had to break in—slim-jim it. The ignition key was at the On position and the alarm not on."

"That's interesting. OK, you'll lead this case until we are clear what actually happened. I'll inform the district. What about Tan Sri KK and YB Ibrahim?"

"KK said that he spoke to KP Selangor, Datuk Jalil, and was assured that the bodies would be released immediately. I'm guessing you'll be hearing from Datuk Jalil or the Tan Sri soon." KP is short for *Ketua Police* or police chief of a state.

"I'll deal with that when it happens. In the meantime, go and get some rest."

"Thanks, ma'am."

"I noticed this is the third year you have not applied for Raya leave. Is there something I should know?"

"Nope. I'm not into festivals, that's all," Mislan answers, not daring to look her in the eye.

"OK, suit yourself. And Lan, you'll not be taken off the roster for the next ten days, at least. We're short. Treat this like any other case and put in time in between shifts."

"No problem."

Back in the office, he tells Johan to go home and to get some rest. His assistant asks if he has any plans for the day.

"I'm thinking of asking Dr. Safia if she's willing to view the vics at the morgue."

"Why?"

"For another pair of eyes to look at them. To ask questions and to give me a layman's explanation. I don't understand most of the medical jargon in the reports. You want to come along?"

"What time?"

"I'll call you once it's confirmed. Maybe after that we could do some more background work on the vics."

Superintendent Samsiah is reading the daily reports when she is summoned by Senior Assistant Commissioner Burhanuddin Md. Sidek. The Officer in Charge of Criminal Investigation's (OCCI) secretary does not say why. She grabs a notepad and goes out. The corridors and the elevators are empty. She relishes the quiet and is surprised by the extra courtesy displayed by the staff. *Most likely brought on by the slow pace and the holiday spirit,* she guesses. Even the ever-constipated looking OCCI is smiling, greeting her warmly as she walks into his office.

"Samsiah, come in, can I get you a drink?

"Good morning, sir. No thank you, I'm fasting."

"Yes, of course you are. Silly me. How are your Raya preparations? Are you going home to Kota Baru?"

"Not this year, the children want to spend Raya in the city," she answers. "I'm sure you did not call me up to ask about my Raya preparations. What's on your mind?"

Upset that his attempt at cordiality is being spurned, the OCCI says, "You know about the murder-suicide of Mahadi and the woman?"

She nods.

"I understand Special Investigations is handling it. What have you got so far?"

"We're still investigating at the moment."

"Who's the lead?"

"Inspector Mislan." She notes the disapproval by his puckered brows at the mention of her officer's name. "Is there a problem?"

"No, no problem. I've received a call from Datuk Jalil . . . Jack, as we call him, asking if we can lend some assistance to the victims' families."

"We'll do all we can to bring the case to closure."

"I'm sure you will. What he meant was, if we could expedite the release of the bodies to the family for necessary arrangements. You know, Raya is only a few days away, and they're expecting to have the burial before that. It's bad enough for the family without the bodies being kept in the morgue. You know what I mean."

"I do, and I empathize with them. I'll speak to Mislan, but it's for the forensic pathologist to decide."

Senior Assistant Commissioner Burhanuddin nods.

"You've heard of Tan Sri Kudin Kudus, KK to most of us?"

"Yes, I've heard of him."

"Well, he called me and said there are certain quarters that would like to see the case solved quickly. It seems the deceased was well-connected, and the case is causing some concern."

"And why is that?"

"He means . . . the bodies found together . . . a lovers' quarrel leading to murder-suicide." The OCCI shakes his head, as though the deceased's affairs matter to him. "What a waste," he sighs.

"Is that what they think it is . . . a murder-suicide?"

"That's what they've hinted, and it coincides with what the district has told me. The district says the deceased were in a love triangle . . . things turned sour, dada, dada, dada. They got into a heated argument, he lost his temper, pulled out his gun . . . bang, bang . . . and we've got two dead bodies. What a tragic end."

"I see, but you missed one bang," she says, smiling, but the OCCI doesn't catch on. "What did the district base their love triangle on?" The OCCI pretends he didn't hear Samsiah's question and continues, "I'll leave it to you to do the right thing. I'll call Tan Sri and Datuk KP and tell them you're taking care of things." He stands and says, "Selamat Hari Raya to you and family," using the customary Malay greeting for Eid.

Leaving the OCCI's office, Superintendent Samsiah smiles to herself. If anything, the meeting has only aroused her curiosity. *Who is pulling the strings and why? Who are you, Mahadi Mokshin?* Back in her office, she calls several of her contacts in politics and business. Then, leaning back in her chair, she wonders whether Mislan might have bitten off more than he could chew this time.

8

Reaching home, he checks on Daniel. His son is playing with the maid in his room. Mislan leaves them and goes to his room. Stepping out of the shower, he slips on a pair of shorts and a sleeveless T-shirt and lies on the bed. Daniel comes into the room and jumps on the bed next to him.

"Daddy, Mummy called."

Mislan looks at his son, saying nothing. Mummy is a sensitive subject with his son, and he prefers not to say anything that may hurt his son's feelings.

"Mummy's coming to pick me up. I'm going to spend Raya with Grandpa and Grandma."

"Do you want to?"

Daniel nods.

"OK, when is Mummy picking you up?"

"She's already on the way."

"Have Sister pack your things."

"Yes, and Sister's coming, too."

"But we've not done your shopping yet," Mislan says, annoyed at the sudden decision by his ex-wife. "Daddy plans to do it this week."

"Mummy said we can do that in Johor."

"OK."

Mislan hugs his son, hiding his disappointment at not being able to do his son's clothing shopping with him.

Getting off the bed, he makes a call to his ex-wife. After several rings, she answers.

"Hi, dear." She still calls him "dear," even after the divorce. "How are you?"

"I'm OK, how are you?"

"I'm fine. Dear, I'll take Daniel for Raya. It's been a while since I spent time with him, and I miss him so much."

"Great, Mi, I'm sure he'll love it."

He used to call her "dear," too, but after Daniel was born he started calling her "Mi," short for "Mummy."

"Thanks, dear. Can I pick him up this evening? His school's already closed, right?"

"Yes, I'll tell Ani to pack his things," Mislan lies, not wanting to let her know that he already knew of her coming. "What time do you want to come?"

"Actually, I'm already in KL. I had something to do this morning. I think I can be there in about thirty minutes. Dear, can you give me his passport? I want to take him to Singapore."

"OK. Mi, I've not had the time to buy his baju Melayu, can you do that for me? Daniel wants one in red or blue," he says with a chuckle. "I'll give you some money for it."

"I already got him one in green. All right, then, I'll get him another one. He can use the green one for his Quran classes. Thanks, dear, and you take care."

"You too, Mi."

Terminating the call, he tells his son to get ready. His mother will be arriving shortly to pick him up. He watches as his son jumps off the bed, telling the maid to get ready since his mummy is coming. Mislan smiles a happy-sad smile at his son's excitement.

After a lot of giggling and bantering between his son and the maid, they emerge from the room with each carrying a travel bag.

"Mummy's already downstairs," Daniel says.

"So soon?"

"Yes. Mummy called Sister."

"OK," Mislan says. "Come here."

He hugs his son, telling him not to be naughty and to listen to his mother. He reminds the maid to look after Daniel and asks if she packed the fever and sore throat medicine. The maid answers yes to both.

Since his wife, Lynn, left, Mislan has not seen her or met up with her. Every time she comes to pick up or send their son back, he just stays in the apartment and looks out from the window as her car enters or leaves the compound. He fears that seeing her will only make him want her back.

After his Daniel has left, the apartment feels empty. He goes back to his bedroom and lies on the bed, missing his son. Exhaustion soon takes its toll, and he falls asleep. When he wakes up, it is almost one in the afternoon. He goes to the kitchen to make a mug of coffee and toast two slices of bread. Waiting for the bread to toast, he realizes he's fasting and abandons them. He leaves the kitchen and calls Dr. Safia.

"Hi, Fie, you busy?"

"Hi, Lan. No, I'm not. I'm home, on leave."

"Oh, going anywhere?"

"Thought I'd visit Mum. I haven't spent much time with her lately. You know, with Raya around the corner and all, just want to cheer her up like the good daughter that I am," Dr. Safia says with a chuckle. "What's up?"

"Nothing much, just woke up from a nap. Hey, you heard about the murder on the DUKE?"

"Read it in the papers. Said they're prominent business people and the police don't suspect foul play because there was no third person involved. Is that true?"

"Did it name the source?"

"No."

"I didn't think so. You should know better than to believe what you read in the papers," he says with a laugh.

"Why do you ask? Are you the lead on this case?"

"I'm leading for the time being, to clear some doubts. When do you plan to go to your mum's?"

"Maybe later in the evening to break my fast with her. Why? You have anything planned?" she asks, expectantly.

"I was wondering if you would like to come with me to HKL Medical Forensics to take a peek at the deceased."

"Why, what's wrong with them?" Safia asks, hiding her disappointment.

"Apart from being dead, I don't know. I was thinking, maybe, if you see the bodies you could explain to me, in lay language, some things I don't understand. You know, those medical terms doctors use to impress the public," Mislan teases her, deaf to her disappointment.

"Oh, you mean like the slang you guys use in the police to sound macho?" she teases him back. "I'm not sure, Lan. The attending forensic pathologist may not like it, and it can cause complications if a formal complaint is filed."

"You'll be coming with me as a friend, not a forensic pathologist. You know, like me showing off my macho police world to my girlfriend."

Dr. Safia laughs.

"What time do you want to go?"

"It's 1 now. What if I pick you up at 2? That'll give you enough time after that to break your fast with your mum."

"Okay, see you then."

At the HKL Medical Forensics, Mislan parks his car by the roadside, tells Dr. Safia and Johan to wait while he goes into the morgue to inquire and to arrange for the viewing. A few minutes later he stomps out, furious and swearing.

"What's wrong?" Dr. Safia asks.

Shaking his head, he walks to the car, unlocks it, snatches his pack of cigarettes from the glove compartment, and lights up.

"Are you not fasting?" Johan asks.

"I was until now."

"You can't smoke here, it's a hospital compound," Dr. Safia tells him. "What happened in there?"

"The bodies have been released," he snarls. "Last night, the doctor said he'd hold on until we talked to our Forensics."

"Calm down. Find out what happened before you blame the doctors," Dr. Safia says. "Maybe there was no valid reason for the bodies to be detained. They're Muslim, and you know that burial should take place at the earliest possible opportunity."

Mislan takes several long drags, drops the cigarette, and squashes it on the pavement.

"I expected it."

"What?"

"The interference."

"What interference?"

"Last night, there was a Tan Sri Kudin and YB Ibrahim here. They're pressuring the pathologist and me to release the bodies. It appears the male deceased was a crony of people in high places."

"All the more reason for you to know the reason for the release. It could give you some idea about what you may face in the future."

Mislan admits she is making sense and calms down.

"Since we're here, it's worth checking out Dr. Safia's suggestion," Johan says.

Safia reaches for his hand and leads him back toward the main gate of the Medical Forensics. His cell phone rings.

"Ma'am."

"Lan, did I wake you up? Sorry," Superintendent Samsiah says.

"No, I'm at HKL Medical Forensics. Anything, ma'am?"

"Just to update you, I was called in by OCCI and he said there are requests from certain parties for this case to be closed ASAP. I made some inquiries about your vic, Mahadi, and as you said, he was very well-connected. I was also told there was something about him in the news a few months ago regarding a run-in with the MACC."

"The Anti-Corruption Commission?"

"Yes, it could be nothing. It may not be related to your case. What I'm saying is, tread with caution."

"Always. Thanks, ma'am."

After leaving HKL Medical Forensics, he drops Dr. Safia off at her condominium and puts through a call to see if Chew is in the office. At the Bandar Tun Razak roundabout, he turns toward the Crime Forensics Laboratory in Cheras.

"What do you make of the release?" Johan asks.

"You heard what Dr. Bakar said. He's a forensic pathologist. Can you blame him for wanting to keep his job?"

"What do you mean?"

"Where else can he work, if not with the government?"

"He's a doctor, isn't he?"

"Yes, a doctor who works on dead people. We do not live in a country where there's a demand for independent forensic pathologists. Look at the Beng Hock case, the independent forensic pathologists were all from other countries."

"Then why become a forensic pathologist?"

"Good question. The next time you see Dr. Safia, you ask her," Mislan says.

Johan laughs.

"Well, at least he was helpful. Remind me to pass on Leha's laptop to Di. I need her to hack the passwords, if any. We must also get Chew to print out the photographs from Dr. Bakar. I'm sure his color printer is better than ours."

"What were you expecting to find? I mean, you wanted Dr. Safia to view the bodies, what were you looking for?"

"Nothing that wasn't found by Dr. Matthews or Dr. Bakar. As I said, I need someone to explain to me in layman's language. Most of the time, when we get an autopsy report, we only look at the cause of death, because we don't understand most of the medical jargon. The vital clues in the report are always elsewhere, like in the defensive wounds, pre- and post-death injury or trauma, things that tell you more about what actually happened."

"Can't you ask the forensic pathologist who performed the autopsy?"

"I can, but the problem is, I don't know them like I know her. The thing with an autopsy report is it tells you what caused the death and what the pathologists observed. With Dr. Safia, I can ask her what may or could have caused what was observed. That's what I need, the understanding of what may and could. She'll answer all my stupid questions without judgment."

"Oh. I always thought you guys understood the reports. So, has my admiration for you been misguided?" Johan says.

Mislan just had to laugh at the way his assistant put it.

9

The parking lot in front of the Crime Forensics building is half empty. The festive season does have its advantages: traffic is light, plenty of parking spaces and people are friendlier. The disadvantages: things move at a slower pace, offices are left with skeletal staff and most of the Malay roadside stalls selling authentic and cheap food are closed. The D9 officers walk up two flights and find Chew in the laboratory examining articles or clothing or belongings of some poor dead person.

"Hey, Inspector, didn't expect you to be here so soon."

"Traffic's light. Are those from my case?"

Chew shakes his head.

"Chew, can you get someone to print out these photographs?" Mislan hands him a thumb drive. "They're photographs of the vics from the forensic pathologist."

"Sure, we can use my printer."

"Is it color?"

"The latest HP Laser color printer in the market. Nothing but the best and latest here."

"I envy you," Johan says.

"Are you done with the cell phones?" Mislan asks.

"Yes, do you want them?"

"Please. Who's doing the gun?"

"We are. I'll be sending it to ballistics once we're finished here. We only got the exhibit this morning. Lily's man sent them over. It'll be a while before we can give you anything."

"Why ballistics? I'm sure the bullets match. I'm more interested in the gun itself. Did you dust it?"

"Yes, I did. We found the victim's prints and no one else's. The bullets in the clip are JHP, and to be sure it came from the recovered gun, we have to do ballistic tests."

"Jacketed hollow points?"

"Yes, you sound surprised."

"I thought JHP weren't available to the public, only for police use," Mislan says.

"I don't know if what you said is true, but your victim managed to get hold of them somehow," Chew replies with a shrug.

"What about GSR?"

"I did the field gunshot residue test at the scene on the victims. The male victim tested positive. But field test is only 90 percent accurate. I've sent the swabs for analysis."

"Did you do it for both hands?"

"Yes, both, and it was only positive for the right hand."

"Can you do me a favor? Can you test the male vic's clothing for GSR?"

"Can do. What are you looking for?"

"Can you trace the GSR spread, the pattern?"

"I don't understand."

"Like how big is the spread? Which part of the shirt is tainted? Argh, how do I explain it? Something like this." Mislan uses his finger to draw an imaginary pattern on Johan's shirt.

"Oh, OK, I got you. You want to know the shot distance. Ballistics can do that for you."

"Great."

"Got any leads so far?"

"Nothing yet, I'm still groping in the dark."

They follow him to his office. Chew opens a steel cabinet and takes out two evidence bags.

"Here," he says, handing him the cell phones.

He plugs in the thumb drives and look for the medical forensic folder. He clicks on it and sends the photos to the printer, then they sit around Chew's table reviewing the printouts. Mislan flips through them, not knowing what he's looking for. The bullet holes look so small, but they were sufficient to kill. Victims on the television and in movies always look better—the handsome still look handsome, and the beautiful still look beautiful. In reality they look pale, ashen and ghostlike, with eyes wide open and eyeballs sucked into the hollows of their skulls.

"Chew, can we look at the vehicle?" Mislan asks.

"Sure."

They walk to the garage on the ground floor, and Mislan stops at the corridor for a cigarette.

"Are you not fasting?" Chew asks.

"Not today."

"Have you had lunch? Do you want me to arrange for something to eat?" Turning to Johan, Chew asks, "Sergeant, you fasting?"

"Yes, for now."

"No thanks," Mislan declines.

Mislan stubs out his cigarette, throws it into the corridor's dustbin, and they continue toward the garage. The black Mercedes E200 is in the middle, unattended, shining like a mysterious dark tomb. He walks toward the front and examines the damage to the right headlight and bumper. The damage is minor—a dented casing and an unhinged fender. *The victim must have slowed before the crash. What could've made him slow down: the act of drawing his gun or the shock of a gun being pointed at him*?

"Chew, in your expert unscientific opinion, at what speed did the vehicle hit the railing?"

Chew walks to the front, squats, and examines the damage.

"Ten, maybe fifteen miles per hour."

"Jo, can you get back to the responding patrolmen and check with them if they examined the road for tire marks? I don't think they did, but ask them anyway."

"Sure."

"Can we look inside? Are your guys done with it?"

"Hang on, let me check."

Chew walks to the office at the end of the garage and comes back with the supervisor, whom he introduces as Gavin.

"Gavin, have you guys finished with the interior?"

"Yes, we've taken the blood samples for comparisons with the victims. There's nothing much else to do. It's a straightforward case."

"Can I see the inside?"

"Sure."

Gavin opens the driver's door.

"Can I get in?"

"Yes, we're all done. Here, put on these gloves, just in case."

Mislan snaps the gloves on and gets into the driver's seat, examining the interior. There are blood splatters on the dashboard on the passenger's side and gear console.

"Chew you got the photos of the vics?"

"Yes. Do you want them?"

"Please."

Chew calls his office.

"Okay, Di will bring them down. What are you looking for?"

"Answers, or in this case . . . questions." He smiles. "Gavin, is there a place to smoke?"

"My office."

"Thanks, anyone want to join me for a smoke while waiting for Di?"

They follow him into Gavin's office.

"I know that look. Something's bothering him," Johan says to Chew.

"Something's always bothering him. It must be tiring working with him. Sometimes I feel as though the dead talk to him."

"I thought I was the only one," Johan says with a laugh.

Mislan lights a cigarette, looks around the office, and walks to the coffee maker.

"May I?"

"Yes, please help yourself."

Fadillah, the computer forensic technician, or Di as she likes to be called, enters the office dressed in a black T-shirt with bright orange prints. The wording on it is covered by her white lab jacket. Mislan suspects it must be something rebelliously interesting.

"Eyeew, you're not fasting?" she jeers, as she hands Chew the crime scene photos. "What's your excuse? Period pains?" she chides.

Johan whispers to her to let it slide.

Mislan grabs the photos before Chew can take them from Di. He spreads them on the table. Examining them, he selects three, squashes his cigarette, and walks back to the Mercedes, followed by the rest of them. He yanks the driver's door open and motions for Fadillah to get into the passenger's side while he gets into the driver's seat. Holding up one of the photos, he guides her into the position of the female victim.

"OK, tell me what is wrong here?"

Chew, Johan, Gavin, and Di look at each other, confused.

"Stay the way you are, don't move," he says, holding her head back.

"Ouch, that hurts."

"Sorry. So, what's wrong with this scene?"

"Her head," Chew says, hesitantly.

"Good. She was shot on the right temple, so the impact would've thrown her head to the left. But in this photo, her head is leaning toward the right. It's not correct."

"How about whiplash? It could've snapped her head to the right," Johan says.

"I thought about that, but the murder weapon is a small-caliber handgun . . . Not enough impact for a whiplash. If it were a bigger gun like a .45 or a 9mm, it's possible."

Without warning, Mislan pulls out his service Beretta, surprising everyone, especially Fadillah, who scrambles out of the car.

"Relax, will you?" He smiles.

Ejecting the clip, he clears the chamber several times to ensure the gun is empty, closely watched by four pairs of concerned eyes.

"OK, the male vic has a gunshot wound on his right temple, right?"

The four anxious onlookers nod.

"That means he used his right hand to shoot himself," Mislan says, lifting the Beretta to his right temple. "Bang, I'm dead."

He lowers his right hand slowly, releasing the Beretta, letting it drop, and it falls to the floorboard. He picks it up again, inserts the clip and holsters his sidearm. Pulling out the photo of the gun, he passes it to Johan.

"What's wrong with this photo?"

"The gun's position," Johan answers.

"But he could have been left-handed," Fadillah suggests.

"He could be, but if he was, he couldn't have shot his right temple with the gun in his left hand."

"You brought the gun down slowly. What if the vic's hand whipped down violently, threw the gun against the door, and it bounced off to the left?" Johan offers.

"Possible. I don't want to create any markings on the door that may be mistaken for evidence. That's why I didn't release the gun forcefully. Gavin, did you find any marking or indentation on the door to indicate a gun bouncing off it?"

"We didn't look for that. I'll get my guys to go over it once more."

"Interesting. So, are you saying this was not murder-suicide?" Chew asks. "You're suggesting there was a third person? But Lily said the car was locked from the inside when they arrived."

"Yes, she did. There are still many questions for which I have no answers."

"Such as?"

"The locked door, how the vic's gun was used in the shootings, and most importantly . . . the motive. For the time being, I have enough to hang on to the case for a little longer. Before I forget, Di can you look at the vic's laptop?"

"What do you want me to look for?"

"See if you can hack the passwords. I don't know what to look for. Just go sightseeing and look for anything interesting or suspicious. Check her social media account, if any."

"Okay and, if there is, do you want copies made?"

"Yes, and please do not change, delete, or add anything."

"Why should I?"

"I'm not saying you would, it's only a reminder."

"Tell you what, why don't I make a copy of everything and give it to you. That way you can go through it yourself at your own pace. I really don't know what you'd consider interesting or suspicious."

"OK, when can I have it?"

"Tomorrow latest. I'll let you know."

"Great, thanks."

"What about their cell phones, can you dump all their messages, call logs, WhatsApps, and whatever else?"

"No problem. Where are the phones?"

"Upstairs in Chew's office. Can I get them tomorrow, too?"

"Sure thing."

"Thanks."

10

By the time they leave Crime Forensics, it is almost 4:15 in the afternoon. On their way back to the office, Mislan receives a call from Audi asking if he'll be at the press conference called by the OCCI at 4:30 p.m. He tells her he's not aware of any press conference, nor is he interested in being present. Leaving the car in the almost empty lot, he tells Johan to debrief the detectives assigned at the morgue to find out what they've learned. He heads for his boss's office to find her staring out the window, deep in thought. He knocks lightly on the door.

"Ma'am, can you spare me a minute?"

She swivels around in her chair and nods.

"What were you thinking about? Missing your hometown?"

She smiles.

"Just taking a brain break. Do you notice how much police work has changed over the decade?"

"You mean evolved, progressed?"

"I mean changed. Maybe it's a trend, and if it is, it's not healthy."

"Sorry, I've lost you."

"You remember the IGP's speech on Police Day about being true to our profession? Not to be influenced by or succumb to third-party pressure."

IGP stands for the Inspector General of Police—the highest-ranking officer in the Malaysia Royal Police.

"It's an old game, ma'am. They'll scream for justice and fair play for the public to hear and then, behind closed doors, it's the same old story. It's not exclusive to us, it's everywhere."

"You seem to be in a forgiving mood today." She smiles. "What've you uncovered?"

"Mounting interference," he replies with a smirk. "The bodies were released immediately after the autopsy this morning. Dr. Bakar said the orders came from the top. See, they, too, have interference."

She shakes her head.

"I guess you're right. We're not the only ones."

"Dr. Bakar was helpful, though. He gave me the photos of the vics off the record. I asked him about the female vic's wounds, and he said both were fatal. Either one would've instantly killed her. I don't understand the need to pump two shots into her, when one had already done the job."

"Rage? Overkill is always associated with lovers—jealousy or despair."

"I don't think the killing was caused by rage."

"Why not?"

"Two shots, one in the head and another in the chest." Mislan shakes his head. "It's a semiautomatic gun. If he was driven by rage, he would have fired repeatedly and the shots would be grouped together. One other thing bothers me: why the head? The body is a bigger target, especially when you're driving. She was not restrained, so when a gun was pointed to her head, she could've turned away. She could have even pushed or grabbed the gun, her hands were free."

"She may not have noticed him pointing the gun at her head," she probes.

"At that range? No way."

Superintendent Samsiah looks at her investigator and wonders, What drives this man in front of her to put everything into his investigations—time, heart, and soul?

"If they were having a lovers' quarrel, wouldn't she have faced away from him? Women do that, don't they?"

"Speaking from experience?" Samsiah says, smiling. "Some, but not all. The emotional ones do, but the strong-hearted ones don't. Anyway, what are you saying?"

"And you think our female vic is strong-hearted. She was shot in the temple, meaning she didn't turn away from the male vic when they argued. It's hard for me to believe it was a murder-suicide."

Superintendent Samsiah remains silent as she looks at her investigator.

After a moment of uneasiness, Mislan asks, "What?"

She smiles.

"What else do you have?"

"Chew's still going over the personal belongings and clothing. The gun was dusted. Only the male vic's prints were found. He'll be sending the gun to Ballistics for matching. Gavin, the garage super, said they've gone through the car and found nothing of interest. I asked him to look for indentations that might have been caused by a gun bouncing around in the car."

"Good. Looks like you've convinced me. Now, all you've to do it get the evidence and convince those who matter."

"Well, with what I have now, murder-suicide is still a possibility. However, if it was not murder-suicide, I've yet to figure out how the vic's gun was used, how the car was locked from the inside and what's the motive. I need to do more digging." He pauses. "I heard there's a press conference today at 4:30. Did you know about it?"

She nods.

He glances at the clock on the wall. It is 4:45 p.m., and he raises his eyebrows at her inquiringly.

"What's on the table?"

"I don't know. I was told but not invited. Why don't you attend?"

"Eh? I don't want to be involved in this press conference."

She smiles.

"Whatever it is, you should thank the coming Raya. It'll buy you breathing space before the pressure is turned on. Why don't you go home and spend some time with your family? You're working Raya, right?"

The word "family" reminds him of his ex-wife picking Daniel up this morning and how much he misses his son.

"You'll be on leave? If I don't see you before then, Selamat Hari Raya, ma'am," he wishes her and proffers his hand.

Shaking it, she returns his greeting, "Same to you and your family."

Mislan tells Johan he needs to go home to attend to some personal matters but arranges to meet him later for breaking of fast and to discuss the progress of the case. On his way home, he stops at an ATM to transfer some money to his ex-wife for Daniel's expenses. He would miss his son this Raya. On the other hand, he is happy that his son will be spending it like other kids, with grandparents, uncles, aunties, nephews, nieces, other relatives, and at least one parent.

After showering, he makes a mug of fresh black coffee, returns to his bedroom, and turns on the news. The newsreader is talking about another stillborn baby dumped in a school lavatory in Terengganu. The baby was covered in dried blood wrapped in old newspaper, with its umbilical cord still attached. A female student and her unemployed boyfriend were being held for questioning. This is followed, as usual, by interviews with prominent religious clerics and politicians. It sounds like a broken record to Mislan.

He lights a cigarette, sits in his wing chair, and thinks of the way the dead are treated. The mention of the Duta–Ulu Klang Expressway attracts his attention and he looks at the television. The woman newsreader starts by talking about the incident in general terms while showing the crime scene before the visuals shift to the press conference. Senior Assistant Commissioner Burhanuddin Md. Sidek is flanked by his two Public Relations dolls. He is beaming, enjoying the limelight. The Officer in Charge of Criminal Investigations gives a narrative of what happened on that fatal night. He said, the police have reason to believe the case was a murder-suicide. He blabbers on about a love triangles and how, although the police are not ruling out other motives, they believe Mahadi shot Zaleha twice in anger before killing himself. The theory was derived because there was no evidence of a third person in the car as substantiated by the expressway toll plaza CCTV. To further support this theory, the car was locked from the inside. However, not wishing to discount other possibility, the case for now was being investigated as murder.

"Bullshit!" Mislan cries out.

His cell phone rings. It's his assistant asking if had just seen the news.

"Yes."

"The case is as good as closed," Johan says.

"Not if I can help it."

"The OCCI just said there's reason to believe it was a murder-suicide."

"He thinks whatever he wants to think, it don't count for shit to me," Mislan snaps. "Ma'am already told me there are pressures from influential outside parties to close the case ASAP."

"That pisses you off, doesn't it?" Johan says, followed by a chuckle.

Mislan laughs.

"Just be careful it doesn't bite you in the ass. What time do you want to meet up?"

"Where are you?"

"At the office going through the vics' cell phone records."

"You want to go home and freshen up first?"

"No time, I'll be breaking fast at the office."

"OK. I'll see you there later."

Terminating the call from his assistant, he makes a call to his ex-wife, asking if they have arrived safely.

"Yes, we just arrived."

"That took a long time."

"The road was horribly jammed all the way from Sungai Besi toll."

The usually four-and-a-half-to-five-hour journey has taken his ex-wife and son almost seven hours.

"That's to be expected with all the people going back for the holiday."

"I know, but it's tiring."

"Can I talk with kiddo?"

He hears his ex-wife passing the cell phone to their son, telling him Daddy wants to speak to him.

"Hi, kiddo."

"Daddy, there were so many cars. Mummy was angry all the way," Daniel says and giggles.

"I know, kiddo. Has Mummy bought anything for breaking fast?"

"Yes, Mummy stopped to buy at the market."

"OK, kiddo. Daddy misses you."

"Miss you, too, Daddy."

11

Mislan hears the Maghrib call for prayer, which also signals the breaking of fast. Putting on a pair of jeans and a polo T-shirt, he leaves. Driving out, he notices the time is 7:32 p.m. Iftar, or the breaking of fast, is 7:29 p.m., and he figures his assistant must had left the office to break his fast. Hitting the Middle Ring Road 2, he lowers the window and lights a cigarette, thinking—*everyone is breaking fast with someone except me.* The thought saddens him. Somehow during the end of Ramadan and approaching Syawal, his feeling of loneliness has grown. He misses his son, his ex-wife, and Fie. He laughs at the thought of how few people in his life matter to him—three. Yes, there are others, like his assistant, Superintendent Samsiah, and his co-investigators, but he doesn't miss them like those three. His boss once said he's not a people person, whatever that meant.

Mislan drives toward Ampang and cuts into Kampung Pandan, intending to take the road above the SMART Tunnel, but gets caught in a traffic crawl caused by a Ramadan market. He swears continually for fifteen minutes as he inches his way through the maze of stalls selling food, Raya cakes and cookies, and traditional clothing put up ad hoc during the fasting month. Ironically, it reminds him of days with his ex-wife and their shopping there. He finally manages to get past the bazaar and the randomly parked vehicles and drives through Jalan Imbi to his office in Jalan Hang Tuah.

Every year it's the same thing, the last-minute shopper crowd. Those bargain hunters looking to save money as Ramadan is coming to its end and stall operators are offloading their stock. His assistant told him that Jalan Tuanku Abdul Rahman, where most of the stalls are located, is like a huge parking lot at night. Traffic control has no effect. Then again, it is the festive mood and the traffic police tend to close one eye and let the situation work out by itself.

He makes a call to his assistant, asking his whereabouts. Johan tells him he's breaking fast in the office with some of the detectives.

"Oh, OK."

"Have you eaten?" Johan asks.

"No, not yet."

"Don't buy anything, we got plenty here."

"OK, thanks."

He makes another call. "Murad, Mislan. Did you brief the OCCI on the case?"

"No, the OCPD and SIO. Why?" The OCPD is the Officer in Charge of a Police District.

"He has just given a press conference, said the motive was a possible love triangle. Also, that the case seemed like a murder-suicide."

"I don't know anything about that. Maybe he talked to the SIO. The OCCI doesn't speak to district IOs like me. I'm too low down the ladder," Murad says, laughing. "Mislan, are you keeping the case?"

"Looks like it."

"Thanks, that's one less on my plate."

Walking to the lobby, he bumps into Superintendent Samsiah coming out. She is on her way home, and he decides to follow her back to the parking lot.

"Just leaving?" he asks.

"Why are you back?" she asks, ignoring his question.

"Why? Am I banned from coming to work?" he jests. "Ma'am, where did the OCCI get the information for the press conference?"

"Which information? He said a lot of things."

"About there being no third person in the car thing, the love triangle . . . Who fed him that crap?"

"Please accept my apologies, I didn't get a chance to ask him," the head of Special Investigation Unit answers sarcastically. "I'll ask the next time I see him."

"I'm sorry, I didn't mean to—"

"Look, Lan, he's the OCCI, he has his sources. And you know what? He doesn't have to clear everything he wants to say with me, like I don't have to explain everything to you."

"I'm sorry. I'm out of line."

"Forget it. I'm sorry, I shouldn't take this out on you. So, what do I owe you for escorting me to my car?"

Her smile reappears.

"Raya lunch . . . the real deal, with rendang, ketupat, and lemang."

She laughs.

"Come over with Jo and the boys if you have some free time."

"For the whole spread, I'll make the time. ma'am, I'm sorry again."

Mislan heads for the detective standby room and finds Johan talking with one of the detectives. On the table in front of them are packs of rice, grilled fish with spicy sauce dip, fried chicken, several Malay traditional cakes, and a large pitcher of syrup.

"Sir," the detective greets him, standing.

Mislan pulls a chair from a detective's table and joins them.

"Syed, you're not off for Raya?"

"I went last year," the detective replies.

Johan pushes a pack of rice to his boss and Syed pushes the dishes closer to him. Mislan washes his hands in the tiny bowl of water and starts eating.

"This grilled fish is good, where'd you get it?" he asks.

"Syed went to Keramat Ramadan bazaar," Johan replies.

"That far?"

"Worth the trip. I've been buying from this stall for years. The fish is fresh and the sauce is tasty," Syed says. "If you go after six, everything is sold out."

"What do we have, Jo?"

"Many unverified stories, both good and bad. I've summarized them into two groups. Here," Johan opens and pushes over his notepad for Mislan to read.

He studies the list.

"Says here, the vics are scamming villagers, stealing their heritage. What's that about?"

"I was just asking Syed the same thing."

"A group of four men were talking about the vics buying kampong land cheaply, on the pretext of developing it for the benefit of the villagers. After that, the vics merely mined the sand and made millions. There was no development," Syed says.

"This one says the vics were married."

"Yes, but I was not able to confirm that. Most said they're a couple and that he employed her to avoid a scandal."

"A scandal because she was his lover?"

Syed nods, smiling impishly.

"Jo, assign Syed and his partner to get confirmation on this, this, and this," he says, pointing to the list. "Names, dates, places, whatever they can get. Get in touch with the Selangor police in PJ and Klang. I'm sure they knew Mahadi. Why don't you guys visit the vic's house, pretend to be one of hundreds attending the gathering, and find out more?"

"Don't forget to dress appropriately," Johan calls after Syed as he leaves.

Mislan finishes his dinner, washes his hands, and thanks his assistant for the meal. He walks back to his office, drops on his chair, and lights a cigarette. Inspector Tee is missing from his desk, probably out for dinner. Dinner was really good and filling, now he feels heavy and lazy. He starts to wonder what was bothering his boss. Superintendent Samsiah is not one to be easily upset by power plays, rank-pulling, and interference. Nor is she one to give in without a fight. Something was bothering her, something personal, or maybe it was him, his attitude. Selfishly putting himself before others, especially her. Johan comes into the office looking questioningly at his boss.

"What are you thinking about?" the detective sergeant asks.

"Eh? Nothing. Did anything happen here while I was away?"

"Like what?"

"I met ma'am downstairs. She seemed a little tetchy, not her usual self."

"Maybe she was tired."

"Maybe," Mislan says and lets it slide. "You said you went through the vics' cell phone records. Who were the last people they spoke to?"

"The male vic's last call was from his son Hashim, while the female's last call was to Ayn. Remember the vic's mother saying Ayn was her close friend?"

"OK, I'm thinking we'll go to Zaleha's house to pay our last respects. What do you think?"

"Let me rephrase that . . . We go snooping to Zaleha's house."

"Hell no. We're going to pay our last respects," Mislan says, grinning.

"You're groping in the dark, aren't you?"

"It's something I've learned about motives: when it's not obvious, examine the vic's life and you'll find it. The other thing is, if the deceased were a couple, the chances are the motive will have something to do with the woman."

"You're only making this up to impress me and justify your intention to snoop."

Mislan laughs.

The shift investigator, Inspector Tee, returns from his break. Seeing Mislan and his assistant, he asks what they're doing in the office.

"You two don't celebrate Raya?"

"We are," Mislan says.

"Here in the office? You don't have a home and family?"

"This is our home, and you guys are our family," Mislan deadpans.

"Yeah, right."

"What . . . you don't want to be family with me?"

Tee and Johan laugh.

12

SINCE MOST CITY DWELLERS have left for their hometowns, Johan decides to cut through the city. They hit the MRR2, making a U-turn under the overpass, and turn left to Beverly Heights. Passing the victim's house, they see through the sliding doors a crowd seated on the floor in the living room. They are all dressed in sarong or the traditional Malay costume, with men wearing songkok or skullcaps. The family must have invited the housing estate imam and Muslim neighbors for the Tahlil, after the burial. When the officers step out of the car, the group is starting with the *Yasin* recital. Approaching the house, they are received by the brother of the deceased, Kamarulzaman. The D9 officers introduce themselves and offer their condolences. Mislan nudges Johan and whispers to him to join the *Yasin* recital group. Johan gives his boss a squeamish look, excuses himself, and walks toward the house. Mislan stays in the driveway, lights a cigarette, and starts a conversation with Kamarulzaman.

"How's your mother?"

"She's still inconsolable. Leha was everything to her. I know that I was the man in the family after Father passed away, but it was she who assumed the role. For mother, it's like losing a husband all over again. To make it worse, Leha was her only daughter." He pauses and looks toward the house to make sure no one is approaching, and then says, "I was told that the police think it was a murder-suicide. Is that true?"

"Do you have any reason to think it was not?"

"Leha was always full of life, optimistic, cheerful and always saw the bright side of everything. She was not one to take her own life. We all went to her for cheering up, for hope, for that extra push. No, I don't believe she'd commit suicide, not Leha."

"How well did you know Mr. Mahadi?" Mislan changes the subject.

"I met him a few times, but I didn't know much about him."

"Did you know he was married?"

"Yes, Leha did say it in passing, but we never discussed it."

"Did you know they were in a relationship?"

"Yes, mother told me. She suspected they were more than business partners."

"How did you or your mother view their relationship?"

"She was okay with it, as long as it was done properly. He could marry four wives if he wanted, he had the means. If they were serious, he could've taken her as his second wife."

"Was he serious?"

"I really don't know. I never spoke to them about it or asked him. Maybe Mother did, but she didn't tell me."

"Did you know her friends?"

"You should ask my mother, she knows more than I do."

The *Yasin* recital ends and is followed by a supplication for the deceased.

Light refreshments are served, after which people start leaving, offering their condolences to the family. Johan asks if they should leave, too. Mislan shakes his head.

"Let's stay a little longer; I want to talk to the mother again."

"I saw you talking to the brother. What did he say?"

"He doesn't know much, but the mother might."

"About what?"

"The relationship between the vics. Did you manage to peek into the kitchen?"

Johan nods.

"See any women of the vic's age?"

"Some. Good-looking, too."

"I'm sure one of them was a close friend of the vic's. Maybe she can tell us something."

"Maybe I could pick one up," Johan teases.

After the last person from the prayer group has left, the two investigators enter the house and approach Kamarulzaman in the living room. Mislan asks if any of the women in the kitchen had been friends with the victim.

"Some of them."

"Is Ayn one of them?" Johan asks.

"I'll check." The brother goes into the kitchen and comes out with a woman about the same age as the deceased. "This is Ayn Raffali."

"Hi, I'm Inspector Mislan, and this is Detective Sergeant Johan. Can we talk to you about Zaleha?"

She nods and sits next to Kamarulzaman.

"Mr. Kamarulzaman, I don't mean to be rude, but can we have some privacy?"

"Sure, I understand," he says, and leaves them.

Mislan takes out his digital recorder from his backpack and switches it on, "Miss Ayn Raffali, can you describe your relationships with the victim?"

"Call me Ayn please. We were BFF."

"By BFF, you mean best friends forever?"

She nods.

"The newspapers say it was murder-suicide. I don't believe it," she says forcefully. Before the investigator can speak, she continues, "Leha told me everything. We shared all our dreams and secrets. Those two were in love, I mean really in love. They were planning to get married after Raya. They were happy and were counting the days, the hours. That was all she talked about. Would a person in that situation commit murder or suicide?" She looks serious, her voice is firm.

"What if there was a snag in their plan?" Johan provokes her.

"If there was, she would've told me. We had no secrets. We broke our fasting together that night. . . . Leha, Mahadi, my boyfriend, and me. They were joking, laughing, and were as cheerful as ever. We talked about the trip and what we needed to bring along. No, there was no snag in the plans, no way." Ayn is emphatic.

"What trip?"

"They planned to get married in Hat Yai and then have it registered here after paying the fine. My boyfriend was going to arrange for another friend to be a witness. Mahadi said that the qadi in Hat Yai needed two male witnesses."

"Can I have your boyfriend's name and contact for us to verify that?"

Ayn hesitates and asks, "Is he going to be involved?"

"I doubt it, but anything can happen."

"Please be discreet. He is, you know . . ." She pauses, letting the sentence hang. Her eyes plead for understanding before handing over her boyfriend's business card.

"Married?" Johan says.

She nods.

"So, when was this trip planned for?" Mislan continues.

"They were talking about the second week after Raya. Mahadi had made the arrangements in Hat Yai."

"Where did you break your fasting with them?"

"Solaris Mont Kiara, the Garden Recipe Café. Then Mahadi got a phone call and said he had to leave. They left before eight."

"Did he say why?"

"No, only that he had to meet some people in KL."

"What was his demeanor—annoyed, calm, or normal?"

"He was apologetic. Mahadi was a gentleman, always pleasant, smiling, and understanding. I knew him for three years and I never saw him angry or abusive. Unlike his children . . . a bunch of spoiled, arrogant brats. I often wondered if they were really his."

"Which one?"

"All four of them. They never did like Leha. They thought she was after his money. It's difficult for some people to accept a young woman's love for an older man. People will always say she's after his money."

"Did Leha have another boyfriend on the side?"

"No! She loved Mahadi and was faithful to him."

"How about ex-boyfriends?"

"She had one ex-boyfriend, a lowlife, a parasite that lived off her, but she dumped him before she met Mahadi. Some months ago, I don't remember exactly when, we're having lunch at the Dome in the KLCC when the sleazebag appeared out of nowhere and sat at our table. He started pestering her to get back together. When Leha told him to go away, he got angry and threatened her . . . said he'd make sure she'd pay for dumping him."

"Then what happened?"

"Mahadi arrived and the lowlife picked a fight with him. But Mahadi just asked for the bill and we left. He continued to follow us, swearing, shouting insults, and Mahadi said to ignore him and to keep walking. It was scary and embarrassing."

"Do you know his name?"

"Hambali something. The last I heard he was in prison for a drug offense. He used to work as an assistant sales manager at the old Hilton."

"The one called the Mutiara Hotel, now?"

"Yes. Inspector, I don't believe Mahadi murdered Leha or that they committed suicide in a pact. The police are wrong. I don't know what happened, but it was definitely not murder-suicide."

Although Ayn expresses her views forcefully, Mislan notes the pleading look in her eyes. It must have been painful for her to lose her best friend, and under such circumstances, too.

"Do you have a number we can call if we need to talk to you again?"

Ayn offers her business card, and Johan is the first to snatch it. Switching off the digital recorder, Mislan thanks her and informs the host that they're leaving. He again offers his condolences to the family, and they walk to the car.

13

On the Middle Ring Road 2, the traffic into the city is light, while that in the opposite direction, to the East Coast, is at a crawl. Operation Sikap targeting irresponsible road users has recorded a double-digit death toll on its first day during this festive season. Mislan looks at the crawl, recalling that his ex-wife and son had taken seven plus hours to reach her hometown. He shakes his head in disbelief at what people are willing to endure during the festive season. And this exodus is not unique to Malaysia; it happens all over the world during major festivals.

"Terrible, isn't it?" Johan says.

"Yup, that's one reason I don't do the back-to-hometown thingy. The best place to be during festivals is here, in the city. Look at that. It'll take them at least eight hours to reach the East Coast, if they're not killed on the way," Mislan says. "Jo, can you check if the detectives are back from the vic's house?"

Johan calls the office.

"They're on their way to the office. Syed says they heard some interesting stories about Leha."

Walking into the empty lobby, they acknowledge a sad-looking policeman on duty and wait for the elevator. Johan tilts his head and says, "I'll bet his leave was not approved."

In the office, Johan goes to the makeshift pantry to make two mugs of coffee. "What do we do now?"

"We wait for Syed and Jeff. In the meantime, let's have another look at the crime scene photos."

He takes out a brown envelope and spreads the photographs on the desk.

Johan picks one up, examines it, and moves on to the next.

"What are we looking for?"

"Anything that doesn't fit or something we can follow up on."

"You mean like this?" Johan hands him a photo. "The male vic was shot on the right, but you don't see blood splatters on the window or the door. This is a picture of the dashboard in front of Leha. Here you can see spots of blood," Johan says.

"Good eyes," Mislan says. "It doesn't make sense, unless the blood was wiped off. But I doubt there was time. I'll get Chew to check the doors for blood traces. They'll spray some magic liquid: If there are traces of blood, it'll turn blue-green. Luminol, that's the name."

"I know it. I've seen it on *CSI*."

Just then Detective Syed and Detective Jeff arrive, joking and laughing.

"What's so funny?" Johan asks.

"Syed, he went into the house and sat with the family, pretending to be a friend of the vic. After a while one of them asked who he was, and Syed lied that he was from a law firm and quietly made his exit."

"OK, you had your fun. Let's hear what you've got." Mislan says.

Jeff flips his notepad, "The female vic, Zaleha, was not well liked by the male vic's family. They called her a bitch, whore, and homewrecker. The children blamed her for their father's death and said she must have cast some black magic love spells on him to make her the managing director of one of his companies, buy her a house, and so on. They said they went to see a shaman in Kampung Broga and were given the remedy, a counterspell. When their father finally snapped out of the vic's love spell, they got into an argument. The female vic threatens to expose their affair, and the only way for their father to save his family was to kill the 'bitch' and take his own life."

"Who said that, one of the children?"

"They all did. It was an open discussion, where they're all speculating why their father acted the way he had. They concluded that their father had reached the limit when the 'bitch' refused to let him go. They were really going at her. Now, here's the eerie part: When the mother came out, everyone shut up. Then, the eldest," Jeff pauses to check his notes, "Latiff . . . no, Hashim, was all over the mother like she was a Mama Bee or something."

"You mean queen bee," Mislan suggests.

"Yes, Mama Bee. You think there's something there?"

"Do you mean kissing up in fear or kissing up as a slave to a master?" Johan asks.

"More like the witch's black cat that purrs on her lap and stares at you with its red eyes, ready to claw your heart out if you make a wrong move." Syed says.

"What movie have you been watching?" Johan asks, raising his eyebrows at the detective.

"Maybe he's concerned for his mother. That's understandable. She just lost her husband, and Hashim, being the eldest, was staking his claim, and assuming the role of the man of the house," Mislan suggests.

"Could be, I didn't think of that."

"All right, what else?"

"There was one guy there, Wan, who said the female vic had a noisy argument with Mokthar, the third son, in her office about a month ago. Something to do with delayed payments, after which Mokthar threatened her and stormed out." Jeff says.

"What sort of threats?"

"Let's see. Ah, here it is: Don't think you can push people around. One of these days you might push the wrong people. You think you're the boss here, that people are afraid of you.'"

"That sounds like a motive to me," Johan butts in.

"Let's get more details on this. Do you have this Wan's contact info?"

"No, but he worked with the female vic. It would be easy enough to find him."

"Good. Anything else?"

"Plenty, but we put most of it down as gossip."

"What about the rumors of the vics being married or having a child?"

"That's what I meant by gossip. No one could confirm it. All claimed to have heard, but no one knew." Jeff explains.

"OK, let's call it a day then. I want you two to contact Wan. I'd like to know more about that argument," says Mislan, giving them their instructions.

After the two detectives have left, Johan says, "What do you make of all this?"

"Hard to say. They could simply be angry with their father's betrayal, especially now that it's public knowledge. The reaction is not surprising, it's to be expected. It is bad enough for the family that the man committed suicide, as a Muslim, and to be found with a young woman . . . Imagine what they're going through."

"Jeff talked about the threats, the rage. That could be a motive."

Mislan shrugs.

"Could be, but I doubt it. You can always tell a rage killing by the multiple injuries. Multiple stabs, slashes, or gunshots, the telltale of an overkill. I don't see that here."

"You're saying it was not murder-suicide. If it was murder, what was the motive?"

"I'm not convinced it's a murder-suicide, but I could be wrong. Jo, can you get a copy of the CCTV from the DUKE tollgate between eight and, say, nine that night? I want to see if we can identify the vic's car. I'm quite sure *he* already has a copy," he says, jerking his head upward, indicating the OCCI's office.

"Why don't we get it from him then?"

"I don't want to give him reasons to think we're checking on his comments at the press conference. He'll jump and put the heat on ma'am."

14

Starting the car, he notices it is almost midnight. He curses himself for not calling Daniel to wish him goodnight. His son is probably asleep by now. Or perhaps he isn't, hyped by the excitement of meeting his grandparents. Pulling out of the Kuala Lumpur Contingent Police HQ, he decides to call anyway, and after a few rings he hears his son's wide-awake voice.

"Daddy, Grandma bought me KFC."

"Hey, kiddo, lucky you. Why are you still awake?"

"I'm helping Grandma make cookies."

"OK but don't stay up too late."

"OK, Daddy, bye."

"Bye, kiddo, Daddy misses you. Love you."

"Hum-hum."

"Miss you, kiddo, miss you, too, Daddy," Mislan does the monologue, chortling, whenever his son goes into his "hum-hum" mode, because he thinks he is too old for such kiddy endearments.

Smiling, he hangs up, happy that he managed to speak to his son.

As he hits the MRR2, Mislan suddenly feels the urge to drive to the crime scene. He makes a left up the ramp to DUKE. The expressway is fairly busy, but vehicles are driving within the speed limit of 60 mph. He keeps to the left, the slow lane and at the eleventh milestone he puts on the hazard lights. He parks in the emergency lane, lowers the window, and kills the engine. The cold night air stirred by passing vehicles is refreshing. Lighting a cigarette, he watches vehicles zoom past and wonders if the drivers or passengers within realize they just passed a site where two individuals' lives were cruelly terminated. He supposes not—their minds are most likely preoccupied with other thoughts, on the Raya celebration.

Why this spot? What's significant about it? He surveys the surroundings for clues but sees none. Farther up the expressway on both sides are high-rise buildings—condominiums or apartments. Apart from roadside lamps and billboards there is nothing that stands out or catches his attention. He focuses on the road divider safety rails: not even a dent and no debris to indicate there was an accident.

If one wants to commit murder or suicide, why not do it in a hotel, house, or office, or jump off a bridge like many other people? Why in a moving car? Why not stop the car first? One could lose control of the vehicle. He flicks his cigarette out and sighs. It just did not make sense. The ringing of his phone startles him.

"Hi," he hears Dr. Safia say.

"Hi, where are you?"

"Bangi, at my mum's. What are you doing?"

"Nothing, just sitting around doing nothing."

"At home?"

"Nope, sitting in my car by the roadside," he says, then realizes how pathetic that must have sounded to her.

"Are you on a stakeout?"

"No."

"Oooh, OK, let me guess. You're in front of the morgue, planning a break-in to steal the reports," she laughs.

"Good guess, but wrong. That's not such a bad idea, though," he says, chuckling.

"Don't you dare."

"I'm only joking."

"Okay, I give up. Where are you?"

"At the homicide crime scene," he answers.

"Lan, you need to get help. I mean from professionals, not spirits of the dead." She laughs. "By the way, are the spirits telling you anything?"

"Sorry, I promised the spirits I wouldn't tell anyone, especially forensic pathologists. Wait, they're telling me something, hum-hum, hum-hum, OK, I'll tell her. Fie, the spirits say that if you want to know, you have to come here."

"Yeah, right. Tell them I'll take a raincheck. Hey, are you working during Raya?"

"Yes, why?"

"Me too."

"Really, I thought that you're on leave."

"Two days, yesterday and today."

"So, Raya's on Friday?"

"Yes, didn't you hear the announcement?"

"No, I was out of the office."

"Lan, got to go. Mum's calling. Tell the spirits to take it easy. Night, Lan."

"Night."

His house is dark. The maid would normally leave the living room lights on at night if he wasn't home yet. He switches on the lights, makes a mug of coffee, and goes into his bedroom. He leaves his backpack on the floor, ejects the clip from his service Beretta, puts everything into his bedside drawer, and switches on the television. He freshens up, changes into his sleeping shorts, and lies on the bed, missing his son.

He turns on the television, and it's showing aerial shots of the rivers of vehicles leaving the city for the festive holiday. The host says that the death toll on the highways has passed the one hundred mark. Visuals of several accident sites, mangled vehicles, black plastic body bags by the roadside, and mourning families follow the statistic. This is followed by interviews with traffic police officers, road transport personnel, and others. Every year it's the same.

He switches channels and stops on the morning news. It is showing a rerun of the homicide press conference by the Officer in Charge of Criminal Investigations. The only addition to the report is that the police have confirmed there was no third person involved. The police are confident they'll close the case soon, with appeals to the public to be sensitive to the victims' families and not to speculate.

He switches off the television and lights, turns on the air conditioner, pulls up the blanket, and tries to sleep. The absence of Daniel, the latest press report, and his visit to the scene stir actively in his head. Sleep doesn't come. He rolls off the bed, switches on the light, lights a cigarette, and sits at his desk. He reaches for his backpack and pulls out the photographs of the deceased, sorting them into two piles, one from the morgue and the other from the crime scene.

The female victim, Zaleha Jelani, was dressed in dark blue slacks, a light blue-and-white-striped blouse, and black pumps. She wasn't beautiful but pleasantly sweet, light skinned, with a short corporate haircut, maybe five foot two or three, and slim. She wore little makeup and few accessories, a gold chain, ear studs, and a sports watch. She had no rings on her fingers. From her dress and the way her best friend described her, Zaleha was probably a simple, easygoing person, Mislan figures.

Mahadi was wearing a cream-colored sports shirt, dark khaki pants, and brown suede shoes, a sports watch, a wedding band, and a magnetic bracelet, the kind used by golfers. Mislan's attention is drawn to the dashboard. All the indicator lights were on, the brake, ABS, battery indicator, and others. He examines the photograph closely, but it is too small for him to read the meters. He looks at his digital table clock. It is 12:40 a.m., too late to call Chew. He sets the alarm on his cell phone to remind him to call the Crime Forensics supervisor first thing in the morning. He switches off the lights and has another attempt at sleep.

15

THE MORNING PRAYER STARTS as usual but with only two investigators present. Inspector Tee the outgoing shift briefs the meeting about two sudden deaths and one armed robbery reported in the last twenty-four hours. The sudden deaths are suspected to be from drug overdoses. The cases are being handled by the districts. Superintendent Samsiah tells them that she is available during the festive period, as she will be in the city. She thanks them for volunteering to be on the roster during this period and ends the meeting by inviting everyone to her open house. Festive open houses are a tradition among Malaysians—Malay, Chinese, Indian, and all other races in the country. The family celebrating will prepare or cater dishes, cakes, and cookies unique to their culture as well as a few that are generically Malaysian and invite their friends over. Children teenage and younger will usually be given colorful packets containing cash ranging from two to ten ringgit depending on the host's status. This is called ang-pow, a Chinese word as it is actually a Chinese custom that had been adopted by all Malaysians.

Mislan follows Superintendent Samsiah to her office and waits for her to sit down before asking, "Ma'am, is everything all right?"

"Why do you ask?"

"Yesterday in the parking lot and just now." He turns his head toward the meeting room. "Am I missing something here, or is the Raya spirit turning you into a different person?"

"I don't know. What do you think?"

"I think I'm poking my nose in places I shouldn't."

She smiles. "Good deduction. Now, unless you've something to update or ask me, I've got work to do."

He tells her how he visited the female victim's house, his chat with Ayn Raffali, and how the victims planned to get married in Hat Yai after Raya.

"Can this Ayn confirm this?"

"I'll be talking to her boyfriend for verification. By the way, her boyfriend's also a married man, so chances are he may not want to go public."

"Don't promise him any exemption from testifying. Anything else?"

He tells her about Detective Syed and Detective Jeff's visit to the male victim's house, the bitching, and Mama Bee.

"You mean queen bee."

"Yes, but Jeff said 'Mama Bee.' Syed also overheard a man named Wan, who worked with the female vic, telling someone about an incident in which he heard Mokthar, the male vic's third son, having an argument with Zaleha about delayed payments and threatening her."

"What were the words used?"

Mislan flips his notepad and reads from it.

"When did this happen?"

"About two months ago."

"What's your take on it?"

"Nothing yet," he answers, shrugging. "Ayn also told me about the female vic's ex-boyfriend, a lowlife who threatened her in the presence of Mahadi at KLCC. That was a few months back. The last she heard he was in prison for drugs. I'll get Jo to check that out, but if he's in prison, I guess he's clear."

His boss nods.

"You asked what's bothering me. Well, I'm going to tell you. Just before I left yesterday, I received a call from Datuk Jalil politely asking me if I could do him a favor by handing the case back to the district. Then I got a call from the OCCI asking me if Datuk Jalil had talked to me. A few minutes later there was a call from Tan Sri KK, asking me if Datuk Jalil had called, and he went on to complain about how rudely he had been treated by my officer in public. As if all that wasn't bad enough for one day, my daughter called, saying she's not coming back home for the Raya, but instead is spending it on some godforsaken island with her college friends."

Mislan tries hard to contain a smile but fails.

"So you think that's funny?"

"Sorry, ma'am, it's just the way you said it. The situation is not funny at all. It's shameful."

She bursts into laughter with him.

"This case is generating more interest that I expected. Tomorrow is Raya, followed by the weekend. I'm sure things are going to cool down a little. That does not mean it will go away. These guys are going to visit each other, and I bet this will be one hotly discussed topic. Come Monday, the wind will have turned into a storm, and I hope you'll have something more concrete. I know a lot of things don't make sense, but sometimes the truth is weirder than we can comprehend. If you really feel this was murder, you'll have to do better. Find the motive and place a third party in the car. Otherwise this case will be closed and you'll not have your closure."

He listens and nods.

"Look, Lan, I agree with you. I believe there is more to what we're seeing, but you must understand what you're up against. If you understand who the victims are, you might know the reasons and possibly, the motive will be there, too."

He nods.

"I suggest you focus around the male vic, the heat is coming from that side. The female vic's side is rather subdued."

"Thanks, ma'am. Sorry for poking my nose where it doesn't belong." He stands to leave.

"It's okay, I know you meant well. Lan, watch your tail."

Back in the office, he calls Chew and asks if Fadillah can enlarge the photographs of the dashboard and email them to him.

"What's in them?"

"Zoom in on the trip meter and the petrol gauge."

"OK, will get Di to do it. When do you want it?"

"ASAP."

"I'll get her to do it now."

He is sipping his coffee when Johan walks in, waving a digital compact disc.

"Took some dancing, but I got it. Are you not fasting again, today? It's the last day, you know."

"Nope, and I know. Here, let's view it."

He slots the DVD into the drive and waits for the video.

"Okay, bring the time to 20:29 and let it run from there," Johan says. "There, that's the car approaching and . . . there . . . it's entering the Smart Tag lane."

Mislan pulls the video counter back and runs it again, pausing just as the car comes in line with the side camera.

"Now, tell me, does that look like the face of a person who is about to commit a murder-suicide?"

"No way. I wish the camera had audio," Johan grumbles.

"Remind me to ask Chew if he knows of a lip-reading service. Get Krishnan to check with the Deaf-Mute Society. I wonder what he was saying to her."

Mislan ejects the DVD and asks Johan to obtain directions to Mahadi's house. A minute later his assistant comes back with a sketch.

"Syed's got the contact for Wan, but he has already left town for Raya and won't be back until Sunday."

"Where is he from?"

"Kuala Selangor."

"It's OK. We don't need to talk to him yet, unless something comes up. I'd like to speak to the vic's widow first."

"Mama Bee?" Johan laughs.

16

THE LATE MAHADI'S HOUSE is a five-bedroom bungalow in an upmarket residential estate. It has been extensively renovated in the style of a Spanish villa, with a thirty-yard paved driveway surrounded by well-manicured green lawns. Under the wide carport, Mislan sees four luxury cars, probably belonging to the family members. The full length of the driveway is double-parked with luxury cars, and so is the road right in front of the main gate, cars all belonging to visitors, the inspector presumes. Johan parks their vehicle, which stands out like a sore thumb from the rest of the cars as far away as he can see. They spot another car that doesn't fit in parked about seventy meters farther on, with two individuals in it.

Pointing to the car, he says to Johan, "Media."

The car's headlights flash twice to attract their attention and Audi steps out, waving at them.

"Oh, shit," Mislan swears.

"What does she want?"

"What else?"

Audi waves more frantically, signaling them to come over.

"Let's see what she wants."

"Inspector, Detective Sergeant, you missed the big boys by about five minutes," Audi says excitedly.

"What big boys, and what are you doing here? Are you following us?"

"What do you mean following you, I was here first, wasn't I? Anyway, KK and a few other big guns were here. They stayed about ten minutes then left."

"What's wrong with that, they're probably paying their respects to the families. Who were they?"

"I know one is a State Executive Council member, and another, if I'm not mistaken, is a district councilor, I've got them on camera and their car registration numbers, maybe you could check," she rattles off in one breath. "I did some digging on the victim, and I found news clippings of his problems with the MACC. My source says the victim's case was still under investigation and they were expecting to make some arrests before this happened. He wouldn't tell me if one of those to be arrested was the victim," Audi finishes.

"Now that the victim is dead, what did your source say is going to happen? Are they still pressing ahead with the arrests?"

"He says there's a lot of buzz but no clear instruction. One thing's for sure, all activities regarding the case have been put on hold."

"So the victim was the key to their case. With him gone, they don't have anything. That's interesting. Who's your source?"

Audi bursts out laughing.

"Like hell I'm telling you. I said I'd help, but I didn't say I'll risk my job for you."

The D9 officers laugh with her.

"OK, now it's your turn to talk."

"We're still chasing shadows. You've got more information than we have."

"Don't give me that shit, I know you. Look, Inspector, I know your weaknesses, and I know your strengths."

"Good, then you can do my annual performance appraisal this year," Mislan retorts.

"Seriously, I'm aware you don't know much about political crap and you don't give a rat's ass about who's involved. But it looks to me like your case smells like Sewage Tank Politics, and without someone like me who understands STP, you'll be drowning in the shit," she says with a swagger.

"That's a colorful appraisal of my weakness. What are my strengths?"

"You have a sharp and keen mind, and you're not easily convinced or fooled by what you see . . . always questioning. In my opinion, your greatest strength is your desire for closure and that you take every case personally."

"OK, now that you have buttered me up, what do you want? I told you, we're still chasing shadows."

"I'll accept that for now. Are you going in?"

He nods.

"Can I come with you? I promise, I'll be a good girl."

"Are you nuts?"

Johan taps his boss's shoulder, and they step away.

"She did give us some good information. I'm OK if you decide to allow her to tag along."

Signaling for her to come out of the car, Mislan says, "That's not my house, so you're free to visit and pay your last respects. If the host thinks you're with us, then it would be his fault for thinking that. Do you understand?"

Audi grins.

"You're good, Mr. what's-your-name."

The three walk to the gate and Johan calls out, "Assalammualaikum," which is responded to in kind. They offer their condolences, and Mislan introduces himself and his assistant. Audi instantly picks up where Mislan leaves off and introduces herself as if she is with them. The host introduces himself as the son Latiff and invites them to the house. There are several guests in the living room, and they go through the formality of shaking hands with them before taking their seats.

"Mr. Latiff, I'm the lead investigator for the case involving your father. I'm wondering if I can speak to your mother. It's purely routine, to tie up some loose ends. I know she's in mourning, but there is urgency for me to tie up this case as soon as possible."

Mislan throws in that last bit knowing it will be the clincher for Mama Bee to grant him an interview.

"I understand. Tan Sri Kudin was just here saying that he'll try to get the case wrapped up so we can continue with our lives. I'll tell Mother," Latiff says.

"Is there somewhere we can talk in private?"

"Let's use the TV room, upstairs."

They follow Latiff and, when Audi follows them, Johan smiles. Latiff shows them into a room with leather sofas and a large Plasma television and invites them to sit while he gets his mother. A minute later, a surly woman in her mid-fifties comes into the room with her son close behind,

"Inspector, what's it that you want to see me about?" she asks sternly.

"Please accept our condolences for your loss and my apologies for coming unannounced," Mislan says, rising to his feet, closely followed by his assistant and the crime reporter. Audi offers her hand in the traditional salam, but Mama Bee does not extend hers.

"Hmmm," is all that comes out of Mama Bee as she takes a seat, while Latiff stands next to her.

"Ma'am, is there anything you can tell me about your late husband's demeanor or anything that was bothering him lately?"

Mama Bee's eyes narrow like a cat's ready to pounce.

"It was that bitch, that's what bothered him," she says without hesitation. "Demanding this and that . . . calling him at odd hours, messing with his head." There is so much venom in her voice that it makes the hair on Mislan's neck bristle. "He had already bought her a house, a car, and given her money. Was that enough? Noo-oo! It was never enough for that bitch. She wanted more, a position in the company, a high position, mind you. Like a whore, she messed with his head, using her young body to squeeze all she could from him. She wanted everything. I mean everything, even things that are rightfully mine and my children's," Mama Bee hisses, spreading her arm to indicate the bungalow. "The bitch threatened to go public with their affair if her demands were not met." She pauses, catching her breath. "He was well-respected, and she tarnished his reputation and destroyed my family's. If you want to question anyone, go and question her family."

"You said Miss Zaleha threatened to make their affair public. When was this?"

"All the time."

"How did you come to know of this?"

"I knew from the way he behaved. He didn't have to say anything, I knew it. He changed when he met her. He started coming home late and taking regular business trips. Two shamans have confirmed what I suspected for a long time. They both said the same thing. The whore had put him under a black magic spell by a Siamese shaman," she snaps.

Mislan looks at his assistant and shares a private smile at the mention of this.

"I'm sorry to have to ask: did you find any note left by your late husband?"

"What note?"

"In most suicide cases, the deceased will leave a note to apologize or to explain his or her decision, action. Did you find any such note?"

"No."

"What about phone calls? Did you receive any from him before the—?"

"No!"

"What about his business?"

"What about it?"

"Were there financial problems, complications, or power struggles that were bothering him?"

"I've told you, it was the bitch that was bothering him. Behaving as if the company was her grandfather's, pushing people around, treating them like dirt, lying and refusing to pay for work that had been done."

"How about the company managed by your late husband, the holding company?"

"Going bankrupt, that's what's happening. What did she know about managing a company? All she was good at was spreading her legs. A *whore*," Mama Bee swears.

"I mean your late husband's company," Mislan insists, trying to keep Mama Bee's attention on the questions being asked.

"There's nothing wrong with the holding company my husband managed. Why do you ask?"

"He was questioned by the MACC about—" Audi butts in, but before she can finish her questions, Mama Bee flares.

"How dare you come into my house and accuse my husband of corruption. How dare—"

"Ma'am, we're not accusing your late husband of anything, we're just asking if the event made him depressed," Mislan explains calmly, trying to contain the situation.

Mama Bee stands.

"I have nothing else to say to you. I want you out of my house, now."

She stomps out of the room with Latiff behind her. A moment later Latiff reappears. He apologizes for the incident and escorts them out.

Standing by their car, Mislan lights a cigarette, takes several long drags, drops it, and squashes it with his heel and says, "I needed that." He gets into the passenger seat, and Johan get behind the wheel. Audi climbs into the back seat.

"Aren't you fasting?"

"What did you think you were doing?" Mislan snaps at her, ignoring her question.

"Where? In there," she says jerking her head toward the house, "or in here?"

"In there. Did I say you could ask questions? You overstepped the bounds and screwed up the interview. And I'll be lucky if that's all you've done. And what are you doing here in the car?"

"To be fair, we didn't discuss anything about questioning rights," she says defiantly.

"Don't be a wise guy, OK? What are you doing in here?"

"Trying to explain what I did in there," she replies, like a child trying to guess the answer to her teacher's question.

The way she's going about it makes Mislan and Johan laugh.

"Well, it doesn't matter, because it's not going to happen again."

"Yes, I promise you it won't."

"I mean you'll not have a chance to make the same mistake. Now, please get out of the car and go chase your stories elsewhere."

She steps out of the car, walks to the passenger door, and smiles.

"Look, Inspector, I'm sorry. I mean it."

"You want a story? Call this number, don't tell her where you got it."

"Girl Scout's honor, thanks," she says, making the sign with her hand.

They leave Bukit Damansara and take the Sprint Expressway into the city, passing by the National Palace. Johan drives to Cheras and the Crime Forensics HQ. Just as they enter the area, the phone rings.

"Mislan."

"Lan, where are you?" Superintendent Samsiah asks.

"Forensics. Anything, ma'am?"

"Just got a call from a very angry KK claiming you're harassing the vic's family. Were you at his house earlier?"

"Yes, interviewing the Mama Bee."

"Any specific reason?"

"Routine interview and checking if there was a suicide note or something from the vic."

"KK said you're making wild accusations against the vic on corruption and the MACC."

"No accusation was made. It was only a routine interview."

"OK, tread carefully."

Johan asks what the call was about. Mislan smiles.

"The usual. KK called ma'am to complain about us harassing Mama Bee and making accusations against the vic."

"That was quick. Was that Ayn's phone number you gave Audi?"

He nods.

"Why?"

"Insurance, I'll tell you why when the time comes."

Johan looks at him with a puzzled expression.

17

Entering the Crime Forensics compound, Mislan tells his assistant to park at one of the vacant shaded reserved parking lots for the senior staff in front of the main entrance. His assistant gives him an incredulous stare. He tells Johan he is 99 percent sure the bosses are all away on leave. Johan smiles and pulls into one of them. Mislan is right, the building is almost deserted, without its usual bustle of staff in white lab coats scurrying about. They find the supervisor is in the laboratory, bent over an examination bench while engrossed in something.

"Hi, Chew."

"Hello Inspector, Sergeant, didn't expect to see you back again so soon."

"Slow day, so we thought we'd come and keep you company," Johan jokes.

"It's quiet here today. Is everyone on leave?"

"Mostly. I've done the GSR tests on the clothing, and the results are interesting." Chew walks over to the examination table where the victims' clothing is laid out. He adjusts the lens of the video camera and an image appears on a big screen in front of them.

"Wow, new toys?" Johan exclaims.

"Only got it working last week," Chew states proudly. "We start with the female victim's clothing. You guys don't have to look at the exhibits on the table, watch the screen."

"Sorry, I'm not used to it yet," Mislan says, laughing.

"Me neither," Chew admits, chuckling. "Gunshot residue traces were found here at the entry," he says circling the spot with his finger. "If you look closely, you can see slight discoloration, but it's not easily noticeable except with trained eyes, like mine." He zooms in closer on the tear hole.

Mislan and Johan bend over the blouse, then abruptly lift their heads, realizing they can see it better on the big screen.

"We've determined the presence of lead and nitrate. The Modified Griess Test results show a deposit concentration of intermediate range, indicating the gun was fired from a distance of more than 12 but less than 36 inches. Again, this very much depends on the caliber, barrel length, and powder type used in the ammo."

"In this case?"

"PPK Walter .32, I'd say ten inches."

"Could it have been closer?"

"It could be ten inches or so but not less than five. I know what you're thinking, and the answer is no, it's not possible. If it was at a three-inch range or if the muzzle was pressed against the victim, what we term Contact or Near Contact Gunshot, there would be an intense ring of residue around the bullet hole. Sometimes you'll get synthetic fibers melting from the burning gunpowder. In this case, all that is absent."

"Fascinating. What about the male vic's clothing?"

Chew moves the camera angle to focus on another exhibit, "We detect very light traces of lead and nitrate particle residues . . . only on the right side of his shirt collar and shoulder."

"Just there? Nowhere else?"

"Just there."

"Interesting."

"I'm saving this for last, and I don't know what you're going to classify it as. Contact or near-contact powder soot was traced with overlaying searing, meaning the gun was fired very close or on contact with the victim," Chew says, bringing up the female victim's photo on the screen. "See this discolored or dark marking around the entry wound?" he asks, indicating the mentioned area. "That's caused by a contact or near-contact shot."

"The same for both victims?" Mislan asks.

"Now that's the puzzling thing, no contact or near-contact trace in the male victim."

"Hmmm."

"OK, you've rated the discovery with one 'fascinating,' one 'interesting,' and one '*hmmm*.' What are you thinking about?" Johan asks apprehensively.

"Yes, what's going on up there?" Chew adds, eager to hear Mislan's analysis.

"Chew, before I forget, can you get Nathan to watch this video and see if he can pick up anything. There's a segment when the vics were at the tollgate, can he make a close-up copy? I want to see if someone can lip-read it."

"Sure, but back to the GSR, what do you make of them?"

Mislan laughs.

"There are traces of GSR on the vic's right hand, collar, and shoulder. That would indicate that the gun was in the vic's right hand, but it just doesn't add up. I need to see the medical forensic report. Thanks, Chew, I've got to go now, but once I have the autopsy report, I may need to speak with you again."

"That's not fair."

On their way back to the car, they stop by the garage. The supervisor, Gavin, tells them there is no trace of indentation or marking made by a bouncing gun.

"Just as I thought," Mislan says.

18

On the way back, Mislan tells his assistant to make a detour to a McDonald's drive-through, where he orders a McChicken to go. As the inspector devours it, Johan shakes his head but doesn't say anything. Mislan wipes his mouth, making sure he eliminates any evidence of the McChicken or fries on his lips.

"You missed a spot," Johan says.

As his boss wipes his mouth again, looking into the rearview mirror, the detective sergeant laughs.

"Funny," Mislan says, lowering the window, and lights a cigarette.

Their office is so quiet they can hear the echoes of their footsteps along the empty corridor. Mislan drops his backpack, lights up another cigarette, and goes into the emergency stairwell for a quiet smoke. Halfway through the cigarette, Johan pokes his head in the stairwell, telling him, "Ma'am is here."

"Shit," Mislan swears. "I thought she was already on leave."

The inspector hurriedly drops the cigarette, squashes it, and follows his assistant into the office.

"What were you doing back there?" Superintendent Samsiah asks, curious. She knows it's his hideaway smoking place, but it's the fasting month.

He smiles and takes his seat at the desk.

"Anything, ma'am?" he asks ignoring her question and knowing stare.

"I don't feel like working today. I guess the festive spirit is getting to me." She smiles. "Jo, come over and join us. *You*'re fasting, I hope?"

"Haven't missed a day yet," Johan answers proudly.

"Good, your boss has a lot of qualities that you should emulate as an investigator but when it comes to religious practices, keep your distance," she jokes. "So, how's the case coming along?"

"We just came back from Forensics. Chew has completed the GSR tests. He said the GSR on the female vic's clothing show intermediate range residue. On the male's clothing, he found traces on the right-side collar and shoulder, and his right hand tested positive, too."

"That's consistent with the shooting," she comments.

"Yes, but it puzzles me that there are no GSR traces on the male vic's shirt, particularly around the front left shoulder or the shirt's pocket," Mislan says, indicating the areas on his shirt with his hand. "If Mahadi shot Zaleha with his right hand, his hand position would have been here," he demonstrates with his hand. "Unless he shot her with his left hand, but that is not possible, because there are no traces of GSR on his left hand. The GSR traces on Zaleha's clothing are of intermediate range, ten to twelve inches. Again, if he had used his left hand, the GSR would be of contact or near contact range. I'm sure the autopsy reports will confirm my suspicions."

Superintendent Samsiah nods.

"Chew said he saved this for last, and I am, too. The swab taken by Forensics of the vics' gunshot wounds found powder soot, which means a contact or near-contact shot. But it was only on the female vic—the head shot."

Superintendent Samsiah raises her eyebrows.

"That would mean the gun was very close to her head. That's only possible if there was a suicide pact and she agreed to it."

Samsiah remains silent.

"Unless."

"Unless what?"

"Unless she was caught by surprise, didn't expect it, and didn't see it coming."

"Your third-person theory."

"The other thing that really bothered me is that there's no trace of contact or near-contact wound on the male vic. No powder soot overlaying the searing."

"Meaning?"

"Who blows off his head in a suicide with the barrel not pressed against his temple or under his chin or jammed into his mouth? Especially if you're doing it while driving. You want to be sure you hit your target—your head."

"OK. That's another indication. You have an idea of how it played out?"

"Nope."

"How about this, they got into an argument, it got heated, he pulled out the gun, shot her in the chest and again in the head. When he realized what he had done, he blew his own head off," Superintendent Samsiah suggests, playing the devil's advocate.

"He'd have had to be really pissed off to do that."

"She might have been playing him behind his back," Johan says, "or cleaned him out. Remember what Mama Bee said?"

"There's no proof of that, it's just angry allegations," Mislan replies. "Let's say he did kill her in a blind rage. Why commit suicide immediately? He could've continued driving, reflected on what had happened, and then acted on it. Surrendered himself, dumped her body, or if he still felt like killing himself, parked the car to do it." Mislan shakes his head and reaches for a cigarette before continuing. "He carried a semiauto. You don't cock your gun unless you're going to use it, and to do that you need both hands. Who was holding the wheel when he cocked the gun? The gun makes a rather loud noise when you cock it, and I'm sure she would have been alerted and panicked or retaliated."

"Maybe he cocked it and put the safety catch on before they left," Johan suggests.

"No, I don't think so. Remember what Ayn said? They're breaking fast together, two lovebirds. He was happy and being his usual self. I don't think the killing was premeditated. Ma'am, do you carry a pistol? Do you cock it all the time and put the safety catch on?"

"No, I don't, and don't you dare smoke. Please respect those of us here who are fasting."

Mislan grins and drops his packet of cigarettes.

"As I thought."

"OK, let's go with your hunch. What was the motive?"

"I think it was jealousy," Johan says. "I'm not being insensitive, but, ma'am, you should have seen Mama Bee. She was so brutally hateful of the female vic, accusing her of seducing and cleaning out her husband. I don't know how to describe her. . . . She was like a character from a bad B movie, stone cold eyes and a stare that could freeze water. She was scary." Johan shivers. "Wooh."

"Her husband has just been found dead with a young woman, what do you expect? I can't imagine what's going through her mind, the public scrutiny of their marriage, her husband's scandalous behavior, the humiliation, her friends talking, joking and laughing behind her back. I wouldn't want to be in her shoes." Samsiah pauses inhaling deeply shaking off the thought of it all. "Are you saying she killed them out of jealousy?"

"She could have done it herself," Johan says.

"I doubt that. She may be capable of plotting it. And there's no way in hell the vic would have let her into the car, not with Zaleha in it. Even if he was somehow tricked into letting her in, she would have been seated in front where she would have belonged, and Zaleha would have been at the back. No, I doubt very much if the vic was so dumb as to let Mama Bee ride with them."

"A contract hit?" Johan suggests.

"Possible, but the thing is . . . contract hits normally are done openly. I mean from outside the car or in some isolated area or, in the more spectacular cases, in the open," Mislan says.

"Good theory, but why kill the husband? Why not just do the woman? She was the threat, not him," Samsiah says. "I agreed with Mislan, the vic has full control of the car and Mama Bee would never have been allowed in with them. But, a contract hit is a possibility. Find evidence of a third party in the car and you'll have a case."

"Well, that's the problem. So far we cannot find any evidence of a third person in the car. The DUKE tollgate CCTV shows only two of them . . . a happy, smiling, laughing couple.

"Twenty minutes later they were dead. It just doesn't make sense. Why would a happy couple do a murder-suicide?" Johan adds.

They ponder in silence.

"Apart from jealousy, do you have other theories?" Superintendent Samsiah asks.

They shake their heads.

Superintendent Samsiah stands, takes a few steps toward the door, and stops.

"There's another reason why I doubt jealousy was the motive."

"The third-party interference," Mislan answers. "That's been bugging me, too."

She nods.

"Tomorrow is Raya, and then it's the weekend. I know the timing is bad, witnesses will be away, but I suggest you use the three days. Come Monday, we don't know what'll happen."

They nod in agreement.

"OK, keep at it. By the way, don't forget to come for lunch tomorrow, if you can," Superintendent Samsiah says as she leaves.

Holding a much-needed cigarette, Mislan takes out the crime scene photographs and spreads them on his desk. He looks at the door to make sure that his boss is gone before lighting up. He puts aside the photos of the victims, leaving only those of the Mercedes E200 spread out.

"What are you looking for?" Johan asks.

"Evidence of a third person in the car. If he was there, he'd leave some sign. What's the one thing we can leave behind without realizing?"

"Prints? But he could be wearing a glove or wiped the car clean."

"I don't think he wore gloves, because that would've alerted the vics. As for wiping his prints, I doubt that he would've had the time or taken the risk of being noticed by passersby. Now, where would he leave his prints? The doors were locked from the inside, right?"

"That's the reason the OCCI gave to justify closing the case," Johan says.

"I think I know how it was done."

"How?"

"The doors were locked from the inside. Come on, let's go before they knock off for the holidays," Mislan says, grabbing the photos, stuffing them into his backpack, and rushing for the door.

19

Traffic is light and Johan decides to turn right at Jalan Pudu instead of making an illegal U-turn at the traffic lights to go to Jalan Cheras. When he drives into a petrol station to top up the tank, his boss takes the opportunity to buy a bottle of 100 Plus. In the car, Mislan says to Johan, "All this thinking and talking makes me thirsty."

Johan smiles at his boss's excuses.

"Can I ask you something?"

Mislan nods, lighting another cigarette.

"What's it about this case that is getting you so worked up? I mean, why won't you accept it as murder-suicide?"

"Well, for one thing, if it was murder-suicide, he must have been in a blind rage. Remember Ayn, the vic's BFF? She said Mahadi was not like that." He pauses and takes a swig of the energy drink. "The other possibility is a suicide pact. In such cases, the preferred locations are bridges, cliffs, and hotel rooms, where they'd have their last romantic, or solemn moment together before they act, normally leaving a suicide note behind." He pauses again and drags on his cigarette.

"I've heard of suicides in cars before," Johan says.

"Me too. But it's normally done in a parked car with carbon monoxide piped in from the exhaust. I've never come across a suicide pact in a moving car, with a handgun."

After a moment, Johan says, "There's always a first."

"I'm not saying there won't be." He flicks his cigarette out of the window and rolls it up. "You know what bothers me? The third-party interference. I know he's one of theirs, but I can't understand why they want the case closed without letting us get to the bottom of it."

"Maybe it's bad for whatever business he was managing for them. Rivalry . . . could it be because of rivalry and one of them knocked him off?"

"Then why kill the woman?"

"Because she was part of his plans, or maybe she was just collateral damage."

Johan drives into the same parking spot they left earlier. Mislan calls Chew, and they arrange to meet in the garage. The Mercedes E200 is still where they last saw it. They decide to wait for Chew outside.

"You said you know how the doors were locked from the inside," Johan says, staring at the Mercedes.

"I said I think I know," he answers. "Most cars now are fitted with a central auto-locking system, right?"

Johan nods. "Especially that beauty."

"I bet the Merc comes with power windows, too. If my guess is right, the driver's window has a one-touch button. If I press it once the window will go down all the way, the same for raising it."

Chew emerges from the stairwell and greets them.

"Hi Chew, sorry to pull you away from whatever you were doing."

"No problem, things are a bit slow today. What can I do for you?"

"Has the Merc been dusted?"

"No, there was no reason to. We did the blood splatters and the photos. I think the car's due for release. Why?"

"I need you to dust it. Can you do it before it is released?"

"Sure, I'll do it now. Give me a minute, I need to get my kit." Chew disappears into the stairwell while Mislan walks to a comer to be by himself. He calls his ex-wife. After several rings, Daniel answers, "Hi, Daddy."

"Hey kiddo, what are you doing?"

"Watching TV."

"Has Mummy taken you shopping yet?"

"Mummy said later, after the breaking of fast."

"OK, don't be naughty. I miss you, kiddo."

"Miss you, too."

"Love you."

"Hum-hum."

He turns off the cell phone off and smiles. Ever since Daniel started Standard Two, he has become unwilling to be hugged, kissed, or even to say "I love you" in public. *How fast kids grow.*

Chew reappears carrying a forensic field kit and motions them into the garage. He enters the office to get the car keys, presses the remote to unlock it, snaps on a pair of gloves, and gives them each a pair.

"Chew, can you do the rear door handles, the central-locking button, and the driver's window button first?"

"Sure, no problem," Chew says, turning on a flashlight-like instrument with blue light.

"Are you looking for blood?" Johan asks.

"Do you want me to?"

"No," Mislan replies.

"What's the blue light?" Johan inquires.

"Oh, this?" Chew says, holding up the instrument. "This is a laser light, to locate fingerprints that aren't visible to the naked eye. It works by spotting chemical residues from sweat."

"OK, OK, we got it. It's another one of your new toys."

They stand back and watch Chew. Gavin, the garage supervisor, appears from his office and joins them. After what seems like ages, Chew says, "Done. Sorry I took so long, too many prints."

"Any from the target areas?"

"Two partials, one from the central-locking button and another from the power window button. There are a few on the rear door handles, but the prints are too smeared for positive matching."

"Chew, can you dust under this?" Mislan points to the auto-button lever for the driver's window.

"Gavin, can you do that?" Chew asks.

Gavin walks to a tool shelf and comes back with a screwdriver. He works on the inner door cover and takes out the button lever, handing it to Chew.

"Can you dust under the lever?" Mislan asks.

Chew turns the button-lever around in his hands and nods.

"Anything?" Mislan asks anxiously.

"I think there's a print. Let me lift it and see if it's usable."

"Great. Gavin, after Chew is done, can you fix back the button?"

Chew comes back and tells them he managed to lift an index fingerprint from under the lever.

"I lifted the print on top of the lever, just in case," Chew informs the inspector.

Mislan smiles, praying silently, *Please let me be right on this.*

"Gavin, can you fix it back?"

After the button lever is fitted, Mislan inserts the ignition key and turns it to the On position.

"Jo, get into the passenger's seat."

He climbs into the back seat and locks the door with Chew and Gavin standing outside.

"OK, here goes."

From the back, Mislan leans to the front, squeezing between the driver's seat and door while pressing the window button lever. The driver's door window smoothly rolls down, all the way down. Then he presses the central auto-lock button to unlock all the doors. He steps out of the car, closes the door, and steps up to the driver's door. Standing by the door, Mislan puts his hand into the car and presses the central-locking button. It is followed by the click of all the locks locking. He flicks the button-lever for the window, and the driver's side window smoothly closes. Removing his hand, he exclaims, "Voilà."

"That was clever," Chew offers.

"That, my friends, was how the car was locked from the inside. I've just proven the possibility of a third person in the car."

He signals to Johan to come out.

"Why did he have to go through all that? Couldn't he unlock the rear door then lock it back by pressing the lock button and holding the door handle from outside as he closed it?" Johan asks. "That would've been much easier."

"Yes, he needed to lock all the doors . . . including the back door that he just came out from. To give the impression that only the vics were in the car. If he left the rear door unlocked, it might create suspicion. That was the ruse, if I may term it that. It fooled us into thinking there was no third person in the car."

Johan, Chew, and Gavin nod.

"Chew, can you do a match on the prints?"

"Yes, I'll get my tech to run them through the system."

As they walk out, they see a tow truck driving into the parking lot, escorted by a policeman and a black BMW behind it. The policeman approaches, asking for Gavin. Chew steps forward.

"These men are here to collect a car," the policeman says, handing him an exhibit release letter.

Chew reads the release letter and hands it to Mislan.

"Can we stop this, now that we've found incriminating evidence inside the car?"

"I don't know, the release was signed by the chief himself and he is already on leave. I can give him a call, but I'm sure he's not going to like it."

"I would like to hang on to the car and for you to give it another go. See if it will yield more evidence."

"I can tell them Gavin is not around and to come back later. By the time he's back, the garage will be closed. Hopefully, they'll accept that. That'll give us at least three days to go over it again."

Mislan gestures to Gavin and Johan standing by the Mercedes in the garage. Chew turns to look in the direction of his gesture.

"That's George," Chew says with a tiny grin.

Mislan gives him a tiny smile. "Try it."

An important-looking Malay man steps out of the BMW and walks toward them.

"Is there a problem here?" he asks curtly.

"I'm Chew, Crime Forensics Supervisor." Chew introduces himself and offers his hand, which is ignored. "This is Inspector Mislan from the Special investigations Unit."

"I'm Hashim Mahadi, I'm here to collect the Mercedes. I've got a release letter and was told by Tan Sri Kudin that everything has been arranged and I can pick it up today," he says, pointing to the car in the garage.

"I'm sure everything is in order, but the person in charge of the garage, Gavin Chong, is out in the field. He'll be back later. I'm sure you understand we're on minimum manpower, most people are away on leave."

"That's your problem, not mine. Get someone else to do it or call him back."

"There's no one around, and by the time Gavin is back, the garage might be closed. Perhaps you'd like to make arrangements for Monday morning?"

"Can't someone else do it?"

"I'm sorry, there's no one else here as most are on Raya leave, and I'm not authorized to call Gavin back from a crime scene unless there's another one of higher priority. You're most welcome to wait for him if you wish."

Hashim frowns and calls someone. After several "Yes" and "Okay, Tan Sri," he hands the cell phone to Chew. He politely identifies himself and explains the situation. From where he stands, Mislan can hear the overbearing voice from the cell phone's tiny speaker. Chew holds the cell phone away from his ear, squirming, and making funny facial expressions. He keeps repeating that the release is not his responsibility and that KK should calm down and take the matter up with the appropriate person, if he's still unhappy. Chew hands the cell phone back to Hashim and signals for the rest to follow him.

"Do you know who that was?" Hashim asks intimidatingly.

"One pissed-off man," Mislan says with a sly grin.

Just then Chew's cell phone rings.

"Yes, Datuk . . . Gavin is out at a crime scene . . . No, there's no one . . . Okay, I'll tell him . . . Sure . . . Selamat Hari Raya, Datuk."

He turns to Hashim, saying, "That was my boss, and his instructions are to release the car on Monday." Turning to the policeman, he says, "Can you please escort them out?"

Hashim angrily storms to his car, swearing and threatening them and the entire police force with a lawsuit. He slams the door and burns rubber as he leaves, followed by the tow truck.

Walking up the stairs to the office, Johan says, "That's one angry, nasty guy."

"Thanks, Chew, but I need to go now. Can you let me know the prints results as soon as you get them?"

"Will do. Hey guys, Selamat Hari Raya."

"Thanks."

20

When they turn into Jalan Cheras, Mislan notices the time is 6:10 p.m. He asks Johan about his plans for breaking his fast. Johan says he is going to be with his girlfriend because she is leaving town that night.

"Why don't you join us?"

"No thanks, I don't want to be the spare tire," he declines.

"It's no big deal. Why don't you invite Dr. Safia? Make it a foursome, that'll be fun."

"She's in Bangi with her mother. You go on ahead. I'll see you tomorrow. Where's your girl from?"

"Ezni? She's from Melaka. Alor Gajah, somewhere," he says, laughing. "I haven't found out much about her."

"Ezni, I thought it was Mahani."

"Mahani is history, broke up about three months ago. She's with some white guy now. I hooked up with Ezni about a month ago. She's moving in after Raya."

"You lucky man," Mislan says.

Johan beams.

"When are you settling down?" Mislan asks.

"I've not met the right girl, yet. Hey, the female vic's BFF Ayn, she's a looker. I don't mind hooking up with her."

"Don't you even think about it. Anyway, what's wrong with Ezni?"

"She's OK, but I don't think she's the wife type. How about you? It's been long enough. What? What has it been two . . . three years now?"

"I'm not looking."

"How do you do it?"

"Do what?"

"Be on your own. Work long hours and take care of Daniel."

"Easy. I love my son and I love my job. Most importantly, it's because I want to. They're both my responsibilities. It's difficult, but it's not impossible."

Johan remains silent the rest of the way. At the parking lot, Johan again tries to persuade his boss to join them for breaking of fast. Mislan again declines, saying he needs an early night. Going home, Mislan takes the Kampung Pandan road through Pandan Dalam, where he buys a stick of lemang, some ketupat, and a packet of beef rendang-tok from a remaining roadside Ramadan bazaar. Raya is not complete without these three specialty food items, at least so the Malay would say. His thoughts drift to Daniel, who is probably having a good time with his mummy, grandparents, and the maid. His heart sinks at not being part of it all. He is resigned to his son having only one parent with him on any occasion.

He leaves the purchased food on the kitchen table and goes to his bedroom, where he goes through the routine of ejecting the clip from his gun, emptying his weapon, and placing it in the drawer. He showers, changes into his shorts and sleeveless singlet and goes back into the kitchen. His movements are deliberate but lifeless, like a zombie's. Lemang are sticky or glutinous rice cooked with coconut milk and wrapped in banana leaves in bamboo tubing. They are roasted over open fires. He splits the bamboo open and extracts the glutinous rice, cutting it into small circular pieces before putting them onto a plate. Ketupat can be made from plain rice or sticky rice. The rice is placed into a small bag weaved from young coconut leaves and boiled. He slices the ketupat to go onto another plate. The rendang-tok is beef sliced thinly and cooked with numerous herbs and spices and coconut milk, Northern Malay style. In the case of rendang-tok, it is cooked until it turns dark brown or black. He pours the rendang-tok into a bowl.

He makes a mug of coffee and sits down for his Raya eve dinner by himself. While nibbling on his food, he hears the call for prayer from the neighborhood mosque. The melancholic call stirs a longing for his son, for his BFF. How pathetic his life is, alone on Raya eve missing Daniel, and his case is going nowhere.

Losing his appetite, he clears the table, takes his coffee to the bedroom, and switches on the television. The local stations are full of Raya stories, musicals, and news that only make his depression worse. He needs to switch off his mind. He sits at his desk and takes out the photos of the victims he got from Dr. Bakar, spreading them out on the desk. He lifts Zaleha's photo and examines the gunshot wounds. He wonders if there is any way of telling which the first shot was—to the head or the chest. He picks up the phone and speed-dials Dr. Safia.

"Hi, you still at your mum's?"

"Yes, thought of going to work from here. What's up?"

Mislan wants to ask her about the gunshot wounds but figures it's not proper, it being Raya eve and all.

"Nothing, just sitting at home watching TV. I thought you'd be back and might like some tea," he lies.

"Love to, but you know, lah, my entire family's here. Don't think they'd understand if I went out."

"I know . . . bad idea. I'll catch up with you when you're back. Hey, Selamat Hari Raya."

"Sure, catch you when I'm back. Selamat Hari Raya to you, too, and, Lan, wish you were here."

He smiles and terminates the call.

He calls Daniel, and his ex-wife tells him his son is asleep, tired from shopping and playing. He tells her he'll call tomorrow and wishes her a happy Raya.

Running out of things to do, Mislan turns on the computer and Googles murder-suicide and postmortem injuries. Just then his phone rings.

"Yes, Audi."

"No Raya greeting? Oh sorry, you don't fast so you cannot celebrate," Audi teases him.

"What do you want? I'm in a rush," he lies.

A crime reporter is the last person he needs at the moment.

"OK, I spoke to Ayn. What do you want me to do with the info?"

"Up to you. I'm not asking you to do anything with it. You do what you want."

She chuckles.

"You're afraid this call is recorded, right? I'm hurt. You still don't trust me."

He can hear a smothered giggle. *Shit, this woman can read my mind.*

After a moment, she says, "OK, I'll hang on to it and when you decide to trust me, we'll meet and talk. Look, Inspector, I'm a friend who happens to like the police. Not all of us are bad, just the handful who are given more publicity than they deserve. By the way, I'll be in town during the festive season should you want to get together. Good night."

"Night."

After ending the call with Audi, he returns to the Internet search. He reads research on murder-suicides, trying to understand motivations. The articles gave love and jealousy as popular motives, as in: He loves her so much that he couldn't bear losing her, and after killing her couldn't face a life without her. "What a load of crap," Mislan grunts.

He keys in: *Cases of committing suicide while driving a car.* No result listed.

His cell phone rings. It's Fadillah from IT Forensics.

"Yes, Di."

"I mailed you the victim's cell phone chats, and you can log into her Facebook account. The user name's Zaleha.J, and the password is D9invest."

"You hacked her account and changed her password?" Mislan is surprised.

"Yes, now only we can view it," Di says, laughing.

"Why?"

"So that if anyone wants to deactivate the account, he can't get in and do it. . . . Diabolical," Di declares with a louder laugh.

"Who's going to do that?" Mislan is puzzled.

"I don't know, but it's no-can-do now."

"OK, thanks, I think."

Mislan calls his assistant and gives him the victim's Facebook username and password.

"Can you go through and see if there's anything interesting?" Mislan asks.

"How did you get the username and password?" Johan asks.

"Long story, tell you tomorrow."

"Why are you not going through it yourself?"

"You know Facebook better than me."

"Sorry, I forgot you don't even have an account," Johan says, chuckling.

21

Mislan wakes up to the call for the predawn prayer from the neighborhood mosque. He stirs in bed and peeks at the bedside clock. His hand instinctively stretches over to the other side of the bed before realizing that Daniel is away with his mother. He knows the traffic on the roads will be light and decides to laze around in bed a little longer. He wonders what to have for breakfast, since all the Malay food stalls will be closed for Raya, including the mamak restaurants.

He rolls out of bed, gulps some stale overnight coffee to wet his throat, and lights a cigarette. He feels sloth, knowing that nothing much can be done over the next few days, with all public and most private offices closed. Most city residents are out-of-towners who'll be away during festive seasons. The only ones in the city during this period will be foreign workers unable to return to their countries. He squashes his cigarette, walks into the kitchen, packs the leftover food, and gets ready for the long twenty-four-hour shift.

Mislan is greeted festively by Inspector Reeziana and her assistant investigator when he enters his office. They have another forty minutes on their shift. Mislan tells her to go home early and that he'll cover the rest of her shift, but she declines, saying that she has no other plans. She goes to the makeshift pantry, makes two mugs of coffee, and gives him one.

"How come you're on, I thought Tee was?" Mislan asks.

"Tee had an emergency, and ma'am called at 1 a.m. to see if I could cover for him."

"What happened?"

"I didn't ask."

"Why didn't ma'am call me?"

"She says you're up today, so she tried her luck with me."

"I wouldn't have minded. Anyway, how was business?"

"Quiet."

"Had breakfast yet?"

"Nope. The canteen is closed, and so are the other stalls."

"I brought some festive food. Want some?" He takes the food out of his backpack. "I bought them at Pandan last night. Are you visiting ma'am later?"

"If I'm up to it," she replies. She nibbles on a small piece of ketupat with rendang. "Hey, this is good."

Johan arrives with a plastic bag of Malay cookies and places them on his desk. Selamat Hari Raya, he greets them, extending his hand. They return his greeting and invite him to share their breakfast. Johan makes a mug of coffee and pulls up a chair.

"Let me guess, these are from Ezni," Mislan says.

"Who's Ezni?"

"His latest love-victim," Mislan says, laughing.

After Reeziana leaves, Mislan boots up his computer and notices an email from Fadillah, with attachments—they're enlarged photos of the dashboard.

"Jo, come and take a look at this. The vic's car's dashboard, look at the trip meter. It shows only 2.7 km, and the petrol gauge is full."

"So?"

"I have this habit of resetting the trip meter to zero every time I top up the tank."

"You're saying the vic had the same habit?"

"Maybe. I know many men who do that. Who are the detectives on standby?"

"Syed and Jeff."

"OK, I want them to scout around and locate all the petrol stations within a three-kilometer radius of the site. Check if they've CCTV, and if they do, see if the vic's car is on it. I know the area, there aren't many here. There's one, I think it's a Petronas, on Jalan Jelatek before the army camp, a BHP near Rampai Court, and a Shell by Carrefour. I don't think the driver filled up at the BHP or the Shell station, because they'd have been on the wrong side of the road for him."

"Will do," Johan says and heads for the detective's room. He comes back after a couple of minutes.

"Next?"

"Ayn said the male vic got a phone call while they were breaking their fast. She said he apologized, said he had to meet someone, and left with Zaleha."

Johan nods.

"Now, if he'd had an appointment, he wouldn't have arranged to break his fasting with them. So the call must have been unexpected and must have been about something urgent or he would've declined the meeting. You said the vic's phone log indicated the last caller was his son, right?"

"Yes, Hashim, the eldest son, the one who came to collect the Merc."

"This is what I need you to do: First, check with the service provider again, just to be sure there are no calls after Hashim's. Second, I need you to check on Zaleha's ex-boyfriend, Hambali. I was going to ask earlier, but it slipped my mind. Ayn said he was in prison: check with Records if it's true. If he's not, find out where he was that night. Ayn said he used to work with the Mutiara Hotel, maybe you can get his details from them."

"What are you going to do?"

"I want to have a chat with Audi."

At 9:30 he leaves his office for the Mid Valley Megamall. He notices that shops are just starting to open as he rides the escalator up to the ground floor, looking for the Coffee Bean. Audi is already seated at one of the tables.

"Selamat Hari Raya," she greets him, offering her hand.

He returns her greeting and asks, "Can I get you anything?"

"I've ordered mine; they'll send it when it's ready."

He walks up to the counter and orders a regular latte. The barista says she has just fired things up and it will take a while. She'll send it over to the table when it's ready. He pays for the drink and joins Audi.

"Are you not going back to your hometown?" Mislan asks as he slides into a chair.

"This is my hometown. My parents and relatives are here. What about you?"

"I drew the short straw," he says. He offers her a cigarette and lights one up himself. "What did Ayn say to you?"

"I thought you don't want to know."

"I didn't say I don't want to know. You asked what I want you to do with the story and I—"

"Now you're being technical with me," Audi says, stopping Mislan midsentence, and grins. "Yes, we met for a drink yesterday. She had some interesting stories."

"Like?"

"What do you want to hear? That your victims were in love, their marriage plans, or that she is unable to accept Mahadi had killed Zaleha and then committed suicide?"

"OK, OK. So you believe her and don't buy the murder-suicide theory?"

"I'm not saying that. I'm asking what you want to hear. Anyway, why did you give me her number? What's the catch?"

"Now look who doesn't trust whom." Mislan smiles. "Can't a friend do another a favor? It's Raya and being a good Muslim, I thought I'd spread the spirit and cheer around."

"Yeah, right," she says, smiling. "So, what's the catch?"

The barista brings their orders and walks away. Their burst of laughter makes her turn around disapprovingly. Early shoppers start coming in. Soon, the tables around them are taken up.

"I need you to keep the coverage alive."

"I don't get you."

"I feel hidden hands want this case to be closed quickly, buried, and forgotten."

"I still don't get you," she probes.

"Don't play dumb with me, OK. You know exactly what I mean," he says, annoyed with the way Audi is fishing for information. "You think you can pull it off?"

"I'll speak to a friend in the print media, she owes me big-time. How long do you want it alive?"

"A couple of weeks."

"I said she owed me big-time, not her life. Two weeks, I'll peddle it but it's a BIG ask. Now, tell me why you need to keep it alive. What's your game plan?"

"I'm still not sure but two things puzzle me. One is the heavy artillery from the male victim's camp, and the other, the absence of any inquiry from the female victim's family. It's like they've been gagged or something."

"And you're expecting?"

"If it was your daughter who had been murdered, wouldn't you want to know why? Wouldn't you want justice? And if you're not getting any, wouldn't you be screaming your head off? Three days have passed, and there's no sound from them."

"Probably because she's a nobody."

"No one's a 'nobody!'" Mislan snaps. "Everyone is a 'somebody' to someone. It's people like you, the media, who like to classify people as 'somebody' or 'nobody.'"

"Hey, cool it. I didn't mean anything by that."

"A life is a life. It shouldn't matter if it belongs to the rich and powerful or an ordinary person. In the eyes of the media, lives are unequal. The rich and powerful, with the titles Tun, Tan Sri and Datuk, get tons of coverage and sympathy. You'll say the murder was heinous, brutal, and whatever other words you dig up. But when an ordinary person gets killed, it's a statistic." He pauses to light another cigarette, but he doesn't offer her one. "Look, a life is a life. Murder is heinous no matter who the victim is. They all deserve the same treatment." His words trail off. He looks at the floor.

"I'm sorry. I didn't mean it that way."

He looks up at her and says, "It doesn't matter. I'm not here to change your perspective. So, will you do it? And for your role, you get the inside stories, the exclusives."

22

Johan is waiting at the covered walkway at the Kuala Lumpur Police Contingent HQ when Mislan drives in.

"Have you eaten?" he asks when his assistant get in.

"Nope, saving my tummy for lunch at ma'am's house. OK, Zaleha's ex-boyfriend, Hambali Mohd Karim, forty-one, was an assistant sales manager, dismissed on disciplinary grounds—drugs. Checked with Record, two previous convictions, both for drugs. Released seven months back and now back in for same offense, been there for almost two months."

"That rules him out."

"The service provider confirmed the last call to Mahadi was from a number registered to his eldest son Hashim. After that, no incoming or outgoing call or message."

"What did Hashim say to his father? I'm sure the breaking of fast was arranged in advance. The call must have been important for the vic to leave and disappoint his friends."

"Let me check," Johan says pulling out his cell phone to make a call. "Hi Miss Ayn, Detective Sergeant Johan . . . normal laa, police have to work." Johan laughs. "Sorry, Selamat Hari Raya to you, too . . . Sorry to ask, that night the breaking of fast, was it impromptu or planned arrangement . . . Oh, OK. Thanks." Johan terminates the call, saying, "You're right, the breaking of fast was arranged three days earlier. It was the vic that arranged it, saying he needed to discuss the trip to Hat Yai."

Mislan takes the Sprint Highway and exits to Taman Tun Dr. Ismail and heads for Damansara Utama. He parks away from Superintendent Samsiah's house, so he won't be blocked when he needs to leave. They are early, and only a handful of people are there, mostly relatives. Superintendent Samsiah, dressed in a blue floral baju kurung, greets them at the front door.

"Selamat Hari Raya, you guys are early," she says with a warm smile.

"Nice dress," Mislan compliments her. "We thought we'd come now when things are slow at the office."

"Thank you. Where are the rest?"

"Sent them on an errand. They'll be coming later."

Superintendent Samsiah's husband and son appear, dressed in traditional baju Melayu complete with samping. They make a lovely couple and family. The husband invites them in and puts plates into their hands.

"Help yourself, don't be shy. There's plenty to go around," he says, ushering them to the buffet table.

The spread is traditional Malay dishes: chicken and beef rendang, chicken curry, lemang, ketupat, groundnut sauce, and since Superintendent Samsiah is from the East Coast, there is laksam, a specialty noodle from Kelantan. Johan decides to go for the laksam.

"I've not eaten this for ages," he says, piling food on his plate.

"Even if it's true, leave some for others," Mislan jokes. "The boss is watching."

Johan turns and sees Superintendent Samsiah smiling approvingly at the pile of her home-cooked laksam on his plate. The two officers take their plates to the sitting area and join the other guests. Mislan starts eating with fork and spoon as Johan watches.

"Boss, that's not the way to eat laksam." Johan tells the inspector.

Mislan turns to his assistant questioningly.

"You eat with your hand, not with a fork and spoon."

Mislan looks around and sees that his assistant is right. All those eating laksam are using their hands to eat.

"That's them, this is me," he tells his assistant and continues eating.

The hosts bring the officers a glass of drink each and sit with them, urging them to go for second helpings.

"Jo," Superintendent Samsiah says, "if you marry a Kelantanese she'll make you laksam every week."

"If he marries a woman who can cook," Mislan adds.

"Jo, go for a second round," Samsiah urges.

"Thanks, ma'am, I'm full, up to here," Johan says pointing to his chest.

"I heard you're the lead for the DUKE murder-suicide," the husband says.

"Darling, you know I don't like to talk about police work in the house," Samsiah admonishes her husband. Turning to her officers she says, "Never bring your work home . . . if you want a happy home. And the second rule as police officers, never let your other half poke his or her nose into your work."

Johan nods eagerly and Mislan grins. After thirty minutes, the two officers thank their hosts and excuse themselves. Walking to their car, Johan asks where they are going.

"Since we're close, I think we should pay the golf club a visit. See if we can chat with the members about the vics. People say, if you want to know someone's personality, talk to their golfing friends."

"Why is that?"

"Golf is a game you play against yourself, so you tend to be hard on yourself, which brings out your true self. The game is challenging and frustrating. It tests your emotions. I used to play golf, and you should see some of the emotions on the course, breaking clubs, throwing balls into ponds, hitting angrily at the fairways, cursing, and swearing."

Driving out, Mislan tells Johan to head for Kota Damansara and swing by the golf club. His cell phone rings.

"Mislan."

"Inspector Mislan, I'm Superintendent Malik from Selangor Police. Are you free to talk?"

"Yes, sir, how may I assist you?"

"I'd rather we meet in person. Where are you? I can come over."

"I'm on my way to Tropicana Golf and Country Club to meet some people."

"How long will you be there?"

"I really don't know, it depends if they're there. What do you want to meet about?"

"I'll tell you when we meet. Can we meet at PJ Hilton in about an hour?"

"I guess so, if nothing else comes up. Why don't I call you once I'm done at the club?"

"Good."

Johan gives his boss a curious stare.

"Superintendent Malik from Selangor Police, do you know him?"

Johan shakes his head.

"What did he want?"

"To meet. Take a left here and go straight."

23

The entrance to Tropicana Golf & Country Resort in the form of a grand arch-gate stands tall about two hundred yards ahead. Johan slows down at the guardhouse, but the security guard waves him on. The road is wide and exceptionally clean, with palms and trimmed hedges lining both sides. They drive past large bungalows and mansions with meticulously manicured lawns. Each bungalow or mansion has several luxury cars and SUVs parked in the driveways. They see two security guards with guard dogs patrolling the road.

"Wow, I feel like we're driving in . . . where's the place that *Miami Vice* movie was made?" Johan remarks. "You know when they drive along the palm-lined road in the convertible."

Mislan observes the surroundings as his assistant drives slowly, admiring the scenery. Only the superrich can afford to own a house here, with a golf course in their backyard and K9 patrols.

"You sure the vic was a member here?" Mislan asks.

"I read in Zaleha's Facebook. She posted a photo of them playing golf and hanging with some of the golfers . . . mostly whites."

"They could've been a guest of the white guys."

"She said, 'At our golf club enjoying a wonderful round of golf with friends.' That means they're members here right? Otherwise why would she say 'our club'?"

"I guess so."

Johan parks in the visitors' open parking area, and they walk to the golf registration counter. He asks to see the manager, and the receptionist points to the golf terrace.

"He is probably having lunch there."

At the golf terrace, he asks a waiter, who points to a man sitting alone at one of the tables.

"Excuse me, are you the manager here?" Johan says.

"I'm the sports manager. How can I help you?"

"I'm Detective Sergeant Johan and this is Inspector Mislan, we're from the Special Investigations Unit in KL. Can we have a word with you?"

"Sure, please take a seat. Would you like anything to eat or drink?"

"Coffee is good," Mislan says.

The sports manager waves for a waiter and orders two coffees.

"Your name is?"

"Subra," he says, giving them his business card. "What can I do for you?"

"Did you know a member, Mr. Mahadi?"

"Yes, a regular. He was here almost every day, except for Saturdays and Sundays. Didn't he pass away a few days ago? There was something in the papers about him committing suicide. Why do you ask? I really didn't know him that well."

Mislan feels the sports manager is building a fence between him and the deceased and is not willing to get involved.

"Golfers normally have their groups—golfing buddies. Did he have one?"

"You see that group?" He points at a table. "That was his golfing group. They call themselves the Blabbers. I can introduce you to them, if you like?"

Mislan has a feeling the sports manager is eager to get rid of them.

"That would be good."

Subra walks them over to the Blabbers and makes the introductions.

"Gentlemen, this is Inspector Mislan and Detective Sergeant Johan from . . . where'd you say you were from, again?"

"Special Investigations Unit, Kuala Lumpur," Johan answers.

"Pull up a chair," an extra-large, bald white man says. "I'm Ed, this is MS, that's Fred the Dutchman, and he's Jim the Texan."

The waiter noisily drags over a second table to join it to the Blabbers' table and another waiter brings over their coffees. The sports manager excuses himself and practically bolts.

"Inspector, what do you want to talk to us about? I hope we're not wanted by the police," Ed jokes, reaching out to touch Johan's arm. "We blabber and bullshit a lot, you know, like you say in Malay, merapu. Perhaps one of the members here reported us, are you here to arrest us under the Internal Security Act?"

Mislan forces a smile at Ed's feeble joke and says, "No, nothing of that sort. We're here to find out more about one of your golfing buddies, Mahadi."

"Great guy," Ed says, and the rest nod in unison. "You know, Inspector, we're all wondering what really happened."

"I watched the press conference by the police chief. He said something about a love triangle. That's a heap of crap, isn't it?" Fred says.

"That was not the Chief of Police. That was the OCCI, Officer in Charge of Criminal Investigation," Mislan corrects him. "Why do you say that?"

"Details, details," Fred laments, followed by laughter from his group. "Well, if he was right, you two wouldn't be here fishing."

"We're looking at all possibilities. Are you gentlemen expatriates?"

"No, we're men of leisure, retired."

"How long have you been in the country, I mean living here?"

"About four years as part of the Malaysia My Second Home program," Fred answers. "Jim is almost a local now. His wife is Malaysian."

"I was married to a local," Ed says. "A Sarawakian. So, what does that make me, Fred?"

"Half-local," MS, a Chinese man and the only local in the group, jests.

"How long had you known the deceased?"

"Three, maybe four years. We meet here every day except for weekends," Jim, says in his Texas accent. "We play a little golf, have lunch, and bullshit around. Mahadi was always cheerful, such a nice guy. Hell, you couldn't get him angry at anything. When Mahadi hit a bad shot, he laughed it off. Fred, here, will go ballistic."

"I knew him for more than five years, fun to be with, very friendly. He knew almost everybody here and would play with anybody, unlike another guy I know," MS says, looking at the Dutchman and flashing him a smile.

"I don't play with Koreans if I can avoid it. I can't stand their lack of golf etiquette. Mahadi played with them, their manners didn't seem to bother him. Like Jim said, he was an easygoing guy," Fred says.

They continue to talk about Mahadi's personality and how he was the joker in the group, always there to assist anyone. Mislan notices that it was Ed, the extra-large bald American, who did most of the talking, his hand touching Johan whenever he speaks.

"Did you guys know he carried a handgun?" Mislan asks when Ed pauses for breath.

The Blabber members nod.

"I saw him putting a handgun into his golf bag and asked if he was expecting trouble," Fred says. "He told me no, but he was afraid to leave his handgun in the car because he'd lost one once. After that, he had it with him wherever he went."

"That's interesting. Can you remember when that took place?"

"Let me see . . . I think it was two, maybe, three months ago. He said he couldn't risk losing it again. I even saw him taking his handgun into the shower a couple of times, seemed like he didn't want it out of his sight."

"When I read Mahadi murdered the woman and then committed suicide, I thought the papers were reporting some other Mahadi. The Mahadi we all knew would not be capable of hurting anyone. It was simply not him," MS says.

Again, the Blabber members nod.

"Did you know the woman, Zaleha?"

"Yes, sometime she joined Mahadi for a round of golf, but we weren't close with her. Mahadi did speak of her."

"All the time," Fred interjects.

"What did Mahadi say about her?"

"Always endearingly. Not difficult to see he was in love with her," Jim says.

"Why didn't she join your group?"

"You see, Inspector, our group is G.O.L.F," Ed interjects.

"I don't get you."

"Gentlemen Only, Ladies Forbidden," Jim says.

Mislan decides he has heard enough and says, "Gentlemen, thank you very much for your time. We'll leave you to your blabbering."

"Come and join us if you ever get the time, we're always here. And good luck with the case."

They fist shake, which according to Ed is the way the Blabber group shake hands, and leave.

At the parking lot Mislan phones Superintendent Malik to inform him that he's on the way to the PJ Hilton. He tells Johan to stay out of sight during their meeting, to keep an eye on them, and, if possible, to take a picture of this Malik guy. He takes out a roll of masking tape from his backpack and attaches a digital recorder to his chest.

"What's with the recorder, you expecting trouble?" Johan asks.

"Nope, but you know me. I always forget what people tell me. Blame it on my age," he chuckles.

"Yeah, especially when it's advice."

He tests the digital recorder to ensure he can capture their conversation.

"Did you hear what the Blabber group said about the vics?"

"I heard them but they may be people who are good at hiding their truthful selves. Put up a happy front for the dead no matter what."

"I know, but he was among friends. Under stress, true natures will surface. As I told you, I played golf before."

"You remember the guy Ed? He couldn't stop talking and touching. . . . Really annoying."

Mislan laughs.

24

Johan drops the inspector off at the main road and drives away, looking for a place to park under the overpass. At the hotel main lobby, Mislan scans the faces of people, trying to spot anyone he recognizes. He sees two men talking in the hallway to the restroom. One of them has a police officer's look and air about him. He switches on the digital recorder and makes a call to his assistant, describing the men and their clothes. No sooner has he ended the call than the two men walk toward him. He pretends not to notice them and walks away to the sofas as if to wait for his appointment. As they approach, one of them asks.

"Inspector Mislan?"

He looks at them and answers, "Yes. Superintendent Malik?"

The man dressed in a white shirt nods and proffers his hand. They exchange festive greetings, and Malik introduces his companion as Daud. He suggests they go over to the coffeehouse for a chat and some drinks. He spots Johan walking into the lobby and gives his detective sergeant a subtle nod. Malik picks a table away from the cashier's counter and orders their drinks. Johan sits in the lobby, monitoring them.

"I don't believe we've met before," Mislan says.

"No, I don't think we have. I was transferred from Terengganu about a year ago. I'm still adjusting, getting used to the pace and feeling my way around. Your boss is Superintendent Samsiah, right? Do you know her G number?" he says, referring to her identity number as a gazette, or senior, police officer.

"Sorry, I don't," Mislan lies. "You're in?"

"Commercial Crimes."

"Mr. Daud, sorry, I didn't get your full name or where you're from."

"Daud Nordin," the man answers hesitantly, "from . . . ah, I run my own business."

"Daud is a friend from my hometown," Malik butts in, cutting off any further inquiry.

The waiter brings their drinks and asks if they wish to order anything else, which they decline. When the waiter is out of earshot, Malik continues.

"I understand you're the lead investigator in the Mahadi murder-suicide case."

Mislan nods.

"How's your investigation coming along?"

"Still digging. Look, sir, I'm not trying to be rude, but I'm on twenty-four-hour today and I really need to be getting back to the office. What's it you want to see me about?"

"OK, let me get straight to the point. I've been approached by certain people who . . . well, let's say are in positions to make or break careers." Malik says it slowly and clearly to ensure Mislan understands what he is hinting at. "They've asked me to see if there's any way to get you to wrap up the case as soon as possible. They've been told it's a murder-suicide, and they would like it to be kept that way. Let the dead rest in peace."

"May I know who these people are?"

"Let's say influential friends of the deceased."

"Don't they want to know what really happened? I mean, being his friends and all."

"It was a murder-suicide, and that was what it was, like your OCCI said. Digging into the life of the deceased will only make things worse than it already is for the families. They've suffered enough from gossip and innuendo. Anyway, what do you expect to uncover?"

"The truth, what really happened, and if, as you say, it was indeed a murder-suicide. Don't they want to know why the woman was murdered?"

"A love triangle was what got her murdered. Jealousy, he may have discovered she was playing him for a sucker. Got into a heated argument, lost his head, and acted rashly. When he realized what he had done, he took his own life . . . a spur-of-the-moment thing."

"I see, and why hasn't this other lover come forward to give a statement?"

"I don't know, fear, embarrassment. It could be any reason. Anyway, what else could it be? The car was locked from the inside, the gun belongs to the deceased, the CCTV from the expressway tollgate and witnesses interviewed all indicate there are only two of them in the car. It looks to me like a simple case."

"Well, if you say so, but I don't have the authority to close cases. It can only come from my boss or the top. I'm only an investigator, and my duties are to investigate, to clear up all doubts. You know that. If you want it closed, I guess you have to reach out to my boss."

"I know, but your investigations will have to support a murder-suicide for your boss to give you that instruction. I'm sure by now you've reached the conclusion that was what happened."

Mislan remains silent, breathing slowly to control himself.

"These people I've mentioned are not ungrateful people. I'm sure they'll remember what you've done for them, and when the time comes, you'll be appropriately rewarded."

"I was informed you're a single parent with a seven-year-old son," Daud butts in. "Here is his angpow." He pushes a thick green packet across the table to Mislan.

"Thank you, but I have to decline. I try not to encourage my son to accept angpow. It's not part of our Malay culture," he replies, pushing the packet back. "I'll speak to my boss about your request and follow up with her after the holidays. I've to go back to the office now. Thank you for the coffee."

He stands, they shake hands, and he leaves.

In the lobby, he lights a cigarette. He then walks toward the main road, switches off the recorder, and waits. Johan, who has positioned himself near the entrance where he can get clear shots of the two men coming out of the coffeehouse, focuses his cell phone camera on them while pretending to speak into it. He takes several pictures of them. Satisfied, he walks to the car, picks up his boss, and drives toward the Federal Highway.

"What was the meeting about?"

"What do you think? Did you get shots of them?"

"Yup, several. They want the case closed?"

The inspector nods.

"Who was the other guy?"

"Gave his name as Daud Nordin, a businessman. Somehow, I doubt the business part. Anyway, Superintendent Malik said he was an old friend from his hometown."

"Something's bothering you?"

"I don't know. The guy Daud knew I'm a single parent with a seven-year-old son."

"And?"

"He gave me a fat angpow for Daniel, which I turned down. What bothers me is how he knew. Even ma'am doesn't know I'm single; not even our HR department, because I've not officially reported it. Very few people knew. They've been digging about me. Maybe their people have even been watching and following Daniel. Perhaps, they're saying, 'We know where you live, who your son is, and where he goes to school.'"

"Are you going to tell the boss?"

"Not yet. I need to know who these people are and their involvements. I need to know their motive for wanting to close the case."

"What about Superintendent Malik's request? Are you going to tell ma'am?"

"I said he'll have to speak to ma'am if he wants it closed. I'll wait until she comes back to the office and let her know. That's if Malik doesn't approach her first."

"I got a call from Syed. He said they've got the CCTV recording from Petronas in Jalan Jelatek with the vic's car on it."

"Good work, let's go back and view it."

On the way back to the office, Johan keeps looking into the rearview mirror, paranoid about being followed.

25

The office is deserted, and there is no sign of Syed or Jeff in the detective's room or the general office. Johan gives them a call.

"They're at ma'am's house and will be back shortly," he says as he picks up an envelope and gives it to his boss. "There's a note in there with the time the vic's car was at the petrol station."

Mislan boots up his computer, slots the DVD into the drive, and drags the timer to the time indicated on the note. A woman is seen entering the station's convenience store. The image is too small to make out her face, but the color and style of her blouse looks similar to that worn by the female victim.

"There's the vic going into the station," Johan says.

A few minutes pass, and the woman reappears and walks to a black Mercedes at one of the pumps. She gets into the car and the Mercedes leaves.

"That's the car," Johan exclaims.

"Can you make out the number?" Mislan asks.

"Too small."

"We need to enlarge these images. It could be anybody and any Mercedes. Is this the best they've got?"

"I guess so, let me check with them." Johan calls them. He tells the inspector the two detectives are already downstairs parking their bikes.

"I'm sure the woman was Zaleha."

"It could be them, but better to be 100 percent sure. Let's get Forensics to look at it, see if they can enlarge it and see more of her and the car."

He calls the Forensics supervisor.

"Hello Chew, Mislan. Sorry to call you during the holidays."

"Selamat Hari Raya. No problem, what's up?"

"Is Nathan working? I need him to look at some CCTV recordings."

"No, he's not. He'll be working on Monday. Inspector, did my fingerprint tech call you?"

"No, why?"

"You remember the prints I lifted from the car? The one on the window auto-button has a match. I told my tech to inform you." Chew sighs, "She must have forgotten. Let me call the office, see if the tech on duty can find it. I'll get him to call you."

"Damn it, when did you make the match?"

"She told me late yesterday evening. Let me call the office, and Inspector, sorry for my tech's oversight."

"Forget it, let me know ASAP."

He hangs up and throws his cell phone onto the desk.

"Damn, they got a match but the tech didn't tell us."

"What match?"

"The prints Chew lifted from the car window button-lever."

He lights up a cigarette to calm himself down. How could the technician have ignored such an important matter?

Syed and Jeff enter the office, each carrying a plastic bag.

"What's that?" Johan asks gesturing to the plastic bag.

"Rendang and lemang. Ma'am packed your dinner," Detective Syed says, handing it to the detective sergeant.

"Did you guys find out how many cameras the station has?" Mislan asks.

"Four. One camera covers the station's entrance and, one the cashier and two the pumps. We spoke to the cashiers, but no one could remember anything."

"How about the other petrol stations?"

"We went to three others, nothing."

His cell phone rings.

"Mislan," he answers excitedly.

"Inspector, I'm Pathma, the Finger Print Technician. Mr. Chew asked me to call you."

"Yes, Pathma. Do you have the print record?"

"Yes, I found it on Yasmin's desk in an envelope addressed to you. Do you want me to send it or do you want to send someone to pick it up?"

"Can you read out the match-number? I'll get his particulars from Records."

Ending the call, he gives Syed a piece of paper, "Go down to Records and get me a hardcopy of this."

"Have we hit the jackpot?" Johan is excited.

"Could be, Jo, could be," he replies, sharing his assistant's excitement and anticipation.

After two cigarettes and several curses from the inspector on why it is taking too long to get a copy of the record of the matched individual, Detective Syed appears at the doorway. Mislan grabs the printout and eagerly reviews it.

"Mahyudin Maidin a.k.a. Mamak Din from Janda Baik, Pahang. One previous record for assault under section 324 of the Penal Code, Serdang Report, fined RM2,500.00 with a year bond for good behavior. Last known address: 12-4, Sutramas, Persiaran Puchong Jaya Selatan, Puchong, and permanent address, 4 Desa Janda Baik. Here," Mislan says handing the record to Johan.

"Is he the third person?" Johan asks.

26

Before leaving the office, Mislan calls Bentong District Police and speaks to Inspector Ooi, the investigator on duty, to ask for interstate assistance. He gives him the suspect's address and asks Ooi if he can dispatch a couple of detectives to the address. Mislan warns him to exercise caution as the suspect may be armed and dangerous. He gives Ooi his cell phone number and tells the officer to call back no matter what time it is. If Ooi takes the suspect into custody, Mislan will arrange for escorts to Kuala Lumpur. Mislan didn't like interstate reaching-out as it was almost always treated with low priority. He would have preferred to drive to Janda Baik to conduct the raid himself, but knowing how hot his case is, he cannot risk news of this interstate adventure reaching the OCCI's ears. He is already skating on thin ice. At the same time, he is also not keen on leaving the office for too long, especially today with most personnel on leave.

On the way to Puchong, he calls the Subang Jaya Police and is told that due to a recent dealignment exercise, the address he requires falls under the jurisdiction of the Serdang Police District. A call to the station is answered by a policeman who is not sure if the address is under them and his call is transferred to the Operations Center. A policewoman answers at the other end. Mislan reads out the address and is told she is unsure which station it is under. He voices his disappointment and the policewoman gives him an excuse, saying that she was recently transferred to the district—two weeks ago. Then, Mislan loses it.

"I don't care if you were transferred there today. You're in the Operation Center. If you don't know your area, then we're in *big* trouble!"

"I'm sorry, sir. Can I have your cell phone number? I'll call you back," the policewoman says.

A minute later his cell phone rings.

"Mislan."

"Sir, I'm Corporal Farid from MPV Unit, Subang Jaya. Have you found the address yet?"

"No, I'm still checking which jurisdiction the address is located in." Mislan says.

"It's under Serdang station, and the police station is Puchong Jaya district. The address you want is just behind the station."

"Thank you."

"Jo, drive to the Puchong Jaya police station."

They stop at the main gate and ask for the investigating officer's office. The sentry tells them he is out. Mislan asks if there is a detective around. The sentry points to a door on the side of the building. Johan parks the car and they walk up to the door, knock, and find a detective watching television. Introducing themselves, Mislan asks, "Are you the detective on standby?"

Detective Tan acknowledges him.

"Are you free to assist us?"

"Yes, nothing else is happening."

"I need to check out Units 12-4, Sutramas, Persiaran Puchong Jaya Selatan."

"That's close by," Tan says, following them out. "Who're you looking for?"

"Have you seen this person around," Johan show him a mug shot of Mahyudin.

"No, I don't think so. Why, what's he wanted for?"

"A witness."

"You want to follow me? I'll be on my bike."

They follow Tan's motorcycle to the guardhouse of a condominium. Tan stops and says something to the security guard, the boom gate is raised, and they drive in. Johan leaves the car in a visitors' lot and joins Tan in the lobby.

"Tan, can you check with the guard if Unit 12-4 has a parking lot?"

Detective Tan walks back to the guardhouse and returns to tell them that the parking spot is in Basement One.

"Let's check the parking spot first, then."

They take the stairs down and locate the parking spot for the unit. A white Toyota Vios occupies it, and as Johan jots down the number plate, Mislan peeks inside the car.

"The car owner is a woman," he says, pointing at some decorative stuff in the interior. "Let's go to the unit."

They take the elevator up to the 12th, locate the unit, and Johan presses the doorbell. Mislan notices several women's shoes but no men's. After another ring, a Chinese woman opens the door.

"Hello, I'm Detective Sergeant Johan," he says holding up his authority card. "Does a Mr. Mahyudin Maidin live here?"

Two more Chinese women poke their heads from behind. One of them asks the one at the door, "Who is it?"

"Cops. Sorry, no man live here."

"Tan, can you ask them if we can come in and ask a few questions?" Mislan says.

Tan says something in Chinese, and the first woman unlocks the grille door. The three curious women step back, allowing the visitors to enter. With Tan interpreting, the Special Investigations investigators learn that the women work in a karaoke bar and that they had rented the apartment about a year ago. They do not know anything about the previous tenant and their landlord is a Chinese man who lives in Kepong. The women give them the landlord's contact. The police officers thank them for their cooperation and leave.

As he is approaching the car, his cell phone rings.

"Mislan."

"Mislan, Ooi here, bad news, lah. Your suspect managed to slip away when the detective approached the house. He bolted through the back into the jungle. The detective gave chase, but he was too quick."

"Damnit!" Mislan swears and promptly apologizes to Ooi.

"No sweat, I understand. Do you want us to keep an eye on the house for a while?"

"I don't think he'll come back. Did your detective talk to the occupants?"

"They're still there, I can ask them."

"Can you ask the detective to find out as much as he can about the suspect's car, bike, cell phone number, last-known address in KL, friends, anything they can get. Please email the info to me immediately when you get it. I'm on a twenty-four-hour."

"Sure. Hey, Mislan, I'm really sorry he got away."

"No problem. Thanks, Ooi."

They thank Tan and drive out to the Kesas Expressway to Sungai Besi and the city. The journey is quiet. Mislan is disappointed and frustrated. It is already evening, and he has achieved nothing because a fingerprint technician failed in her duties. If only he had been told of the matched prints yesterday. He could have gone to Janda Baik himself to lead the raid. He lights a cigarette and frowns. Now that the suspect has been spooked, he'll be flying, and tracking him will be harder.

"Shit," he cries out, flicking his cigarette out the window. At the office, Mislan says to Johan that it's all right for him to go home and freshen up. He tells his assistant to keep his cell phone close.

"I don't think there'll be much happening tonight. In fact, there won't be much happening over the next two days until offices reopen."

27

Mislan is overwhelmed by loneliness as he sits at his desk. The silence is oppressive and depressing. His mind wanders to his son. He wonders what Daniel is doing. Is he having fun with new friends and getting pampered by relatives? His hand reaches for the cell phone and speed-dials his ex-wife. Daniel answers after a few rings.

"Hi Daddy."

"Hey, kiddo, what are you doing?"

"Playing, Daddy, I got lots of money."

"Wow, now we can buy the BMW car you've always wanted," he jokes, and hears Daniel shout.

"Mummy, how much money do I have? Mummy says RM135. Is that enough?"

"Not even close, kiddo, you need much more," he says, laughing.

"How much?"

"At the very least, another two hundred and fifty thousand."

"Ooo. Daddy, can you call me later? I want to play with my friends."

"Okay kiddo. Miss you and love you."

"Love you, too."

And the line goes dead. Mislan smiles.

He remembers the photo Johan took of Superintendent Malik and Daud Nordin at the PJ Hilton. He asks Johan for them. After a minute his cell phone beeps—it is an incoming WhatsApp. He forwards the photos to Audi with a message asking if she knows the man.

Audi replies: *nope, will chk and let u know.*

He looks at the clock. It is only five past six. He sighs, thinking of the long night ahead. Ironically, he wishes for a serious crime somewhere to fill the dreary night. He walks to the makeshift pantry, unpacks the food packages from Superintendent Samsiah's house, makes a mug of coffee, and starts on the rendang. His cell phone rings. It is Dr. Safia.

"Hey Fie, how's your Raya?"

"Quiet. Are you in the office?" she asks.

"Yes. I'm on today. Are you still at the hospital?"

"I left about 5:30. I'm thinking of dinner. Want to join me?"

"Love to, but I'm holding the fort alone. I've sent Johan home to freshen up, and the detectives are out," he says. "I've got some lemang and rendang here if you'd like to come. Anyway, I don't think food stalls or the mamak restaurants are open tonight."

"Is that an invitation?"

"Sure is."

"Sounds good. You want me to get you anything on the way?"

"No, thanks. Are you serious about coming down here?"

"Yeah. I've never been to your office. This is a good time to get a tour of the place where the city's finest work. Unless, you don't want me to come."

"No, I mean, yes. I'd love your company, but don't be disappointed with what you see."

"Hey, I work in a morgue, okay? What could be worse?"

"All right, I'll let the guards know you're coming."

Johan comes around 7:15 while Mislan and Safia are having lemang and rendang at the pantry.

"Doctor, Selamat Hari Raya," Johan greets her. "Am I interrupting anything?"

"Hi Jo, happy Raya to you, too. No, you're not interrupting anything. Had dinner? We're just about to have ours, and I brought some cookies," Dr. Safia says, with a smile.

She is always smiling, always has a smile for everyone, Detective Johan reflects.

"I'm still feeling full from ma'am's open house. You guys go ahead."

"Pull up a chair, come join us," Mislan suggests.

"Let me make a cup of coffee. Doc, you want one?"

"Thanks, I have mine. So, this is what the office of the men in blue looks like. Hmmm, nothing like I've seen on TV," she teases them.

Mislan and Johan laugh.

"We're lucky to have this. On TV, crime is solved in the office, so the office has to look good for viewers. We're the real thing, we solve crimes by hitting the ground, where they are committed," Johan says and swaggers theatrically.

Mislan applauds his sergeant and cheers, saying, "Hear, hear."

Johan takes a bow, grinning.

"Yeah, right. Save the theatricals, OK. It's wasted on me. This is not the Sherlock Holmes age. You guys should prepare yourselves for the new tide where crimes are solved by us, the forensic experts," she says. "Don't worry, you'll still be required to arrest and shoot the bad guys."

Johan laughs, pulls up a chair and joins them.

"Is this your first time in a police office?"

"Office, yes, station no. I've been there a few times."

"It's not all that bad. Before this, I was in the Mobile Patrol Vehicle Unit. I didn't even have an office, we wrote reports in the canteen. At least here, we have our own desks, computers, and telephones, even a pantry."

Detective Syed and Detective Jeff poke their heads in and ask if there are any further instructions for them. Mislan shakes his head, and tells them to wait in the detectives' room.

"Fie, if a person is shot twice, say a few seconds or a minute apart, can you tell which was the first shot?"

"You mean through the autopsy?"

Mislan nods.

"Yes, and no."

"Give me the 'yes' first."

"Yes, there is medical forensic technology to determine this, but it's not used here. However, if the second shot is well after the person is dead and the blood has stopped, yes it can be determined by the wound."

"How?"

"I won't go into the how, it's too scientific and I don't think you should be bothered with it. Just take my word, it can be detected," Dr. Safia says, grinning.

"OK, and the no?"

"It's very expensive and in most cases, what's crucial is the effect or fatality of the shots. So, back to your initial question, the answer is no, but I can only tell you if the shots were fatal."

"Zaleha, the vic, was shot twice. Once in the head and another in the chest. I'm guessing both shots were fatal. If I'm right . . . my question is, why was she shot twice?"

"You've got the autopsy reports?"

"No, not yet. Only the autopsy photos of the vics. I guess the report will only be out when they start working on Monday."

"Can I see the photos?"

"Sure," he says, taking the photos out from his backpack. "Can you tell much from examining these photos?"

"No, only the obvious. During autopsies, I can feel and touch the body. That would give me a better understanding of what I'm looking at. Like a wound, I can touch it, press it, see how the wound and the surrounding areas react it allows me to analyze it better."

She notes the blank looks on Mislan and Johan.

"It's hard to explain. It's like you guys at a crime scene, being there gives you guys the feel. That's the best I can explain," she says, laughing.

"I know what you mean. Tell you what, why don't you feel and press the photos and if you want, smell them?" Mislan mocks her. "Or hold it up against your forehead and go *aummm*, *aummm*, *aummm*, and it'll all come to you."

"Funny. You want me to look at them or not?" she says, regarding him sternly.

"I'm only joking."

She spreads the photos on the desk and examines them, picks one out for a closer look and puts it back, like she is selecting music CD covers. Mislan and Johan watch her silently. Mislan lights a cigarette and passes it to her and lights another for himself. When she finishes, he asks.

"So?"

"By the entry wounds, I'm sure the head shot was fatal, but it's hard to say about the chest shot. If the bullet hit a vital organ, say the heart, yes it was fatal. Otherwise, it may not have been. I don't see any exit wound, so with only these photos to go by, I'd say the shot in the chest could've hit a rib and lodged itself. Or, it may have punctured the heart, hit a rib, and that stopped it from exiting. Until I see the autopsy report, that's my best guess. The key word there is 'guess,' not observation or analysis," she says, grinning.

"What's that around the head wound?"

"See this," she says, pointing at a spot on the head in the photo. "That looks like a burn mark. Heat from the barrel leaves marks like that when the gun is too close or is in contact with the skin. Here, look at the hairs around the wound, see how they're curled. That was probably caused by the heat."

"Forensics spotted that, too. They did a swab and found powder soot to confirm the contact or near-contact shot. Do you see any defensive wounds?"

"No, there don't seem to be any. But here," she points to a photo of the male victim's body. "See this? This mark, something scratched the skin hard enough to lacerate it. What do you think could have made that mark?"

Mislan looks at it. The scratch mark is at the right side of the waist.

"I don't know . . ." He examines it closely. "Could the gun's hammer have done it when it was pulled out of the holster?"

"Is the hammer sharp?"

"No, it's round but grooved."

"Grooved, like what?"

Mislan sketches the hammer from memory. "Something like this."

"Could be, but I can't be sure unless I see the gun. You're thinking they were murdered?"

"Why do you ask?" Johan inquires.

"Because your boss's asking me about differentiating the first and second shot and defensive injuries."

"You're getting good at reading him. We've placed a third person in the car, so my boss's theory of murder could be right, couldn't it?"

"You're saying a third person was the killer and it was made to look like a murder-suicide. *Mmmm.* Even if there was a third person in the car, it doesn't automatically mean he was the killer. He could've been an innocent passenger who bolted when the shooting happened, fearing for his safety or being implicated."

"Why do we always refer to an unknown suspect as a 'he'?" Johan says. "Women kill, too."

"I suppose killing used to be a man thing," Dr. Safia says.

"I think it has more to do with wording of the law, where it says 'he' also includes 'she.' Anyway, I did think of the possibility of the third person being an innocent passenger and hoped he'd come forward to tell us all about it. That hasn't happened. That, my dear doctor, makes me seriously doubt his status as an innocent passenger."

28

Three hours later, the three of them are still debating what could have been or might be the truth behind the murder-suicide of Mahadi and Zaleha as they continue to nibble on the lemang, ketupat, and rendang provided by the thoughtful head of Special Investigations. Safia and Johan throw possible scenarios at him, and Mislan shoots them down with evidence. He is on a roll, when his cell phone rings.

"Mislan."

"Mislan, Ooi from Bentong Police."

"Oh, hi. Anything?"

"Sorry for the delay in informing you. After we spoke, my detectives went back to the suspect's house, and the car was gone. The parents said he came back after they left, gathered his things, and drove off. That was when my detectives came back to the office to prepare the information you require, which I emailed to you earlier."

"Shit," Mislan swears.

"Sorry."

"It's OK, not your fault."

"Why? What's happened?" Johan asks when the inspector has terminated the call.

Mislan tells him, then, "Call Operation Center, ask them to send a be-on-look-out flash to all MPVs. Let's keep it local until we get more intel on him. Jo, if spotted, no one makes a move on him until I'm contacted."

Mislan logs on his email and print out Inspector Ooi's email, handing it to his assistant.

"Got you," Johan says and walks back to his desk.

"Where do you sleep? Is there a room where you sleep?" Dr. Safia asks looking around.

She asks not because she want to know but to temper the frustration emerging from the investigator, to take his mind off the slipup by the Bentong detectives.

"We're not supposed to sleep, and if we're tired, we take catnaps at our desks. Why?"

"Just curious," she answers, smiling.

"It's late, do you want to leave?"

Dr. Safia knows the inspector is boiling inside and wants to get rid of her so he can blow up, feed his frustrations.

"No, not unless you want me to."

He smiles at her, shaking his head.

Johan returns and starts chatting with Dr. Safia about Raya celebrations, a trip down memory lane. They smile as their eyes sparkle with fond recollections. They must have had wonderful childhoods, Mislan thinks. He listens enviously. His mind drifts to his son, and he wonders what sort of memories Daniel will have. He feels Dr. Safia touching his arm.

"Hey, you OK?"

"Yeah, fine."

"You seem distant."

He gives her an awkward smile.

"I was enjoying your stories," he says, and changes the subject before she can respond. "I feel like a teh tarik. Jo, you know where we can get some with all the stalls closed?"

Tee tarik is tea with milk prepared the local way, by pouring and "pulling" the brew repeatedly from one container to another.

"I've no idea. Let me ask Syed or Jeff. They might know."

"Why don't we go to one of the hotels? I know the coffeehouses have it," Dr. Safia proposes.

"I don't like hotel teh tarik, too classy," he says. "They'll charge you ten times more, plus ten plus five, not including the eight-ringgit parking fee."

"Cheapskate," she teases him. "It's Raya. OK, I'll buy."

Johan comes back and tells them a mamak stall behind Istana Hotel is open. They drive in two cars, with Mislan getting a ride from Dr. Safia while Johan drives the investigating officer's standby vehicle. The stall is crowded. Johan asks for a table and they place their orders. While waiting, Johan gets a call.

"Boss, an MPV has spotted the suspect's car."

"Where?" he asks already on his feet.

"Setapak . . . in front of Maybank. The MPV drove past but did not see anyone in or near it. They believe the suspect is in one of the Chinese restaurants and they're monitoring the car, waiting for instructions."

"Tell the MPV to keep out of sight and not to make any moves. Let's go. Fie, sorry, can you take care of the drinks? I'll catch up with you later."

"No problem, I'll take care of it, go on."

As the inspector and detective sergeant turn to leave, she calls after them.

"Hey, be careful, OK?"

Having been with an MPV Unit before, Johan takes the wheel as he knows the city roads better than his boss. He is also trained in offensive and defensive driving techniques. He heads for Setapak, taking the quickest route he knows. Mislan calls Sentul Police, asking for the call sign of the mobile patrol vehicle that spotted his suspect's vehicle. Turning his radio to the Sentul radio channel, he contacts the MPV.

Sentul 2-4, this is Sierra India Inspector Mislan, over.

Go ahead Sierra India.

Echo-Tango-Alpha in 2-0.

Roger that, over.

Traffic is very light due to the festive holiday, and they are making good time. On Jalan Pahang, Johan turns left to Jalan Gombak, driving fast but not recklessly. Mislan marvels at Johan's skill and concentration—his eyes narrowed, forehead wrinkled, and the veins on his neck bulging. The radio crackles.

Sierra India, suspect and a woman are walking toward the car.

Confirm, suspect and one woman?

Affirmative.

"Shit, the suspect's with a woman," Mislan tells his assistant.

Roger that, Echo-Tango-Alpha in 0-5, I repeat Echo-Tango-Alpha in 0-5.

Mislan turns to look at his assistant and gets a firm nod from the detective sergeant. Mislan feels the surge of adrenaline as the engine suddenly vibrates under his feet. Johan guns down Jalan Setapak, heading to the traffic light, and makes a hair-raising U-turn. After about four hundred yards, Johan slows down.

"Over there, that's the Maybank."

Sierra India the suspect is driving off, coming toward us. Do you want us to intercept?

Sentul 2-4, intercept, intercept. I repeat, intercept. Exercise caution, the suspect may be armed and dangerous.

Roger that.

"Cut in here," Mislan tells his assistant. "We'll box him in. . . . Sentul 24 is at the other end."

Johan cuts into the road in front of the rows of shops, aware of the cars and motorbikes parked along the narrow road. Mislan sees the red taillights of a car about two hundred yards ahead, but it's too far to make out its registration number or the model.

"There, can you make out the number," he asks Johan, motioning the car ahead.

Johan shakes his head.

Then the suspect's car brakes hard with tires screeching, making a bootleg 180-degrees turn. In doing so, it clips the row of motorbikes parked by the side of the narrow road. The D9 radio blares.

Sierra India, the suspect saw us and is making a run for it. I repeat, the suspect's making a run. Heading your way.

Johan, alerted by the radio transmission, reacts and barrels the car forward, missing a row of parked motorcycles by inches.

"Slow down," Mislan says, "he's boxed in."

The suspect's car does a tight 90-degree drift spin, clipping a parked motorbike and sending it tumbling into the drain. It stops at a back lane

T-junction behind the rows of shops. The driver revs its engine twice and barrels down the alley, leaving a smell of burning rubber. A few seconds later, they hear the sound of screeching tires again, followed by the roar of the engine.

"Shit, this guy is good, probably had some training," Johan says.

Not to be outdone, he turns right sharply into the alley with the rear of his car skidding. Fifty yards on, Johan jams hard on the brakes at a T-junction. They look frantically to the right and left.

"There, left, left," Mislan shouts.

Johan pulls the hand brake, jerks the steering wheel left, revving the engine hard, burning rubber as the car skids hard left. He releases the hand brake, and the car lunges forward. Mislan holds on tightly to the dashboard with one hand while shouting into the radio.

Sentul 2-4, suspect heading your way through the back lane.

Roger, we see him.

They come to the end of the back lane just as Sentul 24 shoots past, siren blaring, its red and blue beacons lighting up the night, behind the suspect. Johan steps on the accelerator and joins in the chase. The suspect speeds along Jalan Setapak, sidewinding a cruising vehicle, drift skids onto Jalan Gombak, taking down a road sign, doing 90 miles an hour, putting distance between him and the MPV.

"Shit. Did you see that?" Mislan exclaims.

"Hell, this guy is dangerous. He's going too fast and is losing control. We've got to stop him before someone gets hurt. Tell Sentul 24 to drop back and call for backup." Johan says.

Sentul 2-4 pull out, pull out, let us pass and call for backup to cut the suspect off.

Roger.

The MPV moves to the side to open a small passage for Johan to bullet through.

Sentul 2-4, have you called for backup?

Affirmative, Selangor 2-1-1 and 2-2-3 are responding.

"This damn car is old and underpowered," Johan grumbles.

He turns off the air-conditioning for more power and stands on the gas pedal. They start to close the gap on the suspect's car. Mislan waves through the window, signaling the suspect to pull over. The suspect presses harder on the accelerator to put even more distance between them. The high-speed chase approaches a roundabout, and the suspect must have missed the sign, almost going through it. Somehow, he manages to swerve in the very last second and screeches on two tires onto Jalan Batu Caves.

"Whoa, that was close," Mislan says.

Then, for no noticeable reason, the suspect's car slows and comes to a stop. "What the fu—!" Mislan exclaims.

Pointing to the approaching red and blue lights, Johan says, "He's boxed in."

Johan brings the car to a skidding halt about thirty yards behind the suspect's car. Mislan instantly jumps out with his service Beretta cocked and drawn, pointing at the suspect's car. Standing behind his opened door, he shouts.

"Step out of the vehicle with your hands up."

He strains his eyes to see any movement inside the suspect's car. The night is still, except for the blaring siren of the approaching Sentul 24 and the humming of their car engines. An MPV with a red-and-blue swirling beacon approaching from the opposite stops about fifty yards in front of the suspect's car. Sentul 24 finally arrives behind them. Mislan signals it to cut off the siren and shouts again.

"Occupants of the car, please get out with your hands raised."

The passenger door opens and a pair of shiny stilettos attached to a pair of slim legs protrudes. A woman slowly emerges from the open door and turns to face them, shielding her face like a drunk hit by a bright light.

Mislan shouts, "Lady, step away from the car. Driver of the car, please turn off your engine and step out."

The woman looks toward them, not making a move.

Mislan repeats, "Please step away from the car."

She bends into the car's cabin, reemerges, slams the door, and backs away to the curb. In her haste, she almost trips over as her stilettos dig into the soft ground. Recovering, she screams obscenities at the officers and steps farther away from the car.

"Driver of the car, turn off your engine and step out of the vehicle with your hands up," Mislan repeats.

"He's going to make a run. Get in! Get in!" Johan yells.

Just as Johan shouts the warning to his boss, the night is shattered with the deafening roar of a revving engine.

"Get in!" Johan yells again, over the roar.

Mislan jumps into the car and, before he can close the door, Johan guns the car straight for the suspect's. The suspect's car lurches and speeds off just before Johan can ram and immobilize it.

"Damn!" Johan swears.

The suspect's car speeds toward the MPV blocking the road and rams its rear end, spinning the MPV and creating an opening. The patrolmen open fire as the suspect's car veers to the right and zooms past, its dangling front fender throwing sparks like fireworks as it drags on the pavement. Johan speeds through the opening, trying desperately to close the gap between them. A bullet hits their car as they zoom into the line of fire and Mislan crouches for cover, shouting into the radio, "*Stop shooting, stop the bloody shooting.*"

Johan glances at his rearview mirror and sees Sentul 24 frantically signaling and shouting to Selangor 211's crew to stop. When the shooting stops, Mislan shouts into the radio, "*Sentul 2-4, pick the woman up and check on the Mike-Papa-Victor crew.*

Roger.

The suspect makes a sharp left to Jalan Ipoh, heads north for about six miles, and turns right into Selayang Baru at the breakneck speed of 80 to 90 mile per hour. Unfortunately, he loses control of the car, overshoots the sharp bend, and dives into a monsoon drain, kissing the concrete wall at full speed. Johan slams on his brakes, causing the car's rear to slide sideways. Mislan is already out before the car stops. Gun drawn, he rushes toward the suspect's car. The hood is jackknifed, with the engine block pushed into the dashboard. The suspect is pinned between the steering wheel and his seat, his head on the twisted steering wheel, blood oozing from his mouth and ears. His eyes are closed, like he is shutting out the scene of the final impact. Mislan jumps into the waterless monsoon drain, yanks open the door, and feels for suspect's pulse. After a few attempts, he steps back, leans against the wall, and swears, "Damn, damn!"

Johan steps forward and looks at the motionless body of Mahyudin Maidin aka Mamak Din, saying, "I guess he made up his mind . . . Freedom or death, and death prevailed."

Sentul 24 approaches the scene and calls it in. Corporal Lingam tells them that the MPV crew is fine, as they managed to get out of the way before the suspect rammed their vehicle. He also informs them that the scene is under Selangor police jurisdiction and Operations Center has informed the district.

29

The district investigating officer, Inspector Amita Kaur from Rawang Police District HQ, arrives at the scene with Selangor Forensics (D10). The Special Investigations Unit officers step aside and lean against their car, watching the district IO and the Selangor D10 go about their business. Mislan remembers the woman picked up by Sentul 24 and walks to the MPV. He sees her sobbing in the back seat of the patrol car.

"I'm Inspector Mislan from Special Investigations. What's your name?"

"Jamie," she answers despairingly.

Having lost a potential lead, Mislan is not in the mood for sympathy.

"Listen. The rule when a police officer asks for your name is to state your full name."

"Jamilah binti Abu Sibli," she spits out curtly. "My IC is in my bag," holding up her handbag. "Go ahead, take it."

Mislan unzips the handbag, sifts through its contents, and takes out her identity card.

"Good, thank you. Do you want me to address you as Jamilah or Jamie?"

"Whatever."

"Who was Mahyudin to you?"

"What does it matter now, he's dead," she sneers, staring at the lead investigator.

"Look, that attitude won't get you anywhere. Please drop it and answer my boss's questions," Johan says.

"I'm asking you nicely, what's Mahyudin to you?"

"My boyfriend or shall I say my late boyfriend, thanks to you."

"Where were you guys going before all this happened?"

"Home to have sex. You satisfied?" she barks.

"I don't know, I'm not the one having sex with you," Mislan replies, sneering back. "And may I know where home is?"

"Tasik Puteri."

"Yours or his?"

"His, mine, ours, what does it matter?"

"It does matter. Whose?"

"His. Can I smoke?"

"Lose your attitude, and I'm sure I can work that in for you."

Jamie stares at him defiantly. When Mislan holds her stare, she says, "OK, I'm sorry. Now, can I smoke?"

"That's good enough for me, but you have to step out of the car."

Johan opens the door and she alights, wobbling on her stilettos, holding him to steady herself, much to Johan's delight. She sifts through her handbag and fishes out a packet of Marlboro Lights. Her hand is shaking as she lights one and inhales deeply. Glancing at the cadaver, she says, "He could have taken me with him, and I would be dead next to him. He could've just driven on, but he stopped to let me out." She shivers and takes another long drag, "He said goodbye, and I knew—" She stops in mid-sentence and sobs.

Mislan sees Inspector Amita walking toward them and he steps away to meet her halfway.

"Who's she?"

"A friend of the deceased."

"Was she in the car when it crashed?"

"Nope."

"How did she get here?"

"They brought her here," Mislan says, pointing to Sentul 24.

"So she did not witness the crash?"

"I don't know. Why don't you ask her?"

The IO looks at her and Jamie shakes her head.

"OK then, there's no point in recording her statement."

"You're the IO, whatever you say. By the way, are you done with the deceased and the car?"

"Almost. Why?"

"I'd like to take a look. After you're done, of course."

"We'll let you know when we're finished," Amita says and walks away.

"Are you not taking custody of the car?" Johan asks.

"It's their territory. I don't think we can. Anyway, it's too late now. I'll speak to ma'am tomorrow to see if we can get custody and send it to Chew's place."

"But the deceased is involved in our case. Don't we have the right over him and the car?"

"Technically, they've the right over us because the deceased is only a suspect in our case but involved in a fatal accident in an area under their jurisdiction. Maybe ma'am can wangle something. Let's not make it any worse than it is."

"What about the woman? You lied to the IO."

"I did no such thing! She asked a question, and I answered it truthfully. However, she didn't ask the right question. So, if she was misled by my answers, it's her problem, not mine. It's all in here," Mislan says, holding up the digital recorder, and smiles.

Johan shakes his head.

"You've got it all figured out, haven't you?"

Stepping away from them, Mislan pulls out his cell phone and makes a call. "Hi, sorry, did I wake you up?"

"No shit, do you know what time it is? It better be worth waking me," Audi retorts in sleepy voice.

"I think it is. Can you get your crew together and come down to Jalan Selayang Baru?"

"Why, what's there?"

"Let's say something newsworthy. You better hurry, the investigating officer is wrapping things up. If you want the exact location call Selayang police."

"Damn it, Inspector can't you WhatsApp me the location? What's there?"

"You're the investigative news reporter, you find out. And you did not get this call from me."

He hangs up and smiles.

The district IO signals them over, indicating that their D10 is done. Mislan wonders what secret the suspect is taking to his grave.

"You got his ID?" he asks.

"Yes, here." Amita replies, handing it to him.

"ASP Markit, can you do me a favor?"

"Because it's Raya, anything for my Malay brother officer," ASP Markit Singh, head of Selangor D10, jests.

"Can you swab his right hand and the steering wheel for GSR?"

"Why, was he shooting at you guys?"

"No, only to satisfy my curiosity."

"No problemo." ASP Markit instructs one of his team to do the swab.

"What are you expecting to find?" Johan asks.

"Miracles," he answers with a grin.

"Steering wheel positive for lead and nitrate, GSR," ASP Markit says holding up the test kit. "Hand . . . nothing."

"Can you take another swab and bag it? I want to ask Crime Forensics HQ to run another test. And can I get a report of your findings?"

"My friend, is there something about this case you're not letting on?"

"I believe the suspect was involved in a case I'm investigating. I'm trying to find evidence that can link him to it," Mislan answers.

"All right, if it helps solve your case. Give me your contact details, and I'll call you when it's ready."

"Thanks. Can I examine the wreck now?"

"Be my guest, we're all done, but don't take anything."

Mislan bends over and pokes his head into the car's cabin. The humidity and the confined space magnify the stench of stale blood. He hastily withdraws his head, banging it against the door frame.

"Dammit," he cries, rubbing his head.

Johan chuckles. "Careful, you don't want to add your blood to the scene."

"Jo, can you open the glove compartment from your side?"

"Yup," Johan reaches in.

"See if there's a bankbook or anything with an address on it."

"No bankbook, only an Astro bill."

"Pocket it."

Johan glances quickly at the investigating officer, notes that she's engaged with the D10 team, and slides the bill into his pocket. He nods to his boss and steps away from the wreck. They walk over to the district IO and thank her. As they are walking away, Mislan asks, "Amita, did the deceased have bank cards?"

"Two. Maybank and CIMB?"

"Can I have the card numbers?"

She signals to one of the D10 technicians, asks for the dead man's wallet, and hands him the cards. Mislan snaps a photo with his cell phone and hands them back, thanking her again. A D10 technician runs over to Mislan and hands over an evidence bag containing a tube with the swab of the steering wheel.

"Thanks, I totally forgot about this," he says to the technician. "Jo, get Jamie. We're taking her back."

"You want Sentul 24 to make an arrest report?"

"No. For now, she's a witness."

30

THEY DRIVE BACK TO the office under a cloud of gloom, brooding over the loss of a prime suspect. Jamie sits in the back, defeated, staring out the window into the darkness. Mislan debates calling Superintendent Samsiah to update her and seek her assistance in getting the wreck handed over to Kuala Lumpur police. He looks at the dashboard clock. It is 2:25 a.m., and he decides to leave it for a more decent hour. He knows he had the right suspect. He's confident he's on the right track. However, he doesn't know the suspect's link to the murders. As they ride the elevator to the office, he tells Johan to take Jamie to one of the interview rooms and get Syed or Jeff to watch over her.

"Get her some coffee and something to eat. I need to have a wash."

He takes a clean shirt and a face towel from his backpack and goes to the restroom. While washing, he ponders the link between the dead suspect and his victims. He's convinced the suspect knew one of the victims, if not both. That's the only reason his prints are in the car. Was he with them that night? His prints suggest only that he was in the car at some point, but was he in the car when they were killed? Mislan sighs.

He walks back to the office to find Johan sitting at his desk with two coffees.

"Jo, about the bullet hole in the door, can you get a workshop to patch it up?"

"Are you not reporting it?"

"No, just patch it up and get it resprayed. I don't want to complicate the situation more." He sips his coffee, "The MPV crew, didn't they see our car coming through? Hell! If they had aimed a few inches higher, they would've hit the window, and probably me." He lights a cigarette, shaking his head. "I could have been seriously injured or dead," he says and smiles.

"That would make many people happy," Johan says with a chuckle. "I suppose they were shooting for the tires, but you know how it is in real life. Still, you should count your blessings. If those patrolmen were worse shots than they were, we wouldn't be chatting here."

"I suppose so. Jo, don't forget the car. Get it done before someone notices it."

"I'll see to it first thing tomorrow."

"Where's Jamie?"

"Room one, Syed is with her. What's next?"

"I've been thinking. I believe our vics, at least one of them, knew the suspect. We need to find out their relationship."

"What makes you say that?"

"How else would the suspect's prints be in the car? They're lifted from the central locking and the automatic window opener. The suspect had to be in the car recently. Otherwise, the print would have been smeared or superimposed by Mahadi's. He had to be the last person to touch the buttons immediately after they were killed."

The officers ponder in silence.

"The other thing that puzzles me is, why were the vics at the petrol station in Jalan Jelatek? It's off their route. I know there's a Shell and an Esso or a Mobil station down from where Zaleha lived. Farther on, there's a Petronas and a Mobil. Aren't those more likely to be on the vics' route?"

"But they weren't from Zaleha's place. They were having dinner at Solaris," Johan reminds the inspector.

"There are a lot of gas stations from there to the crime scene, but they went to that Petronas. Damn, where were they going? Why the need to tank up before hitting the DUKE? Were they going on a long trip?"

"Ayn said the vic got a call and had to leave. So, I don't think they were planning on going for a long trip. If they were, why arrange for the breaking of fast that night? They would have left in the daytime and broken fasting at their destination or on the way. The son called and they left, remember?"

"Yes, Hashim's call made them leave. What the hell was the call about?"

"Ayn said the vic was annoyed at having to leave. I don't think he expected any other engagement that night, because it was he who had organized the breaking of fast."

"The call from his son was upsetting and made him leave. Hmmm."

He agrees with his assistant.

"OK, let's have a chat with Jamie."

They take their coffee and go to the interview room, where Jamie is catnapping, bent over the table with her head in her arms. The sound of the door opening wakes her, and she opens her eyes, irritated. Johan motions for Syed to leave, and they sit across the table as Jamie resumes her napping position.

Jamilah Sibli is from Kuching Sarawak, East Malaysia. She's in her early thirties, five-foot-two inches tall, average for a Malaysian woman, athletic and slim, with a light-brown complexion and shoulder-length wavy hair, and she is beautiful. When she smiles, she has dimples on both cheeks. She looks educated, confident, and smart.

"Jamie, we'd like to ask you some questions," Johan says softly.

"I'm tired and sleepy. Can I go home now?" she replies, not moving from her position.

"It all depends."

"On what? Am I under arrest?"

"No, but if that's your wish, we can arrange it," Mislan says.

Jamie raises her head and stares at him.

"For what? What did I do?"

"It's not for what you did but, if you recall, you were in a car with our suspect."

"He was my boyfriend. He picked me up and we were going home to have sex. I told you that. How the hell was I to know he was your suspect? When you idiots chased him, he drove off. What do you expect me to do, jump out of a speeding car?"

She snatches her cigarette pack, rips one out, and lights it with shaking hands. Then she asks, "What the hell was he suspected of?"

"Murder."

She stares at them wide-eyed, unbelieving.

"You guys are crazy."

"Maybe we are, but the evidence is not. Look, why don't you calm down, drink the coffee, and we talk? It's not you we're after, you just happened to be with the wrong company."

This seems to pacify her. Mislan places the digital recorder on the table and switches it on. She stiffens.

"What's that for?"

"I'm an old man, and I forget easily. This is to refresh my memory." He smiles.

The calm Jamie reappears. She reaches over the table for the box of tissues, pulls one out, and wipes her eyes.

"I'm sorry. I really don't know what was happening. I was so afraid in the car, and I kept asking him what was going on, why are we being chased, why are we running. He kept telling me everything is all right, nothing is going to happen. When I begged him to stop, he stopped and let me out, said his goodbyes, and you know what happened next."

She starts shaking and cries some more. Mislan pushes the box of tissues nearer to her. He also takes out a Marlboro Light, lights it, and hands it to her.

"Here."

"Thanks."

"Do you want to have something to eat or take a short break?"

She shakes her head.

"No, I'm all right. Can I make my own coffee? This shit stinks," she says, smiling at them, showing off her cute dimples again.

"Sure," Johan answers with a laugh, a little too quickly for his boss's liking.

"Can I make some for you, too?" Jamie offers.

"No thanks, I'm used to Jo's shitty coffee. It keeps me in touch with reality. L-H-L-S."

"Love Hurts, Life Sucks," Johan explains.

After making her coffee, she asks if she can use the restroom. Johan jumps at the opportunity to escort her.

"Are you afraid I'll make a run for it?" she says.

"No, the office is deserted and it can be a little scary. I've heard stories of voices from the restroom at night. You know how police buildings are always haunted?" Johan jests.

"Shit, now you're scaring me," she says, looking genuinely afraid.

She takes Johan's hand and walks to the restroom, chatting with him like an old friend. Mislan watches and feels sorry for her for being involved with the suspect. She is personable indeed, besides being witty and cheeky.

"No thanks, I'm used to Jo's shitty coffee, it keeps me in touch with reality. L-H-L-S?"

"Love Hurts Life Sucks," Johan explains.

After making her coffee, she asks if she can use the restroom. Johan jumps at the opportunity to escort her.

"Are you afraid? I'll make a cup for you," she says.

"Yes, the office is deserted and it can be a little scary. I've heard snippets of voices from the restroom at night. You know how police buildings are always haunted?" Johan jests.

"Shh, now you're scaring me," she says, looking genuinely afraid.

She takes Johan's hand and walks to the restroom, chatting with him like an old friend. Mislan watches and feels sorry for her for being involved with the suspect. She is personable indeed, besides being witty and cheeky.

31

Ten minutes later, Mislan hears Jamie's stilettos on the bare concrete floor, accompanied by giggles and laughter as she and his assistant return to the office. Jamie looks fresh and happy, but once inside the interview room, reality returns. She sits upright, rigidly in her chair. She sips her coffee and lights another cigarette, clearly anxious. Mislan turns on the digital recorder and notices her eyebrows rise.

"Do you really need to record this?" she pleads.

"As I said, I'm old and my short-term memory is fading," he answers, smiling to calm her.

"You're not old, just too serious and grumpy. You should see some of the men that make a pass at me, they're old—Jurassic," she says, grinning.

The two D9 officers laugh.

"Pay no attention to it." Mislan says and lights a cigarette. "How long have you known Mahyudin?"

"About five months or so. We met at a salsa club. I was there to meet some friends, and he was with them. One of my friends said he wanted to learn to salsa and persuaded me to teach him. We became friends. One thing led to another, and I moved in with him about a month back."

"Do you salsa?" Johan butts in.

"Yes, I love salsa. I was offered an opportunity to teach but turned it down. I love to dance. I don't mind teaching a friend but not as a full-time job. It's my way of keeping fit and having fun. Do you salsa?"

"I don't, but I love to watch. It's so physical, so exotic . . . sexy," Johan says.

"Do you know the line of work he was in?" Mislan asks, getting her back on the subject.

"He said he was a personal assistant or bodyguard to a big shot, but he didn't mention a name."

"Have you seen this big shot before?"

"Once, but I wasn't introduced to him. A few months ago, I was with him when we stopped at a Chinese coffee shop in Sri Hartamas because he had to meet his boss. I waited in the car, and when he came back, he pointed out a man to me and said that was his boss. He looked young for a big shot."

"Would you recognize him if you saw him again?"

"Maybe. I don't know. I only had a brief look."

"When was the last time you saw Mahyudin before tonight?"

"Tuesday, Wednesday, I don't remember, why?"

"Where?"

"We were supposed to go clubbing but he canceled, said he had to do something. He drove me to the Petronas in Keramat and dropped me off. Then the idiot told me to walk to my friend's house in Kampung Warisan, a mile away."

Mislan looks at his assistant, lifting his eyebrows. Johan nods.

"Did he say why?"

"He said he was late and if he took me home, he'd have to make a big detour back to the station. He didn't want to be late. What a lame excuse."

"Did he say what he was late for?"

"I was too upset to ask. Anyway, I wasn't interested, but if I had known of its importance to you, I would've asked," she answers cheekily.

"There are many Petronas stations in Keramat. Which one did he drop you off at? What time?"

"It was the Petronas near Kampung Warisan, and it was a little after breaking of fast, close to eight."

"On Jalan Jelatek?"

Jamie nods. Mislan pauses for a moment, then:

"What happened after he dropped you off?"

"I got a taxi and went to my friend's house. He called me again after ten, and we met at the Cuba club."

"Now, I want you to think hard," Mislan says after another pause. "When you met Mahyudin at the club, was he in the same clothes as when he dropped you off at the Petronas?"

Jamie closes her eyes, tilts her head back in deep thought. Opening her eyes, she smiles.

"I don't know about the pants, but I'm sure he had a different shirt on."

"Would you be able to identify the shirt?"

"Of course, I can, it was a maroon polo shirt. I've taken it off him many times," Jamie teases, chuckling.

"Where is the shirt now?"

"I don't know, maybe in his house or at the laundry."

"How about his trousers?"

"They were dark, he had many pairs in dark colors. I don't remember which ones he was wearing."

"OK good. Jamie, I want to visit his house . . . your house. Do you object?"

"No, of course not."

"You have the keys?"

"Of course, I live there."

Bandar Tasik Puteri is twenty-sixty miles north and takes about forty minutes to reach on the North South Highway. It is a fairly new township, built around the Tasik Puteri Golf & Country Club, which is known for its pretty Indonesian caddies. Johan hits the highway, exiting at the Rawang Toll Plaza. The road is narrow, and there are hardly any cars on it. Johan takes the opportunity to speed on the empty road. The bullet puncture on the passenger door whistles eerily in the dark and deserted village road. He makes a left to Bandar Tasik Puteri, where the road widens into a divided highway. Jamie guides them to a two-story link house just before the golf club. Stepping out of the car, they hear the azan for the dawn prayer.

She is already holding the house keys in her hand as they enter the gate. Letting them in, she leads them to the master bedroom. She opens the wardrobe, pulls out the drawers, and shakes her head. Then she sifts through the laundry basket.

"Nope, they're not here."

"Maybe it's at the laundry?" Johan offers.

"Maybe, I don't know. He usually sends and picks them up himself."

"Do you know which laundry?"

"The one down the road. Wait, I need to use the bathroom." She opens the bathroom door, stands at the doorway, and yells.

"I've found it."

Mislan and Johan dash to the bathroom.

"In the pail," she says.

The pail is full of water with a maroon polo shirt soaking in it. Jamie steps into the bathroom toward the pail.

"Stop, don't touch it," Mislan barks, startling her.

Turning to him, she barks back angrily, "I was going bring the pail to you. You don't have to shout at me for wanting to help."

"Sorry, I didn't mean to shout at you. Please don't touch it. Jo, call D10 and ask them to send a team here. I need them to bag the item and send it to Forensics to be logged in with the rest of our exhibits."

Johan steps out into the bathroom. A few seconds later, he says, "D10 is on the way. What's that going to prove?"

"Hey, I need to use the bathroom, I need to wee-wee. Can you step out for a minute?" Jamie says.

"Can you use another bathroom?" Mislan asks.

"The other one is not in use and has nothing in it. Why? Are you afraid I'll steal your evidence?" she asks, daring the inspector.

"Would you?"

"I brought you here, I told you about the shirt, what do you think I'm going to do with it? Stuff it in my panties?" Jamie says angrily. "OK, stand there if you wish, I'm going to pee with you there."

"Sorry," Mislan says and steps out of the bathroom. "Leave the door slightly open."

"You want to peek?" Jamie retorts, laughing.

"Back to your question," Mislan says, turning to his assistant. "The T-shirt puts the suspect in the vic's car at the time they were killed."

"But we already have his prints inside the car and the GSR on his steering wheel."

"The print only puts him in the car but says nothing about timing. The GSR could be pooh-poohed away as transfers when he went to the shooting range with friends. If Forensics finds what I think they'll find, we can put him in the car at a very specific time . . . when the vics were killed."

Johan nods, admitting Mislan is right. This is a high-profile case, and they need to be sure of everything before they act against the killer.

While waiting for D10 to arrive, they go to the living room, and Mislan asks if he can smoke. Jamie brings him an ashtray and goes into the kitchen to make some coffee. When she comes back with three mugs, Mislan asks if she can show him around the master bedroom. She raises her eyebrows and asks mischievously, "Is it part of the investigation?"

Johan laughs, and Mislan realizes how indecent his request must have sounded.

He laughs, too. "What I meant was, I would like to have a look at his things."

"I might consider your offer and maybe show you what a real woman is made of," she teases him.

She walks up the stairs, wagging her firm ass playfully. She points at a drawer.

"That's where he kept all his things. I've never opened it, so I don't know what's inside."

Johan pulls the drawer and empties the contents onto the bed. They sift through the documents and loose items. There are two bankbooks, lawyers' letters, cigarette lighters and matches, a Swiss Army pocket knife, medicines, plasters, condoms, lubricant, flashlight—the sort of junk active bachelors would normally dump into a drawer. Johan picks up the box of condoms and lubricant and tosses it to the middle of the bed, and Jamie grins.

"Woo, those are critical evidence," she jokes.

"Not serious, damning evidence," Johan titters.

Mislan picks up the two bankbooks.

"These must be the two accounts Amita mentioned."

He jots down the account numbers and places them back into the pile. Stepping out of the master bedroom, he asks who occupied the other two rooms.

"There was no one when I moved in, but Din said a couple had occupied one room earlier and his friend Zubir used to stay in the other."

"Does this Zubir work with him?"

"I don't know, I met him a few times at the Cuba club. He gives me the creeps. An asshole. You know the kind that thinks they're so macho they can treat women like pieces of meat."

Johan nods, much to Jamie's delight. They soon start to chat, joke, and banter about music, movies, and hobbies. They're like old friends, oblivious that she could be an accessory to a double murder. She shows off some salsa moves and persuades Johan to try them. Mislan watches and smiles.

When the D10 team arrives, reality prevails again. The mood becomes serious. Mislan leads the team to the bathroom where the pail is.

"Can you bag that?"

"We'll take samples of the water then bag the contents of the pail. Get some photos, first," the supervisor says to the photo technician.

"Let me know when you're done, I'll be downstairs." Mislan returns to the living room and is greeted by a weary Jamie.

"Now what happens?"

"Do you have somewhere to stay for the night?"

"The night is over. I can go to a friend's house in Setiawangsa. Let me call her and see if she's home." Jamie makes the call and says after a while, "She's not answering. Probably sleeping. Can I not follow you to your office?"

"Sure," Johan answers a little too quickly. He looks at his boss and grins. The D10 crew comes downstairs, and Mislan tells them to send the exhibits along with the swab taken earlier by ASP Markit, to Forensics for Chew's attention.

32

Mislan stirs in bed, rolls to his side, and strains to look at the clock. 2:40 p.m. He has slept soundly, exhausted from the long night. It's later than his normal wake-up time after a twenty-four-hour shift. There was no morning prayer or meeting due to the festive holiday. A meeting he now desperately yearns for, a meeting where he can seek assistance from Superintendent Samsiah. His suspect's personal belongings, including his cell phone, are in the hands of Rawang Police, a district under the jurisdiction of Selangor Police, where Datuk Jalil is the Police Chief and Superintendent Malik is stationed. Mislan is certain the news of his suspect's accident had reached him. For Mislan to ask Rawang Police to hand over the suspect's belongings will be met with a firm "no."

He lies in bed for a while, recollecting the events of the night, and remembers Jamie. What the hell happened to her? He recalls Johan saying he would keep her company until she finds a place to stay. She must have many friends with whom she could bunk for a day or two. He reaches for his phone, there are two WhatsApp messages. One is from Dr. Safia asking if he would like to have lunch. Since it is almost three, lunch is out. He WhatsApps her back, apologizing for not replying sooner, and asks if she'd like to have tea later. The other WhatsApp was from Audi, informing him that Daud Nordin has been identified by her friend as the chairman of Serendah Village Development and Security Committee, the JKKK. He WhatsApps Audi, thanking her, and inquires if she made it to the scene last night. Then he speed-dials his ex-wife to speak to Daniel. He hears her calling their son: "Daddy's on the line."

"Hi, Daddy. I'm busy, can you call me later?" Daniel says, panting.

"Hi kiddo. What are you busy doing?"

"I'm playing with my friends. They're teaching me how to play congkak."

"Congkak? Wow, Daddy didn't know you liked playing those games. Hey, Daddy misses you."

"Miss you, too."

"Okay, have fun, kiddo."

Forcing himself to get out of bed, he sips his cold coffee and lights a cigarette. His cell phone rings. It is Superintendent Samsiah.

"Morning, ma'am."

"It's after two, Lan, are you still in bed?"

"Sorry, my brain decided to take a longer rest than usual. Anything, ma'am?" he asks.

"I received a very disturbing call from CP Selangor, something about you conducting a raid in Selayang without coordinating with them and ending up with a dead suspect. Please tell me he's wrong."

"He's wrong."

The line goes silent.

After a few moments she says, "I'm not in the mood for one of your smartass answers. Give it to me straight, what happened last night?"

"Chew lifted two partial prints from the vic's car. One matched an ex-con, Mahyudin Maidin a.k.a. Mamak Din. I got Bentong Police to check his listed address, but he bolted when the detectives arrived."

"I don't need the full report, just give me the short version," Superintendent Samsiah snaps.

"To cut a long story short, Setapak MPV spotted the suspect's car, there was a chase, the suspect rammed MPV blockage, crashed into a monsoon drain, and died."

"If it's Setapak, why did CP Selangor call me saying it was in Selayang?"

"The chase started from Setapak and ended in Selayang. Oh, I forgot to mention that the Selangor MPV crew discharged several shots."

"Anyone hit?"

"No. The suspect died from the crash."

"Anything else I should know?"

"We visited the suspect's house and found some exhibits that may put him in the car when the vics were killed. Our D10 has bagged the evidence and sent it to Forensics."

"I'm not going to ask how you got into the suspect's house. Lan, stay out of trouble and let me know what Forensics finds."

"Will do, and, ma'am, since you're on the line, is it possible for us to take custody of the suspect's cell phone and vehicle, linking it to our investigation?"

"Is it critical to your investigation?"

"The cell phone yes and the vehicle possibly. I won't know until Forensics goes through it."

"Selangor D10 is handling that, right? They'll do a good job. Let the storm settle before we move on that. I'm coming in for an hour tomorrow around ten, drop by my office and we'll talk."

He gets dressed, calls Johan, inquiring about Jamie's whereabouts, detects a slight hesitation, and hears her cheery voice calling out from the background.

"Jo, is that Jamie?" Mislan asks his assistant.

"Yes, and I can explain."

Mislan starts laughing.

"You had better but not to me. Ma'am was just on the phone, and Selangor is pissed. If she finds out about this, make sure you have a bloody good explanation. I'm going out for tea with Dr. Safia. You want to come?"

"Can Jamie come?"

"I guess so. I'm picking Dr. Safia up and will meet you at Starbucks at the Pavilion in about an hour."

Traffic is still light, and it takes him twenty minutes to reach Dr. Safia's place in Cheras and another fifteen to the Pavilion in Bukit Bintang. Pavilion Shopping Center is one of the latest malls to open in the Golden Triangle. Unlike the Golden Triangle of Thailand, Laos, and Myanmar that is infamous for drugs, Kuala Lumpur's Golden Triangle is congested with luxury hotels, malls, bars, entertainment outlets and restaurants—a tourist trap.

As usual, Dr. Safia is dressed casually in jeans and a T-shirt and carries an oversized handbag. They choose a table outside, and he goes in to get their orders.

"You sure you want to sit out here? I'm so hot and sticky," she says.

"I know, but we can't smoke in there." Mislan jerks his head at the indoor section.

"There was some news report on TV this morning about a car chase. It said the suspect rammed into a patrol car. The driver lost control and plunged into a ditch, killing himself. It also said the suspect could be linked to the DUKE homicides."

"Did it?" Mislan shakes his head but cannot hide a smile, "I don't know where these media people get their stories. Was it in the papers?"

She raises her eyebrows.

"You know there's no newspaper today, the press was closed yesterday for Raya."

Mislan smiles, "I don't keep track of all these things. Where did you go after we left?"

"Home. So tell me what happened?"

He sees Johan and Jamie coming.

"That's what happened," he says, tilting his head toward the approaching two.

Dr. Safia turns around and sees Johan and Jamie walking toward them. "What?"

"The chase resulted in her. The suspect's girlfriend or former girlfriend and now I think Jo's new girlfriend."

"You're kidding!"

Her squeal attracts curious looks from the other tables.

"Shhh, not too loud, Fie," he cautions her. "As the saying goes, one person's loss . . ."

"There's no such saying. You guys are unbelievable. You kill a suspect and Jo wins his girlfriend as a trophy. I'm speechless."

"Let's get one thing straight: We did not kill the suspect. He killed himself."

Johan introduces Jamie to Dr. Safia and goes to the counter to place their orders. Seeing Dr. Safia gawking at Jamie, Mislan taps her thigh under the table and gives her an eye signal to stop staring.

Jamie lights up and says, "It's hot out here, don't you guys want to move inside?"

"You can't smoke in there. Jamie, did you have a good rest?" Mislan says.

Jamie jerks her head toward Johan and giggles mischievously in answer to Mislan's question. The two women size up one another up as they chat. As the sun goes down, it becomes a little cooler, but the humidity lingers.

"Hey, how about we go to a karaoke?" Jamie suggests out of the blue. "There's a Red Box up here. I know the manager; he always gives me a good discount. Anyway, it's too hot here," she pleads, giving Johan puppy eyes.

"Yeah, why not," Johan agrees.

Dr. Safia, who is fast becoming Jamie's latest best friend, seals their friendship by agreeing, and they all turn to Mislan for the final vote.

"What the heck, why not?" he concedes.

They take the elevator up to Red Box. While registering for a room, he hears someone calling, "Inspector," several times. Turning around, he sees Audi waving from across the concourse and walking briskly toward them with a man trying hard to keep pace with her.

"Shit! That's all I need, now," Mislan sighs.

"Who's that?" Dr. Safia asks.

"BN," Mislan snarls.

"Huh? Barisan National?" Dr. Safia says, referring to the ruling party.

"Bad News," he says.

"Fancy seeing you here. So, this is how you let off steam," Audi says.

"Audi, this is Safia and Jamie. For your information, this is not how I let off steam. I shoot people like you to let off steam."

"I know you," she says, addressing Dr. Safia. "You're a forensic pathologist with HUKM. His girl," she says nudging Mislan.

Dr. Safia smiles.

"And who's your friend?" Mislan asks.

"Oh, Nazim. Nazim, this is Inspector Mislan, Detective Sergeant Johan, Dr. Safia and . . ."

"Jamie," Johan answers.

"Can we join you guys? I love karaoke."

They look at each other and, before anyone can say anything, Audi is already dragging Nazim into the lounge.

At two in the morning, Mislan feels he has had enough. He announces his intention to call it a day and is bombarded with protests.

"What's the rush? The night is still young," Jamie insists.

"It's a package, we can use the room until closing time. Why waste it?" Audi says.

"Yes, Lan, what's the hurry? Do you have something to do?" Jamie's latest best friend, Dr. Safia, says.

"Nothing. We've been in here for almost five hours. I just think that's more than enough singing or shall I say, in the case of you guys, croaking for one day."

"Something is bothering you, I can sense it," Dr. Safia whispers in Mislan's ear.

"No, I need some fresh air. I can't stand being contained in a box like this for too long."

"OK, let's go. The rest of you can stay if you want."

Dr. Safia stands and presses the service call button.

A waiter enters and Mislan asks for the bill. The waiter informs him the bill has been paid and leaves.

"Jo, did you pay the bill?" he shouts over Jamie's singing, which is more like murdering the song.

Johan shakes his head.

"Listen, did any of you pay the bill?" he shouts.

The group looks at him blank. Mislan steps out and walks toward the registration counter with Dr. Safia close behind. He inquires about their bill and is told all their bills have been settled in full by a man that came in with them. The man deposited RM500 to cover the entrance charges and any additional orders. The girl behind the reception counter says there's still a balance of RM140. The rest of the group catches up with them at the counter. The receptionist offers to give Mislan the balance but he turns it down. Jamie signals the receptionist to hand the money over to her and stuffs it in her handbag saying, "It is bad luck to refuse money."

"Did you know the man? Have you seen him before?" Mislan asks.

"No. I thought he was with your group because he came in after you."

"Is he still here?"

"I don't know, he walked in but I don't know if he is still inside. He could've left, a lot of customers do walk in and out. Is there something wrong?"

"No, no, everything's fine. Can you describe him?"

"Malay, about your height, short hair a little longer than yours, brown skin, around thirty."

"You've given us a description of about a million Malay men," Mislan says.

"Was there anything distinctive about him that you can recall: glasses, scars, accent, anything?"

The receptionist shakes her head.

"It's OK then. Can I have the bill?"

"The one of the million Malay men that I described has taken the original," she chuckles. "I can print you a copy if you want."

"You're a smartass, aren't you? Yes, please print me a copy."

Mislan looks up at the ceiling for CCTV and seeing none he asks the receptionist.

"You don't have CCTV?"

"No, management said people will avoid the place if we install cameras."

"Why?" Johan asks.

"Most customers come here to relax and have fun with their . . . you know. If we put cameras, they'll be afraid their wives or husbands can check and find out," the receptionist explains and smiles.

"Smart," Johan admits.

33

In the car Mislan wonders who paid their bill. The receptionist said it was a man behind them. He tries to recall the faces of those around him at reception. There was a group of Chinese men and women in the waiting area, a Malay couple behind his group, and that was all. When Audi and Nazim approached, he didn't notice a Malay man tailing them.

"You're worried about the bill, aren't you," Dr. Safia says.

He nods.

"It could be an honest mistake, you know?"

"How so?"

"The man could've paid for a bill thinking it was his, but the receptionist confused it with ours. The man could still be in there and will only find out the mistake when he and his friends leave."

"Could be, but I don't think that's the case."

"Why?"

"You only have to settle the bill upon leaving after the last order. So, why did he pay up front? It's not logical."

"I've a feeling there's more than what you're telling me. Something's happened. You want to talk about it? I'm a good listener, you know."

He smiles at her.

"No, I'm not used to someone paying for me, that's all. I suppose, like you say, there might be a reasonable explanation. Let's drop it."

Dr. Safia places her hand on his thigh and squeezes it tenderly. When they reach her house, she goes into the shower and he switches on the news. It is all about Eid, open houses of political big shots, road fatalities, and children injured by firecrackers. He lights a cigarette and stares at the ceiling, pondering the bill. The newscaster's mention of Zaleha's name makes him look at the screen.

This family is not celebrating Hari Raya, says a woman reporter standing in front of the victim's house and goes on to talk about lovers' triangles, the murder-suicide on the DUKE. She talks about the victim's ailing mother and the loss of her daughter, the sole breadwinner in the family. It is difficult for Mrs. Khatijah to accept her daughter was murdered by her business partner, and she pleads for the police to investigate the case thoroughly and reveal the truth. The newscaster moves on to the death of Mahyudin Maidin a.k.a. Mamak Din in an early morning high-speed car chase through the city. The police have denied earlier reports that the incident was related to the DUKE murder-suicide.

Mislan silently thanks Audi for keeping his case alive.

Dr. Safia comes out of the shower with a towel wrapped around her body and another one on her head like a turban.

"Are you staying?"

He nods.

She takes out a pair of shorts from the drawer and gives them to him. "There's a T-shirt on the hanger."

He unclips his Beretta magazine, checks its chamber, and places the gun and the magazine on the bedside table. He takes the shorts and goes to the bathroom.

"You want coffee?" she asks.

"Please."

He stays under the shower longer than normal, enjoying it. The weather has been hot and very humid, and the cold shower is refreshing. He hears Dr. Safia saying something from the living room and realizes he has been in the shower too long. He dries off, puts on the shorts and the T-shirt, and joins her on the sofa.

She gives him a peck on the cheek, leans against the armrest, and stretches her legs onto his lap. They have been seeing one another for nearly a year. He dreads the day she asks him the where-are-we-heading question. Maybe she is waiting for him to raise it, or maybe she only wants his company. As a career woman, a professional supporting herself, why would she want to invite the complications of matrimony into her life?

The night breeze from the balcony is warm, and soon he starts feeling sticky and uncomfortable again.

"Let's move into the bedroom and switch on the air-conditioning."

"Why?"

"It's humid out here, and I'm feeling sticky again."

"Excuses," she teases him.

"What?"

"If you're feeling horny, say so. You don't have to use the humidity as an excuse," she chuckles, digging her heels into his groin. "Naughty."

He blushes, holds her legs, and massages them.

"Now, you're making me horny," she says moaning softly.

She removes her legs, picks up her coffee mug, and goes into the bedroom.

Mislan picks up his coffee mug and follows her. With the television and air-conditioning on, she leans back on propped pillows. He lights two cigarettes, gives her one, and slides in next to her.

"How's your case?"

"Let's not talk about work today. Let's just watch TV and enjoy a quiet night," Mislan suggests, not wanting to discuss his case.

"Oh, my God, you're human," she jokes and snuggles up, resting her head on his chest. She reaches over the bedside table, squashes the cigarette, turns off the light, and pulls up the blanket. Astro is playing a rerun, maybe for the hundredth time, of *CSI: NY.* She mutes the volume, turns toward him, and says, "Are you OK?"

He nods. He kisses her lightly, stroking her hair. Her soft perfume, her warm body soothe away his stress. She senses it and kisses his neck, running her soft fingers along his chest down to his stomach.

He holds her up, they kiss passionately and make love. Breathless, they fall asleep in each other's arms.

34

Mislan arrives at the office around 9 in the morning, makes his usual coffee, and chats with Inspector Reeziana. The makeshift pantry table is stocked with plastic containers of Malay cookies brought by the detectives. There will be plenty for everyone when more return after their holidays. Then, there will be the endless open-house invitations over the entire month of Syawal. *Well, it is only once a year.*

"When is Tee coming back?"

"Tomorrow. I heard about your car chase. I've never experienced one. What was it like?" Reeziana asks.

"Trust me, it's not something you'd wish for. It's not like anything you see on TV. In the movies, they'd drive at normal speed and then make it look like it was going at breakneck speed. I nearly peed my pants, but Jo was fantastic. The way he avoided oncoming traffic, passed cars, made turns by skidding and sliding the rear, missing drains and road signs by inches. Shit, it was scary."

"Drifts."

"Eh?"

"It's called 'drifting.' Don't you watch the movies—*Tokyo Drift, KL Drift*? It's a big sport now. By the way, why are you here?"

"Ma'am said she's coming in around 10. I need to update her. Yana, if you're not too busy today, can you send your detective to the Telco? I need to get some phone listings."

"I don't expect a busy day. Is Telco open?"

"I'm sure the customer service center will be."

Superintendent Samsiah arrives and walks around the various offices offering seasonal greetings to her staff. She then signals Mislan to follow her to her office, saying, "Let's get it over with."

He follows her in, pulls up a chair while she makes herself a cup of tea. "Shoot."

"Where do you want me to start?"

"Why don't you start with the chase?"

"You want the long or short version?" he prods her.

"I noticed you've become a little cheeky lately. Is this your new style?"

He laughs.

"Sorry, I think it must be the festive season, you know how some cosmic changes affect the brain. Anyway, as I said, Chew lifted a print from the car that matched an ex-con. His listed address was in Janda Baik, so I asked Bentong police to check the house, but the suspect bolted. Around 11 p.m., MPV Sentul 24 spotted the suspect's car in Setapak and monitored it while waiting for us." He pauses, reaching for his cigarette, and asks, "May I, ma'am?"

"Since it's Raya, I'll bend the rules a little." She takes out an ashtray from the cabinet and places it on the table.

"Thanks." He lights his cigarette. "As we were approaching, Sentul 24 told us that the suspect and a woman were getting into the car and driving off. We tried to intercept, but the suspect managed to slip away, and the chase started. It went all the way to Selayang Baru, where Selangor 112 did the cutoff. The suspect stopped, off-loaded the woman, and sped off after ramming Selangor 112. We gave chase for about five miles when he missed a turn and drove into a monsoon drain. He died on impact."

Superintendent Samsiah leans against the cabinet, sipping her tea.

"Who's the woman?"

"She claimed to be the suspect's girl."

"Is she in custody?"

"Yes, and no."

"Don't start getting cheeky with me again. Is she in custody or is she not?" she asks firmly.

"No, but Johan is keeping her under close watch. Ma'am, trust me, you don't want to know more. Anyway, there's no reason to put her under arrest. She was dragged into the chase unwittingly." He pauses. "During the interview, she claimed the suspect drove her to Petronas at Jalan Jelatek on the night of the murder and left her there. We have CCTV evidence that the vic, Zaleha, was at that station just before they were killed. Nathan is still working on the footage. Now we have Jamie's testimony that the suspect was there, too."

"We'll talk about Johan later. Go on."

He tells her about the positive GSR test on the steering wheel of the suspect's car, the visit to the suspect's house, and the discovery of the polo shirt that D10 bagged for analysis.

"The fingerprint places the suspect in the vics' car. The positive GSR on the steering wheel proves that the suspect fired a gun. If Forensics finds evidence of the vics' blood on the suspect's shirt, it places him in the vic's car during the shooting or immediately after the shooting."

"Good work. What about the suspect's wreck?"

"Can you charm Selayang into handing it to us, plus the suspect's cell phone?"

"I don't see why you need it now. You've got all the evidence. But, if you really need it, why don't you wait for Chew's results? That'll give you a stronger argument for jurisdiction claims." She pauses and sips her tea very deliberately, deep in thought. "What was the motive? If it was murder, as you are proving it to be, was the suspect acting alone or was he paid? Either way, what was the motive?"

"I'm still at a loss, but my gut feeling says the suspect was not alone in this."

"Keep at it, and in the meantime, I want you to stay out of Selangor until I've had the chance to clarify the situation with them."

"But I live in Selangor," he jokes.

"Don't you start, you know what I mean. Now get out and let me do some work so I can go home and enjoy my Raya."

Leaving his boss's office, he wonders if he should tell her of his dilemma, the meeting with Superintendent Malik of Commercial Crime, Selangor, and the JKKK Chairman Daud Nordin. The casual mention by Daud of his marital status, his son, and the mysterious man who paid his entertainment bill. He decides to leave it until he can get more information. Johan has returned from Forensics HQ when he goes back to his office.

"Was Nathan there?"

"Yes. I've given it to him, and he'll contact me soon as he's finished."

"Jo, did you notice anyone watching us at the Red Box reception?"

"I didn't."

"Sorry, I forgot you were too busy keeping your eyes on your new love," Mislan teases.

Johan grins.

"By the way, where is Jamie?"

"In Setiawangsa at her friend's house."

"Let me make a call first before I forget."

He calls Inspector Amita and asks her for the suspect's mobile number and gives it to Reeziana.

"Where exactly are we going sightseeing?" Johan is curious.

"I've always wanted to go to Kuala Kubu Baru, you know, visit the waterfalls in the forest recreational park. I believe it's cooling, scenic, and tranquil, nature with all its healing goodness. It could be good for the body and mind."

"You expect me to believe that?" Johan says.

35

Serendah is a subdistrict of Hulu Selangor, with Kuala Kubu Bharu as its administrative town. Hulu Selangor literally means "Upstream Selangor" or "Upper Selangor," one of several districts in the state of Selangor—a state that Inspector Mislan had just been told by Superintendent Samsiah to stay away from for the time being. Hulu Selangor is a rural area, known for its forests, waterfalls, whitewater rapids, and the dam. A favorite family picnic destination, especially to those from the city. At one time, it had a Police College that had long since been shifted to Cheras. Kuala Kubu Bharu is about forty miles north of Kuala Lumpur.

It is Sunday, and traffic leaving the city is light, but coming back into it is bumper-to-bumper. The normal workday after the long Eid weekend holiday starts on Monday. They exit the North-South Highway at Bukit Beruntung and drive along the country road. It is a pleasant change from driving among buildings in the city, stopping at numerous traffic lights, constantly caught in jams. On the country road, the going is slow, especially if caught behind a truck, but the scenery is beautiful—green trees on both sides of the road.

At Serendah town, Mislan stops at a gas station to tank up. He goes to the ATM to withdraw some cash. As the inspector is walking back to the car, his assistant notices his red face.

"What's the matter?"

"Here," he says, handing Johan his transaction slip.

"Wow! You're rich."

"I withdrew some money for Daniel's expenses a few days ago, and my balance was RM800. Shit, Jo, I think someone is setting me up."

"Maybe it's a banking error, these things happen, you know. Maybe the money will be debited and you'll go back to being a poor civil servant again," Johan says, chuckling. "I suggest you use this opportunity to dream."

"I'm serious, Jo. First the karaoke bill, now this. Let's stop at Rawang police, I want to make a confidential report."

After the unscheduled stop, they pause at a mamak restaurant for a drink and make some inquiries. They are given directions and told they can't miss the house, a blue bungalow. Driving past the house, they notice several cars in its compound and many others parked along the road outside.

"Jo, I need to ID this guy. Do you feel like role-playing?"

"You want me to go in?"

"I'd do it myself, but he'll recognize me. Who knows, this might be your lucky day. He might have a beautiful daughter," Mislan says.

"Yeah, right. What'll you be doing?"

"It's nearly time for afternoon prayers. I noticed a mosque back there. I think I'll go and perform my spiritual duties."

Johan burst into laughter.

"Text me when you're done submitting yourself."

He drops Johan about thirty yards beyond the blue bungalow and drives to the mosque. The imam and a few elderly men in the prayer hall are waiting for the call for prayer. When Mislan walks in, they greet him, and he joins them. He listens to them talk about politics, the community, and other affairs while waiting for the muezzin's call for prayer. When the time comes, the congregation forms two rows for the midday prayer. After prayer, Mislan approaches the imam and asks if he can talk to him, in response to which the imam invites him and a few others to his house behind the mosque. In the midst of their conversation, he receives a WhatsApp message from Johan asking him what's taking him so long. Mislan excuses himself, thanks the imam, and replies saying he is on his way.

"It's him, Daud Nordin. I don't know the other guests. For your info, he has no beautiful daughter. The women in there are not even remotely beautiful. How was your soul salvation?"

"Pretty good, I strongly recommend it. The imam and some of the villagers recognized our dead suspect. You remember the suspect's assault case? It was for assaulting one of the villagers here who confronted our vic's company representative during a dialogue over sand mining. Dig up the case and see if we can link it to our vics or Daud."

"So our suspect worked for our vic?" Johan asks.

"Looks like it."

"Our vic was sand mining here?"

"That's what they said."

"That's mega-money. From what I heard . . . worth hundreds of millions. One of my uncles is in construction, and he said sand is like gold to them. One ton costs something like RM100 and the miner only pays like RM10 to the council for the mining ticket. Nine hundred percent clean profit. No manufacturing cost, just extract and sell."

"Nine hundred percent . . . *wow* . . . and sand is a natural resource."

"I remember reading about a company being investigated for illegal sand mining in Rasa, Hulu Selangor."

"I know big companies sand mining are mostly owned by politicians or affiliated to political parties. Permits are controlled by the state governments, so you can imagine who will get them."

"Free resources and sold at a premium to contractors."

"Politicians cannot have their names or family names on the permit or company issued with the permits—that'll attract too much attention. Remember, according to Audi, our vic is a proxy holder for politicians. I guess it had to be for sand mining, too."

The inspector's cell phone rings.

"Mislan."

"Inspector Mislan, this is Superintendent Malik."

"Yes, sir, what can I do for you?"

"I was informed you've requested a confidential report be lodged at Rawang station. May I know what the report was about?"

A confidential police report is where a report number is allocated by the police station, but the station itself will not receive the report.

The report will be forwarded to the respective authority that will be conducting the investigation.

"I'm sorry, I can't tell you, but can I assure you it has nothing to do with commercial crime."

"I'm sure it does not. Look, the report was made in Selangor, and I'm a superintendent of police, a superior officer, and I'm asking you, a junior officer. I don't want to take this to your boss, but if you wish I will," Superintendent Malik says intimidatingly.

"I'm aware of all that, and it's your prerogative to do whatever you wish. I'm telling you, my confidential report has nothing to do with commercial crime, and I'm under no obligation to reveal its contents to you. By the way, shouldn't this be the concern of the OCPD and not the head of Commercial Crimes?"

"Listen, you're way out of your league here, Inspector."

"And what league would that be? I thought we were on the same team, playing in the same league."

The line goes dead.

"Superintendent Malik?" Johan asks.

Mislan nods.

"That was quick. What are you going to do?"

"I don't know, yet. I'll talk to ma'am. See what she says. Jo, watch your step, I have a bad feeling about this. Take a break from Jamie for now, you know what I mean?"

The detective sergeant nods.

At the office, Inspector Reeziana hands him the suspect's cell phone call listing. Thanking her, he sits at his desk without looking at it. Reeziana notices his lack of interest, which is not in character for him or an investigator chasing hot leads.

"Hey, you OK?" she asks.

"Yes, why?"

"You didn't even look at the telco listing I gave you."

"I will, just not now."

"Hmmm, losing interest in the case," she says, narrowing her eyes at her coinvestigator.

When Mislan doesn't answer, she walks over to his desk and puts both hands on it, facing him. "What happened?" She stares intensely at him, her face a foot from his. "I know something happened. Tell me what happened."

"Ma'am still around?"

"Left around noon."

Mislan takes his pack of cigarettes, lights up, and hands the pack to Reeziana, who follows suit. Mislan pulls the ATM slip and shows her.

"Shit, Lan, with your smoking and a kid to support, you can still save this much?"

Mislan forces a grin. "The last time I checked I had about 800."

"So where did this money come from?"

Mislan shrugs.

"This is what's bothering you?"

Mislan nods.

"This is serious shit. You got to tell ma'am."

Mislan nods. "I've asked for a confidential report number from Rawang. I need to write it before someone writes one against me."

"OK, I'll leave you to it," Reeziana says and walks back to her desk.

Mislan writes the report, seals it in an envelope, stashes it in his backpack, and leaves for home. As he approaches his condominium's guardhouse, the security guard flags him down.

"Boss, there's something for you."

"What?"

"Hampers, they're in the guardhouse."

He parks the car by the roadside and follows the guard to the guardhouse.

"There."

The guard points to three large hampers. He steps closer and sees a card with his name on it.

"Who sent them?"

"A Chinese man in a van."

"Did you get his name or the van number?"

"No."

"What did he say?"

"He told me he tried to deliver it to your unit but no one was home, so he dropped them here for us to hand it on to you when you came home."

Using his cell phone, he snaps several photographs of the hampers, takes down the security guard's particulars, and puts the hampers in the back seat of his car. Leaving them there, he calls to inform his assistant of what he just received and goes up to his unit.

After a shower, he makes a mug of coffee. He's thankful Daniel and the maid aren't home. Otherwise, they would have accepted the hampers, probably opened them, and eaten some of the goodies. It would have been difficult for him to explain to them. He doesn't want them to be involved in any way. Someone is setting him up. Who? And why? Is it to get him out of the way? Or is it payback, revenge. Over the years, he has made more enemies than friends. Of that he is sure. Whatever happens, he knows he can trust two people to stand by him—Superintendent Samsiah and his assistant. He hears the doorbell.

"Coming," he shouts, thinking it is Johan.

When he opens the door, he sees two men outside the grille gate.

"Inspector Mislan Latif?"

"Yes."

"I'm Senior Enforcement Officer Yusuf and this is Enforcement Officer Redzwan. We're from MACC. May we come in, please?"

"Can I see some IDs?"

The two men show their IDs, and they are indeed from the Malaysia Anti-Corruption Commission. Mislan unlocks the grille gate.

"How may I help you?"

"We received information that you solicited and received some hampers of considerable value," Yusuf explains. He mentions a car registration number and asks, "Is that your car?"

"Let me answer your question in chronological order. Solicited: no, Received: yes. And car: yes. Is all this recorded?"

Yusuf smiles.

"You're a funny guy, aren't you? Would you mind following us to the office for questioning?"

Enforcement Officer Redzwan casually wanders toward the back room, and Mislan stops him.

"Excuse me, I invited you in, but I said nothing about searching my house."

"I was looking for the bathroom," Redzwan offers lamely.

"Don't give me that bullshit. You should stop watching too many police movies. That excuse doesn't work in real life. To answer your question, yes, I do mind, but I'll come anyway. Let me change, and don't you dare snoop around in the meantime. This house is booby-trapped, and you don't want to accidentally set off the nerve gas and get killed."

The two MACC officers smile nervously, unsure if he is kidding. Mislan sees their expressions and walks into the bedroom, grinning. As they come out of the elevator at the basement level, Johan is standing in front of the door.

"What's going on, boss?"

"Jo, this is MACC Senior Enforcement Officer Yusuf and Enforcement Officer Redzwan," Mislan replies, emphasizing their designations. "They've cordially invited me to their office for a chat." Turning to the officer he says, "This is my assistant investigator, Detective Sergeant Johan."

"Questioning for what? Is he under arrest?" Johan stands his ground.

"No, Inspector Mislan is not under arrest," Yusuf answers. "We're only going to interview him over some allegations."

"What allegation? He's being set up."

"It's OK, Jo. I'll be all right. The suspect's cell phone listing is on my desk. Go through it and see if you can match any of the numbers with those in our case."

"Boss, show them the confidential report, that will clear up everything."

"Can I speak to my assistant in private for a moment?" Mislan asks the MACC officers.

Yusuf nods, and they step away.

"Jo," Mislan says softly, bending his head to his assistant's, "I want you to see if there's anyone tailing us. I have a feeling someone is watching me, monitoring what's going on, and giving instructions. Call ma'am and tell her what's happening. I need you to stay calm. Look, I'm playing along so we can draw whoever is behind this out. I need to know what these clowns were told and who is pulling the strings."

Johan nods, and they follow the MACC officers to Mislan's car, where two more officers are waiting, watching over it.

36

MISLAN IS DRIVEN IN the MACC vehicle, while one of the officers drives his car. On the way, Yusuf asks about the confidential report. Mislan tells him it is a police matter, and he is not at liberty to discuss it unless instructed by his superior. His cell phone rings. It is Superintendent Samsiah.

"Lan, what's going on?"

"I'm being picked up by Anti-Corruption."

"I know, Jo told me. Where are they taking you, KL office or Putrajaya?"

"KL, Jalan Sultan Hishamuddin."

"Don't say anything, wait for me. I'll be there as soon as I can."

The call goes dead.

"Who tipped you guys off?"

"Anonymous."

"I'm impressed. Thought MACC didn't act on anonymous tips?"

The two MACC officers do not respond.

"Hell, you guys don't even get cracking this fast on a formal complaint. So, who's pulling the strings?"

"It was an anonymous tip, and no one is pulling any strings. Inspector, please be advised not to make any deprecating remarks about us, we're only doing our duty," Yusuf replies calmly.

"I'm sorry, I'm tired. Please accept my apologies, my remarks were uncalled for."

"Forget it, only don't repeat it. Some of my colleagues might not be too understanding."

At the MACC office, Mislan is taken to an interview room where the officers ask him about the hampers. He tells them exactly what had happened.

"So you did not solicit them?"

"Not to my recollection."

"Do you know who sent them?"

"Nope."

"If that was the case, why did you take them with you? Why not just leave them at the guardhouse?"

"Because they're exhibits, and I wanted to take them to the office. If I had wanted to keep them, I would have taken them into my house and not left them in my car in plain sight."

"Maybe you were taking them somewhere else and you didn't expect us to come, like the tough police inspector you think you are," Redzwan says sarcastically.

"Maybe I was going to bring them here to surrender and confess personally to you, how about that, smartass?" he lashes back.

"Cool it, guys," Yusuf intervenes.

"What's the deal here? Are you recording my statement or interrogating me?" He takes out the digital recorder from the backpack, switches it on, and places in on the table.

"What's that for?" Redzwan barks. "You're in our office. You don't get to do as you wish. This is not one of your goddamn police stations."

"Shut up and sit down," Yusuf snaps. "Inspector, there's no need for that. You're not under arrest, and we're only conducting an interview. At present, there's no necessity for us to record your statement. So, let's all remain calm."

"What's with him? You'd better keep him on a leash before he hurts himself."

"Is that a threat?" Redzwan hisses, staring at him menacingly.

"It's brotherly advice," Mislan replies calmly.

He hears soft knocking on the door, and Superintendent Samsiah enters with Johan close behind. She introduces herself and asks if she could have a word with Senior Enforcement Officer Yusuf privately. Yusuf nods and follows her, closing the door behind them.

Johan slides into a chair next to Mislan, whispering, "You're right, got the bike number. I'll check it tomorrow when the office opens. So, what's happening?"

Redzwan pretends not to care what they're whispering, but it's obvious he's straining to listen.

"Careful, you may burst your eardrums," Mislan tells him.

"You think you're smart, don't you? Well, let's see how smart you feel after we're done with you," Redzwan threatens him. "You don't know who you're dealing with. They eat people like you for breakfast."

"Really! Wow, they must be wild animals, then," he replies, laughing with Johan.

"Laugh all you want. When Tan Sri—" Redzwan pauses, checking himself. "I mean when they're done with you, you'll be lucky if you can get a job as a security guard."

"You know what, Redzwan? When all this is over, I suggest you start looking for another job, because Tan Sri is going to find out it was you who fingered him," Mislan says, pointing to the digital recorder.

Redzwan lunges across the table for it as Mislan snatches it away. Johan leaps up, going for Redzwan. Just then the door opens, Senior Enforcement Officer Yusuf and Superintendent Samsiah standing in the doorway. All three stop still in mid-action and look at the door. And as if on a count of three, they slowly return to their original positions, pretending nothing has happened.

"What's happening here?" Samsiah asks firmly.

Mislan is about to answer when Superintendent Samsiah gives him a stare to shut him up.

"Is this how professionals act? We're on the same side and going at each other's throats will only benefit them." Turning to Yusuf, she says, "Thank you, it has been a pleasure meeting you, and please advise me of the outcome. I'll forward a copy of the confidential report and their statements by tomorrow evening."

"Likewise, ma'am. Thank you."

She motions to Mislan and Johan to follow her, and Yusuf hands the car key to the inspector as he walks by.

"Thank you, and sorry," he says to Yusuf, extending his hand.

As they wait for the elevator, Mislan starts to explain to his boss the sequence of events, but she holds up her hand and says, "I don't want to hear anything from you now. I want both of you to go to the office, write out your statements, and go home. Hand them to me first thing tomorrow morning."

Mislan and Johan nod.

"If I find out that you've left anything out, intentionally or otherwise, I'll make sure you regret it. And Lan, I mean it."

He nods and looks at his assistant, who is grinning at him like a mischievous child. When Superintendent Samsiah is gone, he asks his assistant.

"What did you tell ma'am?"

"I told her you were picked up by MACC."

"And?"

"She gave me the third degree."

"And you told her everything?"

"I'm sorry, boss, she was scary. You know how she is when she gets into one of her moods."

Mislan laughs.

"You're weak, Jo. She plays you like a fiddle."

"I know, I'm sorry, boss."

"I think Yusuf, the senior guy, is OK, but the other one may be under the control of KK."

"Hoping for a favor in return, a promotion."

"I know many of these guys are pally with politicians or is it the other way around? That's why you don't see many politicians arrested and charged with corruption."

"I wouldn't be surprised if the asshole is one of them."

37

At the MACC lobby, Mislan asks Johan if he has the victim's cell phone listing. Johan tells him it is at the office.

"Are you not going back there?"

"I thought of writing my statement at home, to stay out of trouble," Mislan says laughing.

"With you it doesn't make any difference. Trouble follows you."

"Jo, let me leave first. You watch my back and see if I grow a tail again. Let me know if I do, and let's try to collar him. If not, we meet back at the office."

"OK, but that's like looking for more trouble, if you ask me."

"Did I ask you?" Mislan replies.

Mislan walks down to the basement, locates his car, and casually walks toward it, imperceptibly glancing at the reflections on the windshields and side mirrors of other parked cars to see if he's being followed. He unlocks his car, sits in it, and lights a cigarette, glancing at the rearview and side mirrors for any movement. He strains his ears, listening for a car door or the sound of an engine. Seeing and hearing nothing, he presumes the tail must know the model of his car, make, and number and is waiting outside to follow him. He drives out slowly, offering his tail every chance.

When he reaches Jalan Sultan Ismail, Johan calls to tell him that he has grown a tail. Mislan tells his assistant he's going to take a detour to let tail become overconfident, and when he gets to Jalan Tun Perak, he will stop next to the LRT station. If the tail stops, too, Johan is to collar him.

When Mislan pulls over at the LRT station, he notices a motorcycle stopping by the curb about twenty yards behind. The rider pretends to inspect the engine of his motorcycle. Mislan watches Johan walking up to his tail, surprising him. The tail tries to ride off, but Johan grabs the ignition key. The tail jumps off the motorcycle and makes a run for it. When he's about ten yards from Mislan's car, the inspector jumps out, levels his Beretta, and shouts, "Freeze, police!" The tail tries to cut to the right, loses his footing, and hits the pavement. Two overzealous onlookers jump on him, grab him, and punch him. Mislan walks over, his Beretta lowered to his side, saying, "Thank you, that's enough." Johan arrives at the scene, flips the tail on his stomach, and cuffs him.

"Jo, I'll take him in. Call for a detective to pick up his bike," Mislan says, yanking the tail up by the arms harder than necessary. Aware of public sentiments against snatch theft, Mislan announces to the onlookers, "Snatch thief." The huge crowd applauds and some of them snap photos. As he walks the tail to his car, an MPV shows up. Mislan tells them to transfer the tail to the Special investigations Unit.

Back in the office, he tells the duty detective to put the tail in an interview room and waits for his detective sergeant. When he arrives, Johan asks, "Do you want me to make a report?"

"Yes, link it to a suspected recent snatch theft or for suspicious behavior."

"OK. Do you want to hold him?"

"For what, riding his bike behind me?"

Johan laughs.

"Let's talk to him and decide later. Jo, you take the lead."

"You're the boss."

Mislan's cell phone rings. It is an unknown number.

"Inspector Mislan," he answers

"Mr. Mislan, this is Daud, you remember me? Superintendent Malik's friend."

"Yes, how may I help you?"

"I was just told you have arrested my nephew, Arif. May I know for what offense?"

"Suspected snatch thief."

"Snatch thief! I think you're mistaken. Can I arrange for him to be bailed?"

"I'll tell you what. He's being interviewed at the moment, and when it's done, I'll call to let you know the situation."

"I'd really appreciate it if you can release him on bail. His mother is here with me, crying and pleading. Can I come and see you?"

"I don't think that's necessary. I'll call you as soon as they're done."

Mislan enters the interview room, and Johan introduces him to Arif.

"Now, let me ask you again, why were you following Inspector Mislan?"

Arif keeps looking at the floor, not saying anything. It's obvious to Mislan that Arif is not a seasoned criminal.

"Your uncle, Daud, just called me." At the mention of Daud's name, Arif's face lights up. "He wants to bail you out. Guess what my reply was?"

Arif looks at him fearfully.

The inspector walks to the chair next to Johan, and sits down. He can sense Arif's anxiety building. He continues, "I told him, murder is a non-bailable offense."

The word "murder" strikes panic into Arif and he snaps.

"What are you talking about, what murder? I didn't murder anybody. I was asked to follow you and report back."

He realizes he's said too much and shuts up.

Johan slams the table with both hands, startling both the detainee and Mislan. "Who told you to follow Inspector Mislan? Was it your uncle?"

He nods timidly, watching Johan like a frightened rat. With this admission, Johan grabs the initiative, trying his luck.

"Did he also ask you to pay for our karaoke at Red Box?"

He nods.

"Where's the bill?"

"I gave it to him."

"What about the hampers, did you order the hampers?"

"No. I was asked to observe and to call my uncle when the hampers were collected."

Arif timidly shifts his eyes momentarily to Mislan.

"How about the money, did you deposit the money into his account?"

"What money? I don't know anything about any money."

Mislan's cell phone rings. It is his boss. He steps out of the room to answer it.

"Yes, ma'am."

"Didn't I tell you not to get into any more trouble?" Superintendent Samsiah asks, her voice sounding tired.

"Yes, you certainly did, ma'am."

"And which part of . . . not getting into any more trouble don't you understand? The OCCI just called me saying you've just made a spectacular arrest at LRT Jalan Tun Perak with your gun drawn in a crowded place."

"Oh boy, I'm in deep shit, aren't I?"

"Lan, use your head," she sighs. "You're making a bad case worse. I know you're angry at them for trying to frame you, but you're making it easy for them. Your conduct will cloud everything you've worked so hard for."

"Ma'am, the person we detained was my tail, he was reporting back to them. He is my link to Daud and maybe to others," he argues. "I don't know how they're linked to my case, but with this guy, I'm sure I can get to the bottom of it all."

"Get Reeziana to record a caution statement from him. Lodge an arrest report linking him to your confidential report and we'll hand him over to MACC tomorrow. Lan, please go home and stay home."

"Thanks, ma'am, I will. And, ma'am, I'm really sorry for my temporary loss of sanity," he says, chuckling.

"I'll deal with you and Johan later."

He informs Inspector Reeziana and Johan of the boss's instructions, lodges the arrest report, and goes home.

38

Mislan, slumped in his wing chair, lolls his head against the soft cushion and closes his eyes, feeling exhausted and frustrated. He dozes off and dreams. He is alone in a train, looking out of the window. It's dark outside, but he can sense the trees, houses, and bridges whooshing by. He has always been fascinated by long train rides and has always wanted to take one through Southeast Asia, into China and ending in Russia. It is on his to-do list—to take Daniel along on a father-and-son trip. In his dream, he is finally taking that trip but without his son and best friend. He sees a group of foreign backpackers talking in a language he doesn't understand, probably German or Dutch, he thinks. One of them starts plucking her guitar and sings what sounds to him like a folk song. He doesn't know what the lyrics mean, but by her sweet voice and the slow beckoning melody, it has to be a sad love song. He looks away from the window and watches them enjoying their carefree lives. He hears the sound of whistling but can't figure out where it's coming from. After a while, the whistling stops and he continues watching the backpackers. The blonde girl starts another song, and he recognizes a few of the words as being Malay: *Where is my house?* He asks the singer the title of the song, and she tells him it's called "Rumah Saya." It is a Dutch evergreen and the title is Indonesian, meaning "My House." He smiles. He asks himself, *Where is my house?*

The whistling starts again and becomes louder. He snaps out of his dream, opens his eyes, and realizes it is his cell phone ringing. Reaching over he answers, "Mislan."

"Mislan, this is Superintendent Malik. I understand you arrested a man by the name of Arif, suspected of snatch theft." It was a statement rather than a question.

"Eh, oh yes."

"Since when has D9 started going after petty criminals, like snatch thieves?" Malik mocks him. "Look, don't you give me a cock and bull story! You cut him loose, and we'll forget all about your little activities."

"Since the power of arrest was given to all police officers by our laws," Mislan replies sarcastically. "Since when is Selangor Commercial Crimes interested in KL D9 arrests? So, you knew about my little side business. Damn, I thought I was discreet."

"Listen," he hisses, "one of these days, you're going to be working under me, and when that happens, you'll regret we ever crossed paths."

"You must remember that when your days in the force are over, I'll still be serving. So the regret thingy might well become reversed."

The line goes dead.

He checks the WhatsApp messages on his cell phone—one from Inspector Reeziana informing him the detainee has been processed, another from Johan asking how he was. The last was from Audi, asking if he has seen the prime news. *Shit, I overslept.* He replies to Reeziana's and Johan's WhatsApps, gets dressed, and drives to the mamak restaurant near his condominium for dinner. While waiting for his order, he calls Daniel. As usual, his son is busy and asks if he can call back later. He tells Daniel it is all right, that he only wanted to hear his voice, missed him, and for him to have fun. He reflects on Superintendent Malik's call. He had heard whispers of Team A and B in the police force but hadn't paid any attention to them. In the old days, it was about clean cops and dirty cops, my men versus your men. Now, a new dimension has crept in—politics. It was tough to stay neutral.

When he returns home, he makes some extra-strong coffee, takes out the suspect's cell phone listing, and sits at his desk. He WhatsApps Audi to inquire what was said on the news. She calls.

"*You*. By the way, there's also an upload of the video on YouTube. Boy, you looked good . . . just like Horatio," she says, chuckling. "Have you guys run out of serious crimes for you to go after snatch thieves?"

"Funny. What's the YouTube title?"

"Try . . . *Vote KL versus LA Cop.* You know what, I voted for the KL Cop."

"Hey, I need another favor from you."

"You've not even returned my first one, but since I voted for the KL Cop, this is FOC. Shoot!"

"Can you find out from your MACC friend the names of all those involved in the allegations against the deceased? I mean all."

"All may not be possible, but if you're specific about who it is you want, it'll be easier for me to get something out of him."

"OK, how about those closely related to the case?"

"Easier, I guess. I'll check if he's on duty tomorrow. Otherwise, I'll arrange lunch with him when he's back."

"Thanks."

"Just so you know . . . the lunch will be on you."

He returns to the suspect's cell phone listing, searching and highlighting frequent incoming and outgoing phone numbers. He does the same with the Mahadi listings. He leans back and cross-references the two. One number matched and he jots it down. It is Hashim's cell phone number.

"Bingo," he says, smiling, and he rewards himself with a cigarette. This discovery excites him, and he calls his assistant, "Jo, I found the link."

"What link?"

"Between the suspect and our vic. It's Hashim, the vic's son."

"How?"

"Phone listing, there are numerous calls between the two of them. Didn't Jamie say the suspect was a bodyguard for a big shot?"

"Yes, but she didn't know his name."

"But she had seen him before. You have a photo of Hashim?"

"No."

"Can you get one?"

"I can try."

"Do that and show it to Jamie, see if she can recognize him."

"OK."

Mislan returns to the listing and makes a note:

On the night of the murder
Hashim called the suspect—7:40 p.m.
Hashim called his father—8:02 p.m.
Hashim called the suspect—8:04 p.m.

Mislan theorizes:

The first call was to inform the suspect it was going down tonight. Mahadi and Zaleha are breaking fast with friends and if Mahadi is to leave, they'll leave together.

The second call was to tell Mahadi something to make him leave the breaking of fast.

The third call was to inform the suspect where to rendezvous with Mahadi.

Jamie told them the suspect received a call and canceled his plans and dropped her at the Petronas gas station around 8 p.m. That would have been after the suspect received the call from Hashim at 7:40 p.m. Then at around 10 p.m. the suspect called, and they went clubbing. Mislan checks the listing and finds the call to Jamie made at 10:15 p.m. It had to have been made after the suspect went home to change his shirt.

Mislan plays the scenario in his head: so, how did it go down? *Hashim makes the call, gets his father to pick up the suspect, who then kills him and Zaleha.*

He laughs at how stupid he sounds.

You don't need to be a criminal lawyer to get the judge to throw your theory out the window, Lan. "How about the gun, how did the suspect get hold of the vic's gun? Remember what Fred the Dutchman from the Blabber group said? He said the vic even took his gun into the shower, that he wouldn't let it out of his sight. Then, what about the getaway?"

He knows he is on the right track, but he has to work out the modus operandi to get his closure. He needs someone to kick his thoughts about, someone with a wild enough imagination, someone not afraid to challenge his theories.

39

Mislan arranges the meeting at McDonald's at The Weld because it is not too crowded and it has an outdoor section where they can smoke. His only concern is that it may not be a twenty-four-hour outlet. They could adjourn to a mamak roadside stall behind Istana Hotel if the need arises. He looks at the dashboard clock. It is 8:45 p.m. The meeting is at 9:00. He dresses, gathers the documents, and drives out, stopping several times to see if he has grown another tail. He is late, Johan is already waiting at the entrance when he arrives.

"Have you solved the case?" Johan asks excitedly.

"Close, but I need to plug a few holes. What do you want to eat?"

"I'll have a McChicken, I'm hungry. You have a motive?"

"That's one of the holes." He grins.

He orders the food and Johan takes the tray to their table. They see Dr. Safia walking in. He calls her over and asks what she wants.

"Why couldn't we meet at my place?" Dr. Safia asks, her smile ever-present.

"Because of him," Mislan gestures to his assistant.

"I don't mind."

"I didn't want to embarrass him. Anyway, let's see how this goes."

"I've eaten. I'll just have an apple pie."

Mislan goes to get her order. When he returns, he explains what they had uncovered. Dr. Safia listens intently.

"So, you were right all along," she says.

"On the murders, yes, but there are still many holes in the case."

"Like what?"

"The gun belonged to the deceased. How did the killer get it?"

"The killer could've taken it from him, snatched it from him from behind," Johan suggests.

"Not likely. Forensics found a holster clipped to the vic's waist. It's a clip holster, so the gun is inside the trousers. It would not have been easy to snatch it. Besides, the suspect would've had to know which side of the victim's waist the holster was. If the suspect starts patting the vic's waist, I'm sure the vic would've stopped him. If that happened, the car could've gone out of control and crashed or the vic would've pulled over to the roadside."

"What if the suspect pulled a knife on one of the vics and demanded the gun?"

"Possible, but the deceased could've pretended to hand over the gun and blown the suspect's head off. Self-defense. Anyway, the suspect would've been a fool to try using a knife against a person with a gun."

"What if the vic left his gun unguarded and the suspect got hold of it?" Dr. Safia probes.

"How?"

"Stole it?"

"I'm certain the vic would've reported it. One of the vic's golfing buddies said the deceased never let his gun out of his sight. He had lost one before, so he was fanatical about its safekeeping."

"Even took it into the shower at the club," Johan adds.

At that point, the lights in McDonald's go off.

"Damn, the place is closing," Mislan says.

"How about my place?" Dr. Safia offers. "We can sit on the balcony, it's cool and breezy. And we can go on till morning with no one disturbing us."

Mislan sees Johan nod.

"Can we stop at a 7-E and get some chips or something?" Dr. Safia asks, grinning.

Dr. Safia makes coffee while the two men stand on the balcony, looking at the city's night skyline.

"Nice," Johan says.

"Yeah," he agrees. "How are things with you and Jamie?"

"She's great, but I have to be realistic. She's high maintenance."

"Hmmm."

"How about you and . . . ?" Johan jerks his head toward the kitchen, "Any plans?"

"For now, we're going with the flow, and I like to keep it that way."

"Not ready to take another leap?"

"Hey guys, why don't we talk here, it's more comfortable," Dr. Safia calls from the living room.

They sit down, and Dr. Safia takes her usual position, leaning against the armrest with her legs on his lap. Mislan waits for Johan's cheeky comment, but none comes.

"Let's leave the gun for a while and figure out how it was done," Johan suggests. "How did the suspect get away after killing the vics?"

"Yes, how did he escape?" Dr. Safia asks.

"That's the easy part. Have you ever seen a road accident or stopped to gawk at one?"

Both acknowledge having had such an experience.

"Would you remember the faces of other onlookers?"

No response.

"Precisely, unless you know each other beforehand, none of us would remember the onlookers. That was how he got away. Most people do not even witness an accident. They hear a bang and by the time they turn toward the sound, the accident itself is over. Those who do witness accidents normally drive on because they're too close to stop or do not want to get involved, although they could report it to the police or the emergency services center."

"So, you think that's when the suspect got away," Dr. Safia says.

"Maybe he understood human behavior, or it was sheer daring on his part," Mislan says. "My guess is he had an accomplice following in a car or on a motorbike. When the job was done, the suspect got out, pretended to be one of the onlookers, and when more and more people stopped to assist or gawk, he casually slipped away with the accomplice."

"You already have it all worked out."

"Not all of it. Who was the accomplice? Jo, do you remember Jamie mentioning the suspect's housemate, Zubir? We have to track him down. Talk to Jamie, see if she can give us a clue."

"By the way, how is Jamie?" Dr. Safia asks Johan.

"OK, I guess."

"You're not with her anymore?"

Johan grins.

"You think it was him?" he asks changing the subject.

"I don't know, but he's the only one I can think of. Anyone else have any suggestions?"

"What about this Daud, the JKKK chairman?"

"Possible, but I doubt if he'd want to get his hands dirty. His type would use others to do the dirty business."

"If he can frame you for—"

"Frame you! What did he do?" Dr. Safia shrieks.

"It's nothing, just a misunderstanding," Mislan says, warding off her query, signaling Johan not to say anything more.

Dr. Safia sits up and looks at him in distress and disappointment.

"It was just a misunderstanding," Mislan repeats and avoids her gaze. "Let's get back to our objectives. Any other suggestions?"

She shakes her head, continuing to stare at him.

"This is going nowhere. I need you to throw me your theories. It doesn't have to be right. I need a new angle. Something, anything," Mislan pleads.

Mislan takes out his cell phone and calls Audi. He puts her on speaker mode for the benefit of the others.

"Hey, have you got anything on the victim's MACC case?"

"Do you know what time this is? Don't you ever sleep?" Audi snaps.

"I thought investigative reporters didn't sleep, prowling the street for news," Mislan teases "I'm putting you on speaker so that Dr. Safia and Jo can listen in, too."

"Hi Audi," Dr. Safia greets her.

"Hi Doc, what are you doing with the crazy inspector at this hour?" Audi jokes.

"Keeping him sane," Dr. Safia answers with a chuckle.

"OK, I spoke to my friend, and we're having lunch tomorrow. He's not willing to talk over the phone, saying it might be tapped. They've become paranoid since the Beng Hock saga."

"OK, let me know when you speak to him."

"I'll call you as soon as we finish lunch."

"Thanks." Mislan terminates the call and sighs.

"Why do you need to know the victim's MACC case?" Dr. Safia asks.

"I need to understand why there's so much outside pressure."

"You think they're involved?"

"In the absence of any other reason, it does point in that direction."

"To shut your victims up?"

"Could be or could be due to money. I read on the Internet that sand mining is big business. Money's always a good motive for killing."

At 12:15 a.m., Johan announces he is leaving.

Mislan gathers up the documents while Dr. Safia cleans up the mess of leftover chips, crackers, and drinks. With Johan gone, the house is quiet. He reflects on what he has achieved through the discussions. Not much, but he did get some weight off his chest. Dr. Safia comes back with two mugs of fresh coffee.

"You staying?"

"Better not. I'm up for a twenty-four-hour tomorrow."

"You mean today; it's already Monday morning," she corrects him, putting the mugs on the coffee table. "Lan, about the accomplice, have you given him . . . what's the son's name . . . a thought?"

"Hashim?"

"Yes. You said he was probably the one who set up the meeting. The last call to the victim was from him and to the suspect, too. And there's no call from him to the suspect or the suspect to him after the killings."

"He's a strong possibility, but apart from the phone calls, there's nothing to link them."

"If you commit a murder, you want to be sure. I mean, you want to be in control to make certain everything goes according to plan. At the same time, you don't want too many people involved," Dr. Safia reasons. "Even if he was seen at the scene, he would have a good and believable excuse to be there . . . like he was passing and noticed his father's car, thought it was an accident, and stopped to help."

"So, you're saying he trailed the vic's car and picked up the suspect after he whacked them? That could explain why there were no calls between them afterward. He was there, so there was no reason for the suspect to call and report."

He lights a cigarette and hands it to her, lights another, and slumps back. She looks at him in silence.

"What was Hashim's motive?" he asks.

40

Monday is the first day of work after Eid holidays; the office is still not fully alive. Superintendent Samsiah is already at her desk, going through the reports when Mislan arrives. He greets her in passing and goes to his desk, where Johan is waiting with hot coffee.

"Morning, did you make any headway after I left?"

"Morning. Dr. Safia did bring up an interesting theory about the accomplice. Jo, did you manage to get a photo of Hashim?"

"Not yet, but I asked Syed and Jeff to run over to one of the media offices in the city. I'm sure they'll have one. I'll see Jamie once I have it. What is Dr. Safia's theory?"

"Hashim's the accomplice."

"Based on?"

He explains to his assistant what was discussed and the reason for the absence of a call between the two after the killing.

"That makes sense. So, you're going to pick him up?"

"Not yet, I need more than phone calls or their absence as evidence. I'll discuss it with ma'am, get her opinion and advice."

The morning prayer is more like a tea party, with plastic containers of Eid cookies, coffee, and stories. The mood is festive. After almost fifteen minutes, the meeting is called to order, starting with the outgoing investigators' briefing. Kuala Lumpur will be quiet for another week. Then, the return of city dwellers and foreign workers will mean an increase in crime rates. For the time being, crime investigators are enjoying slack time, while the traffic police are inundated with accident reports. Inspector Krishnan finishes his briefing in two sentences, followed by Inspector Reeziana in five.

"Do you want me to brief you on the confidential report?" Reeziana asks.

"See me after this," Superintendent Samsiah says.

The meeting is adjourned, and before leaving Superintendent Samsiah says to the inspector, "See me after Reeziana."

After about fifteen minutes, Reeziana returns from her meeting with Superintendent Samsiah.

"What did you gals talk about?" Mislan asks.

"Your report and what to do about it."

"How's her mood?"

"Can't tell. Her phone was ringing constantly. I think it's about your case."

"Shit."

He grabs the documents and heads for the office of Superintendent Samsiah. She is on the phone when he pokes his head around the door. She waves him in, points to a chair, and continues talking on the phone. When she finally puts the phone down, she disconnects the line.

"What's that about?" he asks, referring to the fact that she disconnected the line.

"Time out. I've been getting calls from people I don't even know."

"That sounds like the lyric from 'Rhinestone Cowboy,'" Mislan says, smiling.

Superintendent Samsiah laughs. "It does, didn't it?"

"My case?"

She nods.

"Which?"

"All three."

"Three? I thought there were only two."

"Count the car chase as well. The OCCI wants me to keep your confidential report internal."

"Translated, he wants it buried," Mislan sneers.

"Due to the fact that you discovered the money in your account in Rawang and that the report was also made there, he wants to let the

Selangor police handle it. He insisted that there's no necessity to bring outsiders in, by which he means the MACC. I'm giving you the option to decide, as it involves you."

"I never thought I would say this, but I'll take my chances with the MACC."

She nods. She tells him how she'll be going about it and advises him not to have high hopes and to let it take its course. In the meantime, she suggests he stay away from people he has identified in his confidential report.

"There's no telling what else they'd be willing to do when they get wind of MACC's investigation."

"I don't understand it, ma'am. Why do they want the case wrapped up so quickly? It makes me feel like they're involved."

"Lan, sometimes when people want cases closed, it's not because they're involved but because they've other things to fear and hide."

"I never thought of that."

"Well, you should."

"Ma'am, I need to run some discoveries by you and tap your wisdom," he says, smiling. He explains his theory of an accomplice, the modus operandus, and the escape.

"That's a serious allegation, Lan. Besides the calls between them, what else do you have?"

Mislan shakes his head.

"You know what would happen if you're wrong?"

"I can guess."

"Are you prepared to face the consequences?"

"I'll start going through the job openings," he jokes. "What about you?"

"I can take care of myself. Anyway, I've reached my optional retirement age. I may quit and look after my family."

She reconnects the telephone, and it rings instantly. Waving him out, she answers the phone. As he rises, he uses hand signals to ask for her decision. She covers the mouthpiece and says, "Do it by the book."

41

It is 11 a.m., and the courthouse corridors are empty without the usual witnesses and journalists. Normally, an officer requesting a warrant is accompanied by the court prosecuting officer, but Mislan decides to go alone this time. He knocks lightly on the magistrate's chamber, enters, stands in front of her desk, and hands over his request. The magistrate reads the request, asks a few questions for clarification, and issues the warrant. Walking to his car, he is overwhelmed with the anticipation of where the warrant in his hands could lead. What if he's wrong? Is he prepared to face the consequences? Never mind him, what about his boss, the head of Special Investigations? Over the years, she has taken a lot of beatings on his behalf, probably even risked her career for him.

Shit, Lan, this is not the time to lose your balls. He calls his assistant and asks his whereabouts. They arrange to meet at the office in half an hour. He calls Chew and inquires about the results of the analysis carried out on the T-shirt and water sample. Chew tells him that both tested positive for human blood and have been sent for DNA testing.

Sitting in the car, he says, "Yes!" Then he feels alone and trembles with mixed emotions. He is excited about the positive forensic results but fearful that his suspicion of those involved may well be wrong.

Hashim Mahadi's office is on the second floor of Wisma MM Harapan in Jalan Kelana Jaya. The same office he shared with his late father. Arriving at the building, Mislan and his assistant approach Detective Syed and Detective Jeff, who were assigned to watch the building. Syed informs him that Hashim arrived around 10:10 a.m. and has not left the building. Mislan instructs Syed to monitor Hashim's car and Jeff the lobby. He and Johan take the elevator to level two. At reception, he introduces himself and asks for Hashim Mahadi. He is told that he has moved into the executive chairman's office on the third floor. They take the staircase up to level three, and when they step into the lobby, two men stop them.

"Can I help you?"

"Yes, I'm Inspector Mislan from D9, Kuala Lumpur, and this is Detective Sergeant Johan. We'd like to see Mr. Hashim Mahadi."

"Is he expecting you?"

"No, but I have a special pass from the court," Mislan says, holding up the warrant.

The office door bursts open, and Hashim appears in the doorway.

"It's you! What do you want?"

"Mr. Hashim, we have a search warrant to take possession of your car for forensic examination," Mislan says.

The two men step between their boss and the two police officers. Johan gives them a stare and says, "You don't want to do that," and the men melt away, letting Mislan pass.

"Zubir, call my lawyer," Hashim snaps. He pulls out his cell phone and speaks urgently to someone on the other end.

The man named Zubir rings a bell, and Johan steps closer to him, saying, "Mr. Zubir, can I see your IC, please?"

Zubir turns to his boss for advice, but his boss is too engrossed with his telephone call to notice.

Johan repeats firmly, "Can I see your IC, please?"

The man takes out his identity card and hands it to Johan, asking, "Why do you need my IC?"

"Sit down here," Johan says, holding on to his identity card.

Mislan follows Hashim into the large office and waits for him to finish his call. Before Hashim can make another call, he steps closer to him.

"You can make all the calls you want after we're done here. In the meantime, please follow me to your car."

"What's this about? How do I know this is issued by the court?" Hashim barks, holding up the warrant.

"It's all stated in the warrant and you know exactly what this is about."

"What do you mean by that?"

"When I served you the warrant, you did not ask me any questions. Instead, you asked for your lawyer and called whomever it was you just spoke to. If you really didn't know what the warrant was about, you would've asked me instead of doing what you did. So, please take me to your car."

Hashim remains seated, his face growing redder, staring menacingly at him.

Mislan knows Hashim is buying time, and he's not looking forward to being caught in a circus of arguments with lawyers and others.

"Look, we can do it quietly, and you can continue with your work after it's over. Or we can turn this into an ugly scene. You have five seconds to decide."

Hashim remains silent, his eyes unblinking.

"Time's up. Mr. Hashim, please stand, you're under arrest for refusing to comply with a warrant issued under section 54 (c) of the Criminal Procedures Code."

Mislan steps forward, and Hashim abruptly jumps out of the chair, backing away toward the window, screaming, "You *stupid fool.* Do you know who I am? I know people who can destroy you just like that." He snaps his fingers. "You think you can come here and threaten me. You've no idea what trouble you're already in!"

He pulls out his phone and makes another call, urgently telling the person on the other end he needs to speak to Tan Sri immediately.

"Let's not dwell on my future," Mislan replies with a smile. "For now, you should be worried about yours. I'm asking you for the last time: are you coming peacefully or do I have to put these on you?" Mislan asks, holding up a pair of handcuffs.

The voices of men talking loudly from the elevator lobby momentarily distract the attention of the two Special Investigations officers and the bodyguards. The acting executive chairman of MM Harapan Holdings, however, breathes a sigh of relief. Two men dressed in white, long-sleeved shirts, complete with cufflinks and neckties, barge in at the outer office and the one talking the loudest asks, "What's going on here?"

Hashim dashes out of his office, yelling, "What took you so long to come here? Your office is just next door."

"What's going on here? Who are you people?" the loud man asks.

"I'm Inspector Mislan from Special Investigations, Kuala Lumpur, and this is my assistant, Detective Sergeant Johan. And if my guess is right, you're his lawyer."

"Damn right, I am. I'm Manikam from V. Manikam and Partners. We're the company's solicitors. Why are you arresting our client?"

"For refusing to comply with a search warrant."

"What search warrant?"

Hashim runs back to his office, takes the warrant, and hands it to his lawyer. Manikam examines it and hands it to his assistant.

"Let's go into the office," Manikam says.

Inside the office, the acting executive chairman and his lawyers stand behind the desk engaged in whispered consultation, which is regularly disrupted by Manikam's phone ringing that causes further annoyance to his already agitated client.

"Shut the damn thing up," Hashim snaps.

The lawyer does as he is told, and the consultation continues with the client violently shaking his hands, protesting or rejecting his advice.

"What exactly are you looking for?" the lawyer asks.

"It's all stated in the search warrant, if only you care to read," Mislan answers.

"It states here evidence link to the murder of Mahadi . . ." Manikam stops and stares at the inspector. "You're saying my client killed his own father? How dare you make such absurd malicious accusations?"

Mislan grins at the lawyer's display of being lawyerlike.

"What evidence . . . What do you think you'll find? I was told the case was classified as murder-suicide, what's this rubbish of murder?"

"If you're so confident of your client's innocence, why are you and he protesting. What are you afraid of?" Mislan dares them.

The lawyer looks at his client. Mislan spots tiny fleeting fear in Hashim's eyes.

"My client will comply with the warrant. Let it be on record that his compliance is under protest."

"Whatever. Please advise your client to come with me to hand over the vehicle."

"There's no need to arrest my client, he is complying with the warrant."

"I'm not arresting him, I'm asking him to come with me to point out the car and hand it over to us. Those are the procedures."

Their elevator ride down to the basement and the short walk to the car are accompanied by a chorus of threats and profanities by Hashim. Passersby and visitors amused by the ruckus form a line behind them, turning the short walk into a mini parade. Chew's team is waiting as they approach the car. Mislan goes through the formalities of taking custody of the vehicle and hands it over to Chew's team.

Before leaving the building, Mislan instructs Jeff and Syed to take Zubir to the office. In the car, he switches on his cell phone and is instantly greeted by numerous missed calls and messages. He scrolls the missed call listing and is surprised by who has called. He listens to the voice messages and reads the text messages, shaking his head. "Well, you were warned," he says to himself.

"Sorry, what did you say?" Johan asks.

"No, nothing. I was only thinking aloud."

"I stole a few snapshots of Hashim and Zubir. I'll see if Jamie can recognize them."

"Do that, and get Jeff or Syed to run Zubir's particulars through Record, see if he's on record before we interview him. By the way, Chew said the water sample contains human blood, he has sent the samples for DNA matching."

"When will we get the results?"

"He didn't say. I hope soon, because the heat's past boiling point. The city's eyes are on us."

"What are all the voice messages about?"

Mislan shrugs and smiles. "Let's stop for lunch, I'm starving. Jo, let's go to Bangsar, there's a restaurant next to CIMB, across Bangsar Village. I don't know its name, but it sells the best biryani I've eaten."

"You mean the one with the morning wet market?"

"Yes, just before that area."

Johan manages to find a parking space about a hundred yards from the restaurant. "Don't look back, but I noticed a blue car, a Myvi, on our tail since we left MM Harapan's building," Johan says.

"I spotted it, too. I'm going into the bank. Why don't you go to the restaurant and find a seat? I want to see if they're following us."

Johan walks toward the restaurant as Mislan heads to the bank. Through the glass wall he observes two men coming out of the Myvi and walking toward the restaurant. He allows time for them to enter the restaurant before coming out of the bank. The two men are seated a few tables behind Johan, who is placing his order. Mislan walks to their table, sits down in front of them, and places his authority card on the table.

"Now it's your turn. Can I see some identification?" he asks, surprising them.

"Why?" one of them asks.

"Because I showed you mine and because I asked you to," Mislan replies, staring at him.

The two men look at one another in disbelief. Mislan's reply is something they had not anticipated.

"Look, either I see some identification or you two are coming with me to the police station for failure to produce valid identification or give reasonable explanation of your identity."

The thinner of the two pulls out his wallet and produces an MACC identity card, sliding it across the table to Mislan as Johan joins them.

"How about you?" Mislan asks the more senior-looking of the two.

"I'm his superior."

"No shit. Can I see what a superior MACC ID looks like?"

The man pulls out his identification card and slides it to him.

"OK, Mr. Agus and Mr. Lambuk, why were you following us?"

"We're not, we came here for lunch," Agus answers defensively.

"I'd buy your story if your office was located near MM Harapan's building, but it's not. May I suggest you guys go for surveillance training? We spotted you the moment you were on our tail. What's the deal?"

"Our boss, Senior Enforcement Officer Yusuf, assigned us to keep an eye on you. He said someone is after you and was concerned for your safety."

"Please tell Mr. Yusuf I really appreciate his concern, but I'm perfectly capable of taking care of myself. I have his number, and, if I need assistance, I'll call him. Meanwhile, enjoy your lunch, and please don't follow me anymore, because I get jittery when I grow a tail. When I get that way, I'm bound to do something silly, which I know I'll regret. You know what I mean," Mislan says. He winks, slides their identification cards back, and with Johan moves to their table.

42

THEY KEEP LOOKING IN the rearview and side mirrors driving back to the office. Johan takes the precaution of making sudden right or left turns without signaling and pulling over by the roadside. After several such countermeasures, he feels confident no one is following them and drives to their office. Mislan's cell phone rings.

"I could really do with some good news."

"Wow, no hello or how did the lunch go?" Audi taunts him. "We had a wonderful lunch, thank you, and you owe me RM135."

"What did you guys have for lunch, gold nuggets?" Mislan chides.

"Western, for privacy. Anyway, it was worth every sen. The story's that your victim, Mahadi, was the front man for a few well-connected individuals. He ran the business, and the others made sure his applications for permits were approved and there was no interference. The investigation was with respect to overmining, mining outside the permitted area, under declarations, and malpractices in permit approvals."

"No surprises there. You got names?"

"A few. Inspector, I heard something happened yesterday. Something you're not telling me. Tell you what, let's trade the names for the inside story of what happened yesterday."

"Look Audi, I can't tell you what happened because it's not in my hands anymore. However, I can point you to the right person. You give me the names and I'll tell you who to pester and make his life miserable."

"Deal. You go first."

"You didn't get this info from me."

"What info?" she asks, laughing.

"Senior Enforcement Officer Yusuf Alamin, MACC, KL. Now the names, please."

"KK, Daud Ibrahim, and I get first crack at the story, okay?"

"OK, thanks."

Once they reach the office, Mislan calls Inspector Reeziana from the parking lot, asking if she could do him a favor. He gives her the necessary information and tells her to keep it between them. Walking into the office, they see a group of men and women crowding the front desk, making loud threatening inquiries: who is the person in charge, where is she now, call her now, who is this Inspector Dahlan or Mislan. He and Johan walk behind the crowd into their office without the front-desk clerk noticing.

"The gang's here," Johan says, jerking his head toward the front desk.

"I would be disappointed if they were not."

"Now what?"

"Now we interview Zubir. Check with Jeff if he has a record."

He takes out the digital recorder and goes to the interview room.

"Jo, WhatsApp their photos to Jamie."

"OK."

Zubir stops talking to Syed when Mislan walks into the interview room and motions for the detective to leave. He sits in the vacated chair, staring unblinkingly at Zubir. So this is the guy, the arrogant jackass that Jamie told them about. Well, he doesn't look so macho now.

"What's your position in the company?" Mislan asks.

"Bodyguard," Zubir answers smugly.

"Woo, that's a powerful position, the boss's bodyguard. So, are you trained in close-escort protection?"

"Eh?"

"Forget it. Do you know a person by the name of Mahyudin Maidin, also known as Mamak Din?"

"Yes, he died in a car accident a few days ago. Why?"

"Was he also a bodyguard for your boss?"

"No, he was my boss's friend."

"Did he do any work for your boss?"

"Yes."

"What kind of work?"

"Meet people, talked to people for my boss. . . . You know, that kind of thing."

"No, I don't. Why don't you tell me?"

"He was like my boss's messenger. When my boss wanted someone to back off or to be paid off, he would be sent. You know, that sort of thing."

"When your boss wanted someone to back off, what did Mahyudin do?"

"Talk to them and sometimes rough them up a little. I never saw him doing it, but I heard him telling my boss what he did."

"So he was your boss's muscleman, his henchman?"

Zubir nods.

"Who did he work with?"

"I don't know. He was alone whenever I saw him. He never had anyone with him when he came to the office or met my boss."

Johan enters and whispers to Mislan that Zubir is clean.

"Where were you last Tuesday night, between eight to ten?"

"That's the night the chairman committed suicide, right? I was at my mother's house in Melaka. We're having prayers for my late father. You can check that out."

"Do you know where Mahyudin was?"

Zubir shakes his head.

The front desk clerk pokes his head in the doorway and tells Mislan that the boss wants him in her office. Before leaving, he tells Johan to take down the alibi's details and cut Zubir loose.

Superintendent Samsiah's office is packed with family members of the male victim. Mama Bee is seated in one chair and a middle-aged man in another, while three other men and two women stand behind them. All eyes stare at him as Mislan squeezes to the side and leans against the filing cabinet.

"You wanted to see me, ma'am?"

She nods and, addressing her guests, says, "This is Inspector Mislan.

He's the lead investigator in this case." Turning to him, she continues, "The deceased's family are concerned with the seizure of the eldest son's car and the arrest of . . . his bodyguard. Do you care to enlighten them?"

"As you're aware we're investigating the murder of Mahadi and Zaleha—"

"What murder? I was told by Tan Sri it was a murder-suicide," Mama Bee snaps, cutting him off. "Why are you doing this, who paid you to reopen the case? It was that bitch's family, wasn't it? What else do they want from us? She has stolen enough from me and my family."

"Mrs. Rahimah, the case was neither reopened nor has it been reclassified. I don't know what you've been told by Tan Sri, but it was never classified as a murder-suicide," Superintendent Samsiah says calmly, trying to pacify Mama Bee.

"It was in the news, the press conference by the police," the man sitting next to Mama Bee butts in.

"It was one of the theories that the police are not discounting," Samsiah explains.

"Why has my son's car been taken?" Mama Bee stares at Mislan like she is casting an evil spell on him.

"To clear any doubts that we may have about the case," he answers, trying to be diplomatic.

"What doubts?"

"I'm not able to divulge that information, as it is an ongoing investigation. However, as soon as we clear our doubts, the car will be released immediately."

"And why has one of our employees been arrested?" one of the men barks. Mislan figures the questioner must be Mokthar, the youngest of the three sons, who was reported to have threatened the victim Zaleha.

"He was not arrested. He was brought in for questioning. He was released before I came here."

"You think you're smart. . . . Got all of the answers, don't you?" Mama Bee snarls. "I promise you, this will not be the end. I'll go right to the top if I have to. Just you wait and see. I'll have your job, like that." She snaps her fingers, stands, and walks out. The rest of her gang-members follow suit.

When they are out of hearing distance, Mislan lets out a low whistle. "Now you know why Jeff called her Mama Bee."

Superintendent Samsiah smiles. "It's starting. You'd better be right on this."

"Well, if I'm wrong, I'll take full responsibility. It's all on me, no one else."

"That's what you say, but that's not how the game is played."

He smiles. "I know, and I'm sorry for any shit that might fall on you."

"Do your job, and the shit will not fall."

43

As he leaves his boss's office, Mislan is met by his assistant in the corridor.

"Jamie identified Zubir but is not sure of Hashim. She said the image in the photo looks like him, but she's not sure."

"It's OK, Zubir already confirmed the suspect is his boss's friend, his henchman. Jo, call Melaka and ask them to verify Zubir's alibi. I'm sure it'll all true up, but let's be sure."

The front desk officer stops them and tells Mislan he has been summoned by the Officer in Charge of Criminal Investigation and ma'am, too.

"Damn, what is it now?" Mislan sighs. "Jo, I need you to follow up with Chew on the car. Text me, once you have it. The result will determine which way this case is going."

Superintendent Samsiah approaches them.

"Remember I told you, come Monday the blizzard will start. I hope you're ready."

"Always."

They ride the elevator to the OCCI's floor in awkward silence. The outer office is still deserted except for the OCCI's personal assistant and a few clerks. The personal assistant ushers them into the meeting room, saying the OCCI is waiting for them. Superintendent Samsiah knocks lightly on the door, opens it, and is greeted by a room full of people. Most of them were in her office earlier.

"Come in," the OCCI says, introducing them. "This is Superintendent

Samsiah, head of Special Investigations, and Inspector Mislan. Please sit," he says, not realizing there are no more seats.

None of those seated make any move to offer theirs, so the two D9 officers stand in front of the whiteboard.

"Samsiah, can you update us on the murder-suicide case?"

"Apart from the family members who were just in my office, may I know who are the rest of them?" she asks, looking at the two new faces seated at the table.

"They're family of the deceased, their lawyer, and business partners. Datuk Jalil has asked me to update them as a favor. You know, to keep them informed. I'm sure it's all right with you."

"The case is ongoing, and I don't think it's appropriate for me or my officers to divulge information pertaining to it at the present moment, especially to interested non-personnel."

"I'm not asking you to divulge any sensitive information. Just give them an update," the OCCI says rather sternly.

"In that case, there's nothing to update, as we're still waiting for results and confirmations from various parties."

"Don't give me that bullshit. They told me Mislan arrested one of their employees and seized the deceased's eldest son's car. What's going on?"

"I'll brief you if you wish, but not with them present," Samsiah answers defiantly.

"You're a stubborn woman, aren't you?" Mama Bee sneers.

"I'm not getting into an argument with you. I already explained things to you and your family in my office."

"How dare you speak to my mother that way," Mokthar snarls. "I'll make a report to Datuk Jalil against you for being rude."

"You may do as you please," Samsiah replies unperturbed. "In the meantime, I suggest you let us do our work. Sir, if there's nothing more, may we be excused?"

"Can you excuse us for a minute?" the OCCI says to his guests.

Standing up, he signals for the head of Special Investigations and Mislan to follow him to his office.

Once inside his "ego" chamber, the OCCI snaps, "Do you know who those people are? They have connections. Tan Sri KK, to name just one of them. Mislan, this time you're way over your head. Don't fool around with these people. And Samsiah, you're a fool to back the wrong horse. I hope you know what you're doing, and I suggest you pray damn hard you're right." Senior Assistant Commissioner Burhanuddin pauses for breath. "I've already said the case is a murder-suicide, but your hardheaded investigator here chooses to ignore it. Then he goes poking his nose into a hornet's nest. Well, this time you're not getting my backing."

Mislan thought of asking, *What backing?* but bites his tongue.

"Whether it's right or wrong, we have to investigate every lead. That's what we're doing, to prove or disprove—"

"Don't give me the bullshit sermon, I'm not one of your probationary inspectors," the OCCI's retort cuts her off. "Now we're alone, so brief me."

Superintendent Samsiah nods to her lead investigator to go ahead. Mislan briefs him on the evidence gathered from Jamie, the suspect's house, and Forensics' analysis confirming the samples to be positive for human blood. He leaves out the probability of an accomplice. Instead, he cooks up a story about the suspect killed in the car chase having connections with someone in the victim's company who has a grudge against the victim. The problem is they are not able to establish the link, as the suspect was dead by the time they got to him. He goes on to say that the seizure of the car was a planned sting to make the unknown accomplice think the police are barking up the wrong tree. He hopes the real accomplice will lower his guard and make a mistake.

"We have a team monitoring the real suspect, and we're confident he'll make some move soon, now that he feels the heat is on someone else," Mislan adds.

"What move?"

"We're hoping he'll be confident enough to start disposing of incriminating evidence so that we can catch him in the act."

The OCCI nods his approval. "What about the car?"

"To make it look real, we called in Forensics HQ to take the car to their garage. We could've asked D10 to do it, but we didn't want the car here. Forensics has been instructed to only keep the car out of view for a while."

Again, the OCCI nods his approval. "Who's the real suspect?"

"At this moment, we believe he's part of the vic's business or someone who benefited from the victim's sand mining operation," Mislan lies confidently.

"What's the grudge?"

"Money. We heard the victim was short-changing them for years, and has been channeling it to the woman," he answers, the lie becoming easier.

Mislan knows the eager-to-please OCCI will relate all these lies to the victim's family and from them to the prime suspect. He is banking on his prime suspect's arrogance, his feeling of being untouchable, to bury him.

"And by seizing the car, you're shifting the heat from the real suspect, drawing him into the open. Good work, I'm sure the family will be happy to know that," the OCCI says, smiling. "What if you're wrong about the real suspect? What if he does not make any mistakes?"

"We'll release the vehicle and try some other approach," Superintendent Samsiah answers, playing along with her officer's lies.

"The more appropriate answer would be, it'll be the end of your career in the force," the OCCI remarks with an easy laugh. Standing, he says, "You're excused."

Leaving the ego-chamber, the two D9 officers restrain themselves from discussing what just happened. They walk in silence, but Mislan can see his boss is suppressing a smile. She avoids looking at him and walks briskly to her office. He knows he just committed a willful breach of officers' conduct, yet he feels great about it. Stepping into her office, she motions for Mislan to close the door behind him.

Once the door is closed, she bursts out laughing, joined by her investigator.

"Where the hell did you pull the story from?" she says, still laughing. "That was one hell of a brilliant lie."

"I really don't know. He wanted a story, so I gave him one."

Superintendent Samsiah suddenly turns serious, gazing at her officer.

"What?"

"Have you ever pulled such a tale on me?"

"No way," Mislan replies, trying hard to keep a straight face.

"Hmmm."

"I'm hoping he tells the family the story and makes the suspect feel he's not the target. Hopefully, he will feel confident and make mistakes."

"What if he does not?"

"Then, I'll start reading the help-wanted section."

Mislan goes to his office to look for Johan, who tells him Chew is still waiting for the DNA test results and expects them later on in the evening. Inspector Reeziana comes in, and Mislan immediately turns his attention to her.

"Have you got it?"

"Yes and no," she replies. "The money was banked through a cash deposit machine in Serendah, but the machine is not fitted with a camera. However, the bank does have CCTV covering its ATM area. It's too blurry—you'll need to get Video Forensics to work on it. Perhaps, they can get facial images of people using the machine."

"Thanks, I'll pass it on to Nathan."

"Hey, I saw two officers from the ISCD in ma'am's office. What's going on?"

ISCD is Integrity Standard Compliance Division, formerly known as the Disciplinary Department—Internal Affairs.

"I've no idea. We've just come back from the OCCI's office."

Mislan's cell phone beeps, indicating a message. He reads the text, grabs his backpack, and signals for Johan to follow him. Turning to Reeziana, he says, "You did not see me," and disappears through the emergency door with Johan.

"What's going on?" Johan asks anxiously.

"Here," he says, handing his cell phone to Johan. The text was from

Superintendent Samsiah: *I've got ISCD officer ASP Amir in my office looking for you. Be prepared.*

"What's this about?"

"The eye of the hurricane," he answers, laughing as they hurriedly go down the deserted staircase.

44

THEY EXIT AT LEVEL four, walk casually to the lobby, and hop into an open elevator, avoiding eye contact with anyone. When the elevator door opens on the ground floor, they walk hurriedly to his car. Standing by his car, Mislan smiles.

"What's so funny?" Johan asks.

"Us, sneaking out like fugitives. Now I know what it's like to be a wanted person."

They laugh.

"Where to?"

"Forensics, I need to see Chew."

In the car, Mislan calls Audi.

"Hey, you want something juicy?"

"How juicy?"

"Very juicy. But you must put it on air ASAP."

"No promises, but if it's juicy enough, I can try. Shoot."

They walk up to Chew's office, where they are told he is in the garage. Mislan asks for the video technician Nathan, and is directed to the laboratory. Nathan is reviewing a clip of a robbery in action.

"Hi, Inspector, I worked on your video from the Petronas station, but as you said, nothing much can be done about the car's image. But all is not lost. I managed to enlarge and enhance the woman's image enough to be identifiable," Nathan says.

"Great. Nathan, I need you to view this video, kind of urgent. Do you mind?"

"Not at all. I'm just going over this video for a court case next week, to refresh my memory. Let's see what you have." He slots the compact disc into the player. "What exactly do you want me to do?"

"The cash deposit machine at 13:12, can you blow up the image of the person making the deposit?

"Let's see." Nathan moves the timer to 13:10, and lets the video run. "The video is quite blurry. I don't know if I can do any better."

"There," Mislan says.

Nathan pauses the video, highlights the image of the machine, and punches some keys. The image zooms in on the machine and a person standing in front of it. He repeats the same with the person's head and says, "Not a good angle."

"Can you zoom in on the machine's display screen?"

Nathan does so, but the reflective screen makes the wording illegible.

"OK, let's try this," Mislan suggests. "You rewind the video slowly and trace the person's movement coming into the kiosk. Then play it back and see if you can get his face."

"OK."

Nathan runs it several times until he establishes the best image he can get and freezes the frame. "That's the best." He zooms in and enlarges the face. "If I enhance this, I think you can make a positive identification of him."

"That looks good, Nathan. I need the part from when he walks in, until the moment he finishes making the deposit. Can you enlarge the face and make an insert at the top?"

"I can do better than that. I'll circle his head walking in all through the video and pause for a moment at this part, and insert his face's image on the top right corner here."

"Wonderful. When can I get it?"

"Before the end of office hours, today."

"Great. You're the best," Mislan says, patting Nathan's shoulder.

They go down to the garage to find Chew and his men busy working on Hashim's car. Mislan stops midstep and says, "Jo, can you ask Jamie if she has ever seen the suspect with a gun?"

"Why?"

"We have almost all the evidence needed to prove murder, and only two things can throw our case out the window. One is the gun: how did the killer get hold of the vic's gun?"

"And the other?"

"The motive."

Johan calls Jamie. His assistant rings off and shakes his head.

"Damnit," he swears.

"Inspector, you don't look happy," Chew says.

He smiles. "Running low on ideas and fuel."

"You! Never. OK, today, I'll be your genie in a lab-coat. Make your wish and I shall grant it," Chew jokes.

"OK, I wish to be a millionaire so I can quit this miserable job and live by the beach in the Bahamas with the woman of my dreams."

"Not that kind of wish. I'm a forensic genie. Now, you make a wish that the car will yield conclusive evidence. Go ahead, make the wish."

"Ok, I wish the car would yield conclusive evidence," he says, humoring Chew.

"Your wish is my command, Master Inspector," Chew replies. He goes through the abracadabra motions, complete with old-fashioned Arabian bowing. "Behold, Master Inspector, we found tiny traces of blood on the passenger's door handle, armrest, and seat. By the smear patterns we're confident that they're transfers. They tested positive for human blood, and I sent swabs for DNA matching. How's that, Master Inspector?"

Mislan and Johan beam.

"That's the best news I've had in a long time," he says, bear-hugging Chew. "If it weren't against my religion, I'd kiss you," he says. "When can I have the DNA results?"

"Earliest will be tomorrow morning. If it helps, the blood type is the same as the victims', but that's not something you can use as conclusive evidence, because there are millions of others with the same blood type."

"That's good enough for me. I bet my job the DNA will match the vics. Can I see it?"

They walk to the car. Mislan and Johan examine the door handle and the interior where tiny markings have been drawn.

"I don't see anything," Johan says.

"You can't, not with your naked eye. The car has been cleaned inside out. Here, put these on," Chew says, handing them what look like sports glasses. They put them on and Chew shines blue light at the markings. Tiny chemiluminescent blue specks appear. "We sprayed the parts of the car where we believed blood would likely to be found with a chemical called luminol. Then we shine this baby on the spots. If there's blood, it'll give out a blue glow just like you're seeing now."

"Just like *CSI* on TV," Johan says.

"Some of what they show on TV is real, but some is only movie science. Maybe in a decade or two they may become real, too. In the meantime, it's only a crime-forensic dream."

Mislan's phone rings. It's Audi.

"Yes."

"I met with him and nothing," she says, disappointed.

"Yusuf?"

"Yes, Yusuf the tight-ass lips."

Mislan chuckles, "Your friend's in there, does he know Yusuf?"

"I don't know but I don't think it matters, his lips are tighter than a bank vault."

"OK try and work on this. The car chase suspect is known to be connected with someone involved with the victim's business. That's all I can feed you. Audi, I need this aired ASAP, like tonight. I need it to be breaking news, not another story to fill in airtime."

"Why? What's going to happen?"

"I'll tell you the next time we meet. And can you somehow squeeze something in about the MACC's investigations on the vics' business?"

"That's old news, but I'll try."

"Thanks, I'll catch you later."

45

Driving out of Crime Forensics HQ, Mislan calls his boss to update her on Chew's findings. He asks her the purpose of the ISCD officers' visit and is told that there was a police report lodged against him by the victim's family.

"For what?"

"Inappropriate conduct, use of vulgar language while executing a search warrant. Soliciting favors to reopen the case."

"You're kidding."

"Do I sound like I'm kidding? Lan, I have a feeling you're knocking on the right doors and these people have been shaken. They need something to stop or at least delay you so they can regroup and cover their tracks. The report against you was only a firefighting measure to slow you down, not an act of containment, which they're probably still working on. My advice to you is to watch your back and go in for the kill. You're on roster today, right?"

"Yes."

"I'll get Reeziana to cover your shift until 8 and you can arrange to cover hers when all this has blown over. I don't want you coming into the office unless it's really necessary or until the building is empty."

"Thanks, ma'am."

"And, Lan, good police work on the car. That was a gutsy call."

He makes another call but does not get through. He tells Johan to take a detour for Hospital Kuala Lumpur. It is always easier to drive there than to get your calls answered, he concludes.

"What's there in HKL?"

"Test our luck, to see if the postmortem report is ready. Jo, we're to stay away from the office until about 8, until it is empty."

"Why? What about today's shift?"

"Reeziana's team will cover our shift and we'll cover for her later. Ma'am's instructions."

"Does it have something to do with the ISCD officer?"

He nods.

"They received a complaint?"

"The vic's family lodged a police report against me."

"What! For what? For trying to find out who killed their father? They must be crazy."

"For using foul language, for soliciting favors, for improper conduct, I suppose someone's advising them."

"And ISCD's investigating it. Someone's pulling strings. ISCD don't simply jump, they're too seasoned for that."

Mislan is silent.

"You know, that's the trouble with being a police officer. Anyone can make a police report and you're marked. It doesn't matter if you're right or wrong, you're marked. Then when you're exonerated, there is not a bloody thing you can do against that person for making the false and malicious allegation. Heads, you lose, tails, you lose," Johan moans.

"The law does provide for acting against people who make false reports."

"What good's the law when we're not willing to use it? You know the excuses the brass will give: We don't want to aggravate the situation. To hell with the situation, aggravate it as much as we can and make them pay for their lies." Johan is livid.

Mislan smiles. Johan is right, but he knows how it is. Until the top brass has the will to do something, police officers will have to suffer these punches in silence.

The morgue is as crowded as always with grieving families, relatives, and funeral-home touts. They walk into the Medical Forensics reception and ask for Dr. Bakar Sulaiman or Dr. Matthews. The receptionist tells them Dr. Bakar Sulaiman is still on leave, but Dr. Matthews is available. She calls the doctor and tells them to go in.

"Good evening, Doctor," Mislan greets him.

"Inspector, Selamat Hari Raya."

"This is my assistant, Detective Sergeant Johan. Doc, sorry to pester you, but is the report ready?"

Matthews acknowledges Johan and then says, "Yes, but I'm not sure about Dr. Bakar's report. Let me check." He turns to the computer, taps some keys, and says, "Yes."

"Can I have a copy?"

"Mine sure, but Dr. Bakar's report has to be authorized and signed by him. He's still on leave and will only be back next week, Monday."

"It's OK if it's not signed. I need it more for my investigation. For the documentation papers, Inspector Murad will get the signed copies."

"Well, in that case, let me print it for you."

"Doc, were there any peculiarities in the postmortem?"

"Everything seems to point to murder-suicide, except for two points."

"What are they?"

"One is the skin laceration on the male deceased around the waist about here." Dr. Matthews points to the right waist. "It's more of a scratch. I assume that was where the victim scratched himself when pulling out the gun. The scratches are consistent with an upward movement."

"What's the other?"

"The gunshot residue, the concentration of lead and nitrate on the hand of the deceased is too low for a man who had fired three shots."

"Very interesting, Doc. Were the two injuries on the female victim fatal?"

"Let me see . . . . ah . . . yes, both shots damaged vital organs. Either one of them would've killed the victim instantly."

"By instantly, what does that mean?"

"Well, it's like popping a balloon with a needle, it bursts and there is no more balloon. All that's left is a piece of rubber. It's the same with vital organs, when the bullet hits a vital organ, there is no more vital organ, just flesh and other stuff."

Matthews smiles and hands him the reports.

"Would a shooter know that the victim is dead before shooting the victim once more?"

"All depends. If the gunman shoots rapidly, no. But if the person shoots once then waits before shooting again, possibly. Again, it depends on postmortem spasms. The shooter may think the victim's still alive."

"What do you mean?"

"You see, sometimes the central nervous system still sends signals to parts of the body after the heart has stopped, causing limbs or the head to twitch, so it looks like the victim is still alive. You've heard of a chicken running around after its head has been chopped off? That's a postmortem spasm," Matthews says. "But, Inspector, you have to understand: if the shooter is not a trained medical practitioner, chances are he or she may not know. Why do you ask?"

"Covering all possibilities."

They thank Dr. Matthews and leave. Outside the morgue, Johan remarks, "That was easy enough to understand."

Mislan's cell phone rings. It is Audi. "Inspector, catch the 6 o'clock news."

"What's up?"

"I don't want to spoil the surprise."

"Jo, you know a place we can watch TV around here? I need to catch the news."

Johan looks at his watch. "That's in 15 minutes. There's a karaoke place in the Seasons Hotel across the road. I know the manager. Maybe we can use one of the rooms. What's on?"

"I don't know. Audi refused to say."

Kamilia Karaoke Lounge is on the mezzanine floor. It's happy hour, and the early crooners and drinkers are drifting in. Johan asks for Jeffery Koning, the manager, and is led to one of the rooms where he is just finishing dinner. Johan introduces Mislan and asks if they can use one of the rooms.

"Sure, for how many people?" Jeffery asks.

"Only the two of us, we want to watch the news," Johan explains.

"You can use this one." Jeffery switches on the TV to the news channel. "You want anything to eat or drink?"

Mislan shakes his head.

"OK, I've got work. Call me if you need anything."

The news has already started, and the female newsreader is reading out statistics for road fatalities, which have risen to three digits. Mislan lights a cigarette and leans back as she rambles endlessly on the same subject. A string of advertisements fills the screen and finally the newscaster touches on his case.

It starts with a brief background, some old clips, and then moves on to the field reporter. Audi appears in front of the Malaysian Anti-Corruption Commission building, announcing a new development in the investigation of what had earlier been claimed by the police to be a case of murder-suicide, a love triangle gone sour. It was confirmed by MACC that the lead investigator for the case was brought in for questioning regarding some allegations of corruption. However, the MACC senior enforcement officer in charge of the investigation refused to comment, except to say, "It is an ongoing investigation." The police, too, when contacted, refused to make any comments, and the lead investigator cannot be contacted. Undisclosed sources close to the MACC say the corruption case may have some links to the investigator's probes into the victims' business activities. There is also talk that MACC is restarting its investigation into the victims' affairs after it was temporarily suspended following the victims' sudden deaths. It is believed the MACC is ready to make several arrests and is rumored that it may include several prominent individuals. Audi ends her report by promising that updates will be aired as information is obtained.

"Wow, where did she get all of that from?" Johan asks.

"She's an investigative reporter, I'm sure she has her sources."

"Someone's going to hit the roof."

"Not someone . . . many someones."

46

Superintendent Samsiah is just about to leave her office when she is summoned by the Chief Police Officer. Taking the elevator up, she is joined by the Officer in Charge of Criminal Investigation. It is not often that the top brass summons a head of unit, and her brain rushes through the outstanding cases of public interest being handled by her unit. She has several, the most recent being the armored car heist, the killing of a prominent market analyst, and a series of armed robberies by a yet-to-be identified group. But somehow, she has a feeling this is about Mislan's case.

"Do you know what this is all about?" the OCCI, Senior Assistant Commissioner Burhanuddin, asks as they step out of the elevator.

"Not a clue."

The Chief Police Officer, Deputy Commissioner of Police, Datuk Zaid Zainal, is with a guest when they enter. DCP Zaid makes the introductions, and they move to the sofa. "Have you met Tan Sri Kudin?"

"No, but we've spoken over the phone," the OCCI replies proudly.

Superintendent Samsiah shakes her head.

"I understand your unit is investigating the death of Mahadi," Zaid says. "Tan Sri is concerned that the investigation is attracting undesired media attention and is volunteering to assist in any way to bring the case to a close."

Superintendent Samsiah notices there was no mention of the other victim, Zaleha.

The OCCI immediately becomes defensive and says, "I have told Samsiah the case should've been classified as murder-suicide and be closed, but she feels otherwise. And of all the officers, she has appointed Inspector Mislan as the lead investigator. This Mislan is a maverick. He thinks he is beyond reproach—"

"I'm not interested in what you think of Inspector Mislan," Zaid snaps, shutting him up. "Samsiah, what's the status of the investigation?"

Superintendent Samsiah briefs them on the investigation's progress and states that the evidence points to a double murder. When she finishes, Zaid asks, "Do we have suspects?"

"The suspect is believed to be Mahyudin Maidin, who died in the car crash during a high-speed chase. At present, Inspector Mislan is working on the possibility of him having an accomplice or accomplices. Mislan believes it won't take too long for him to make the connection."

"Good, that will bring the case to a close." Turning to Tan Sri KK, Zaid says, "Well, it looks like it's going to be over soon."

"May I know who this suspected accomplice is?" KK asks.

Superintendent Samsiah looks at the Chief Police Officer for a sign, then answers, "I'd rather not reveal our suspicions at the moment. It may jeopardize Mislan's investigation."

Deputy Commissioner of Police Zaid agrees.

"Tan Sri, may I know the reasons for your interest in the case?" Superintendent Samsiah asks, drawing a disapproving snort from the OCCI.

"The victim, Mahadi, was the executive chairman of MM Harapan Holdings, a company that . . . how shall I put it?"—KK pauses searching for words—"holds the interests of several individuals, and I am one of them. I'm sure you've heard I dabble in politics. Well, half of what you hear about me is rubbish. Politics is a very expensive game. To meet these expenses, we hold unregistered interests or become advisers in these companies for a small fee. Let me come clean here, and I hope this stays within these walls."

The Officer in Charge of Criminal Investigation nods in earnest, while the Chief Police Officer and head of Special investigations remain silent.

"With his demise, these individuals fear the investigations may uncover or stumble on some issues that are better kept away from the public eye." KK pauses as if unsure how to continue. "Lately, sand mining has been making the headlines, and MM Harapan's one of the companies the MACC has targeted. The company has been operating for more than a decade, and no one has ever cared about its activities. Then, about a year ago, the MACC came knocking. It's all politics, that much I can tell you. Anyway, the deceased was questioned and when one looks hard enough, one is bound to find something." He pauses again. "His death does not help our situation. The timing was wrong, and the circumstances, well, unimaginable."

"So, you're saying his death has nothing to do with his business activities or the MACC investigations?" Samsiah asks.

"Yes. It has only attracted attention . . . negative attention. That's not something we care for, not at this moment."

"How long have you known the deceased?"

"For as long as I can remember. We grew up together."

"Do you know of anyone who would have wanted to harm him?"

"Mahadi? No. You see, Mahadi was the kind of person who did not get into arguments or trouble. He was not one to go around offending people. He didn't hold grudges and was always ready to lend a hand. Mahadi was the kind of person you would want as a friend, not as a political candidate. A good man to call a friend."

"Tan Sri, I'm sorry to have to ask you this, but I need to be sure. Did you or any of your friends have a hand in setting up Inspector Mislan?"

"Samsiah! You are stepping way out of line with that question," the Officer in Charge of Criminal Investigation admonishes her. "Do you—"

The Chief Police Officer holds up his hand, "Oh, shut up, Burhan. Why don't you sit back, observe, and listen. She is not trying to offend Tan Sri. She's only being there for her men."

Tan Sri laughs. "I agree with Datuk. No, I did not, and if any of them did, it was not with our common knowledge or blessing. There was some talk about this Inspector Mislan. It sounded to me like he's a straight shooter with two balls. I'd like to meet him one of these days, after all this is over."

"I'll tell him of Tan Sri's wish, and I'd like to take up Tan Sri's offer to assist, if I may."

"By all means, say the word and it's done."

"It will help, if Tan Sri and his friends can let Inspector Mislan do his work undisturbed. That way, should the interference persist, we'll know it's not business related. That'll allow Mislan to focus his attentions on other motives."

"You have my word. Inspector Mislan will not have any interference from us."

"In return, I'll instruct Mislan to stay away from MM Harapan business activities, unless it is a motive for murder."

"Thank you. Is there anything else I can help you with?"

"Not at present, I'll keep Tan Sri informed, should there be anything else."

"May I ask what makes you think I was behind the actions to set up Inspector Mislan?"

"One of the MACC officers mentioned Tan Sri by name, claiming that you were calling the shots."

Tan Sri KK laughs, a sincere genuine laugh. "I've gotten used to people dropping my name. It's a curse for being successful and may I also say influential. My name is used to protect illegal activity and actions all the time."

"I understand," Superintendent Samsiah, says feeling sorry for the Tan Sri.

"Samsiah, you asked me who might want to harm Mahadi. Well, if he had anyone to be afraid of, I'd say his wife. When she got wind of Mahadi's intention to marry Zaleha, I was told by my wife that she went berserk. She confronted Zaleha, and my wife said, she assaulted and threatened to destroy her. My wife might have exaggerated a little about the assault bit. You know how some women are."

Superintendent Samsiah smiles. "Do you remember when the incident happened?"

"I think it was about five or six months ago."

47

LEAVING THE KARAOKE LOUNGE, Johan drives to the Damai Complex behind the hotel. They stop at a roadside stall selling Thai food. They select a table by the pavement and order seafood tom yam, salted fish kailan, onion omelet, chili fried fish, two plates of rice, and two iced lemon teas. The night is humid, and the hot air is blown away from the road by passing cars.

"You know the tom yam here and that in Thailand is very different," Johan says, making small talk. "I've been to Phuket Island and Krabi, but I still like this better."

"That's because the tom yam here is cooked to our taste. It's the same with most foreign food, even Western food. Otherwise, they'd have to close shop." Mislan lights a cigarette and watches people walking by.

"What's on your mind? Since we left HKL, you've seemed distant. Something's bothering you. Is it the police report against you? If it is, I'll give them my statement. I was there, too."

"No, that doesn't bother me. I've been through worse."

"No wonder you're still only an inspector," Johan teases him.

"I'm lucky to still be one," he says with a chuckle. "It's about the scratch marks on the vic. You remember, Fie noticed them, too."

"What about them?"

"The vic had the gun for many years, and he'd have pulled it out hundreds if not thousands of times from his waist. By now, he'd have been able to do it without scratching himself. I mean, do we scratch ourselves when we take our guns out every night or at the office?"

"What if he pulled it quickly, you know like in a quick draw?"

A waiter brings their food, and just as they start eating, Mislan's cell phone rings."Yes, ma'am . . . Having dinner . . . He did? Wow. . . So far there's no reason to—? No kidding, when— I'll try and get more info on it. . . . Thanks."

Johan looks at him. "What's up?"

"Ma'am just had a sit-down with the CPO and Tan Sri KK. KK told her that neither he nor any of his people were involved in setting me up. He also denied any involvement in the case. His interest to wrap up things quickly was to avoid unwanted attention on their business activities. Anyway, he gave ma'am an assurance there'll not be any further interference from him or his people."

"If he's not the one setting you up, who is? Remember the fat MACC guy mentioned a Tan Sri?"

"He may have said it to scare us. Anyway, there are many Tan Sri around, and he might not have meant KK. Then again, that was what KK said to ma'am, and he's a politician."

Johan laughs.

"Well, the vic's son takes the number one spot, I guess. KK also said the vic's wife, Mama Bee, assaulted and threatened Zaleha about five or six months ago. We need to get more on that. Can you set up a meeting with Ayn? She'd know."

"Sure, when?"

"Tomorrow."

Chew answers Mislan's call after several rings.

"Inspector, are you still working?"

"I'm on a twenty-four-hour. You still in the office?"

"Just about to leave. Why?"

"Small favor, where's the vic's gun now?"

"Safe, in my exhibit cabinet. Why?"

"Can you do a swab on the hammer?"

"Sure, what are you expecting to find?"

"If my guess is right, nothing. Otherwise, skin cells."

"Do you need it urgently?"

"Not really, because there's nothing much that can be done tonight, but I'll sleep better knowing," he says, laughing.

"I didn't think you were supposed to sleep on a twenty-four-hour shift."

"Only a figure of speech."

"Okay, I'll get on it now. By the way, remember you wanted someone to lip-read the video of the deceased?"

"Yes, did you manage to find someone?"

"I gave it to a friend who does a little lip-reading, but he couldn't make out what the deceased were saying. He said the image wasn't clear enough."

"It's OK, it's not important. Thanks."

They finish dinner and drive back to the office. At the guardhouse, the sentry stops them and hands Mislan a note. It is from Assistant Superintendent of Police Amir of the Integrity Standard and Compliance Division, asking him to drop by at his office in the morning before knocking off for the day. Mislan squashes the note and drops it as Johan drives into the parking area.

"You're going to piss him off," Johan warns him.

"He has to join the queue," Mislan says.

Inspector Reeziana is still in the office covering for him. She tells them that nothing much has happened—one sudden death that is being handled by the district.

"It's still very quiet, enjoy it while it lasts," she says.

"It won't be long before things get back to the normal madness. I kind of miss it," Johan says.

"You're like Field Marshall Rommel."

"Who?"

"The Desert Fox. He commanded the Ghost Division during the North African Campaign. Anyway, he said, it's a love-hate affair. When he was in the desert he hated it, but when he left the desert, he missed it."

"How do you know all these facts?" Johan asks.

"From the History Channel," Mislan says with a laugh.

Reeziana laughs, too. "Okay, City Foxes, have a good night. Catch you tomorrow."

Chew calls to tell him the gun's hammer is clean. Mislan thanks him and smiles. He is right, and it only puts him in a bigger predicament. What scratched the victim's waist? Who had the victim's gun and why did the victim not know his gun was missing? There must be an explanation. He must have overlooked something.

48

Mislan decides to bring forward the meeting with Ayn. Johan calls her and asks if they could make it tonight. They agree, and the meeting is fixed for 9:30 at a mamak restaurant in Sunway Damansara. Ayn, still in her office clothing, comes with her married boyfriend. They go through the formalities of introduction, place their orders, and settle down to some small talk while waiting for their food. Ayn's boyfriend appears uncomfortable about sitting out in the open. His eyes dart about, observing customers entering the restaurant. *What if he is spotted here with Ayn by someone he knows, what would be his excuse?* Mislan wonders.

The Bangladeshi waiter serves their food, places their bill on the table, and leaves. Ayn, who has not had dinner, starts attacking the *mi goreng*, while Johan and her boyfriend sip their drinks and make small talk. Mislan waits for Ayn to finish her dinner. She finally puts down her cutlery and smiles.

"Sorry, I was starving."

"We could see that," the boyfriend jests.

"Inspector, what did you want to see me about?"

"Please call me Lan, 'Inspector' sounds a little formal," he says, smiling, and receives an uncomfortable look from her boyfriend. "I was told the vic, I mean the victim, Zaleha, had a confrontation with Mahadi's wife. Do you know anything about that?"

Sucking on her straw, she nods. "That was some time ago, about four or five months."

"Can you tell us what happened?" Johan says.

"I was at home when she called, rambling and crying from a clinic in Taman Melawati. When we got there, she had just come out of the doctor's—"

"We?"

"We," she says, smiling to her boyfriend. "When she came out, her left eye was swollen, her shirt torn at the collar, her left cheek red, and she was shaking with fear. She refused to go home, so we took her back to my place."

Ayn reaches for a cigarette. Mislan notices her trembling hand. He waits for her to light her cigarette and compose herself.

"Leha, she said she was on her way home from the office when a car cut her off at a traffic light near her house," Ayn continues. "She said, it was so sudden that she couldn't stop in time and hit the other car." Ayn sips her drink to wet her throat. "When she stepped out, a woman and Mahadi's sons got out of the vehicle that had blocked her. They rushed toward her, swearing and calling her names. Then the woman slapped Leha across the face and punched her in the eye. The woman screamed at her to stay away from her husband and threatened to harm her if she continued seeing him. One of the sons pulled her by the collar, dragged her toward a monsoon drain by the side of the road, and said, this is where they'll find her body if she didn't stop seeing their father. Then he kicked her. She fell to the ground, and the other son kicked her, too. One of the sons went over to her car and scratched it. Before leaving, they spat on her saying, this is the last warning."

She stops talking, gropes in her handbag for some Kleenex, and wipes her eyes.

"You said the victim's sons. Did she tell you which ones?"

"Hashim and Mokthar, the two bastards."

"So the woman was the victim's wife?"

"Yes, the woman, Leha did not know who she was until the woman told her to stay away from her husband. Leha had never seen her before."

"Did she make a police report?"

"No, she was too frightened and she didn't want Mahadi to be involved in a public scandal."

"Then what happened?"

"She was too frightened and ashamed to go out because of the black eye and bruised cheek, so she stayed at my house. She was afraid to go home because they knew where she lived and could send someone to hurt her again or her mother. After three days, Mahadi found out because she hadn't gone to work, and came for her at my house. He was furious. It was the first time I had seen him angry, but Leha persuaded him not to do anything about it and to let it go."

"Can you remember the name of the clinic?"

"I can't, but I know where it is."

"How about her car? Where did she send it for paintwork?"

"In Ampang, we went together. Sorry, I don't know the workshop name, either. It was a Chinese workshop, on the way to Bukit Belacan. I can show you the clinic and workshop if you want."

"That would be very helpful. Was Zaleha ever assaulted or threatened again?"

"She told me there were some anonymous calls."

"Man or woman?"

"Man. Leha believed it was the son because the voice sounded the same, although she said he was trying to disguise it. She didn't know who the caller was because the calls were made to her office phone. Then, about three months before she was killed, the calls stopped."

Mislan's cell phone rings. It is the front desk reporting an armed robbery at a cyber café in Chow Kit. The robbers were armed with a handgun and a knife. One patron put up a fight and was stabbed in the stomach. According to the paramedics, the wound isn't fatal, and they're taking the victim to HKL. Special Project Team has been informed and is already at the scene. Mislan excuses himself and tells Ayn he'll call her should they need more information. In the car, Mislan asks his assistant, "What do you make of Ayn's story?"

"Interesting, but were the threats carried out? It could've been empty threats by an enraged wife and angry sons. These threats are rarely carried out. The silent threats, they're the dangerous ones."

"Could be, but I think it was more than that. Ayn said they cut off Zaleha's car at some traffic lights near her house. So, they either waited in ambush or followed her. Either way, it was planned."

"You have a point."

"Then there was the threat of killing her. The two sons dragged her to the monsoon drain and told her that's where her body would end up. To me, that's serious. It's quite unusual for sons to be involved. Usually, confrontations of this nature are by the aggrieved wife, sometimes with a confidant, a busybody friend. But in this case, Mama Bee had two of her sons."

"So, you think the threat was real?"

"Let's do some more digging before we conclude."

The cyber café where the robbery took place is along Lorong Haji Taib 2, an area renowned for its cheap boarding, red lights, drugs, petty crimes, scam rackets, and gambling. An area that never sleeps, it is a favorite haunt of the city's more colorful inhabitants as well as foreigners, mainly from Thailand, Indonesia, and Africa. Johan finds a place to park the car, and they walk toward a group of onlookers behind the police line. Johan asks for the investigator. It's Inspector Wee of Dang Wangi.

"Is he still here?"

The policeman points inside the cyber café. Mislan sees ASP Ghani of Special Project talking to the IO and elbows Johan.

"Dracula and his vampire squad are here. Let's split. I'll call the IO later for details. I don't feel like meeting him tonight."

They walk toward a nearby stall and several of its customers hurriedly leave.

Johan laughs. "Illegals or druggies."

"Jo, can you arrange for Ayn to show you the clinic tomorrow? I need to get the vic's medical report and see the extent of her injuries."

49

THE NIGHT ENDS WITHOUT any further events. Mislan and Johan use the slack time to review the evidence and testimonies to present to Superintendent Samsiah. Mislan is hoping she will grant him her blessing for the arrest. He's convinced he has a strong enough case and is confident his boss will see it, too.

His boss is ready for them when they enter her office with their night's work and case log. She tells Johan to close the door and motions for them to sit.

"Let's hear it,' she says without formality.

"Can I smoke?" Mislan asks, trying his luck. "It's been a long night, and I need my nicotine to keep me sharp and awake."

"If it makes you present your case factually, I'll make an exception. You know where the ashtray is, get it yourself."

"Thanks. Can I make Jo and myself a cup of coffee, too?"

"Why not? And how about breakfast, can I get you something?"

Johan doesn't get her sarcasm. "Thanks, but no thanks, we had some leftover Raya cookies," he replies.

"OK, let's get on with it."

Mislan starts from the very beginning, covering information that his boss already knows, but she allows him to go on without interruption. Johan hands her the documents as his lead investigator makes reference, pointing at the specifics. Superintendent Samsiah is proud of the enthusiasm of her two investigators. She admires their strength and relationship, supporting and standing by one another. In her four years as the Head of Special Investigations, she has seen several teams grow into responsible law enforcement teams, but these two went beyond that—they became good friends. Mislan wraps up his presentation, and Johan waits anxiously for her comments.

"Impressive, very impressive work," she comments.

Her two officers look at one another and grin.

"However—"

"Damn, here it comes," Johan says.

Superintendent Samsiah and Mislan laugh at his remark.

"Jo, I was just about to say: however, I suggest you wait for the DNA report before making any move on the suspect."

Johan goes red with embarrassment. "Chew said, the earliest he can get it is this morning. We'll pull him in for questioning and when Chew gets the result, we'll make the arrest."

"What's the rush?"

"You know how these people are. By now, they'd have gathered their resources to set up obstacles."

"Lan, you may have an airtight case, but the gun is your weak link, and the lawyers can use that to blow it apart."

"I have a theory, but I have nothing to support it. I asked Jeff and Syed to get the investigation paper on the vic's lost gun from the Petaling Jaya police. I spoke to the firearm licensing clerk and was told the vic's lost gun was a Walther PPK .32, the same make and model as the one he bought to replace it. He's probably comfortable with the model."

"What's your theory?"

"It sounds stupid, but I believe the vic's first gun was stolen by one of the sons. Then before the murders, it was switched with the vic's current gun. After they're killed, the killer retrieved the stolen gun, which the vic was carrying. It was hastily yanked from the holster, thereby causing the scratch mark on the vic's waist."

"And how was that possible?"

"The gun the vic lost he would place in the glove compartment while he was playing golf. That was why his golfing buddies said he carried the new one around even when he showered at the club. The sons would probably know where the gun was kept when their father was on the course. And I'm also sure there is a spare remote to their father's car either in the office or at home."

"So, what you're saying is that the suspect had the vic's gun that was stolen by the sons?"

Mislan nods.

"If that was the case, why not simply use the stolen gun to kill them?"

"Then the case wouldn't look like a murder-suicide, it would be murder because the gun used was the vic's reported lost gun. They don't want that. They need the case to be closed ASAP as murder-suicide. They'd be home free."

"It makes sense."

"So, are we good to go?"

"I still say we wait for the DNA results because all you got for now is theories."

Mislan's cell phone rings. It is Nathan, the video technician, calling to say the video footage enhancement is ready for collection. He asks Inspector Reeziana if she can collect it and hand it over to MACC Senior Enforcement Officer Yusuf. Jeff and Syed return with the copy of the police report from Petaling Jaya police. Mislan almost snatches the envelope from Jeff's hand, rips it open, and starts reading the report.

"Yes, the gun was stolen from the golf club parking lot," Mislan says aloud.

"Whose gun?" Reeziana asks.

"Oh sorry, the vic's gun."

"The DUKE murders?"

"Yup. Jo, can you ask Jeff and Syed to keep the suspect under surveillance? Please tell them to be discreet."

"You want another team to back them up?"

"I don't think it'll be necessary, it's only until we get the DNA result and the warrant. By the way, what's the status of that? It's nearly 10, what's holding it up?"

"I'll call the court and find out."

"Thanks."

Mislan calls Petaling Jaya police and asks for Inspector Norehan. After several minutes, he is put through, "Norehan here."

"Hi, I'm Inspector Mislan from D9 KL; I understand you're the IO for the loss of a firearm reported by the late Mr. Mahadi Mokshin."

"What's the report or IP number?"

Mislan reads out the report number and date.

"Yes, I remember the case. I've never investigated a case with so many big shots calling me. Why?"

"Any one still on the case?"

"What case? It's already CFF." She giggles.

"Closed For Filing? But there's nothing here to say that it was CFF."

"It's not on the report heading, it's in the minutes."

"OK, so no suspect?"

"No, but if I had to pick someone up as suspect, I'd pick someone who could open the car door without triggering the alarm. Anyway, it's all academic now. Why are you going through this case? I thought the gun owner is dead, a murder-suicide."

"Yes, he is."

"Did the gun resurface?"

"No," he answers a little too quickly.

"You don't sound convincing," she says, laughing. "Well, just between you and me," she says lowering her voice, "my money is on the gun resurfacing. No one breaks into a car to steal a handgun unless he or she intends to use it."

"Why steal when you can buy one from the underground market or from up north?"

"Good question. My guess is, he or she didn't have the connections to or was not in the crime business but had a need for hardware that could not be traced back to him or her."

"Good deduction. Hey, thanks."

"No problem."

Johan enters, informing him that the warrants are on their way to the office and should arrive any minute. Mislan makes a call to the forensics supervisor, Chew.

"Just got it. Confirmed it's the victims' blood," Chew says before Mislan can ask.

"Both the victims?"

"Yes, both."

"Can you scan the results and email it to me?"

"Doing it now."

"Thanks.

Mislan goes to Superintendent Samsiah's office, shows her the DNA result, and gets her blessing to move on the suspect.

50

Two searches are to be conducted simultaneously—one led by Mislan at the suspect's office and the other by Inspector Krishnan at the suspect's house. Stepping out at the elevator lobby on the suspect's office, they see the two bodyguards seated at the front door. They immediately spring to their feet and Johan stares at them, pointing to the glass door. Zubir immediately swipes his key card and holds the door open for the police team, and the other meekly sits down again. Mislan marches his team straight to the suspect's office. The secretary just gawks at the team, too shocked to react. He knocks on the door and walks in, followed by Johan and the two detectives.

"Mr. Hashim, I have a warrant to search your office," he announces.

Hashim, who is with his lawyer, is caught by surprise and immediately launches into a verbal assault.

"Who the hell do you think you are, barging in here again? I don't give a damn if you have a court warrant, get the hell out of my office, no, my building. Zubir! Jalal!" he screams. "Get them out of here."

Detective Jeff and Detective Syed shake their heads at the bodyguards, and they remain seated.

"Zubir! Jalal! Get in here, now!"

"I think they're smart enough to know not to interfere with a court warrant," Johan says.

The lawyer, Manikam, stands up slowly and asks to see the warrant.

"This is preposterous! What evidence do you have that makes you think my client has anything to do with his father's death?" he declares, handing the warrant to his client.

"You're my lawyer, do something."

"Inspector, if you do not cease this madness now, I promise you, I'll be filing a complaint against you. This is police harassment. When this charade's over, I'll take the utmost pleasure in suing you and the police force for everything you're worth," Manikam says, putting on a display worthy of his retainer.

"That's your prerogative. I suppose you can step aside now. I'm sure your client's already impressed by your showmanship. I have a search warrant to execute, and I intend to execute it. Please sit down and stay out of our way."

Hashim and Manikam continue abusing the detectives as they're escorted to the sofas.

The only respite the detectives get from the verbal harangue is when one of them makes or answers a phone call. The search is tedious, made worse by the nonstop verbal abuse from the suspect. No drawer, cabinet, compartment, or box file is left unopened. Every table and chair is examined, even the carpets, but they uncover nothing. While his team searches, Mislan notices a large framed portrait of the Twin Towers on the wall. He steps toward the portrait and notices a flicker of anxiety in the suspect's eyes. He pushes the portrait slowly to one side to find a wall safe. Taking the portrait off the wall, he says, "Mr. Hashim, can you open this safe, please?"

The suspect starts to object, but his confident lawyer says, "Go ahead, humor the inspector."

"Yes, humor me."

Hashim walks hesitantly toward the safe, stops, and turns to look at his lawyer as if to say something. He decides against it, faces the safe, and starts turning the combination. Mislan notices the suspect's hand shaking as he turns the knob to the right and left. Then, he stops and twists the handle. Nothing happens.

"Is something the matter?" Mislan asks.

Hashim shakes his head and starts over, his hand clearly shaking. Mislan notices drops of perspiration on his forehead and his labored breathing. He stops turning the knob and twists the handle, again nothing happens. He turns to Mislan, fear in his eyes.

"I can't remember the combination," Hashim stutters.

"Try again, the third time's always the charm," Mislan suggests.

"I can't remember it," he snaps, and turns to his lawyer. "Can't we do this later?"

Manikam looks at Mislan.

Mislan shakes his head.

"Give it another go, and if you still can't open it, we'll get our Forensics colleagues to break it open. Whichever way, it'll be opened in your presence."

Hashim slumps into his swivel chair. Mislan observes closely, knowing he is thinking of a way out. He knows he must not allow the suspect time to think and says sternly, "Do you want me to call Forensics now?"

Hashim stares at him and snaps, "I'm trying to remember the combination, OK?"

"Write down the two combinations that you tried, that will help you figure out the right one."

Hashim stands and faces the safe. He turns the combination, and Mislan hears a click and tells him to step aside. He waits for the suspect to be out of arm's range before grabbing the handle. The brass feels cold in his grip. He feels the eyes of his search team anxiously watching the drama. His heart pounds so hard he is sure the entire room can hear it. *This is it, Lan,* he says to himself, *the fate of ma'am and your career will be decided by what's in this safe.* He slowly opens the safe, sees the black butt of a pistol he recognizes as a Walther PPK .32, and says a silent prayer. His heart still beats fast and he takes several deep breaths to calm himself. When he finally finds his vocal cords, he asks for a detective to photograph the contents of the safe. When the detective steps away from the safe, he snaps on a pair of gloves, takes out the gun, and puts it in an evidence bag, which he tags. He turns to the suspect.

"Mr. Hashim, you're under arrest for the murders of Mahadi Mokshin and Zaleha Jalani. Please stand and turn around." Those words give Mislan the greatest satisfaction he has had in a long time. "Jo, cuff him."

Manikam jumps from the sofa to protest the arrest and the seizure of the weapon and threatens them with every imaginable lawsuit. Surprisingly, the suspect loses his gift for colorful vocabulary and submits quietly. Only his eyes remain defiant. As Johan cuffs the suspect, Mislan administers the cautions, informing the suspect of his rights under Section 113 of the Criminal Procedures Code. The lawyer continues his war dance, although no one pays him any attention. Mislan steps out of the office to make three calls—one to Chew, one to his boss, and one to Audi. Stepping back in the office, he calls Inspector Krishnan, telling him to abandon his search.

They wait until Chew and his forensics team arrive. Mislan hands the evidence bag with the Walter PPK .32 to him for processing. Detective Jeff and Detective Syed are given the honor of escorting the suspect out of the building. He and Johan keep their distance. When they leave the building, Audi and her cameraman rush forward, shoving the microphone into the suspect's face.

"Mr. Hashim, I was informed you've been arrested for the murder of your father and Miss Zaleha. Any comment?"

"This is ridiculous! This is all a big mistake, and we intend to act against the arresting officer and the police force for their incompetence and the humiliation caused to my client and his family," Manikam replies.

"Mr. Hashim, you have any comment?" Audi persists, ignoring the lawyer.

Detective Jeff and Detective Syed are having the time of their lives, basking in the limelight.

"No comment," Manikam says.

"I was also informed the police recovered a gun believed to be the murder weapon from your office. Any comment on that?"

"No comment." Again, it is Manikam.

Lowering the microphone, Audi snaps at the lawyer. "I'm not interested in what you have to say. If I want your comments, I'll ask you."

Raising the microphone, she shoves it into the suspect's face and asks again, "Mr. Hashim, do you have anything to say at all?"

"How did you know about this arrest and the gun?" Manikam retorts. "Who called you?"

"My sources are confidential and protected by law. As a lawyer, you should know that," Audi snaps back.

"This is a deliberate act by the police to humiliate my client, to tarnish his reputation. I'll sue your station if you air this," he threatens.

As the suspect is taken into the car, Audi and her cameraman ignore the lawyer and rush over to Mislan and Johan.

"Inspector, can we have some comments from you?"

Mislan smiles at her and shakes his head.

Sitting in the car, he watches Audi standing in front of MM Harapan building to give on-site commentary of what happened. As Johan drives off, Mislan smiles and nods at her.

"You tipped her off, didn't you?" Johan says.

"Why would I want to do that? She probably has someone inside the company on her payroll."

"Yeah, right. I saw her thank you with her eyes as we passed."

"I have no idea what you're talking about, Jo. Anyway, I'm happy she was tipped off by someone. She deserves it. She's been working hard on this case."

"You can drop the act now. I would've done the same for her."

"I wouldn't make that statement in public, Jo. It's against the force's policy to tip off the media. You can get yourself in trouble for saying it," Mislan says, laughing.

His cell phone beeps, indicating a text message. It is from Audi: *Thks, knew u'll keep ur word. Call me ltr.* He smiles, feeling no guilt.

51

THE JOURNEY BACK TO the office is quiet. Mislan chain-smokes as Johan drives at a leisurely speed. When they reach the city, Johan asks his boss if he wants to have a quick lunch before they go to the office. Mislan shakes his head and silence returns. Mislan replays the search scene in his head repeatedly, trying to recall if he missed out any procedure that could make it all invalid. After several reruns, he is confident that it was done in accordance with procedure. His mind shifts to Audi and her appearance in front of the building as the suspect was escorted out. The suspect's lawyer had been suspicious. Mislan is confident it won't jeopardize his case, though there could be disciplinary issues. What would Audi say if she was hauled up? Would she squeal on him? He shakes his head.

Johan notices the head shake and asks, "What's the matter?"

"Nothing . . . just trying to clear my head."

Johan knows not to push it. After years with Mislan, he knows when to and when not to press matters. At the guardhouse, Mislan notices the corporal in charge make a call as they drive through into the compound. Several parking spots are still available, as many officers are still not back from the festive break. As they approach the lobby, Johan spots Mama Bee in the center of a large crowd walking up from the visitors' parking lot.

"Shit, Mama Bee and her swarm are here!" he says. "Let them go up first, I don't want to have a confrontation with them in the lobby."

They move out of sight and watch in disbelief as the noisy swarm of killer bees make their way into the lobby. An elevator door opens and before the people inside can step out, the swarm pushes its way in. Policemen at the lobby intervene to avert a shoving match.

"Did you see that?"

Mislan just shakes his head, squashes his cigarette, and enters the elevator lobby. At the office, they expect to find the swarm in their boss's office but, surprisingly, they are not there and neither is Superintendent Samsiah. Mislan asks Johan to check on their suspect while he writes the search and arrest report. Jeff asks if they want lunch. Mislan gives him RM50 and tells him to get lunch for all four of them. His cell phone rings; it's Chew.

"Inspector, you struck gold with the gun. I managed to lift several prints from it and traces of skin cells. I've sent the cells for DNA and the prints for matching. Keep your fingers crossed."

"Great job, and Chew, please let me know as soon as you can. I'm standing in quicksand here."

"I'll let you know the minute I have it."

A uniformed officer approaches him just as he puts down the receiver. "Inspector Mislan, I'm Amir Muhammad from ISCD. Can we talk?"

"Sir, can we do this later? I've got to lodge an arrest report."

"I can wait," Amir says, sitting down.

"What's this about?"

"Go ahead, lodge your report first, then we can talk."

"I have a suspect in the interview room, and I've not had my lunch or any sleep for the last thirty hours. And looking at the situation, I don't think I'll get any sleep for the next ten."

"I understand and appreciate your situation. I, too, was an IO once. But you have to understand: Contrary to your assumptions, we like to perform our duties and responsibilities to the best of our abilities, too." Amir pauses. "Did you get my note from the guardhouse?"

"Yes."

"You could've at least called me. I would've gladly rescheduled our talk. That way, I wouldn't have to wait around for you and get more and more pissed off. You can go about doing whatever needs to be done. The police force is not about you and your responsibilities alone."

"I'm sorry, I wasn't thinking," Mislan says.

"Mislan, many here have heard about you and your reputation.

Most of us think highly of your dedication and audacity. But, at the same time, many think you're condescending, and this attitude will be your downfall. You need to start being a team player, start trusting your fellow officers by showing them the same courtesy and respect for their duties and responsibilities. It really doesn't take much to do that."

"I'm truly sorry," is all Mislan manages to say.

"There's a report filed against you. I did some inquiries and I'm convinced the allegations are baseless, intended to derail your investigation. However, I still need to record your statement to complete the investigation and put it to bed. For your information, I know about your brush with the MACC and your confidential report. It saddens me to know you put your faith in the hands of a third party rather than your fellow officers. I'll leave you to your duties. Call me for your statement as soon as you're finished and have had a good rest. Let's not drag this on for too long."

"Thanks, sir. I will. Again, I'm sorry."

He sits staring at the door for a long time after Assistant Superintendent of Police Amir Muhammad from the ISCD has gone. "You are a certifiable prick, Lan," he says aloud.

Johan enters and sees his boss brooding "What?"

"Eh . . . nothing."

"You're staring at the door. Were you expecting someone?"

"Thought I heard Mama Bee," he lies.

"You're serious? Are they with ma'am?"

"I don't know. Is the suspect ready?"

"Yes."

Mislan takes his digital recorder and a copy of a blank caution form and follows Johan to the interview room. The suspect is dismissive and unconcerned by what is happening. The lead investigator sits across from him and puts the digital recorder and a blank caution form on the table while Johan sits next to him. Mislan switches on the recorder and speaks into it, stating the date, time, and names of those present.

"Please state your name and identity card number for the record," he says, pushing the recorder closer to the suspect. Hashim does as he is asked, without looking at either of them.

"I'm going to caution you again, please listen carefully." Mislan reads out the caution and asks, "Do you understand the caution?"

Hashim nods and says, "Yes."

"Please acknowledge it by signing here," Mislan says, pushing the caution form across the table.

"Do you wish to make a statement with regards to the murder of Mahadi Mokshin and Zaleha Jelani?"

"No."

"Do you wish to answer any question with regards to the murder of Mahadi Mokshin and Zaleha Jelani?"

"No."

Mislan switches the recorder off and lights a cigarette. Nothing is worse than interviewing a suspect who decides to turn mute on you. It is easier to deal with lying and smartass suspects. Lies will always lead to the truth, eventually. A soft knock on the door and the front-desk officer pokes his head in, informing him that he is wanted by Superintendent Samsiah. He is expecting the boss's office to be swarming with killer bees, but she is alone, looking dejected. She invites him in and asks, "Where's Johan?"

"With the suspect. Do you want him, too?"

"Might as well."

Mislan calls his assistant on his cell phone and instructs him to join them. He senses something bad. Johan enters and sits next to his boss.

"I've just come down from the OCCT's office," Superintendent Samsiah starts.

Johan lets out an "Oh-oh," drawing a tiny smile from Superintendent Samsiah.

"Mama Bee has admitted killing the victims, and her admission is being recorded as we speak," she says.

"What the—!" Mislan snaps.

"Don't you use that tone on me," she admonishes him. "You heard me the first time."

Johan stares at her, speechless.

After a long silence, Mislan says, "I'm sorry. What did she say in her admission?"

"I don't know, I was only just told by the OCCI. It's still being recorded."

"Who is recording it?"

"ASP Nasir."

"Nasir from Admin, oh my God," Mislan heaves. "Why can't we do it, ma'am? It's our case."

She gives him the don't-ask-me-silly-questions look.

Mislan desperately needs a cigarette. His head is spinning, and his thoughts are scrambling in a thousand directions. Superintendent Samsiah recognizes the look on his face, goes to the cabinet, takes out the ashtray.

"Here, have your fix."

He lights a cigarette, and Johan, too, reaches for the pack on the table.

"Jo, don't you start," she warns.

Johan's hand stops halfway, and he smiles.

After several long drags, Mislan asks glumly, "So, what's going to happen now?"

"Have you interviewed the son?"

"Yes, but he has turned mute on me, staring into space. You think he knows what is happening? You think they planned this?"

"I don't know. Whatever it is, until we get a copy of the admission, don't assume anything. You go back in there and break him down, see what he says. You said he has shut down. I suggest you figure out where his switch is. Provocations usually work. Don't say anything about the admission, but use his mother as leverage. The way I see it, if she's willing to take the fall for him, there must be something between them that we're missing."

52

In his office, Mislan notices the packed lunches on his desk. He tells Johan to take one. He sits at his desk and smokes. Although his stomach is growling, food is the last thing on his mind. Johan goes to his workstation, slumps in his chair, and stares at his desk, looking defeated. Mislan wishes he had something comforting to say to his assistant, but he, too, is shattered by the new development. His throat is dry and sore from too much smoking, his brain overheated from too many distractions, and his body screaming for rest. Yet he cannot bring himself to stop smoking, nor his brain from crunching on, and his eyes from staying awake. He needs to focus if he wants closure. He has never experienced a situation like this before. There must be a catch; she is not going to deny him his closure.

"Jo," he calls, snapping his assistant investigator out of his silent sulk. "Are you dreaming of Jamie?" he jokes to lighten the situation.

Johan gives him a tight smile.

"Can you tell Jeff or Syed to take the suspect for processing?"

Superintendent Samsiah strolls into the office, looking her usual elegant and formidable self in her uniform. She pulls over a chair and parks herself in front of her lead investigator.

"Did someone die?" she asks, chuckling.

Johan walks over and joins them.

"Any news, ma'am?"

"The admission, nope," she says, shaking her head. "It'll be a while before we're given a copy, that is, if he chooses to give us one. Lan, I heard you had a visitor today; how did it go?"

Mislan smiles meekly, embarrassed at the realization of his boss's knowledge of his run-in and lecture from Amir Muhammad of ISCD.

"I hope you take heed of what he said. I know Amir, a good officer, always fair. Are you two done with your brooding, fretting, and blaming the world? If you are, please get back to what you do best."

They look at her.

"Police work, investigations, you know, looking for evidence, solving crimes. You still remember that, don't you?"

Mislan and Johan nod, bashfully.

"Where's the suspect?"

"Jeff and Syed took him to Records for processing."

"I doubt he'll have any records."

"Something is not right," Mislan says.

"What's not right?" she asks.

"It's too quiet."

"By that, you mean . . ."

"When we picked him up, his lawyer, Manikam was jumping mad. Threatening civil suits, harassment charges, you know . . . the defense lawyer's war dance. Then it goes all quiet, like no one gives a damn anymore."

Superintendent Samsiah laughs. "It'll come, that I can promise you. In the meantime, let's figure out how to milk this stone. How do you want to go about it?"

"Like you said, I'll use the mother to provoke him into talking."

"I'm sure that will work. Perhaps, Lan, you guys might want to map out your evidence to support your theory first. Leave gaps where the results are not in yet and lure the suspect into filling the gaps with his stories. Once you receive the results, use them to catch his lies."

"The problem is, he's not talking."

"How many people do you know who can listen to a story without commenting, especially if they're a part of it?"

Mislan and Johan nod.

"People always want to be heard, to say something, even when they've nothing of substance to say. They like to hear their own voices. That's how politics started." She chuckles. "Mostly, they make fools of themselves. I'm sure your suspect is no different. With his aggressiveness and flaming ego, he'll jump at the first opportunity to challenge your theory."

The two remain silent. Jeff informs them that the suspect has been processed and is back in the interview room. Mislan tells the detective that Hashim hasn't had lunch and gives Jeff his packed lunch.

"What about you?" Jeff asks.

"I lost my appetite."

"Eat something, Lan. Your brain might not think it wants food, but your body needs the energy," Superintendent Samsiah says as she leaves. "Never let your emotions rule your head."

53

They enter the interview room to see Hashim pushing away the Styrofoam food pack. He barely touched it. His face shows disgust, implying the food is unfit for him. Johan takes offense of the suspect's snobbish attitude.

Mocking the suspect, he says, "The rice's not up to your standards? Well, you'd better learn to enjoy it, because where you're going, that's gourmet food."

"You eat it," Hashim sneers back, pushing the packet carelessly toward Johan.

Johan turns red, takes a menacing step toward the suspect and is stopped by his lead investigator. They sit and Mislan tells Syed to clear the lunch pack. He lights a cigarette, leans back, and stares at the suspect without saying a word. He finishes his cigarette and lights up another one, continuing to stare at the suspect without flinching or saying anything.

"What?!" Hashim finally snaps.

Mislan remains silent, keeps staring, and continues smoking.

"What the fuck are you looking at?" Hashim barks.

Mislan smiles, an act he knows will agitate the suspect further. He knows the suspect has taken the bait and is ready.

"What's so damn funny?"

"I'll tell you what's so damn funny. You, that's what . . . a middle-aged mama's boy trying to act macho. I'm sure Mama will be proud of you."

The mention of his mother pushes Hashim to explode—his fist

clenched, his eyes bloodshot, and the veins in his neck bulging. "Don't you ever dare mention my mother, you pile of cow dung," he hisses.

"Woo, I'm scared," Johan says, laughing.

Hashim turns to him.

"You'd better be. I'll have your job before all this is over."

"So, mama's boy, did mama tell you there's nothing to worry about and that she'll take care of everything?"

"*I said not to bring my mother into this,*" Hashim screams at Mislan. "*You fucking shithead!*"

Mislan knows he has provoked the suspect to a point where his ego will rule his brain. It's time to start the interview. Mislan switches on the recorder and asks, "Did you have a Mahyudin Maidin working for your company?"

Hashim stares at him, not answering.

"I understand. Mama told her little boy not to say anything to us, right?" Mislan provokes him.

The suspect hisses at him like a king cobra. Mislan can see him grinding his teeth.

"Do you know of a person by the name of Mahyudin Maidin a.k.a. Mamak Din?" Mislan presses on.

"Yes, damn it, yes," Hashim says, leering at the inspector.

"Was he an employee of your company?"

"No, he was a friend."

"What sort of friend? A business friend . . . a social friend, or an acquaintance?"

"A friend friend."

"I heard he was more than a friend. My source says he did work for you."

"He ran errands for me and many others. Is that a crime?"

"What sort of errands did he do for you?"

"Business."

"You mean like bribing, muscle-flexing, arm-twisting?"

Hashim stares at him, saying nothing.

"Were you with him on the night your father and Miss Zaleha were killed?"

"I was with some friends at breaking of fast."

"Was Mahyudin one of them?"

"No."

"Did you meet him on the night of the incident?"

"I've already said *no*."

"What about after the murder, did you meet him?"

"I did not meet him, and the last I heard he died in a car chase that you provoked him into. Why are you asking me about him?"

Mislan smiles and says to himself, *strike one*. He knows the lies are coming, and there is no stopping.

"Do you know why he ran away from us?"

"Because you shitheads are so ugly he thought you were the walking dead," Hashim says, and laughs at his own joke.

"Maybe he thought we were your ugly mama's twin brothers," Johan responds, drawing another venomous hiss from the suspect.

Mislan laughs at Johan's response, making the suspect furious.

"Why did Mahyudin run?" Mislan repeats his question.

"How the fuck should I know?"

Mislan lights another cigarette, giving the suspect all the time he needs to fan his anger. He switches to another topic.

"Whose office were you in when we arrested you?"

"Mine."

"I thought that was your father's office. Your office is on level two."

"I've been appointed the executive chairman of the company, so it's my office," Hashim replies scornfully.

"Who made you the executive chairman? You?" Johan pokes.

"None of your fucking business."

"Mama?" Mislan guesses.

"You go to hell!" Hashim screams.

Mislan knows he has the suspect's brain pumped and goes into rapid questioning mode."The safe in your office. Do you use it?"

"Yes,

"Who has the combination?"

"Me."

"Who else?"

"No one."

"What about your brothers?"

"No."

"Your mama?"

"No!" Hashim snarls.

"When you opened it, was that the original combination?"

"No, I changed it when I moved into the office." Straightaway, Hashim knew he had fallen into the interviewer's trap.

You are not as smart as you think, dumbass, Mislan says to himself and pushes on.

"The Walther PPK .32 found in your safe, it's the gun your father reported stolen from his car at the golf club, is it not?"

Hashim shuts down again, staring at him.

"Can you explain how it got into your safe?"

The suspect keeps staring at Mislan, not answering.

"Can you explain how a gun reported stolen by your father three months ago was found inside your safe?" Mislan repeats firmly.

"I bet you, sir, it was his mama who put it there," Johan says to Mislan.

The suspect lunges at Johan, the fist of his one free hand missing the detective sergeant's face by a few inches.

Johan smiles, saying, "Temper, temper."

"How did the gun get into the safe in your office?"

"I don't know. It must have been in there from my father's time."

"You said earlier that you changed the combination. How did you do it without opening the safe?"

Hashim thinks for a while and lamely offers, "Maybe someone put it there."

"Who might that someone have been? You just said that you changed the combination when you moved into the office, and you're the only one who knows the new combination. So, who could've put the gun there?"

The suspect remains silent, and Mislan registers *strike two.* He sees the suspect reverting to his mute mode. It's time to provoke him further.

"Maybe your mama knows the combination and she put it there."

The mention of his mother makes the suspect snap. "I told you not to bring my mother into this. She does not know the combination. Only I know it."

Mislan decides it is time to change the line of questioning. He brings the suspect back to the first subject.

"Did you meet with Mahyudin before your father was killed?"

"I already told you, NO. How many times do I have to tell you? *No, fucking no.*"

"Did you call and speak to Mahyudin an hour or two before your father was killed?"

"*No*, I did not."

"Did you speak to or call your father an hour or two before he was killed?"

"No."

"Then how do you explain your cell phone call listing, which shows you made a call to your father then to Mahyudin before your father and Zaleha were killed?"

"I don't know. OK, maybe someone used my phone, maybe I did but I don't remember."

"That's odd. I'm sure you'd remember if you spoke to your father before he was killed. It's something a son would cherish and tell others. That is, unless you don't want people to know. So, which is it?"

"I already told you, I don't remember," Hashim snaps. "It's all hazy, and I'm confused."

As the interview continues, more and more lies pour out from the suspect. Mislan and Johan have a field day recording them. Superintendent Samsiah was right—arrogant people have little control over their desire to show off. After nearly three hours, Mislan ends the interview. He asks Johan to arrange for the suspect to be sent to detention for the night and for his remand application the following day.

54

Mislan is exhausted. He asks Johan if he wants to go for some teh tarik and get something to eat. They decide to go somewhere besides the usual mamak stall where other personnel hang out. Johan drives to Taman Maluri and parks the car in front of a stall.

"The food here is not too bad," Johan says as they take their seats. "I come here for supper sometimes."

They order chicken tandoori and teh tarik.

"You know what puzzles me? Why did he keep the gun in the safe?" Johan says.

"Sheer arrogance, because he thinks he's untouchable. He thought the police would take the case at face value and classify it as murder-suicide, and that would be the end of it."

"Well, he nearly got that right." Johan shakes his head.

"In this case . . . nearly was not good enough."

His cell phone rings. It's Audi asking if he has seen the news. He tells her he has not.

"Too bad, there is some great footage of you, Johan, and the victim's son," she said, chuckling.

"I'll try and catch it later tonight."

"Where are you? Can we meet?"

"Not now, maybe later."

"I heard there's going to be a press conference by the OCCI at 6 today. Do you know anything about it?"

"No idea."

"Don't kid me. The word is, the OCCI is going to announce the killer of the DUKE murders. You have to know about it, you arrested him."

"I arrested Hashim Mahadi. I don't know who the killer is, at least not yet."

"If not him . . . who?"

"I really don't know. Why don't you go to the press conference and find out, then you can tell me."

"I will, and Inspector, if it's about DUKE, I should be told first. We have an understanding, remember?"

Mislan tells his assistant that Audi said there will be another press conference by the OCCI.

Johan looks at him, disturbed. "The admission?"

"I don't know, but I wouldn't bet against it."

"We're screwed then?"

"We're always screwed, but we have the tools to unscrew it," he says, laughing.

The food comes, and they eat in silence. They order another drink each and lean back, allowing the food to settle. The evening air is humid, and it looks like it is going to rain. Mislan feels uncomfortable, as his overnight clothes are sticky and smelly.

"Jo, it's already five. Let's go home, shower, and change. The humidity is making me lethargic."

"OK, I'll drop you off and pick you up later."

"No, I don't feel like going to the office tonight. Why don't you drop me off and take the car with you? I'm going to try and catch up on my beauty sleep," Mislan says, "Pick me up tomorrow at seven."

"OK, call me if you need the car. I can always take a taxi or borrow a friend's bike to the office."

Mislan is unable to get used to the empty house—the absence of Daniel's voice, his inquisitiveness, and the sound of him playing. He peeks into his son's empty room, sighs, and goes to his bedroom. It has been a while since he spoke to his son. He speed-dials his ex-wife and waits.

"Hi, Daddy, I'm busy, can you call me later?"

"Are you playing with your friends, kiddo?"

He hears his ex-wife's voice in the background telling their son to tell his daddy that they're watching a movie and to call later. He feels good hearing her voice, although she's not talking to him.

"I'm watching a movie," Daniel says.

"Oh, OK. Miss you, love you, kiddo."

His cell phone rings just as he terminates the call to Daniel.

"Yes, ma'am?"

"Can you talk?"

"Yes, I'm home, thought of taking a shower and a nap. Anything?"

"I have inside information that Mama Bee is undergoing treatment for some critical illness at University Hospital. Why don't you pay them a visit and find out about it? Perhaps it'll shed some light. By the way, what's happening with the suspect?"

"In our lockup, enjoying our hospitality. Who knows, it may be good for his soul."

"OK."

"Thanks, ma'am."

"You can thank me by heeding Amir's advice."

University Hospital, renamed University of Malaya Hospital in Petaling Jaya, is a teaching hospital once reputed to have the best equipment and staff. That was before the country became a hub for private specialist hospitals. Johan takes the Federal Highway, exiting right at the Employment Provident Fund building. The drive is filled with anticipation.

As they expected, at the hospital, the D9 officers are confronted with unyielding bureaucracy. Even the mighty police authority card is powerless. Armed with only the patient's name, Mislan and Johan are directed and redirected to several sections on different floors of the complex. After twenty minutes, Mislan feels as though they have covered the entire hospital. He stops a group of interns in the corridor and asks for directions. At the general administrative office, he introduces himself and asks for the person in charge. Without a word, the receptionist points to another member of staff, whom he approaches. He introduces himself again and asks to see the administrator. She asks his reason, and when he explains, he is told the administrator is not in. Sensing his boss is about to lose his cool, Johan comes forward and asks if there is anyone who can assist them. The clerk suggests they check with the Clinical Support Section at the Patient's Information Desk down the hall.

Johan takes the lead, introduces himself, and asks the desk clerk if the hospital has a patient by the name of Rahimah Mat Jan. The clerk keys in the name and says, "We have three of them. Which one are you referring to?"

Johan looks at Mislan, who shrugs.

"Do you have her identity card number?" the clerk asks.

"Sorry, I don't. Can you tell me their ages?"

"One is thirty-two, one is fifty-three, and the other fifty-four?"

"Forget the one who's thirty-two. How about the two others, can you check their personal particulars and see if the husband is named Mahadi Mokshin?"

The clerk keys in some data, looks up, and says, "She's under the care of Professor Dorai, Radiation Oncology."

"Is the professor in?"

"Let me check."

She talks to someone on the other end of the phone and says, "Yes, but he's leaving soon."

"Where can we find him?"

"Take a left and go right to the end, past the imaging department."

"Thanks, you've been a real help."

They bump into Professor Dorai, who is about to leave. Mislan introduces himself and asks if the professor can spare them a few minutes. The professor steps back into his office.

"Yes, Inspector, how may I help you?" he asks rather hastily.

"I'll get straight to the point. I understand you have a patient by the name of Rahimah Mat Jan. May I know what her illness is?"

"I'm an oncologist, what do you think my patients' illnesses could be?"

Smiling, Mislan answers, "I'm sorry, but I'm not familiar with medical terms."

Dorai smiles. "Sorry. An oncologist deals with cancer. Who is it again?"

"Rahimah Mat Jan."

"Yes, she's a patient of mine, but I'm not at liberty to reveal to you her illness or condition, unless she consents to it. It's the patient-doctor privilege."

"I understand that, but I'm investigating a double murder. It would be really helpful if I could get some information, especially on her condition."

"I'm sorry, but I'm bound by my code and hospital, and I can be sued. I suggest you get a court order, and I'll be very glad to give you a copy of her records. I really must go. I have students waiting."

They walk with Professor Dorai. As they walk past the clerk stations, Mislan asks the professor the way out, pointing to the general direction of the clerks. He makes sure the clerks notice them and his pointing.

After they part company with the professor, Mislan motions Johan to follow him back to the general office. He seeks out the clerk whose name he noted earlier.

"Miss Norliza, Professor Dorai said he has students waiting and asked us to check with you on Mrs. Rahimah Mat Jan's record."

The clerk looks at him doubtfully.

"Oh, sorry, I'm Inspector Mislan, and this is Detective Sergeant Johan," he says with a smile, displaying his best impersonation of a holy man blessed with a police authority card. His impersonation does not fool the clerk, but the authority card does the trick. She retrieves the record on her computer screen.

"What do you need to know?"

"Her illness, condition, and the treatment she's undergoing."

She reads it out to them, the patient's illness and the type of treatments, pointing to the screen that only she can see.

"I really don't understand medical lingo. Can you print it for me so that I can just include it in my file for future reference," Mislan says, playing the role of a not-too-bright police officer.

"I'm not sure if I should. Normally, all printed records must have the approval of the Prof."

"It's OK, we're not using it for anything official. I only need it to show my boss that we've come here as she instructed." To further convince the clerk, he says, "If you wish, I can call the professor, but I'm sure he's with his students now and wouldn't like to be disturbed."

Mislan takes out his cell phone and pretends to punch in the professor's number.

"It's OK, you don't have to bother him," the clerk replies, punching the print key.

55

THEY WALK BRISKLY TO the car, looking over their shoulders more than once, expecting the professor or the clerk to come chasing after them. Once in the car, Johan starts the engine, puts the car into gear, and drives out of the hospital compound. Only when they hit the street do they breathe easy. They look at each other and laugh.

"That was smooth. You think the professor'll find out?" Johan asks.

"Does it matter?"

"He can file a complaint."

"About whom?"

"Us . . . tricking the clerk into giving us the records."

"I doubt it. It'll only highlight his department's vulnerability." Mislan reviews the report and sighs. "I can't understand a damn thing. I can't even pronounce some of the words. Like this one, neo, ad, ju, vant therapy. What the hell's that?"

He speed-dials Dr. Safia, asks if she wants to have dinner, and tells Johan to drive to Dr. Safia's place.

Johan laughs. "They need those big words to justify the fee they're charging. Are you going to ask Dr. Safia to look at it?"

Mislan nods.

"She's a 'stiff' doctor, will she understand it?"

"She's a doctor, isn't she?"

In the car, Dr. Safia says she feels like having mutton curry, and Johan declares he knows just the place. They drive through Loke Yew to Jalan Cheras, past the Kuala Lumpur Badminton Stadium, toward the old Cheras police station. He turns into Jalan Peel, and about a hundred yards up the street, he pulls up in front of a restaurant that says Cheras Fish Head Curry.

Johan clarifies, "Don't be misled by the name, this place sells the best mutton curry in town."

They take their seats, and since Johan knows the restaurant, he orders the food. The restaurant begins to fill up, and they notice that many of its customers are Chinese, all ordering mutton curry.

"I didn't know the Chinese liked mutton," Dr. Safia says.

"Not all mutton, only the one here," Johan says. "Go ahead, try it and save your comments until after."

They dig in. After a couple of mouthfuls, Safia says, "This is really good. The gravy's thick, and the mutton is sooo tender."

Johan grins with delight.

"How do you know of this place?"

"My MPV buddies from Cheras police took me here once, and since then I've been coming here if I feel like mutton curry."

Mislan's cell phone rings.

"Yes, Audi?"

"Thought we're meeting up?"

"Sorry, no can do, I'm a little busy now. How did the press conference go?"

"The OCCI announced he had solved the DUKE murders, and a suspect has confessed. He did not reveal the name. The admission will be forwarded to the Public Prosecutor's office for further action. In the meantime, the suspect is under police bail. As the suspect surrendered under her own accord, the OCCI feels there's no threat of her absconding. Did you hear me say 'her'?"

"Yes, I did."

"And you did not stop or ask me. So you knew, didn't you?"

"Yes, I did."

"And you didn't let me in on it? I thought we had a deal," Audi says angrily. "You allowed me to waste my time sitting in a press conference for that horseshit."

"Look, I know we have a deal, but I don't want it to be obvious. Go with the crowd, and when the time is right, you'll get the edge you want. Trust me. As a crime reporter, you should have figured it out."

"Figured what out?"

"You got the inside on Hashim's arrest, so when the OCCI called for a press conference, the fact that I don't give a damn about it should have flashed you a signal."

"What signal?"

"That we're walking two different paths. Look, I've really got to go now. I'll let you know once I have something newsworthy."

They finish their dinner and decide to go somewhere else, because the restaurant is getting busy and noisy. Mislan pays the bill, and Dr. Safia suggests that they go to the mamak stall near her place. That way they won't have to make another trip to send her back.

At the stall, they pick a table farthest away from the crowd and order their drinks.

"So, what do I owe you for the best mutton curry dinner in town?" Safia jokes.

"Nothing, but since you asked, do you mind looking at this report and explaining its contents in English?"

Mislan pushes Rahimah's medical report toward her. He lights a cigarette and hands it to her, lighting another for himself.

"I knew there was something. Let's see."

She reviews the report and asks, "Who is Rahimah?"

"The vic's wife."

"The report says she has colorectal cancer, advanced stage, and is undergoing neoadjuvant therapy."

"What's that?"

"Radiation therapy."

"When you said advanced stage, what does that mean?"

"Cancer's referred to by its stage, which determines the treatment needed. In her case, she is T3, N3, and M2, which means the cancer has spread to other adjacent organs."

"What's the highest stage?"

"Four."

"So, she's close to the top. She's dying."

"Well, you might say she is terminally ill. Doctors can only give professional opinions or a guesstimate of when death will occur by the patient's response to treatment and the rate of deterioration. We're not always right. New medicine and technologies can radically alter a patient's survival chances."

"Let's say, if everything else is constant or if she doesn't get any treatment, how long would she live?"

"It all depends on how many lymph nodes have metastasized and spread to other organs. This report's only the covering page, where are the treatment records?"

"I don't have them."

"Then, I can't give you an opinion."

"But she's terminally ill, and chances are that she doesn't have long to live. That makes sense."

"What makes sense?"

"The admission."

"You mean, she admitted to the DUKE murders?"

"Yes, earlier this afternoon."

"Wow."

56

Mislan drops Dr. Safia off at her condominium and drives Johan back to the office. Before going home, he tells his assistant to get a good night's rest, as he anticipates tomorrow to be a long and trying day. He thinks of calling his boss to update her, but changes his mind and decides to do it in the morning, after morning prayers. He remembers the DNA samples taken from the suspect's car. Chew said the results were supposed to come in before the end of office hours. *I'll call him first thing in the morning,* he reminds himself. Not trusting his overworked brain, he takes out his cell phone and writes reminders under tomorrow's calendar: *call Chew for DNA results, check on remand for suspect, write official letter of request for medical report under section 58 of CPC, brief ma'am.* He thinks of other tasks that need to be done and remembers the victim's notebook. Fadillah, the Forensics computer technician, gave him a thumb drive containing copies of the contents of the female victim's laptop, and he adds to the list: *review Zaleha's laptop contents.*

After a cold shower, he makes a mug of strong black coffee and sits at his desk. Switching on his laptop, he plugs in the thumb drive labeled Zaleha Laptop Contents. Several folders appear, most of them containing business-related documents. One folder, Memories, contains photos of her, Mahadi, family members, and friends. A file named Draft Report catches his eye. Opening the file, he finds a draft police report of the assault. The draft is brief but detailed, naming Mama Bee, Hashim, and Mokthar as the assailants. There is also an account of the allegations and threats:

If you see him again, there, inside there's where your body will be, understand.
Whore, you think you can steal another's husband.
You think you can steal our inheritance.
Even if you die, no one will care.

He calls Johan and gives him the name of the twenty-four-hour clinic Zaleha visited, telling him to visit the clinic on his way home and get a copy of her medical report. He scrolls down and opens another file, titled Preparation List. The file contains travel plans, invitees, events, and items needed for her impending marriage ceremony. He leans back and wonders what their lives would have been like, married. Then his cell phone rings.

"I'm about to sleep," he says.

"No, you're not," Audi says.

"And how do you know that?"

"I just do, OK. Hey, do you know that Mahadi's wife has cancer?"

"Nope," he lies.

"Well, she does and she's undergoing treatment at University Hospital. I just found out from my source. It seems she's really ill."

"So?"

"Just thought you might want to know. Wait a minute. You knew, didn't you?"

"Nope, but thanks for the info. Look, I'm really beat. I need to get some sleep or I'll get grumpy and unfriendly. Good night."

Audi's call brings his mind back to the case. The threats and assaults on Zaleha provide the keys to the motive. Money—a piece of printed paper with pictures of dead people. A piece of paper that is not even big enough to wipe your ass, but people will slave for, cheat, lie, die, and kill for. It always has been that way, still is, and will continue to be. Men created money and sell their souls to have it. He turns off his laptop, gets under the blanket, and sleeps restfully.

57

THE CITY SLOWLY RETURNS to normal with its traffic jams, noise, pollution, and crime. Roadside stalls reopen for business, catering to two million hungry city dwellers. Mislan stops at one on his way to the office to buy two packs of fried noodles with sunny-side-up eggs topped with a touch of chili paste and some curry puffs. It has been a while since he has had a decent Malaysian breakfast. The Police Contingent HQ elevators are crowded again, and the noise level has increased noticeably. Johan comes up behind him with carrying a plastic bag.

"What's that?" Mislan asks.

"Your favorite nasi lemak. The stalls are open today."

"I've got you fried noodles and curry puffs," he says, chuckling at the thought of how much they both miss their normal breakfast. "Did you check out the clinic last night?"

"Yes, I've got the report right here," Johan replies, patting his sling bag.

"You know who is on remand detail today?"

"Inspector Tee's team. I already told the front desk to include our suspect."

"Good. Let's go eat in the canteen before going up."

The morning prayer is dominated by ASP Ghani, with his insistence that the Petronas and cyber café robberies were committed by the same gang. He urges Superintendent Samsiah to request that the districts turn the cases over to Special Projects, meaning to him. To his dismay, Superintendent Samsiah is not convinced and tells his team to focus on the armored car robbery. Should more supporting intelligence become available, she says, she might reconsider. Mislan marvels at Ghani's incessant enthusiasm for firearms cases—criminals he can shoot to kill.

After the meeting is adjourned, Mislan asks Superintendent Samsiah for some face time. She tells him she has an urgent matter to address first and to come in thirty minutes. At his desk, Mislan calls Chew and is told the DNA results are delayed and will probably arrive during the course of the morning. He prepares a request letter under Section 58 of the Criminal Procedure Code, addressed to Professor Dorai at the University Hospital, asking for the medical records of Rahimah Mat Jan.

He signals Johan to follow him, and at the front desk they bump into Assistant Superintendent of Police Nasir from the Administration Department asking for Superintendent Samsiah. They walk together to her office and, when they're seated, Superintendent Samsiah says, "I've invited Nasir to sit in before he goes to see the DPP with the admission," referring to the Deputy Public Prosecutor. "Is that all right with you?"

Mislan nods.

"Jo, please get another chair. I don't like you standing." Turning to ASP Nasir, she says, "I'm sure you know each other."

They nod.

"OK, Nasir, why don't you go first?"

Handing her a copy of Rahimah's admission, Nasir says, "It's a straightforward admission. As you can see, she refused to answer any questions or provide any specifics as to how the murder was committed."

"What do you make of it?"

"This is my first experience with admission, but I always thought if someone admits to doing something, he or she would want to let it all out. In her case, she only said she did it. Period. It's questionable, at the very least."

"She gave jealousy as her motive. Do you buy it?"

"Possible, but why kill the husband?"

"Lan, Jo, what do you think?"

"I think she's protecting the real killer. I found no evidence of her involvement. She could've planted the seed, instigated, or even masterminded it, but she did not execute it. She does not have the means, ability, or the opportunity. As the instigator or mastermind, she can only be implicated by the killer's testimony."

"Why don't you update us on what you have? Then, when Nasir briefs the DPP, he can at least caution him."

"Chew lifted some prints from the gun recovered from the suspect's office. They match those of the suspect, Mahyudin, and the vic, Mahadi. Nothing of Mama Bee, I mean Rahimah. We've reviewed her phone records and Mahyudin's, both cell and landline, for the past three months. There was no communication between them. Unless they met in person, there's no way they could've planned and executed the killings."

"You said that her admission is to protect the real killer, how so?" Nasir asks.

"She's terminally ill with colorectal cancer. Here," Mislan says, handing the report he and Johan obtained through questionable means to Superintendent Samsiah. "The cancer's at an advanced stage, and I was told she's losing the battle."

"She's dying?" Nasir asks.

"Dr. Safia says the cancer is at T3, N3, M2, which is the medical way of saying it's bad. She can't say if the patient is dying unless she views the treatment records. I've formally requested those records and should get them by this afternoon. My guess is, Rahimah knows she is dying and, by confessing, she also knows she won't be held in detention because she needs treatment. And by the time the case goes to trial, she'd probably be home with her Creator."

The group nods its concurrence.

"What's the motive?"

"Money. Zaleha was assaulted by Mama, sorry, Rahimah, and her two sons. The vic did not file a police report, because she didn't want to involve Mahadi in a scandal. I found a draft police report on her laptop, and she wrote, verbatim, the threats the sons made. Here, I've copied them down." Mislan hands his notepad to his boss. "These are serious threats. The vics continued to see one another and went on to plan their marriage. Hashim felt Zaleha was going to strip them of their wealth, their heritage, so he got Mahyudin to pop her."

"Why kill the father?" Nasir asks again.

"I don't think there was any love between them. From the first interview, I noticed he's fiercely loyal and protective of his mother. I see the elimination of the father as an act to protect the mother and make sure she gets what she deserves as the only wife. Anyway, he had to make it look like a soured love-triangle murder-suicide. Mama Bee has them all under her spell, and the suspect deemed or was brainwashed into believing the father was a threat—as someone who betrayed his mother's love, sacrifice, and loyalty."

"Nasir, can you ask the DPP for a little more time before deciding on the admission? Let's give Mislan a couple of days to work on his theory and get the evidence to support it."

"I don't think *he*'ll like it," he says, implying the OCCI, "but I'm sure I can convince the DPP."

"Good, let's get to work then."

Mislan looks at ASP Nasir and then at his boss.

"What is it?" Superintendent Samsiah asks.

"Will *he* be briefed about our discussion here?" he asks, jerking his head upward.

They both look at ASP Nasir.

58

Mislan reexamines his evidence and testimonies while waiting for Hashim to be brought back from the court. He figures he has one shot at breaking the suspect before a brigade of lawyers and those with vested interests descend upon him. By now, the family would have engaged a whole band of criminal lawyers to represent the suspect. He wonders about the reactions of Tan Sri KK, YB Ibrahim, Daud, and Superintendent Malik when they heard of Hashim's arrest. Did it scare, shock, or please them? Could Mama Bee's admission be a strategy they cooked up? One question bugs him: Did they know of the plot and were they coconspirators? Did they nod their approvals through nonaction, nonintervention to serve their own needs? If so, did that make them somehow less guilty than the killer and his accomplice? This is something he will probably never know, something they will ensure he is not given the opportunity to pursue.

"Jo, are they back yet?"

"On the way. You want him taken straight to the interview room?"

"Yes, I want to start before it rains politicians and lawyers. Can you call Syed and tell him to show the report to Dr. Safia before bringing it back here? I'll let her know Syed will be stopping by."

"Sure."

Mislan calls Dr. Safia and asks if she can run through the report and make notes in plain English on the patient's chances of surviving the illness. He calls Chew and is told the results will arrive hopefully in a couple of hours.

"Chew, can you ask them to inform you verbally of the results? I'll be conducting an interview shortly, and it would be helpful if I could know the results."

"Sure, I'll call them in thirty minutes and ask. Hey, I'm sorry about this delay."

"No problem, I know you tried your best."

Johan informs him that the suspect is in room one, and there are several men claiming to be his lawyers at the front desk.

"Who're they looking for?"

"I don't know, probably ma'am."

"Is Manikam one of them?"

"No, I didn't see him."

"I'm not in the mood to dance with lawyers today. Tell the front desk I'm not available should any of them ask."

"What if ma'am asks?"

"I'm in an interview. Come on, let's go."

Hashim Mahadi is slouched in a chair, staring blankly at the wall. He looks haggard, with sunken eyes, overnight stubble, and a rumpled shirt, and he stinks. *He probably hasn't had a shower since yesterday, yet there's still an air of arrogance about him.* Maybe one night is insufficient to wipe away the sense of privilege cultivated over more than thirty years. Their presence makes the suspect stage an air of confidence, sitting upright and staring at them.

"Good morning, Mr. Hashim, have a good night's rest?" Mislan asks casually.

The suspect sneers.

"Had your breakfast?"

His question is met with another sneer.

"I'll take that as a yes. And in any case, if it's a no, I can't help you now because you might use my kindness against me later on claiming inducement." Mislan chuckles. "Let's see, where shall we begin?" Switching on the digital recorder and placing it in the middle of the table, Mislan lights a cigarette and leans back. He states for the record the date, time, those present, and that this interview is a continuation. Before he can start, the front desk officer appears, informing Mislan that he is wanted in the boss's office. He reminds Johan not to ask the suspect any questions, as whatever the suspect says to a police officer below the rank of inspector may not be admissible in court.

Three men are in his boss's office when he enters. She introduces them and says they represent the suspect and would like to have a word with their client.

"I don't think it's appropriate now, maybe in a couple of days or when we take him to the court."

"Are you charging him?" one of them asks.

"It has yet to be decided."

"What are you detaining him for?"

"Possible involvement in the murder of Mahadi and Zaleha."

"The DUKE Murders? At the press conference, it was stated that the police already have a confession."

"Correction, we have an admission. A confession is only if it's in front of the judge. Anyway, that doesn't mean we'll drop everything. You know how admissions are recanted all the time. Statutory declarations, confessions, admissions, they don't hold much water anymore, don't you agree?" Mislan says with a tiny smile.

"So, even with the confession, you're still going to pursue your harassment of my client."

"It's an admission, not a confession. Yes, we're pursuing every lead, and no, we're not harassing your client."

"I want it placed on record that we're denied access to our client."

"What record?" Mislan asks, irritated by the lawyer's language. "We're not in a courtroom, and your client's not here to admire your performance."

Superintendent Samsiah shoots him a vile stare and turns to the lawyers saying, "We'll take note of your request and our refusal of access at this juncture."

"You're the Head, you can overrule him."

"Yes, I can, but I do not overrule my lead investigator simply because I can. Contrary to what the public thinks of us, we do practice professional courtesy among ourselves. I'm sure as practicing criminal lawyers you're aware that while under remand, access to legal counsel by a detainee is not a statutory right but a police discretion. We'll try to fulfill your request at the earliest possible opportunity. And in this case, it's the lead investigator's view that now is not an appropriate time for counsels' visit."

"Can we have a copy of the confession?"

"As Inspector Mislan has repeatedly tried to correct you, it's an admission, not a confession. And no, you can't, mainly because we don't have it."

"Who has it then?"

"You have to check with the Officer in Charge of Criminal Investigations."

"Ma'am, if there's nothing else, may I be excused?"

She looks at the three lawyers and nods to Mislan.

"I guess we have to take our request higher then," one of the three threatens.

"I guess you should," Superintendent Samsiah replies. "That's why we have higher authorities, so people not satisfied with our answers and decisions can refer upward for more acceptable answers and decisions."

59

In the interview room, Johan asks what the meeting was about. Mislan tells him and notices the suspect's eyes lighting up. Turning to the suspect, he says, "Don't hold your breath, you won't be seeing them for a while. Let's say, not until you are charged."

The suspect flashes him a smug smile.

Switching on the recorder, he says, "OK, let's continue. In the last interview, you said you didn't know how your late father's lost gun got into your office safe, is that right?"

Hashim nods.

"Please answer verbally."

"*Yes, yes, yes,*" he snaps.

"Did you, at any time, handle the gun before it was found in your safe?"

"No."

"Can you then explain how your prints were found on the gun?"

Hashim remains silent.

"Mr. Hashim, can you please answer the question?"

"You're lying," Hashim explodes. "You're trying to trick me into admitting."

"Forensic does not lie," Mislan answers calmly and pushes the fingerprint match across the table.

Hashim stares at the printout, his eyes red with anger, and Mislan thinks his stare might set the printout on fire.

"I'll tell you how your prints got onto the gun, and you can correct me if I'm wrong." Observing the suspect's face for giveaway signs, he says, "You knew your father kept his gun in his car when he played golf. You knew this because you've been with him to the club to play golf. Your father's golfing buddies, the club sports manager, and the security guards can testify to that. You also knew where the spare remote key to your father's car is kept. You, or someone on your instructions, stole the gun when your father was playing golf and used the remote key to unlock your father's car and steal the gun. Then you stashed it away to be used later. You knew your father would use his connections to get a replacement and that would be the end of the story about the lost gun. That was how your prints found their way onto it."

The suspect remains silent, but his eyes tell Mislan he is right. "I figure you aren't too bright, so who planned the break-in to steal the gun, your mama?"

"*Leave my mother out of this!*" the suspect screams. "*Leave her out.*"

"Ooo, touchy," Johan teases him.

"You claimed earlier that you did not meet Mahyudin Maidin a.k.a. Mamak Din, after your father was killed. Is that right?"

Hashim nods.

"Does the nod mean yes?

"*Yes.*"

"How do you explain the bloodstains found on the passenger seat of your car?"

The suspect stares at Mislan, his eyes narrowing, burning with rage, "You're lying. You planted it there, you're trying to frame me."

"And why would we want to do that?"

Hashim remains silent, his eyes blinking rapidly. Mislan spots panic in his eyes.

"I take your silence to mean that you do not have an explanation. The blood DNA results will be in soon, and I bet my career they'll match your father's or Zaleha's or even both."

The suspect remains silent.

"You don't give me the impression you're smart enough to plan the murders, so someone must have done that and then you executed it. Maybe it was one of your brothers. Or was it your sister?"

The suspect lunges forward toward Mislan but is held back by his hand cuffed to the chair. "*I said leave them out of this*," he shouts. "They've nothing to do with it. Do you understand? *Nothing*!"

"Are you saying, you have something to do with it? Maybe not all of them are in on it, just the hotheaded brother of yours, Mokthar."

"You leave my family out of this. Do you fucking hear me?!" he hisses, still standing, staring at Mislan menacingly.

"You're in no position to make any demands, so please sit down," Johan advises.

"And why is that? Why should we leave your family out of this? Unless you can give us an acceptable reason, they're all potential suspects," Mislan taunts.

Hashim slowly sits back in his chair, realizing his relatives have somewhat implied having knowledge of the murders. The room is quiet, except for the humming sound of the air-conditioning.

"I think, your little sister, Laila, may have been in on it, too," Johan says, adding to the provocations.

The suspect stares at Johan, then Mislan, his jaws clamped and the fingers of his free hand clenched. For a moment, Johan thinks he is going to snap the cuffs and beat the hell out of his boss. Keeping one eye on the suspect, Mislan nonchalantly lights another cigarette. The wall clock shows five minutes to 1 and they have been at it for almost two hours. He'll have to stop soon and allow the suspect to have his lunch and a reasonable period of rest, in compliance with the Lockup Rules.

"I'm going to allow you time to think about what I've just said. If you do not wish your family to be pulled in for questioning, give me plausible reasons." He stands, switches off the recorder, tells Johan to arrange for the suspect's lunch, and leaves.

An envelope with Rahimah's medical report is on his desk when he returns to his office. In it he finds a note from Dr. Safia summarizing Rahimah's conditions in lay terms:

Discovered the cancer late, it was already at an advanced stage

- *has been undergoing treatment for six months but not responding well*
- *has been treated four times with radiation with no improvement shown—tumors are spreading to other organs rapidly*
- *recommended for brachytherapy (planting of radioactive seeds in the body)*
- *by the look of things, patient may not have long to live*

"Just as I thought," Mislan says. He calls Dr. Safia and thanks her for the note. He walks to his boss's office, finding her enjoying a home-cooked lunch while catching up on the news.

"Sorry to disturb your lunch. May I come in?"

"Sure, had your lunch?"

"Not hungry. What happened after I left?"

"They went upstairs, I suppose. How was the interview?"

"Slow, but I think he is about to cave in. I have a feeling the suspect feels it's his responsibility to protect his family . . . not only his mother but the entire family."

"So, he's playing the alpha male."

"That's what I think."

"We live in a vicious world, Lan. Lives are worthless. Money has risen to the top. Nothing surprises me anymore."

His cell phone rings, it's Chew telling him that the blood samples from the polo shirt, water in the pail, and the suspect's car match the DNA of both Mahadi and Zaleha. He'll fax over the report once he receives it. Mislan thanks Chew and informs his boss.

"Good job, Lan. Go get your closure."

60

Mislan notices a packed lunch on his desk. Johan tells him it's his favorite, sambal petai, fried beef and petai beans cooked in spicy chili sauce.

"I know you don't feel like eating, and I hope the petai will spur your appetite."

Mislan smiles. "Thanks."

"I've not eaten, I was waiting for you to have lunch together. Also, I got you some iced syrup."

He picks the packed lunch and goes into the makeshift pantry. He doesn't really have an appetite, but he doesn't want to disappoint his assistant. Johan calls after him.

"Go ahead and taste it. Bought it from a new stall near Puduraya. I asked the seller for plenty of petai for you."

Mislan starts eating, and the sambal petai is very good, "How do you know about this place?"

"One of the detectives told me, said it's a relative of his."

"You know what the English term for 'petai' is? Smelly beans . . . *Parkia speciosa*. I Googled it, can you believe that?" He laughs.

"To white people, everything good is smelly, like durian. They just don't know what they're missing," Johan says, chuckling. "In China, these things are worth their weight in gold."

"The DNA results matched."

"Yes! We got him," Johan exclaims excitedly.

Mislan nods.

"You don't seem excited. Is something wrong?"

He sighs. "Somehow, I wanted to be wrong, I wanted the DNA not to match. I still have a desire to believe in the human race. I guess, ma'am is right. Nothing is beyond us anymore when it comes to money." He finishes his lunch, lights a cigarette, and asks, "Has Hashim had his lunch?"

"Yes, Syed bought something for him."

"OK, let's end this today."

The suspect's food is again untouched. Syed tells them the suspect refuses to eat but did drink the iced tea. Mislan excuses Syed, and they take their seats.

"Why don't you eat something? We can wait."

Hashim ignores him, remaining silent.

"Suit yourself." Mislan pushes the packed lunch aside and switches on the recorder. "Let's continue from where we last stopped. You asked us to leave your mother and siblings out of this case. Do you know something that'll prove they're not involved?"

"Just leave them out of this. They don't know anything," Hashim says softly.

"By that, are you saying you do?"

Hashim turns his head toward Mislan, looks him in the eyes. Mislan holds his stare. As he continues staring into the windows of the suspect's soul, he sees the rage and resentment fading, slowly being replaced by equanimity. As if the suspect is discovering an inner peace.

"They deserved what they got," Hashim says softly, like he's talking to himself.

"What did you say?" Mislan asks, surprised.

"They got what they deserved. The bitch thought she could destroy my family, steal from us. . . . She was wrong. And the old man, an ungrateful old man whom my mother stood by from when he was only a clerk. When he became rich, he discarded her like an old hag and screwed around with the bitch. Bought the bitch a house, car, and gave her a company while my mother suffered at home. Afraid to go out, afraid to be ridiculed by her friends, and because of him she became ill. They didn't deserve to live."

"Tell me what they deserved and how they got what they deserved."

Leaning forward, Mislan pushes the recorder closer to the suspect. He sees a subtle transformation in the suspect's manner, a part he has not seen or believed the suspect had in him. His voice is soft, almost pleasant, and he appears to be at peace. Mislan thinks he sees a hint of relief and resignation.

"Can I get a drink?" Hashim asks politely.

Mislan nods, and Johan leaves to get one.

"How about a cigarette?"

Mislan nods and watches the suspect calmly reach for the cigarette, light it, and take a long drag, letting the smoke out slowly. Johan comes back with a plastic cup of cold water for the suspect.

"Thanks," the suspect says, surprising Johan. He sips the water. "They were going to get married, you know. My mother nearly died when she heard that, when the old man asked for her consent. She was hospitalized for three days. She refused to eat, and the doctors had to force-feed her. The old man knew she was dying, that she has advanced-stage cancer. He could've waited until . . . until"—Hashim just couldn't bring himself to say the word *died*—"when she's not around, to marry the bitch. He could've spared her the humiliation and suffering. No, he had to do it now, when my mother needed him most." Hashim pauses, takes another sip of the cold water, and lights another cigarette. After a long silence, he continues, "I tried reasoning with him, pleaded with him to postpone the marriage, at least until Mother was gone, to spare her the shame. He agreed, but the next thing I heard, the marriage was being planned for two weeks after Raya. That's next week. They had planned to get married in Hat Yai. That's when I knew I had to put an end to it."

Mislan looks at the suspect and feels sorry for him, carrying the burden of seeing his mother suffering and dying while his father had already found a replacement. Being the eldest, Hashim must've felt it was his responsibility to hold the family together and to keep his ailing mother happy until her last day. *No one should be made to shoulder such responsibilities.* However, whatever his feelings, Mislan has his responsibilities as a police officer to bring closure to the case and for justice to take its course.

"Tell us how you planned and executed their murders."

"You know how it was done. You have all the evidence. You know, when I first saw you at the morgue and our eyes met, something inside me said that you're someone I had to be wary of. Something about the way you brushed powerful people aside, not cowering in their presence. I made some inquiries about you, and I learned that you're a worthy adversary," Hashim says, laughing. "I tried to buy you, but you didn't take the bait. Most people would've taken it. I applied pressure, you grew stronger, and when I set you up for a fall, you simply kept fighting back." He lights another cigarette, "Even my supporters backed out," he says, shaking his head.

"Your mother has admitted to the killings."

"Rubbish, she is only protecting me. She doesn't know anything about it. Ask her how it was done, and you'll see she knows nothing."

"What about Tan Sri KK, YB Ibrahim, and Daud?"

"They're just protecting their own asses, afraid of being implicated for their roles in the business. With the MACC investigation going on, it was easy to make them believe the case was going to reveal everything. People like them, they're the first to come at the smell of money and the first to run for cover at a sign of trouble," Hashim says with a cynical smile.

The room falls silent.

"What will happen to me now?"

"You'll be charged with abetting the murder of your father and Zaleha."

"And the punishment?"

"If found guilty, it would be the same as if you had committed the murders yourself."

"Death," Hashim says.

Mislan nods, searching the suspect's eyes. They are clear and calm, with not the slightest sign of fear.

"Can I see my family?"

"I'll arrange it as soon as it's possible."

"Thank you."

61

It is six in the evening when Mislan ends the interview and the suspect is sent to the lockup for the night. The revelations have mentally and emotionally drained him. He goes to his boss's office to brief her. Superintendent Samsiah offers them tea and places the ashtray in front of Mislan without him asking.

"Go ahead, you need it," she says, taking her seat.

Mislan lights a cigarette, toys with it, and then stubs it out.

"He admitted to being an accomplice," he mumbles.

"How did it go down?" Superintendent Samsiah asks.

"On the day of the murders, the suspect knew his father was going for breaking of fast with his future wife. That afternoon, he swapped his father's reported lost gun with the new gun. They're both of the same model and caliber, so it was hard to tell the difference unless you checked the serial numbers, which, as you and I know, no gun user does. When it's in a holster, it is near impossible for even experienced individuals like us to tell the difference. The suspect then gave the new gun belonging to the vic to Mahyudin." Mislan pauses and lights up another cigarette, again toying with it.

"If you're not going to smoke it, don't waste your money lighting up," Superintendent Samsiah says.

Mislan grins and takes a puff. "At around eight, the suspect called his father saying there was an emergency at their sand mining site and the village folk were gathered and waiting. He lied to say that he was already there and asked his father to pick up Mahyudin because his services might be required. He also advised his father to send Zaleha home, as her presence might not be appropriate or welcomed by the villagers."

"Why not ask the father to take Zaleha along? That would have given them more time to execute their plan."

"The suspect wanted it to look like they were on their way home, to her home, so that the lovers' quarrel cover line appeared more authentic. The suspect knew where Zaleha lived, so making the father pick Mahyudin up at Petronas in Jalan Jelatek, which is on the way to her house, was convenient."

Superintendent Samsiah puckers her lips, nodding.

"The suspect then followed his father's car when it left Petronas. After it went down, Mahyudin came out of the car and pretended to be one of the onlookers. The suspect pulled over by the roadside, Mahyudin got into the suspect's car, the suspect drove off, and he dropped him off at Petronas. The suspect then went to a coffee shop and waited for the news of his father's death."

"That was how traces of the vics' blood were transferred into the suspect's car?"

Mislan and Johan nod.

"What do you think happened in the car?"

"The way I see it, Mahyudin must have got into the back of the car, sat in the middle between the two vics, grabbed Zaleha's head with his left arm, and popped her in the head. The gunshot must have startled Mahadi into slowing the car. Then, he moved to the right and popped Mahadi in the head, causing him to lose control of the car and ram it into the road divider. He then put the gun into Mahadi's hand and popped Zaleha again, this time in the chest. He tossed the gun between the seats and pulled out the reported lost gun from the holster clipped to Mahadi's waist." Mislan sips his tea to wet his throat.

"How would you support the theory?" she asks, testing her lead investigator.

"Zaleha's head was tilted to the right and that could only have happened if someone was holding her head when she was popped. Otherwise, the impact would've moved her head to the left because she was shot in the right."

Superintendent Samsiah nods.

"Mahadi's head is slanted to the left, as it should be, so the killer must've moved to his right, sliding between Mahadi and the door. The body and arm of the killer blocked the splatter of blood from Mahadi, and that was the reason the driver's window and door panel had no blood splatters. Then the killer moved back to the middle, placed the gun in Mahadi's hand, and fired another shot into Zaleha. That was the reason the GSR on Mahadi's hand was too diluted for a person who had shot three rounds."

She nods.

"That was also the reason why the gun was found in the middle of the car, at the bottom of the gearshift, and not on the driver's side, Mahadi's side."

"Apart from Hashim's admission of swapping the gun, what supporting evidence is there?"

"Mahadi's body had a scratch on his waist. It's recorded in the autopsy report. Chew examined the hammer of the lost gun recovered from Hashim's safe and found traces of skin cells that matched Mahadi's DNA."

"The motive?"

"Extreme hate and money . . . in this case the fear of losing it. Hashim blamed his father for his mother's sufferings and illness. His mother blamed Zaleha for stealing her husband and the family's wealth. When Hashim discovered they planned to get married two weeks after Raya, he knew all would be lost for his mother and siblings. He decided he had to put a stop to it. You know the rest."

The room goes silent. No one wants to comment or say anything.

"Good job, both of you."

Mislan and Johan each flash a fleeting smile, acknowledging her praise.

"Look, you did not plan this. You did not write the script. You followed the evidence and it led you to the truth. You don't have to like it, and you don't have to dislike it. You only have to accept it."

62

Leaving Superintendent Samsiah's office, Mislan lumbers to his desk, collects his backpack, and goes out. Johan walks next to him, not saying a word, only being there for his lead investigator, his friend. They walk to the car, and Mislan pats his assistant on the shoulder, congratulates him on a job well done, and advises him to go home and rest.

Johan nods.

"Hey, call me if you need to talk. Anytime."

Mislan manages a smile, gets into the car, and drives off. As he hits the main road, his cell phone rings. It is Dr. Safia.

"Hi?

"Hey, like to go for a drink?" she asks.

"Thanks, but I'm feeling a little tired and thought I'd go home and catch up on my sleep."

"Lan, are you OK? Jo called, he's worried."

"I'm fine, thanks."

"You sure?"

"Yes, I am . . . really, just a little tired."

"Call me if you want company or to talk, okay?"

"Sure. Thanks, Fie."

For some strange reason, Mislan decides to take the DUKE home instead of his usual route. At the eleventh milestone, he slows down and looks at the site where two lives were taken. Innocent lives or not, it is not for him to judge. What matters is that they were lives wrongfully taken. He drives past and notes there is nothing at the site to indicate anything had happened there. No traces or telltale signs to remind a passerby that this was where Mahadi Mokshin and Zaleha Jelani lost their lives to anger and greed. He takes the slip road down to Middle Ring Road 2 and makes a U-turn at Hujung Pasir. Mislan stops at the guardhouse, produces his authority card, and is waved on. He parks the car, flicks the cigarette into the gutter, rings the gate bell, and waits. The hall lights come on, the front door opens, and a woman pokes her head through the doorway and he greets her with, "Assalammualaikum."

"Waalaikumsalam," a woman's voice replies.

"I'm Inspector Mislan. Is Mrs. Khatijah still awake?"

"Yes, let me get her."

After several minutes, the gate swings opens, and a very frail-looking Mrs. Khatijah appears, inviting him in. Mislan is shocked at how much she has aged since the last time they met. There are bags under her eyes, probably from the lack of sleep, and she has lost weight. Her maid holds her arm, steadying her as she walks to the living room and sits in the first chair she reaches.

"I'm sorry to disturb you at this hour."

"No, you're not disturbing me. I was reading the Yasin before sleeping. You look very sad and tired. Is there anything I can do for you, Inspector?"

Mislan shakes his head.

"I'm fine, thank you. I came to inform you that Zaleha was neither killed by Mahadi nor did she commit suicide. We've arrested the killer and will be taking action against him soon."

Khatijah breaks down, sobs, and hugs the maid, praising Allah Almighty. She thanks him profusely for bringing closure to her misery. Now she can sleep in peace, knowing that her daughter did not take her own life in a suicide pact nor was killed by the man she loved. Now, she can pray for her soul with confidence.

Mislan leaves her to grieve her loss.

His house is dark and eerily quiet when Mislan enters. Preferring the darkness, he moves around without switching on the lights. After showering, he turns on the air-conditioning, gets under the blanket, and closes his eyes, missing his son. Soon, he is on a train with Daniel, looking out of a window into the darkness as they roll through the night across unfamiliar territory. No worries in the world—just him and his son looking ahead to fun, adventure, and new discoveries.

and closes his eyes, missing his son. Soon, he is on a train with Daniel, looking out of a window into the darkness as they roll through the night across unfamiliar territory. No worries in the world—just him and his son looking ahead to fun, adventure, and new discoveries.